# OUT OF TIME

A Nine Minutes Novel
By Beth Flynn

**Out of Time**
© 2015 by Beth Flynn
All Rights Reserved

Edited by Jessica Brodie and Cheryl Desmidt
Cover Photo by Chelsea Cronkrite
Cover Design by Nisha E. George
Interior Formatting by Allison M. Simon

ISBN-13: 978-1515111504
ISBN-10: 1515111504

*Out of Time* is book two in a series. It is not a stand-alone novel. I highly recommend that you read my first novel, *Nine Minutes*, to be able to understand the background stories of the main characters. There are many twists and turns in both books that can best be connected if read consecutively.

Although I do answer the outstanding questions from *Nine Minutes*, there is more to this story and some readers may consider it a cliffhanger. If you do not like cliffhangers, you may want to wait until the third novel is released in 2016. Other readers may be satisfied with the answers and the ending. Regardless of which category you fall into, I hope you enjoy the story.

For those of you ready to take the plunge, it's going to be a crazy, exciting, and somewhat complicated ride. I hope you enjoy it. And remember: Things aren't always what they seem.

*For Jennifer Hewitt.*
*Because a million thank-yous could never be enough.*
*I love you, Jenn!*

"Oh, what a tangled web we weave ... when first we practice to deceive."

—Walter Scott, *Marmion*

# Prologue
## 1950s, Central Florida

THE SLAP WAS hard and almost knocked him to his knees. They wobbled for a split second, but he managed to regain his stance and glared hard at his father.

"Your mother said you missed the bus and had to hitchhike home."

He tasted blood in his mouth where the slap had caused him to bite the inside of his cheek. He knew his next comment would bring another blow. He braced himself.

"Ida is not my mother."

Another hard one, this time to the side of his head, which caused a ringing in his ear. This was nothing. He'd endured worse. He didn't know why it bothered his father so much when he said this. Ida herself was the first to remind him that she wasn't his mother.

"Don't fuck with me, boy. Where were you?"

"It's the last day of school. Some of us had to stay after to help the teachers clean out their classrooms." This was a lie. He'd gotten in a fight that day. He'd snapped when a snooty rich kid made fun of him.

The kid was new and had only been enrolled for the last two weeks before school let out for the summer. He was too new to have been warned. The new kid had asked him in the boy's room if he picked his clothes out of the garbage can that morning. He'd left the idiot dazed and bloody on the bathroom floor, then calmly washed his hands and went back to his classroom. He'd looked at the big clock over the blackboard. Less than fifteen minutes until summer started. Hopefully, his dad wouldn't work him to death and he'd be able to keep an eye out for her. For Ruthie.

He'd been on the loaded school bus, ready to pull away, when the driver reached over and opened the door. The substitute principal stood at the front of the bus and quietly perused the group of kids. When he saw who he was looking for, he pointed and indicated with his finger. Follow.

Damn. He'd almost made it out of there.

They never discussed the alleged crime as they made their way back into the school and to the principal's office. He simply bent over the desk and endured the paddling. It wasn't so bad and didn't even compare to the beatings he'd received from his father. Beatings that had left permanent scars on his back and other parts of his body. He may have been young, but he knew this fucker, a temporary replacement for the school's regular principal who was out recovering from surgery, was enjoying this way too much. Would probably lock his office door and jerk off after sending him to find his own way home. Fucking pervert. The world was foul.

So, he'd hitchhiked and ended up walking the last seven miles to get home and now stood there, facing the wrath of his father. His stepmother stood off to the side leaning back against the kitchen counter, her arms crossed and a smug look on her face. A hot, stale breeze floated in from the window above the kitchen sink.

His stepmother. Ida. He'd hated her for as long as he could remember. He had no memory of his real mother. He was told she'd died in this house giving birth to him. It wasn't really a house so much as a shack in the middle of nowhere. A two-bedroom hovel situated on several acres surrounded by orange groves as far as the eye could see. His father was a skilled carpenter by trade, but for reasons that made no sense to his son, he preferred this destitute existence. He could have made a decent living, could've lived in a home not so far from the modern world—as modern as you could get in the fifties. He chose instead to live in a dilapidated old house that had been passed down for generations. He never once used his carpentry skills to make it into a real home. He'd slap some tar on the roof if it leaked or replace a busted pipe, but other than some hodgepodge repairs, he never lifted a finger. It was crumbling around them.

Maybe it was because his father considered himself the king of his castle and he could hold reign over his unworthy subjects. Maybe the brutality he unleashed here made him feel an iota of power that he didn't feel in the real world. Maybe knowing that he could provide a nice and safe environment, but purposely chose not to, was part of the psychotic seed that had been implanted in his personality. He wasn't just a bad man. He was worse than that. He prided himself too much on withholding any good he could do for his family.

That made him pure evil in his son's eyes.

Before she'd married, Ida had worked as a maid for a wealthy family in West Palm Beach. His father had met up with a couple of other laborers to make the long drive down to a mansion situated on the beach to spend a few days doing carpentry work and repairs. He returned with his three comrades and a glowing Ida, who had finally, finally snagged herself a man. She had become tired of being someone's maid, and when a hardworking, widowed family man came along and showed a hint of interest, she jumped. Unfortunately for her, she jumped too quickly and without hesitation. She hadn't realized then that she was jumping from the frying pan right into a fire that was even worse. Overnight, she went from being a lonely, overworked maid to a lonely, overworked, and abused housewife.

No, he had no good memories of Ida. Maybe she'd started out trying to do her best. To make their shack a home, to be a mother to her new husband's young son. But if she had started out that way, he had no recollection of it. Maybe she wasn't always the horrible person he knew. Maybe his father made her that way. It didn't matter. He hated her no matter what. He hated her because he knew what she was doing to her own daughter. His half-sister, Ruthie.

Ruthie was a sweet and trusting child who'd captured his heart since the day she was born. She was a happy little girl who was always smiling in spite of the mistreatment her mother inflicted. He spent every second that he wasn't at school or working caring for his little sister. He adored her and did everything he could to protect her from his parents, especially Ida. He made sure she ate when she was sent to bed without supper. He made sure she was bathed. He couldn't do it every day, but he did it as often as he could manage. He erased evidence of her bathroom accidents, making sure to wash out her clothes in the creek and let them dry before returning them to her dresser. He wiped away her tears and kissed her boo-boos.

Unfortunately, there were too many even for him to kiss away.

Every night she'd say, "Brother, tell me a story. Tell me a happy story where things don't hurt and everybody is nice."

He would pull her close in the bed they'd shared ever since she was a baby and, ignoring the stench of their unwashed bodies, he would make up happy stories to tell her. Anything to make her forget, just for a little while. They would watch the stars from their bedroom window and sometimes he'd even use them in his stories.

"See the brightest star, Ruthie?" he'd tell her as they gazed out their window. "That's you. You're the brightest, most beautiful star in the sky."

"Where are you, Brother? Are you there, too?" she asked him once.

"I'll always be the one that's closest to you."

He didn't know if the stories he made up were happy ones. He didn't know what happiness was himself, so how could he tell a four-year old? But he tried.

Once in a while, after he was certain his father and Ida were asleep, he'd go to the back screen door and let Razor in to sleep with them, too. Razor was a big black Rottweiler that had wandered up to their house one day and never left. His father refused to let the dog stay and insisted he didn't need another mouth to feed, that he'd shoot the dog if it didn't leave on its own. The dog was smart. Sensing the father's animosity, it would come around only at night and wait for the handout left for him on the far side of the barn. His father finally relented; he decided maybe the dog wasn't so bad after all when his barking woke them up one night to warn them that a wild animal was trying to get into the chicken coop. The hen's squawking never reached their sleeping ears, but the stray dog's barking and pawing at their back door did. His father let Razor stay, but he had to be kept outside.

Now, the beating done for the day, his father stared at him for a few seconds. Finally, he said, "Get your fucking chores started. Don't come back in until they're all finished. You don't get done before supper and you don't eat."

The boy didn't need to glance at his stepmother to know she would purposely serve a very early supper that day. He headed out the back screen door and let it slam behind him.

"C'mon, Razor," he said as he headed for the ramshackle barn.

It was dark outside when he finally finished his chores. He found some food he'd stashed in the barn and silently ate, sharing half with his dog. After washing up in the rain barrel, he headed into the house and crawled into bed with Ruthie, pulling her close. She moaned.

"Brother is here, Ruthie. Do you want a story?" He was exhausted, but couldn't fall asleep thinking he would let her down without a story.

"My stomach hurts," she whispered.

"Do you need me to take you to the bathroom?" he whispered back.

"No. It's not that kind of hurt."

"What kind of hurt is it? Are you hungry?

"Mommy stepped on it."

He stiffened, then squeezed his eyes shut. He was glad she didn't want a happy story tonight because the only one he could think of was one where he strangled Ida with his bare hands.

**********

The next day, he was walking back from the groves carrying the three squirrels he'd killed with his slingshot. Ida could make a decent stew out of these. He'd watched Ruthie that morning at the table as she slowly ate her breakfast. She seemed okay, and he'd left to hunt before she finished. He shouldered the squirrels and imagined the look on Ruthie's face when she saw what he'd caught.

That's when he heard it. A shotgun blast coming from the direction of the house.

He'd heard the shotgun before, when his father caught rare sight of a deer or other animal that was either a predator or something that would end up on their dinner table. But his gut told him this was different.

He broke into a full run, then came upon a scene that brought him up short. He tensed as his mind started to grasp what had happened.

There, right beside the clothesline. His father holding the shotgun. Ida cradling a bleeding arm. Razor on his side and lying in a puddle of blood.

And Ruthie, on the ground and flat on her back, her arms at her sides. Ruthie.

He broke into another run.

"Your fucking dog was attacking your sister, and when Ida tried to stop him, he went after her, too," his father said coldly, a finger still resting on the trigger. "I had to kill him."

Razor attacked Ruthie and then Ida for trying to stop him? Impossible. Razor would never hurt Ruthie.

Ida held her arm up for him to see. She didn't have to. He had already seen it and there was no doubt it was a bite from Razor. More like a mauling. Like he'd grabbed on and was wrestling with her.

He dropped his dead squirrels and knelt at Ruthie's side. And then he knew for certain the concocted story wasn't true. His sister was lying on her back, her eyes closed. Soft blonde curls framed her face. She looked more peaceful and beautiful than he had ever seen her. A tiny smile curved her sweet, innocent mouth.

Of course she was smiling. She had just escaped from hell.

He knew she was dead. He also saw nothing on her body that indicated Razor had attacked her.

They were lying. But he'd already known that.

He couldn't stop himself. The words were out of his mouth before he could think.

"Doesn't look like Razor attacked Ruthie. No bites or anything. Just Ida's bruises."

The blow was hard, but not unexpected.

"Get the shovel," his father ordered. "Pick a place way out past the house and bury your sister. Don't care what you do with your dog. You can drag its lousy ass out to the groves if you want and give the vultures some supper." Scooping up the three squirrels that had been dropped, he grabbed his wife by the uninjured arm. "You ain't hurt so bad you can't make supper."

As he headed back to the house with Ida and the dead squirrels, he yelled over his shoulder, "And when you're done you get your sorry ass back here and put out the rat poison like you were supposed to do yesterday."

He stared after them as they made their way back to the house and tried to imagine a world without Ruthie.

A world without light.

\*\*\*\*\*\*\*\*\*\*

Two weeks later, he was sitting in the passenger seat of a strange man's car. The man had introduced himself when he picked up the young hitchhiker, and he didn't seem bothered by the fact that the boy just stared at him and refused to say anything. The boy now turned to gaze out the car window as he reflected on what he'd done.

He'd buried his sister like his father had told him to, taken his shirt off and covered her body with it before retrieving a shovel and heading way out on their property where he dug one large grave.

Leaving the shovel at the gravesite, he'd headed back to the house. He went into the barn and retrieved the rat poison, shoved it down into his pants.

He'd gone into the house, noticed that Ida had cleaned up and was working on their squirrel stew. He could tell by her movements she was in a lot of pain. Razor had done a decent job of tearing up her arm. She probably needed to go to the hospital, but his father would never take her, nor would he allow her the use of their one vehicle. It wasn't at the house anyway. He must've gone somewhere.

It was obvious what had happened. Ida had been giving Ruthie another beating and Razor had stopped her. Unfortunately, Razor hadn't stopped her in time.

The boy had no way of knowing that Ruthie had been slowly dying of internal injuries sustained from her mother's brutal beatings, culminating in the final stomp to her tiny stomach the day before. He was certain Ida had always inflicted her brutality on Ruthie inside the house, where Razor wasn't allowed. That day must've been different. She was probably dragging a crying Ruthie out to the yard to help her with some chore and started whaling on her when the little girl wouldn't, or most likely couldn't, do as she was told. There was no doubt Razor had been trying to defend Ruthie by grabbing Ida by the right arm. Ida was right-handed.

Leaning back from her spot at the stove, Ida looked out the back window and spied the little girl's body in the yard. She gave her stepson a level look. "You're not finished. What are you doing in here?"

Her voice was steady and without emotion. She could've been asking him if he'd fed the chickens or painted the fence. It revolted him to think that this was how she thought of her daughter's burial: a chore. She was more of a monster than his own father. She had given birth to Ruthie. She had shared the same body with her only child for nine months. He didn't know anything about mothering, but even he could see how there could be, should be, a special bond between a mother and her child.

Without looking at her he answered. "Hole's dug. Came back in for something to wrap her in. Was gonna take my bed sheet."

They'd always shared a bed and it had only ever known one sheet. He would use it to wrap Ruthie's tiny body.

He didn't know what caused Ida to say the next thing. She countered with an offer that surprised him but also provided him with an opportunity.

"I have something you can use. Got it as a going away gift from where I used to work."

She took the big spoon she had been stirring with, tapped the side of the pot and laid it down. Cradling her sore arm against her chest, she headed back toward the bedroom she shared with her husband. He knew her arm was hurting, knew it would take a few minutes to dig out whatever it was that she was going to get. He could hear her clumsily rustling around for something.

He seized the chance to retrieve the poison from his pants and dump the entire contents of the container in the stew. He hastily stirred it, grateful that it seemed to quickly dissolve, and returned the spoon back to its place. He was standing by the back door when she returned with a blue piece of fabric draped over her good arm. He realized that it was a bathrobe of some type. It was thin and he didn't need to be educated to know that it was high-quality and expensive. *Going away gift my ass,* he frowned. She stole this. She held it out to him while avoiding his penetrating green eyes. They'd always unnerved her, at least that's what he'd heard her tell his father, and for a split second she seemed to hesitate, to waver.

She must have regained her bravado and, without waiting for him to take the robe, snapped, "Wrap her in this." She tossed it at him and headed back over to the stove to stir her stew.

At the freshly dug grave, he gently cloaked Ruthie's little body in his own shirt. "Brother is always with you, Ruthie," he said quietly. He then wrapped Razor in Ida's expensive bathrobe and snorted to himself as it occurred to him that even his dog was too good for Ida's supposed going away gift. He gently laid his little sister in the very deep hole and placed Razor next to her.

"You were a good boy, Razor. You did the right thing trying to protect her. Now you can always protect her."

He knew he wasn't going to mark her grave for anyone to know where she was. Only him. He knew nobody would be looking anyway. It wasn't like she was going to be missed. Like him, she hadn't been born in a hospital. He doubted she even had a birth certificate. He wasn't sure if he had one himself, though he guessed there was one somewhere, since he'd been enrolled in school. Do you need a birth certificate to go to school, he wondered? He didn't know.

He stood over his sister's grave and stared at the freshly compacted earth. It was missing something. He wandered off and soon came back with an oversized rock. The stone was heavy, massive really, and he had exerted an enormous amount of energy to carry it to her gravesite. He dropped it with a thud. He had chosen it because of its size and unique shape. He would remember it.

Falling to his knees, he began to weep. He never remembered crying even once in his life. Not even as a child, enduring horrific abuse that was tantamount to torture. He couldn't comment on why his father hated him. He couldn't figure why his stepmother hated Ruthie. He didn't want to think about them, anyway. After he was finished, he'd never think of them again.

A low wail that didn't sound human began to build, a cry that came straight from the pit of his empty stomach and found its way up his chest, through his throat and out his mouth, taking his soul and any semblance of light with it. The light that had been Ruthie.

He wasn't sure how long he'd knelt sobbing at Ruthie and Razor's grave. His eyes stung and he had a combination of dry and wet snot all over his bare arms as he tried to swipe away the grief. His sore back eventually brought him out of his mourning, the pulse of the sun reminding him of the lashes his father had inflicted a few nights earlier. He was physically and mentally exhausted, but his job wasn't finished yet.

He was worn out, but somehow he gathered the strength he needed and headed out further to an even more remote location.

He had one more grave to dig.

He would bury them together, not for the same reason that he buried Ruthie and Razor together: to offer protection and comfort to one another. No, he dug one mass grave because they deserved to be dumped like garbage.

And that was exactly what he was going to do.

**\*\*\*\*\*\*\*\*\***

"Kid? Kid, you need anything or have to use the bathroom?"

He'd fallen asleep and jumped when he was touched. It took him a split second to remember where he was. A car, now parked. The man who'd picked him up was looking at him, waiting.

The man nodded out the window. "I'm getting gas. You need to use the john or something?"

"Where are we?"

"Fort Lauderdale. Getting some gas and heading to Miami."

He nodded his head, starting to sit up. He was sore. The last few days had taken a toll on him physically and he was feeling it.

"Yeah, I gotta go."

He went around the side of the little gas station and let himself into the restroom. It smelled like crap but was surprisingly clean. His mind wandered as he relieved himself, memories rolling over him.

He'd returned to the house that night to find his father and Ida sitting at the dinner table eating stew. He reached up on the shelf and took down an old jelly jar, using the kitchen tap to fill it up. Leaning back against the counter, he drank his water as he watched them eat their dinner. Nobody bothered to offer him any. That was okay. He would've refused it anyway.

"Tastes like shit! How the fuck can you mess up squirrel stew?" When Ida didn't answer, his father backhanded her across the face.

Taking his glass of water, he'd gone to his bedroom and shut the door behind him. He laid down on the bed that he'd shared with Ruthie, hugged the only pillow close to his chest, and fell immediately into a dead sleep.

He was awakened that night to the sound of violent vomiting and retching. The next couple of days were a blur as he tried to pretend to help his extremely sick parents. Keeping buckets by their bedside, bringing them liquids to drink. Liquids he had continued lacing with more poison from the barn.

He remembered the instant his father realized what was happening. He was trying to get out of his bed, insisting that his young son take him and his wife to the hospital. The boy wasn't old enough to have a license, but he knew how to drive. He'd let his son drive their beat-up old station wagon to haul things around the property.

"You're gonna drive us to the hospital, boy," he said, voice laced with pain.

"No, I'm not." He just looked at them, a small smile on his lips. "I'm going to watch you both die a slow and painful death. I'm kind of glad you never bought us a TV. This will definitely be much more entertaining."

Bloodshot and pain-filled brown eyes met hard green ones as realization dawned. His father glanced around his bedroom and noticed his shotgun was not in the corner. It was gone. Even if it had been there, he wouldn't have had the strength to get up and get it.

His father fell back onto the bed and turned to look at his wife. She was curled up with her arms wrapped around her knees, which were pulled up to her chest. She had heard the conversation and opened her eyes long enough to say to her husband, "We both deserve this."

His father rolled onto his back and looked at his son, who stood at the foot of the bed, arms crossed, green eyes cold and staring.

"Shoulda known you were the devil's seed." Without waiting for the boy to comment, he added, "I loved your momma and thought I did the right thing by marrying her when she was pregnant by another man. Shoulda known you were evil when you killed your own mother, you no good piece of shit."

Finally, an answer. Although it didn't matter now. The man who'd raised him wasn't his father. The man who'd raised him resented him for taking his mother's life in childbirth. Another man's bastard had killed the woman he loved and he was going to make that child pay. Had been making that child pay ever since.

In a way, he could kind of understand that. He almost allowed a stab of conscience in, telling him he should take them to the hospital. Maybe it wasn't too late.

But then he remembered Ruthie. There was no excuse for what had happened to Ruthie. No excuse at all.

He stared coldly at the man he'd thought was his father. "I'm just sorry I didn't do this before you let her kill Ruthie."

Then he went to the kitchen and made himself something to eat.

After they were dead, he loaded them both in the back of the family car and drove them out to the second grave. He dumped their bodies with as much care as he'd show a pile of old chicken bones and flung the dirt back in. He hurled the shovel in the back of the station wagon and drove back to the house.

He wanted to draw as little attention to the shack as possible. He would not burn it down, but he would give careful thought as to what it should look like if a family just up and left, taking only things they could load in their one car. He went to work, packing up what few pictures they had, their personal papers and clothes. He sneered when he saw a picture of his father as a boy. No. Not his father. His stepfather. He looked like a miserable piece of shit even back then. He tossed it in with the other things. He never came across a single picture of himself or his mother.

He carelessly threw everything he could into the old car, barely leaving room for himself to fit into the driver's seat. He went into his bedroom and retrieved the brown bag that held the few things he'd set aside to take with him. It contained some clothes, along with thirty dollars and twenty-six cents that he'd scavenged from his stepfather's wallet and Ida's money cup, which he'd found hidden behind some dishes in the kitchen. He reached into his pocket, retrieving something he hadn't known existed until he'd started cleaning out their personal items. It was a picture of Ruthie and Razor. It had obviously been taken at their house, but he didn't know when or by whom. He never found existence of a camera when he was going through their belongings. He had no way of knowing where the picture came from and he didn't have time to ponder it.

He looked at it again. Ruthie was sitting down in the grass and looking up and smiling. She was leaning against Razor, who had himself wrapped around her like a cocoon. Her knees were pulled up to her chest and she had her arms wrapped tightly around them. Her blonde curls were shorter then. The two of them looked happy. Like they had been romping in the tall grass and had taken a break to pose. He knew neither Ida nor his stepfather had taken the picture. If that had been the case, he was certain his baby sister wouldn't have been smiling. He carefully returned it to his back pocket and continued his cleanup.

Hours later he stood in the middle of the little house, surveying it. He wasn't certain, but he was pretty confident he'd loaded up the important stuff. It was the fourth of the month. The electric and water bills wouldn't need to get paid again until the thirtieth. School was out, so he wouldn't be missed until September. And even then, he was doubtful anybody would care. His stepfather wasn't regularly employed, so he wouldn't be missed, either. They had no phone to worry about.

Yes, it looked like the family that lived here decided to move with their most personal possessions. The small amount of mail they got could stack up for months in their little slot at the post office. Nobody would notice. And by the time they did, it wouldn't matter. He'd be long gone.

He headed out to the chicken coop to set them free when he noticed laundry on the clothesline. He would grab those clothes and toss them in the car before leaving. After retrieving his brown bag and canteen, he carefully drove the family's car to the nearest, deepest canal he knew. It was off the beaten path and he didn't have to pass any houses or civilization to get there. It would be a long, hot walk to hitch a ride somewhere, but he only had a brown bag to carry and his canteen, which he'd filled with water.

Now, in the gas station restroom, he splashed cold water on his face and dried off. He reached into his back pocket before leaving the restroom and took out the picture of Ruthie and Razor. He would never hold her again. He would never hear her voice asking for a story. He would never wrap his arms around Razor's neck and nuzzle his short fur. He swiped away the tears that had started forming in his eyes and returned the picture to his back pocket.

He'd taken a vow that day at Ruthie's grave. No more crying. Ever.

He was starting to get hungry and decided to go back to the car to get some money. He would see what the gas station had in the way of food. Hopefully, they had some candy bars and soda pop. He'd tasted soda only once and was looking forward to the sugary drink.

He made his way around the side of the gas station and stopped dead in his tracks. The car he had been riding in was gone. He blinked to see if his eyes were playing tricks on him. They weren't. That son-of-a-bitch drove off with his brown bag that contained his few items of clothing and all of his money. He had left his canteen on the front seat. Even that was gone.

The world was rotten and so was everybody in it.

# Chapter One
## 2000, Two Days After Grizz's Execution


"YOU'RE SAYING YOU would rather see Leslie dead than read in some stupid magazine article that I'm Grizz's son? That doesn't sound like you, Ginny."

Tommy tried to remain calm and focused, but he could see the life he had patiently waited for with the woman he loved evaporating before his eyes.

"Of course I don't want Leslie dead! I'm just in shock. How could you and Grizz have kept this from me? I feel so stupid. Foolish." Ginny crossed her arms and rubbed her hands up and down as if to ward off a chill. She wouldn't, couldn't, look him in the eyes. Not yet.

Finally, she stood, her voice quiet. "I can't do this now, Tommy. I'm too angry. I cannot talk about this. I need to leave."

"Look at me, Ginny." He stood too, grabbing her by both shoulders. "Look at me!"

She shrugged him off. "No. I can't look at you. I can't believe the lies you let me live with all these years."

"Ginny, I didn't always—"

She interrupted him as something occurred to her. "Oh, no. No. Mimi is your sister! Our daughter is really your half-sister."

This time she did look at Tommy, and what he saw on her face filled him with dread.

"Get out. You need to leave *now*," she spat. He'd never seen Ginny angry like this. Never.

"We need to talk, Ginny. I'm not leaving. This is my home, too."

"It's not anymore."

Ginny strode to the front door, hands shaking. "I have to pick Jason up at Max's house. Don't be here when I get back. I mean it, Tommy. I want you out."

She picked up her purse and car keys from the little table that sat next to their front door, accidentally knocking over a framed picture as she did. It was a photo of the whole family—Ginny with Tommy,

Mimi, and then-newborn Jason. She had just brought him home from the hospital and couldn't remember a time when she'd been happier. Her friend, Carter, had taken the picture, presenting it to them in a homemade frame as a gift. She started to pick it up to set it back in place, then realized the picture was nothing more than a reminder of her fraudulent life. A life based on lies.

She left it face down on the little table and turned to look back at Tommy once more.

"You said you talked to Grizz right before he died and he said he was sorry. I don't believe you." Tears threatened, but she didn't let them fall. "I only heard Grizz say he was sorry for one thing and that was twenty-five years ago."

She slammed the front door behind her.

Backing out of the driveway a little too quickly, she sped off. Her shoulders shook as she drove and she gasped when, in her careless haste, she almost sideswiped someone. When she reached the stop sign, she looked in her rearview mirror. The vehicle she'd almost hit was a courier van and it was now pulling into her driveway. Doesn't matter, she thought. Whatever it is, Tommy can sign for it.

She turned on her car radio, punched the button for her favorite station, one that played music from the seventies. "Nights in White Satin" by the Moody Blues was playing. She turned it off, took a quick right into a strip mall and found a shady parking spot under a tree. She put the car in park, draped her arms across the top of the steering wheel, laid her head down.

And sobbed.

# Chapter Two
Thirty Minutes Earlier,
Offices of *Loving Lauderdale* Magazine

"BUT THE LOVE story. That's what I really want to play up. The love between the hardened criminal and the sweet, innocent girl. That's what the readers want, a love story, and I need something to make the conclusion pop."

Leslie cradled the phone against her ear as she spoke, trying to make her voice as convincing as possible. What she'd failed to mention—and didn't intend to reveal—was that she already had her conclusion and, boy, would it pop. But did Ginny know?

She knew she was just pushing the envelope here, stretching the boundaries of this interview. She wasn't just being nosy. She was being downright greedy. But she had to push.

"That signal he gave you," Leslie prodded. "It must have meant something. Can't you give me anything here, Ginny?"

Ginny's sigh was audible over the speakerphone. "The only thing I can tell you, Leslie, is that I've spent three months letting you interview me and the real love story was right under your nose the whole time. You just didn't see it. A story about a man who has loved me from the very beginning, from the first glance. The man who always was and still is my soul mate. That's the only love story now. Yes, I loved Grizz, that's true. But that story is over. Don't romanticize it. I've built a new life with—"

That was it—there was no way in hell Ginny knew her husband was Grizz's son. Leslie was certain of that now. Nobody was that forgiving. Leslie cut her off and went in for the final kill.

"She doesn't know, does she, Tommy?" Leslie asked sweetly, knowing full well Tommy was sitting right next to Ginny. "You haven't told her yet?" She tsk-tsked. "Well, I suggest you do so before she reads it in my article."

But instead of the torrent she'd expected, there was nothing but silence. Leslie waited a beat, then two, for Tommy's answer. There was no reply. She'd been disconnected.

*Damn!* She'd wanted to get the story behind that signal Grizz had given Ginny; she just *knew* there was something to it. But nobody would tell her a thing. Truthfully, she was a little surprised to realize Tommy had never revealed to Ginny that Grizz was his father. In her experience, most people couldn't keep secrets like that to themselves.

Leslie didn't purposely set out to be mean or rude, but she liked having the upper hand in an interview. She probably came across as pushy, but she didn't care. Especially now—this article was too important to her career. It could be her big chance with a popular, renowned magazine. She had told a white lie when she'd originally approached Ginny about the interview. She didn't actually *work* for the magazine in question, but she knew that after submitting this story she would have a shot at it.

And Leslie had proved to be a good investigator. She knew how to coerce people. How to get them to talk to her. That's how she got this interview. She did her homework and went to the one person who could influence Ginny to open up. Her daughter, Mimi. Yes, she knew Grizz was Mimi's father. Leslie was surprised when she realized the fifteen-year old, unbeknownst to her own parents, knew it, too.

Leslie swiveled back to her computer screen and did some final edits on the article. It would still be a great story, even without the answer to the question she'd asked Ginny. A few more tweaks and then she'd be done, maybe go home and spend a real Sunday with her mom and sister for once. She was the only one in the tiny magazine office today, a small remodeled gas station located off the beaten path. The owners—Don and his wife, Irene, a natural redhead with a bouffant hairdo who always smelled like cotton candy—were rarely around, and Leslie ran the day-to-day operations. In a way it was a good job. But Leslie had grown tired of being in charge. She didn't care about keeping up with advertisers, subscriptions, payments, any of it. All she wanted to do was write. That's all she'd ever wanted.

Less than an hour later, she was putting the finishing touches on her story when she heard the door open. Without looking up from her computer, she said, "Office is closed today. You can come back tomorrow morning. We open at nine."

She heard the door shut and didn't realize the person had closed it from the inside until she heard the creak of the chair right in front of her desk. She turned to look and almost gasped.

It was Keith Dillon. Gang name: Blue.

Blue was one of the gang members who hadn't gotten the immunity some of the others had. He was too high up in Grizz's organization for that. Blue had gone to prison with Grizz and a few others. Got a lousy ten years and was out in two.

Blue had visited Leslie a week or so after Grizz had attacked her in the prison interview room, right after Grizz gave her the phone interview. Right before the execution. She'd known Grizz did it out of anger and she'd had to swallow her pride after the beating, eat a little crow when she talked to him, but her instincts had been accurate. She knew she'd angered Grizz enough in that first meeting that he just might give her something.

Boy, did he. When he told her during the call that Grunt—Tommy—was his son, Leslie had almost dropped the phone. He wouldn't answer any other questions. She'd wanted to get more details, like whether Grunt knew and, if so, for how long. He wouldn't give her anything else.

The first encounter with Blue was when Leslie had just come out of the grocery store and was putting bags in the trunk of her car. The sun was hot and she felt a trickle of sweat make its way down the center of her chest. She had allowed her pain medication to wear off so she could drive herself to the market. The heat and renewed pain were making her woozy, but she was still feeling a little high, too. She knew the secret Grizz revealed was going to make her article. Make her career.

She didn't know where Blue had come from, didn't see or hear him approach her car. He was just there, standing silently with his arms crossed. He didn't ask her not to print the secret. He demanded it.

"Grizz changed his mind." Blue looked her up and down. "Don't print whatever it was he told you during the phone interview."

Leslie just stared at him. She knew who he was, but he didn't incite the same sense of fear that Grizz did. So instead she took her cart back to the return, left him standing behind her car. Like an afterthought, she called out over her shoulder, "You don't even know what it is, do you?"

He didn't answer.

She stashed the buggy and strode back toward him. "The big secret. You don't know it, do you?" she asked a little too smugly.

Blue waited for her to return. "Doesn't matter. Don't print it. This is just a courtesy call. You don't want to be seeing me again."

He turned around and walked away.

Now, two days after Grizz's execution, Blue was back. He sat in the chair and looked at her. Didn't say a word. She wouldn't allow herself to be intimidated. A quick stab of terror at the memory of Grizz's brutality jolted her, but she quickly replaced it with confidence. That bastard was dead. She was safe. She wouldn't let Blue get the upper hand.

Blue gazed around the room, taking in the fake leather sofa, the framed poster art on the walls, the cheap paneling. "Wow, this must be the white trash satellite office for your big magazine." A laugh escaped his lips.

She stiffened. "I didn't say I worked for them. I just said—"

"I already knew that. So did Grizz. That's not why I'm here." Before she could comment, he asked, "So, it's not getting printed. Right?"

"What does it matter now, anyway?" She shrugged with a little more confidence than she actually felt. "He's dead. Besides, I didn't use any real names. That was part of the deal I made with Ginny. Who's going to care?"

"I care. You took it out of the article, correct?"

"What if I didn't? What if it gets printed? What's going to happen?" She gave him a fierce look. "You're going to slash my tires? Beat me up?"

Blue stared coldly. "It's obvious you want to play games here. So the rules have changed. Now there will be *no* article."

Leslie sat back in her chair, sighing. She tilted her head to one side as she looked at him, trying to determine her response. Truth be told, she didn't want to get the shit beat out of her again. Okay, so maybe she wouldn't print the secret. Not this time, anyway. But she would certainly hold on to the information and use it when needed. It was obviously important. She would try calling the Dillon's again. The Dillon's? Ha! They weren't really the Dillon's. They were the Talbot's—if that was even Grizz's real last name. She wanted—needed—to ask about the signal, the nod. She would get them to tell her. She would get what she wanted, eventually. She always did.

"Okay," she relented finally. "The secret won't come out in my article."

He leaned forward, his words like ice. "It's too late. You shouldn't have fucked with me just now. There will be no article. You'd better erase its existence right now. If I even think you have a copy of it anywhere, or that it might show up someday—"

"What? You'll do what?" She glared at him. She was getting angry and more than a little tired of being bullied. "I already know what it feels like to swallow my own teeth. It's not great, but if that's what it takes, I'll do it. I'll handle whatever it is you think you can do to me. You know why? Because my future is at stake here. My career. My chance to get out of this crappy little rat-hole of a job and make something of myself. So you know what, Blue?" Her eyes blazed. "You can just deal with it. I won't print that Grizz is Tommy's father, but that article is getting submitted."

She sat back in her chair and took a deep, triumphant breath. She was shaking, but not with fear. She was mad.

As if on cue, her telephone rang. It was Sunday; the answering machine could pick it up. Irene's sweet voice filled the tense air between them. "Thank you for calling the *Loving Lauderdale* office. Our hours are Monday through Friday, nine to five. Leave a message and your call will be returned promptly. Thank you and have a great day!"

Just then a woman's frantic voice could be heard over the answering machine. "Leslie! Leslie! Oh God. Leslie, please be there!

Please answer. If you're there, pick up. Please!"

It was her mother's voice. Leslie looked at Blue and was instantly filled with unease. As she reached for the phone, her mother's panicked cries continued.

"I don't know what to do! Please call as soon as you get this." She choked back a sob. "It's Hannah. Your little sister is missing!"

Leslie picked up the phone. "Mom, I'm here. Calm down. Calm down and tell me what happened."

She listened intently as she stared into Blue's cold eyes. He got up and quickly walked out the door.

Leslie dropped the phone, the receiver landing with a loud thud on her desk. She could hear her mother's voice fading as she ran out after him, as he strode toward an idling sedan. She put her hand to her brow to dim the sunlight. The glare was blinding. Was that a woman in the passenger's seat?

Blue had started to climb into the driver's side when Leslie finally screamed after him, "You win! Okay? You win!"

Blue nodded at her and got in the car. It sped off.

Leslie stood there a moment, paralyzed with unmistakable fear. Funny—she remembered thinking when he'd first confronted her in the grocery store parking lot that he didn't incite the same sense of fear that Grizz did.

She was wrong.

Leslie didn't bother trying to get a license plate. She didn't bother trying to get a better look at the woman. It didn't matter.

What she'd said was true. He'd won. That bastard was dead and he'd still won.

Tears rolled down both cheeks as she went back inside to comfort her mother and delete her file.

# Chapter Three
## 2000

TOMMY HADN'T MOVED from his spot in the den. He was still in shock over how his life had taken a detour in less than five minutes.

Hell, he wished it was a detour. This was more like a complete U-turn.

He understood why Ginny was upset. Of course she was. But he never expected the anger and hatred he'd seen on her face. She was devastated.

He couldn't blame her. They'd had such a good marriage and he couldn't bring himself to believe that this could ruin it. He'd never even gotten to tell her that he didn't always know about being Grizz's son. He just didn't see how it could matter so much now. He hadn't thought it was something Ginny had needed to know. It wasn't something anybody needed to know. Damn Grizz for telling Leslie out of anger. He swiped his hand through his hair and sighed. This wasn't part of the plan. This fucked everything up.

"Fuck you, Grizz. You said you had Leslie handled," he said to no one. "You were locked up in jail for fifteen fucking years. Then I watched you die two days ago. Yet all along you *still* found a way to screw with me. I thought we settled things. I thought this was over. Son-of-a-bitch!"

He leaned back and allowed his mind to drift. Memories invaded his senses. His hands tightened into fists as he thought about the abuse he endured as a child. He couldn't stop the thoughts from coming. When he'd left that life behind, he thought no one would ever screw with him again. Especially not Grizz.

But he was wrong. Grizz had screwed with him worse than any of them. Grizz, even beyond the grave, had messed with the one thing that mattered most.

He could almost smell the rotting garbage and cat urine in Karen and Nate's house. The sour sponge that Karen made him use to wash the dishes. The stale cigarettes and weed. His own rancid, neglected body. He could feel the constant itch of his lice-infested scalp.

He subconsciously rubbed his arms as he recalled the painful blisters. The broken bones.

His mind drifted back to a time he wished he could forget. He couldn't stop the flood of memories.

He remembered what it was like living in hell.

# Chapter Four
## 1969

TOMMY WATCHED FROM the shadows of the hallway. He had woken up thirsty, was going to sneak into the bathroom to drink from the faucet. But the big man was there. He was bringing Karen money again.

He had seen the big man before. He was scary looking. Tommy didn't know why he gave Karen money. He never got close enough to hear their conversations. But he could hear them tonight.

"Is he okay? Got everything he needs?" the big man asked.

"Yes, of course he has everything he needs. Why wouldn't he?" Karen took a long draw on her cigarette and tapped her ashes into an open beer can.

The big man walked to the refrigerator and looked inside. "Because there's nothing but beer in your fridge and this place is a shithole."

Now the big man was pacing the room, opening cabinets and drawers. Tommy realized he'd never seen him inside the house before. He'd watched from a window as Karen or Nate would meet the big man outside. They could always hear him coming, heard his motorcycle when it rounded the corner a few houses away. But tonight there had been no warning. Guess he didn't ride it tonight.

"What? Are you saying I don't feed him?" Karen started to add something, but before she could, the big man grabbed her by the throat and lifted her off the kitchen chair. She dropped both her cigarette and her haughty attitude. Tommy had never seen her afraid before tonight.

"Who the fuck do you think you're talking to, bitch? Are you taking care of the kid like you're supposed to?"

The kid? Tommy's thoughts kicked into high gear. The big man was there for him! He was giving Karen money to take care of him. Why? Did he care about Tommy? He must have cared a little. But why would he? And why would he give money to people who neglected and abused him?

Tommy was young, but not stupid. If he was ever going to get out of there, now might just be his chance. Even foster care was better than this nightmare. The big man could help him or leave him with Karen and Nate. The way Tommy saw it, the worst that could happen was that Karen would beat him after the man left. Maybe Nate would, too, when he got home from work. Tommy didn't have to think long. He'd take his chances. Quickly, he tore off his filthy, ripped T-shirt and tossed it on the ground. He moved quietly from the shadows of the hall to the rundown kitchen.

"Karen, I'm thirsty," Tommy said, rubbing his eyes. "Can I have something to drink?"

He saw instant regret flash in Karen's eyes and knew he'd been right to make himself known to the big man.

Karen looked at Tommy, then at the big man, who was staring openly at the battered boy.

"I don't hit on the kid! It's Nate—Nate does it. Ju-just when he needs discipline."

"And I suppose Nate, who doesn't smoke, uses your cigarettes to burn him?" The big man lashed back without taking his eyes off Tommy.

"Uh, yeah," she stammered. "When he needs it."

His eyes still fixed on Tommy, the man reached behind him and pulled out a gun. Without a word, the big man turned toward Karen and put a bullet between her eyes. Tommy heard a gasp and saw Nate, frozen in fear by the front door. Nate spun around to flee, but he wasn't quick enough. The big man nailed Nate in the back of the head.

Then the big man tucked the gun away and looked at Tommy.

"You don't need to be afraid of me," the big man said in a gentle voice. "I'll make sure you're taken care of from now on."

"I'm not afraid of you," the little boy replied.

The big man nodded. "Anything here you want to take? Grab it now, because you won't be coming back."

Tommy ran to his room. He put on his tattered and stained T-shirt and slipped his feet into sneakers with no laces. He went to his bottom dresser drawer and slowly pulled it out. He reached in and retrieved a small box. It contained his most prized possessions. His only connections to her. He returned the drawer to its place and slowly scanned the room. No, there was nothing else there. He returned to the living room.

"I'm ready."

Tommy was surprised when the big man took off his jacket and wrapped it around him, then effortlessly scooped him up and walked outside to an old pickup truck. They didn't speak as they drove off.

After twenty minutes they pulled into a little bar called The Red Crab and parked close to the door, which was propped open. The big man told him to wait in the truck as he went inside. Tommy sat as quietly as possible, strained to hear. He chanced a glance inside the door, saw the man go to the phone by the cash register and dial a number.

"I'm gonna need a dark clean up at a house in San Carlos Estates." After rattling off an address, he hung up the phone and turned to the bartender. "Mike, call Blue at Sissy's and tell him to get his ass over here now. Tell him not to bring his bike and to come alone."

"Sure thing, Grizz."

"I'm gonna need your truck a little longer."

"No problem, man," the bartender said and picked up the phone.

Grizz went outside and climbed back into the old pickup truck. He looked at Tommy.

"They've been hurting you." It was a statement, not a question.

Tommy nodded as he looked at his hands resting in his lap.

"They been feeding you?"

Tommy shook his head.

"You hungry now?"

Tommy looked at the big man. "Yeah, I'm really hungry." After a brief pause, "Who are you?"

"Are a burger and fries okay?"

"Yes, please. And can I have ketchup and a drink?"

"Yeah. Stay here."

Grizz went back inside and Tommy could hear him order a

burger with fries and a soda. He told Mike he'd be back in ten minutes.

"I'm sitting in your truck. Don't bring the food out to me. I'll be back."

"Yeah, whatever you say, Grizz."

Grizz went back to the truck. He looked at Tommy while Tommy continued to stare into his lap. He wasn't sure how much he should tell the little boy. He'd only found out about him a few months ago.

"You can call me Grizz. You don't tell anybody about what happened tonight. Is that clear?"

Tommy nodded.

Before ten minutes had passed, a shiny light blue Camaro pulled into The Red Crab and parked a few empty spaces away from the truck. Grizz got out and walked to the car. Tommy noticed he held up his hand like he was telling the driver to stay put. The man did just that, rolling down his window. Grizz rested his forearms above the opening, leaned down and spoke. Tommy's window was up now, so he couldn't hear them. Eventually, the other man got out of the car, then he and Grizz walked toward Tommy. Grizz opened Tommy's door.

"I'm going inside to get your food. This here's your big brother, Blue. You're gonna live with him now."

And with that, Grizz walked back into The Red Crab.

Tommy stared at Blue with a look of trepidation. He wasn't as big as Grizz, but he looked just as scary. *Should I have kept my mouth shut and stayed with Karen?*

Blue must have been reading his mind.

"Don't be scared, runt. I won't hurt you."

# Chapter Five
## 2000


THE RINGING DOORBELL brought Tommy back to the present. For a moment he allowed himself to think Ginny was back, that she had just locked herself out of the house. But instantly he knew there would be no truth in that split-second thought.

A young man with bright red cheeks wearing a courier's uniform was at the door holding a clipboard, a large package on the porch next to him.

"I have a delivery for Dillon. Can you please sign here, sir?" the courier said as he swiped his brow with his forearm.

"Not expecting a delivery." *Especially not on a Sunday.* "Who is it from?"

"Don't know. Just initials from a Florida address. Should warn you though, it's heavy."

After Tommy signed his name, the apple-cheeked courier took the clipboard from him and stuck it under his right arm as he struggled to pick up the weighty package and deposit it in Tommy's hands. He whistled to himself as he sauntered down the front steps and out to the driveway, got in his van, and left.

Tommy stood there wondering what the package could possibly be. The kid was right. It was heavy.

Kicking the front door closed behind him, he headed for his home office as he easily hoisted the mystery parcel and set it on the desk. Did Ginny order a set of exercise weights or something? Without looking at the return address label, he ripped it open, then sat down with a heavy sigh. This was unexpected. What did it mean, if anything?

"Shit," was all he said.

# Chapter Six
1969

"SO HOW'S THE kid doing at night? Still having nightmares?" Grizz asked Blue as they sat at the bar and drank their beer.

"He's getting better, but he still won't go to bed unless the door that connects our rooms is left open," Blue answered, then paused to give Grizz a look. "You never mentioned a little brother before."

Grizz thought carefully. He would have to be cautious with his answer. He never told Blue that Tommy was his little brother. He'd just told Blue the boy was going to be living at the motel and that Blue should pose as his older brother. Blue had just assumed Grizz was the kid's older brother.

Grizz took a sip of his beer and answered casually. "Wasn't around much. Was gone by the time he was born. You know I didn't stay in touch with my family. I don't think he has any memory of me."

Of course this was all a lie. Tommy wouldn't have any memory of Grizz because Grizz didn't even know he existed until a few months ago. Before Blue could reply, Grizz added, "You keep working on him. Keep convincing him. He's young enough that he'll believe what we tell him."

Blue didn't say anything, just nodded. He'd known Grizz as long as he could remember and he'd never heard him mention a family. Didn't mean he didn't have one. He just never talked about them. He also knew Grizz would never let people know he had a younger brother who lived at the motel. It would make Grizz too vulnerable and probably wouldn't be safe for the kid. Grizz had some serious enemies.

"You know Misty's been picking on him."

"Yeah. It's okay. It'll make him tough."

"Did you know how smart he is? I mean he's, what, ten and he was arguing with Chip about the Cuban Missile Crisis. Made Chip look like an idiot. Everyone is starting to call him grown-up runt instead of just runt."

Grizz looked directly at Blue. "Is that where they came up with Grunt? Short for grown-up runt?"

"Yeah, a couple of the guys are calling him that. I don't think they mean anything by it. It's just easier to say. Want me to make 'em stop? It's kind of rude."

Grizz didn't answer right away. He took another sip of his beer and stared at something on the back wall of the bar. With a nickname like Grunt, there was no doubt he would probably get picked on by someone. "No, let them call him that. Like I said, the kid needs to be tough."

Blue didn't reply. He disagreed with Grizz on this point. The kid had been through enough. The first time Blue saw him without a shirt he'd had to hide his surprise. The kid was full of scars and mottled bruises. If he let himself think about it, Misty's bitchiness was probably nothing compared to what he had already experienced. Still, maybe he'd tell her to back off in spite of what Grizz said.

When they got back to the motel, there was a small group gathered around the pit. As they approached the fire, Blue asked no one in particular, "Where's the kid? Did Sissy get back with him yet?"

Sissy was Blue's girlfriend. She'd driven the little boy down to Miami to get him some more clothes and books. The kid wouldn't be attending school, but he'd still be getting some lessons. Upon first arriving at the motel, he'd immediately asked for books. "Learning books," he'd called them. When Grizz and Blue saw the type of books he picked out, they were shocked. Nobody at the motel would be giving the boy lessons. The books he'd selected were out of their range of knowledge. They got him what he'd requested and left him to educate himself. He'd already devoured the ones he'd received when he first arrived. This was his second shopping trip.

"Yeah," someone answered. "Sissy left. I think he's in Misty's room folding laundry or something."

Blue gave Grizz a sidelong glance and Grizz signaled him to let it go. *Damn. Why isn't Grizz stepping in here? And why do I care so damn much?* If Blue was honest with himself, the boy was growing on him. He was a smart and gentle child. He'd fascinated everyone in the couple of weeks that he'd been at the motel, dazzling them with his intelligence and showing a strong resilience to Misty's verbal abuse. Even Chip was more captivated by him than mad when they'd started discussing politics and world events.

But truth be told, if the kid was going to be living here, he would have to be tough. Maybe Grizz was right to let some things go. To let him have an undignified nickname like Grunt.

It wasn't until a few weeks later, after Grizz cut out Misty's tongue for an off-the-cuff comment, that the child's true intelligence came out. Without any medical experience, or at least none Blue knew of, the kid somehow managed to nurse her back to health by himself. Nobody had really liked Misty and most of the regulars weren't even fazed when Grizz had come out of his room that night with blood all over him. Grunt was the only one who jumped up immediately and, seeing Grizz wasn't hurt, had enough intuition to know something was terribly wrong. Misty hadn't come out of Grizz's room.

That night, Blue had watched from the pit as a hysterical Misty leaned heavily on the child she had been so mean to while he slowly and gently guided her back to her room.

*That kid is way too good to be living here.* Blue sighed and took another swig of beer.

# Chapter Seven
2000

IN THE CAR outside the strip mall, Ginny dried her eyes with the last of the tissues she'd found in her glove compartment. She needed to clean up before going to pick up Jason.

She got out of her car and headed for the yogurt shop at the end of the mall. Without looking at anyone, she headed straight for the ladies room and locked the door behind her, almost gagging at the overwhelming scent of lavender air freshener. The mirror showed her eyes were still red and swollen, and her nose was starting to run again. She unwound some toilet paper and blew her nose, then splashed cold water on her face. She had already cried off all of her makeup. Thoughts of Grizz, Tommy, the kids, everything, all swirled around her. She didn't know how long she stood there, bent over the sink, taking in large gulps of lavender air.

Someone jiggled the door. "Be out in a sec," she said flatly.

She used a paper towel to dry her face, then headed back out to her car without making eye contact with anyone in the store.

Less than ten minutes later, she pulled up to Max's house and beeped her horn. She could've gone inside to get Jason. She liked Max's mother. Denise Reynolds was genuinely sweet, but Ginny just didn't have it in her to make small talk. Besides, she couldn't trust herself not to fall apart. She needed to talk to someone. *Carter*. She would call Carter when she got home.

Sarah Jo wouldn't have been a good option. Ginny knew how much Jo loved Tommy. Jo and Tommy had a special history, and even though Carter had become close to both Ginny and Tommy over the years, she could be counted on to be more loyal to Ginny.

Did Sarah Jo know? Ginny's heart pounded. Oh no. She couldn't even bear to think about that. No. She wouldn't jump to conclusions.

Just then, the front door of Max's house swung open and a miniature version of Tommy bounded out, calling over his shoulder, "Later, dude."

She stared at her son. The son that Tommy had suggested they name after Grizz. Now she knew why. Grizz was actually Jason's grandfather. Her head started spinning. This is not happening.

Something nagged at her as she watched Jason approach the car. When they made eye contact, he broke into a wide grin. Her heart swelled with love for him. He looked just like his father. She had a déjà vu moment of a memory she couldn't place. She'd had it before, but could never conjure up a specific incident. Was it something she remembered about Tommy at this age? No. It couldn't have been. She didn't know Tommy when he was this young.

It was something else, but for the life of her, she couldn't remember what it was.

"Hi, Mom!" Jason tossed his bag into the back seat and climbed into the front passenger seat.

Ginny smiled at him, leaning over the console for a hug. He was such an affectionate child. Just like his father. She kissed his forehead as he started to buckle his seatbelt.

"How was your stay with the Reynolds? Did you have fun with Max?" she asked as she backed out of the driveway.

Max's mother had come out to the front porch and waved. Ginny beeped the horn twice in acknowledgement as she drove off.

"Yeah, a lot of fun. Mrs. Reynolds made homemade ice cream last night! Can we do that some time? It was really good."

"Yeah, sure, I guess."

"Mrs. Reynolds told me to tell you all my clothes in my bag are clean. She did laundry last night. She didn't want me to go home with dirty clothes." Before Ginny could comment, he added, "I got to help Polly wash her car this morning after church."

Ginny glanced at her son. "You *got* to help her?" she asked, laughing.

"Yeah, she said I was the best washer!" he replied excitedly. "And an even better drier!"

"I'm sure you are, honey. I'm sure you are." Ginny smiled to herself. Max had two older sisters, Sarah and Pollyanna. Jason had been in love with both of them since he was eight. He could never decide which one he loved more. Of course, they were way too old for

Jason. Polly was a senior in high school and Sarah was in college. She was sure both girls loved Jason like a little brother. More than likely, they found him as annoying as a little brother, as well. But they were nice girls. Always sweet to him. She appreciated that.

She wished Mimi were nicer to Jason, she thought as she drove the short trip back to the house. It wasn't that Mimi wasn't nice. She just wasn't interested in her little brother. Ginny couldn't explain it. It was something she had discussed more than once with Tommy. Mimi was never outright mean to Jason, but she wasn't a loving older sister. At least not anymore. Call it mother's intuition, but to Ginny, it sometimes seemed as if Mimi was incapable of feelings. Ginny couldn't put her finger on it. And to make matters worse, Tommy couldn't see it, always saying she was imagining things. Once he'd even told her she was too paranoid about Mimi being Grizz's biological daughter.

"Gin, you are subconsciously afraid that Mimi is too much like Grizz," he'd said. "I told you more than once that Grizz wasn't born that way. Grizz had a horrible childhood. Mimi didn't inherit Grizz's inability to care about people. It was something he turned off as a result of his abuse. Stop thinking about it."

But she couldn't help it. She knew about Grizz's childhood. He'd told her a little bit about it when she was pregnant that first time and they were still living at the motel. It was a neglectful childhood, not abusive. But Ginny had been neglected as a child, too, and she didn't murder people.

Mimi hadn't always been that way. Something had changed in Mimi a couple of years ago, almost as if a switch had been flipped. Mimi went from being a sweet, thoughtful child to a distant and detached one. Ginny wanted to have her daughter talk to someone, but everyone insisted that Mimi was just being a typical teenager.

Jason chattered non-stop the entire ride home. Ginny felt a little guilty for blocking him out, but her mind was elsewhere. She hoped Tommy would be gone when she got home. She didn't think she would be able to face him.

"Mom? Mom? How come you won't answer me?"

Ginny gave Jason a sidelong glance. "Sorry, sweetie. Did you ask me something?"

"Yeah, I asked if you thought Dad had the strap on my helmet fixed. He promised before you guys went out of town that we could take a ride on his motorcycle when I got home today."

Before she could even answer him, Jason continued, "Where were you guys the last couple of days?"

"I don't know about your helmet, but if your father told you he had it fixed, then I'm sure he had it fixed. And you know where we were. We told you we went to see an old friend before he left town."

"That's not what Corbin said." And before Ginny could respond, he blurted, "Corbin said you and Dad went to see some guy get fried."

# Chapter Eight
1969

GRUNT HAD BEEN living at the motel for a couple of months when Grizz said to him one day, "C'mon, kid. Let's go for a ride."

"On your motorcycle?" Grunt asked excitedly.

"No, we'll take one of the cars."

"Okay, let me check on something real quick." Grunt hurried off.

Grizz shook his head. He watched as the boy went into Misty's room. Why the kid gave a damn about Misty was beyond Grizz's understanding. Enough time had passed. She had healed and was fine. Grunt could be a mystery.

Grizz headed toward the cars he kept parked on the far side of the office. He wouldn't be taking his red convertible Mustang. With its loud engine and shiny chrome wheels, he'd stick out like a sore thumb. He wouldn't take the Cadillac either. Just a little too classy for where he was going. Might get noticed. He settled on the average-looking four-door sedan. He didn't say anything when Grunt climbed in the passenger seat.

"Where are we going?" Grunt asked.

"To check on a friend's daughter."

Grizz then turned on the radio at almost full volume. The kid was a talker and he just wasn't in the mood for conversation. A couple of miles before they reached their destination, Grizz glanced over at the kid. Grunt. That was his new name and it was starting to stick. He turned the radio volume down.

"Friend of mine died a few years back. Left behind a daughter. Her mom and stepdad aren't real stable. Kind of neglect her. I made a promise before he died that I would step in when I could and just keep an eye on things. Make sure she's being taken care of."

Grunt didn't say anything at first. Grizz could tell that he was thinking. Finally, he said, "What do her mom and stepdad think about you checking on their daughter?"

This surprised Grizz. The kid was perceptive.

"They don't know. And it's not something I can do myself. Besides, when the hell would I have time?" He glanced over at Grunt. "Mavis keeps an eye on her for me. Just tells me when she thinks I need to do something. That's why we're checking on her today."

Mavis was an older woman who did the bookkeeping for the couple of bars Grizz owned. They were his only legitimate businesses and the older woman had grown on Grizz. Mavis was rail thin and overly tanned. She had short cropped bleached blonde hair and the kind of gravelly voice that came with sixty years of chain-smoking. Grizz had realized early on that Mavis could be trusted and was only too eager to take on the role of Gwinny's guardian angel. A widow with no children and no family, she had worked at a convenience store near The Red Crab. Grizz used to go in all the time to buy cigarettes. He didn't remember exactly how the friendship started. Probably Mavis first engaged him in small talk, knowing her. Later, he found out through casual conversation that she'd run an accounting business with her husband before they retired. Her talents were being wasted behind a cash register. Offering Mavis a job was one of the best decisions he'd ever made. She used the office at The Red Crab and was dearly loved by even the roughest characters.

Not just that, but Mavis was also more than happy to insinuate herself into Gwinny's life. She managed to get a part-time job at Gwinny's elementary school, as the cashier in the cafeteria line, and was loved by all of the children. It was one way she could keep an eye on the little girl and strike up an occasional conversation with her without being obvious. Mavis looked forward to the days she got to work at the cafeteria. She loved not just Gwinny, but all of the kids. Except for one. She was having a hard time warming up to the school bully. As she said, that Curtis Armstrong was a troublemaker.

Grunt gave Grizz a questioning glance. "How do you check on her without anybody knowing it?"

"I thought it would be hard, but the sad truth is, this little girl is so alone nobody has ever noticed me. And I think I'm kind of noticeable. But the few times Mavis told me something was up and I've had to see for myself, I've been able to stay in the background." He didn't know why, but he felt prompted to continue. "Mavis told me one day that something was wrong. She suspected that Gwinny wasn't being fed much at home. She was getting her free school lunch, but kept asking for seconds to take with her."

Grunt looked at him. "Her name is Gwinny?"

"Yeah. Her name is Gwinny." He paused reflectively, subconsciously tugging on his beard before continuing. "Gwinny walks up to the convenience store once a day, like clockwork. One day after Mavis told me her concern, I decided to just hang out there, lay low, see if I could figure out what was going on. That day I saw her go into the store with a brown bag. She came out still holding the same bag and she looked upset. I went in after she left, and the lady behind the counter looked upset, too. I asked her if something was wrong. She said she felt awful because the little girl who'd just left was trying to sell some of her personal things to buy food."

"Why didn't her parents feed her?"

"I thought they did, but I guess they were gone so much, they ate at the bar they hung out at and would forget to make sure she had food." Grizz gripped the steering wheel. "It really pissed me off. It bothered the clerk at the store, too, because she told me she was a working mother and didn't even have a dollar to give her. And to make matters worse, the little money Gwinny did have, she used to buy her mom cigarettes."

"So what did you do? Did you help?" Grunt's eyes were wide.

"Yeah." Grizz shrugged. "I got Mavis to start leaving a bag of groceries on their doorstep here and there. One time I left a bag by the door myself when I knew nobody was around."

This shocked Grunt. He couldn't imagine Grizz grocery shopping. Grizz must have read his mind and gave Grunt a half smile. "I had the girls get some extra stuff when they went shopping. I was just the deliveryman. And I only did it once when Mavis couldn't."

"Are we delivering groceries today?" Grunt asked as he turned around and eyed the back seat. He didn't see anything.

"No, Mavis said things have gotten better since then."

"So she looks like she's getting fed?"

"Yeah, I guess so. I haven't actually seen her in over two years.

But I'm sure Mavis would've told me. Besides, she's older now and I guess she makes sure she gets money from her parents. Mavis said she used to walk to the grocery store because it's cheaper. But it's a lot farther away than the convenience store." Grizz looked at Grunt a little sheepishly before he told him, "I bought her a bicycle. Left it when nobody was around. I guess her parents think the neighbors must be helping out. They honestly don't seem to give a shit."

Grunt smiled up at Grizz. "You bought her a bike or you got someone else to buy her a bike?"

"Mavis picked it out. What the hell would I know about a girl's bicycle? Mavis outdid herself. It was purple with a sparkly banana seat and tassels on the handlebars. The whole nine yards," he laughed.

What Grizz didn't tell Grunt was that it never occurred to him that Gwinny had nobody to teach her how to ride it. Mavis mentioned her skinned knees and elbows a few weeks after he left the bike. But she eventually got the hang of it and was able to fit a small grocery bag in the basket. He was glad she was using it. He still couldn't believe her parents let her ride that far to the grocery store on her own. She was still only nine.

Grunt interrupted his thoughts. "Your friend would be happy to know you're looking out for his daughter."

Grizz didn't answer him and wouldn't meet his eyes. The kid seemed just perceptive enough to detect that he was lying. Gwinny wasn't the daughter of a friend who'd died. She was just a little girl who'd offered him a kindness once and he was trying to anonymously return the favor the best way he knew how. He never did use the bandages she'd handed him that day outside of the convenience store, but he'd kept them. They meant something to him.

That day, those bandages—it was the first time he ever remembered someone giving him something without expecting something in return.

Grunt looked up and realized they were at the end of a cul-de-sac. He hadn't been paying attention to where they were going. Grizz was turning around. Eventually they edged slowly past a house with thick hedges along its driveway. Grizz went past it just a little, then backed far up into the driveway, hidden from sight. He cut the engine and looked at a house across the street to their left. It was two houses down from the one they were facing.

He pointed. "That's where she lives."

Grunt looked over the dashboard and strained to peer above the hedges that were camouflaging the car. He didn't see her. He looked at Grizz questioningly.

"Mavis said the school bus should be dropping her off at the end of the block."

Just then, Grizz was interrupted by a loud noise. A lawn cutting service had been unloading their gear at the house next to Gwinny's when they first drove past. They had just started up their equipment and were now busily mowing the lawn, using an edger and trimming up some bushes. The smell of fresh cut grass mixed with gasoline from the lawn equipment wafted into the car.

Grizz continued, "I've never watched her house, but Mavis told me this lawn service is new. I don't know if these guys realize she's alone. I just want to make sure they're not gonna cause trouble for her. She's so vulnerable."

Grunt looked back toward Gwinny's house. A little girl was making her way down the street, ponytail swaying. She walked with long, deliberate strides. He gulped back his surprise as his eyes widened.

"Is that her?" he asked, as he sat up to get a better view.

Grizz didn't answer. She made her way up to the front door and took the key from around her neck to unlock it. But Grizz wasn't watching her. He was watching the lawn guys. Nobody seemed to pay her any attention, he thought with satisfaction.

"Are we leaving now?" Grunt asked, sounding disappointed, like he wanted to stay a little longer.

Before Grizz could answer, she barged out of the house carrying something large and heavy. They realized it was a table. They sat quietly as they watched her quickly and expertly set up a card table on the sidewalk.

Grizz was surprised by how tall she had gotten in the two years since he'd last seen her. But she looked healthy enough. She carried the card table out effortlessly. *Good, she's being taken care of. But why is she wearing a sweatshirt? It's fucking a hundred degrees out here.* He swiped his brow, sweat trickling down his back.

She went back into the house and came out with a large sheet of construction paper. She taped it to the front of the table. In large block letters that had been neatly written, it read, "Fresh squeezed lemonade, 25 cents."

"Can we get some?" Grunt asked.

"No, we can't get some," Grizz growled. He was starting to get upset. Here he was worried that the lawn guys would notice her and he was relieved when they didn't seem to. But now, she was outside with her lemonade stand. *Calm down. They don't know for sure that she doesn't have a parent or other adult in there. She could have someone who works nights and sleeps during the day, so she would have to let herself in.*

Grunt interrupted his thoughts. "If you don't have any money, I have some," Grunt said, reaching into his pocket and pulling out an impressive wad of cash.

"Where the hell did you get all that money from?"

"It's mine," Grunt answered defensively.

Before Grizz could comment further, Grunt sat up straight. "What's she doing now?"

She had finished setting everything up and was sitting in a lawn chair when she looked over at the guys mowing the lawn and stood up. She was watching them. Then she took five paper cups from the stack and set them on the little tray she'd used to carry her supplies. She filled up each cup and proceeded toward the house next door. Grizz shook his head. *She was bringing the lawn guys lemonade! Damn!*

She approached each man and offered him a cup. The first guy reached into his pocket, but she shook her head and smiled. She did this with each person, and each time they tried to pay her, she refused to take the money.

Grunt looked at Grizz, then her, then back at Grizz.

"You told me she used to barely have money to get food and now she's giving away her lemonade?"

Grizz sighed and swiped his face with his hand. "Yeah. She's giving away her lemonade."

By now Gwinny had made her way back over to her table and sat down.

Just then, Grunt said excitedly, "Look, she has new customers!"

Then his excitement seemed to ebb as he squinted to get a better look.

Grizz glanced at the three boys approaching Gwinny. They were on bicycles. He stiffened. He recognized one kid. Curtis Armstrong. The boy who had bullied her the first day Grizz saw her a few years back. Curtis had grown a little. Were they friends now? Mavis never mentioned him, so maybe he left Gwinny alone. He didn't have to wait long to find out.

Gwinny stood as the three boys approached her. They got off their bikes, letting them drop on her front lawn. Her body language told Grizz she was ready for a fight. Dammit.

They couldn't hear the conversation, but they could tell Curtis spoke first. They watched as he leaned over her pitcher of lemonade and quickly poured a bag of dirt in it.

All three boys starting laughing.

The muscles in Grizz's jaw tightened and he looked away. "I can make sure she's fed and has a bike to ride to the store, but this is one thing I can't get involved in."

Grunt was staring out over the dashboard as Grizz spoke. Finally, he turned back to Grizz, smiling broadly. "Doesn't look like she needs you to get involved."

Grizz glanced back over at the lemonade stand and laughed out loud.

Gwinny had dumped her pitcher of muddied lemonade right on Curtis Armstrong's head.

Grizz and Grunt watched in amusement as a humiliated Curtis and his friends rode off in the same direction from which they'd come. Gwinny quickly packed up her lemonade stand and went into the house. Grizz kept an eye on the lawn guys, who didn't seem to notice what had happened.

Finally, it was time to go.

They silently pulled out of the driveway and slowly drove down the block. They had passed about ten homes when Grunt ordered, "Stop!"

Grizz jammed on the brakes, and before he could stop him, Grunt jumped out of the car. Grizz watched as he ran back toward a house they had just passed. Grizz started to back up and follow him, but then stopped when he realized what Grunt was doing. Grunt ran halfway across someone's yard, removed a pocket knife from his back pocket and, in the span of ten seconds, had expertly punctured the tires of three bicycles left lying on the lawn. Then, he trotted back to the car, got in without a word, and slammed the door.

Grizz looked at him and nodded. *The kid was learning.*

After a couple of miles, Grizz finally asked, "You wanna tell me about the money?"

Grunt looked over at him. "I didn't steal it."

"I didn't ask if you stole it. Where'd you get it?"

"I earned it."

"How'd you earn it?"

"When Doc came last month to sew up Chip's arm, he gave me ten dollars for being a good helper."

"That was a helluva lot more money than ten dollars," Grizz said, giving him a sidelong glance.

"It's sixty dollars," Grunt replied, and before Grizz could say anything else, "The rest of it's hidden in a good place."

"The rest of it?"

"Yeah, I have four hundred and sixty-two. I just keep the sixty on me in case I need it. Like today. I could've bought you a cup of lemonade."

"I could've bought my own damn lemonade. How the heck did you get all that money?"

Grunt gave a hint of a smile. "I won it playing poker."

This surprised Grizz. He knew some of his crew had a weekly poker game in one of the rooms. He'd never really bothered with it and hadn't noticed Grunt had been playing.

"Who taught you?"

"Nobody. I taught myself. I was helping Moe get the guys their beers and stuff and I just started watching real close. I figured it out."

"Who the hell is Moe?"

"You sure do cuss a lot," Grunt remarked, then added, "It's Misty. Sometimes I call her Moe." And before Grizz could ask, he added, "Some of the new people call her Moe. Someone asked her once what her name was, and she made an M kind of sound, but she couldn't say Misty. So I guess the guy thought she said Moe."

"So it's Moe now," Grizz said matter-of-factly.

"I asked her if she liked it and she nodded 'yes.' She wanted a new name to start over," Grunt told him thoughtfully. "She writes me notes a lot."

He looked at his lap.

Grizz didn't say anything for a while. He wondered what the kid thought of what he did to Misty, or Moe, or whatever she called herself now. Was the boy judging him? He started to wonder if he cared, but was instantly reminded of the earlier conversation.

"So you taught yourself to play poker and won a ton of money. Does Blue know you're playing poker with the guys?"

"Yeah, he knows. He told me it was okay, but he said I had to be careful with my money. Having some is a big responsibility and it might make some of the guys mad. He even said that some of them might be mad enough to try and steal it back from me so I had to learn how to protect what was mine."

Grizz glanced at him. "He's right. You being Blue's brother might scare some of them off, but that's a lot of cash, kid, and someone might just be gutsy enough to try and get it back from you."

"I know. That's why I hid most of it. I picked a really good place where nobody would look."

The conversation was starting to amuse Grizz. "So, where'd you stash it? The freezer? The A/C vent?" He paused. "The floor?"

"No way," Grunt said emphatically. "I had to pick a place where they'd be scared to look."

"Ah," Grizz said. "The swamp. I'll tell you what. You better be super careful out there. You go out there burying your money and you better be watching your surroundings. An alligator could snap you up and disappear in seconds."

Grunt looked over at him. "It's not hidden in the swamp. I told you, Blue told me to pick a scary place." He paused before adding, "I hid it in *your* room."

# Chapter Nine
## 2000

TOMMY LOOKED UP when he realized someone was talking to him. It was Mimi. She was standing in the doorway of his office. He didn't hear her come in. The thought occurred that maybe she'd been home this whole time. Had she heard their fight? Did she know?

"So is it okay? Can I go?" she was asking Tommy. She didn't look like she'd heard anything.

"Sorry, hon, I didn't hear what you asked me. Go where?"

"To Courtney's. She invited me over to hang out by the pool. She said I could stay for Sunday dinner and movie night. Can I go?"

"Yeah, sure." He blinked, tried to shake the fog from his head. "Do you need me to drive you?"

"Nope. I'm walking down to Lindsay's. She's invited, too and can drive us both. She can bring me home later." Lindsay was Mimi's friend and a year older. She had a license and use of her mother's minivan whenever she wanted.

"Ten-thirty."

"Ten-thirty? C'mon, Dad, it's summer," she wheedled. "There's no school tomorrow. Midnight. Pleeeaaase?"

Tommy was too distracted to argue with her. If Lindsay's parents didn't have a problem with their daughter being out that late, he could give in, too. Giving in, he realized, was something he'd been doing more and more lately.

"Yeah, sure, honey. But not one minute later."

"You're the best." She beamed from the doorway of the den.

Tommy didn't even hear her leave. He was too lost in thought over what had happened between him and Ginny.

Mimi, meanwhile, walked down the tree-lined street. She passed Lindsay's house and took note of the missing minivan. *Good, they're still out of town like Lindsay said. Thanks, Linds.* She continued on her way, glancing around occasionally. She didn't see anyone she knew. It was a lazy Sunday and most people weren't outside in the Florida heat. They were inside their air-conditioned homes enjoying a cold one while watching sports on their oversized TVs.

She heard a couple of kids' voices and splashing as she passed houses with swimming pools. She smelled chlorine and fresh cut grass in spite of the fact that there was nobody out mowing their lawn. A loud humming was coming from somewhere. Probably a beehive tucked up under someone's mailbox, she thought to herself as she confidently made her way down the street.

She noticed a small car approaching and casually looked at the sidewalk as she took quick note of the driver in her peripheral vision. It was a woman and she was squinting at the mailboxes. *She must be looking for an address,* Mimi thought. She didn't pay any attention to Mimi and they passed each other without notice or incident.

Mimi quickened her pace. She rounded the corner at the end of her block. She spotted him immediately and started jogging toward him. When she got to him, he grabbed her around the waist and pulled her close, kissing her hard.

"Let's go, baby," he said as he handed her a helmet.

She jumped on the back of his motorcycle and they sped off.

# Chapter Ten
1969


IT WAS A few weeks after the lemonade incident when Blue told Grizz, "There's gonna be some business at the motel today. Can you find someone to take the kid out? Get him outta here for a while?"

"What business?" Grizz frowned at him.

"Slash" was all Blue said.

Grizz nodded. He knew Slash had been sharing gang secrets with a woman he was seeing from a rival gang. Grizz planned on making an example out of him. He didn't realize Blue was having him brought to the motel today. Blue went on to explain that he'd put the word out and they were expecting a big crowd and were going to put on a little show of what would happen to someone who defied the gang. Worse yet, someone who defied Grizz.

"Didn't know it was today. I'll handle it," he told Blue. "You can take the kid somewhere."

"No, if you don't mind, I want to handle it myself, Grizz. If I'm going to earn the kind of respect you have, I need to show them I'm not afraid to get my hands dirty, or in this case, bloody."

Grizz thought about it for a minute. "They already respect you, Blue. But fine, I have business at the bar with Mavis. I'll take him with me."

Blue nodded.

"And don't kill him," Grizz added. "Just make him wish he was dead."

An hour later, Grizz and Grunt pulled up to The Red Crab on Grizz's motorcycle. Grizz purposely took his bike so he didn't have to answer a million questions. The few times he'd taken Grunt on outings it always felt like an official interrogation. The kid's brain and mouth were non-stop. He was too smart for his own good.

This would be the second time Grunt would meet Mavis. Grizz had taken Grunt with him once to Mavis's house to pick up some paperwork. It was when Grunt first came to live at the motel. Mavis had been recovering from minor foot surgery and had been working from her home during that time. She'd stared at the little boy that day with horror. Grunt was still extremely underweight at the time and it was obvious he had been a mistreated child. Grizz quickly explained to her that the kid was Blue's younger brother and had been abused at home. Blue stole him away from his family. Mavis had nodded with understanding. She didn't ask questions. She didn't pry. She accepted what Grizz told her and never addressed it again. That's why he liked her so much.

The realization that he actually liked someone surprised him as he was brought back to the present by Grunt's voice.

"Is this the bar we came to the first night?"

"I told you to never mention that night again," Grizz said in a low voice.

"I know that. I just wanted to see if I remembered right. Are we going in? Are we going to get to eat here? Do you know if there's a pinball machine in there? How about a pool table?"

Grizz didn't answer him. It was going to be a long day.

As they opened the door, their senses were attacked by the ferocious stench of stale cigarettes and a grease-laden grill. Grunt waved his hand in front of his face as if to chase away the smell.

"It really stinks in here," he said to no one in particular.

"White Room" by Cream was blaring on the jukebox. As Grunt's eyes adjusted to the dim light, they widened.

"Hey, the girls in here aren't wearing any shirts!" He elbowed Grizz. "Where are their shirts? Why aren't they wearing shirts?"

Grizz looked down at the boy, tried not to smile. "Is this your first time seeing tits?"

Grunt didn't answer, he just stared as he followed Grizz back to a small office. Mavis was sitting at a desk and smiled when Grizz walked in. She stood up and went to give Grunt a hug after she noticed him behind Grizz.

"Well, hello, young man. You have certainly filled out some since I saw you last. And you got a haircut. It looks nice. You still going by Runt?"

Grunt looked at Mavis shyly. "Everybody called me Runt at first.

Then Grown-up Runt, but that was too long. So now it's just Grunt. It's my own special name. Everybody has a special name at the motel." Before Mavis could comment, he added, "Did you know the girls out there aren't wearing any shirts? You're probably the only girl in here wearing a shirt. How come you're wearing a shirt and they're not?"

Grizz looked at Mavis and said, "I'll let you handle this one. I'll be back in a minute. Kid, you hungry?"

"Yeah. Can I get a hamburger? Wait, no, a cheeseburger and a soda. Oh! And French fries, too."

"Sure, I'll be back in a little while with it. You stay here with Mavis until I come back."

"Okay, Grizz," Grunt said.

When Grunt turned back to look at Mavis, something nagged at her. She thought he seemed familiar, but she couldn't grab hold of a memory. Maybe she was remembering the first time she saw him when she was working from home that day, and Grizz dropped in with him. He looked different now. Healthy and strong, even if he was short for his age. But when she gave it more thought, she remembered she'd had this same feeling the first time she had met him, too. She frowned, then decided to dismiss it. With all of the children at the school, it was very possible he looked similar to one of them, that was all.

Giving him a kind look, she asked, "So, I take it this is the first time you've seen female breasts?"

She knew it wasn't any of her business, but she thought Grizz was wrong to not give any thought to the fact that this child was probably being exposed to things that were too mature for him. Maybe she could gently and tactfully explain some things to him.

"They're not breasts," Grunt said matter-of-factly. "They're tits."

Before Mavis could reply, something caught his attention in the office. "What is that? Is that some kind of game?" he asked, pointing to the top of one of the filing cabinets.

Mavis turned around and saw he was pointing to her chess set. "That's a game called chess," she answered him. She was secretly glad their topic had turned from breasts to chess.

"Whose game is it?" Grunt asked inquisitively as he walked over to the filing cabinet and stood on his tiptoes to get a better look.

"It's my game," Mavis answered, smiling at the memories. "I played with my husband every night before he passed away. When I found out Grizz played, I brought it here so we could play occasionally. And thanks for asking. I need to remind him that it's his move."

"Can I learn to play chess? Can you teach me to play it?"

"Sure, I'll teach you."

He sat down in a chair across from her desk and reached behind him. He whipped out a small notebook. Then he took a pen that was behind his ear and looked up at her. Mavis hadn't noticed the pen until he retrieved it.

"What have you got there?" she asked.

"It's my learning notebook. Okay, tell me the rules and I'll write them down. I write everything in my learning notebook. That way, I remember to study it later."

Mavis smiled warmly. She liked this child. She really liked this child.

Grizz returned ten minutes later with Grunt's lunch order. Grunt was writing in his notebook. Mavis looked up and told Grizz before he could ask, "He's writing down everything he thinks he needs to know about chess. Why don't you take this set back with you and play with him? You don't bring him here enough for me to play with him."

Grizz didn't say anything, he just nodded. Maybe it would be a good idea to play chess with the kid. If he found something else to occupy him other than poker, Grizz wouldn't have to worry about the guys getting pissed off that the kid was winning all their money. Yes, maybe chess would be a good distraction from poker.

Mavis stood up and took the food from Grizz's hands.

"Grunt, honey, why don't you sit over here in the corner and have a picnic on the floor? We'll bring the chess set over and you can familiarize yourself with the pieces."

Grunt shoved his notebook in the back of his pants and put his pen behind his ear. He stood up and carefully lifted the chess set off the high filing cabinet and walked it over to the corner where Mavis had set up his picnic. She had even laid down a spare tablecloth to use as a blanket. He'd never had a picnic before.

After settling him in, she went back to her desk. Grizz sat in the chair that Grunt had just deserted and they discussed business: tax issues, payroll, expenses. When they were finished, Mavis looked around Grizz to see if Grunt was still occupied. She wasn't sure if Grizz would want Grunt to hear the other thing she wanted to discuss.

In almost a whisper, she said, "I want to talk about Gwinny." She nodded toward Grunt to let Grizz know that she was being considerate of the fact that "young ears" were in the room.

Grizz turned around and stared at the boy. He looked like he was immersed in his new game. "It's okay. What's up?"

"Summer is what's up. School is almost out. I'm not sure how I can keep a watch on her for you when I won't see her for a couple of months."

Mavis knew that Grizz hadn't thought about summer, but he never had to in the past. Mavis purposely made it a point to accidentally run into Gwinny at the convenience store over the last couple of summers. She concocted a story that she lived close by, which she didn't. It was actually a few miles out of her way to go there, but she really had become fond of the little girl and was concerned about her well-being. Truth be told, there was more than one child at Gwinny's school that could have benefited from her watchful eye. She wondered if Grizz's friend was watching down from heaven with a grateful sigh of relief that his daughter had some human guardian angels.

Grizz scratched his chin and tugged absentmindedly on his long beard. Before he could reply, she added, "That convenience store. Why don't I get a part time job there? Maybe that would help."

"I couldn't ask you to do that, Mavis," he said. "You've already gone above and beyond."

"Look," she answered. "I don't mind it, really. I hadn't realized how lonely I was until you asked me to keep an eye on her. I mean, yeah, I've come to love the regulars here at the bar, but I've never had the chance to have a child in my life. Truthfully, I love all of the children at that school. Well, most of them," she added with a knowing smile.

"That's a long time to be on your feet every day. At least here you get to sit. At the cafeteria, too. You have a chair at the register, right?"

"Yes, and I can have a chair behind the register at the convenience store, too. I do have experience, so I can't imagine the owners having a problem with me sitting behind the counter off and on. Really, I'd like to try it. But remember, we don't even know if Mindy's is hiring part-time."

"They'll hire you," Grizz added. "Convenience stores are always turning over employees." Before Mavis could comment, Grizz asked, "Why now, Mavis? She seemed okay last summer without you having to take on a summer job to keep an eye on her."

"That's the other thing I wanted to talk to you about," she said quietly.

"What? What is it?" Grizz sat up.

"I know she's only nine, but she's a mature child, Grizz. I didn't even notice until I heard that brat Curtis Armstrong say something."

"Say something about what?"

Mavis looked at him and gestured toward her own chest. She nodded at him as if she expected him to understand what she was trying to say.

"What? What are you talking about?"

She rolled her eyes. "Boobies, Grizz. She looks like she's starting to develop. Not a lot, but noticeable enough for that little shit, Curtis, to say something. I've heard him commenting to his friends. And she's started wearing a sweatshirt. It's ninety degrees outside and she's wearing a *sweatshirt*. She's trying to cover them up."

"Are you kidding me? She's only nine. Isn't that early?"

"You're asking me? I didn't get mine until I was—um, actually, I still don't have 'em—but yeah. She might be young, but children develop at different ages. She's what? A year younger than him?" she asked nodding over at Grunt, who still seemed involved in his food and the game. "And she's definitely taller. I just think maybe it's time for some training bras. I can't see that ditzy mother of hers taking her to get any, either. I've seen that woman just a few times and I'm pretty certain she doesn't even own a bra."

Grizz looked uncomfortable at the idea. "So what are you going to do? Wait until she comes in to buy her mom's smokes and say, 'Oh, by the way, Gwinny, I found these training bras and thought you might like them?'" He made a face. "And what the hell is a training bra?"

"Stop being a smart ass. A training bra is just a little starter bra. I was thinking of going down to the thrift shop and picking up some used clothes that I know would fit her. I could toss some bras in with the clothes and then tell her my neighbor's granddaughter left some of her things here while she was visiting, and my neighbor asked if I knew any little girls they might fit."

Grizz leaned back and sighed. This Gwinny thing was getting to him. He'd never once considered what he would do as she got older. He guessed he naively assumed that she would stay a sweet, little girl who needed someone to keep an eye on things. He never imagined he'd be dealing with bullies and bras. He dragged a hand through his hair, letting out a long sigh.

"Yeah," he said finally, "get the job for the summer. Get the bras. I trust you to handle it and let me know if I'm needed."

He started to stand up to leave when she stopped him, a hand up.

"And there's another thing."

He sighed again and sat back down. "What? What else is there, Mavis?"

She nodded at Grunt. "I think he might be a little young to be coming here. He already informed me that the girls had 'tits,' not 'breasts.' You think you could've at least started him out with something a little milder?"

Grizz looked at her like he didn't know what she was talking about.

"Maybe you could have told him they were boobies, or ninnies or something. You had to tell him they were *tits*?"

"They are tits, and boobies is something a ten-year old would say."

"He *is* a ten-year old!"

"Fine, okay," He swallowed back a grin and stood up. "Grunt, time to go. Pack it up."

Grunt stood up and walked over to him and Mavis. He reached behind his back and whipped out his notebook. He took the pen from behind his ear and started writing.

"What are you writing down now?" Grizz asked.

"I'm taking notes to research something later."

"What do you need to research?"

"I need to learn why Gwinny's boobies need training."

# Chapter Eleven

2000

TOMMY HADN'T REALIZED how quiet the house was until he heard the automatic icemaker on the refrigerator dump a load of ice into the bin. He inhaled deeply and could smell apple and cinnamon spice, but he didn't know where it was coming from. It was one of those mystery scents Ginny had placed somewhere in their home.

He knew she'd meant it when she said she wanted him out of the house.

He also knew he wouldn't be leaving.

He stared at the heavy box on his desk and sighed. Memories continued to swirl, pressing down on him like a weight. It all suddenly felt like too much.

The doorbell rang. He left the box on his desk and wandered to the front door. It wouldn't be Ginny, not this soon. He opened the door to find a woman there, clutching some kind of notebook to her chest. *Oh brother, not another reporter.* He stiffened as the last few months with Leslie flashed through his mind. Even though she didn't spend much time interviewing him—she mainly spoke with Ginny—Tommy decided early on that he didn't care for reporters or journalists. The experience with Leslie had only cemented that. He would be nice to this woman, but firm. No interview.

"I'm looking for Tommy or Ginny Dillon. I have something—"

"Look, you seem like a nice lady. But we're not doing interviews. I don't want to be mean or rude to you, but please leave us alone." He started to close the door but she appeared startled, holding up a hand.

"I'm not a reporter! Please—I have something to give you."

He turned back and sized her up. She seemed familiar, but he didn't know why. He was certain he'd never met her. She was a nice-looking woman—average height and just a little on the heavy side, with brown hair with blonde highlights, intelligent brown eyes, and a warm smile. He couldn't guess her age. Before he could continue with his mental assessment, she spoke.

"I'm Louise." She cleared her throat. "Louise Bailey."

Tommy didn't say anything. He shook his head.

"I'm Rhonda Bailey's daughter."

The name was familiar, but Tommy still couldn't make the connection.

She looked at him and smiled kindly. "You knew her as Chicky."

Chicky. Tommy's mouth went slack. That was a name he hadn't heard or thought about in years.

"You're Chicky's daughter?" He found himself smiling now, picturing the no-nonsense voluptuous blonde with the cheerful eyes. Truthfully, it had been so long he wasn't sure when he'd last laid eyes on the woman. "Come in. Tell me how she is. We haven't heard anything about her in years. Last we did hear, she owned her own bar somewhere up in South Carolina."

He showed Louise into the living room and motioned toward the sofa. "Here, sit down. Can I get you a drink?"

She smiled again, and he suddenly saw her mother in the crooked grin and warm eyes. "No, thank you. I'm not thirsty."

Tommy took a seat on the chair directly across from her. "I haven't thought about Chicky in a long time. How is she?"

"That's why I'm here. Fulfilling her last wish, I guess you could say."

"Her last wish?" Tommy asked, realization dawning.

"Mom passed away a few years back. Cancer."

"I'm sorry," he said with genuine sympathy. "Chicky was one of the good ones."

"Yes, she was. Thank you for saying so." After a beat, Louise quickly added, "I don't want this to be awkward, so I'll tell you up front that I know about my Mom's earlier life with the gang and everything." She paused, fingering the notebook. "She held on to something for years."

Louise looked up at him and smiled again, this time more sadly. "This. She said on her deathbed that it should be given to you or your wife after Grizz was gone. I don't know if his death is significant or not. Just something Mom felt specific about. She went to see him in prison a couple of times before she died. Did you know that?"

"No, I didn't know," Tommy said quietly.

"I think he was fond of Mom. A beautiful bouquet of flowers showed up at her funeral. There was a card with just the initial 'G' on it. I think it was from him."

This surprised Tommy. He couldn't imagine Grizz sending flowers to a funeral. Even Chicky's.

"She told me what a rough character he was, but she was fond of him, too," Louise shrugged. "He always treated her right no matter how rotten he was to the others. I don't know, maybe there's something in here that could have hurt him. Or maybe something that would've made him mad. That might be why she never wanted him to know about it and why I've held on to it this long. I've never read it. I don't know what's in it. I honestly don't care."

She stood and offered the notebook to Tommy. He got up and took it from her outstretched hands.

"What is this?" he asked, looking down at it, then back up at Louise.

"It's Moe's journal."

**********

*Moe's Diary, 1969*

*Dear Elizabeth,*

*I hate him. I hate him so much. I can't believe how bad he hurt me. I used to love him. I would have done anything for him. I did do everything for him. I don't understand why he got so mad.*

*I was cleaning up his kitchen and I made some comment about seeing him with some guy in a suit. I had been hitching rides and wound up somewhere near the beach. I saw two men get out of a fancy car. One was all dressed up and the other was Grizz. I saw them go into a building. I just told him that his new friend looked nice and would he be bringing him around the motel?*

*He got real mad then. Like he thought I was purposely spying on him. He threw me up against the refrigerator and started asking me stuff. I told* him the truth. I didn't know anything. I just happened to see him and thought the fancy suit guy was handsome. Thought maybe I could make some extra money by getting to know him better.

He said I could die for just seeing that and that I had a big mouth and couldn't be trusted. Then, he took his knife off his belt and told me that he was doing me a favor.

I heard him telling Blue later that he'd asked for a blow job and that I'd told him to let Grunt do it. That's why he cut me. I didn't say that, but it does sound like something I would've said.

I've been really mean to Blue's little brother. It was just easy, I guess, and for some reason, it made me feel better. But not anymore. I feel so bad now. Everything and everyone that has ever been good to me, I've hurt in some way.

I'm sorry I saw Grizz that day and had to ask him about the guy. I'm sorry I was mean to the one person at the motel who was ever nice to me. Grunt. That's what some of the people call him now. He is now my best and only friend.

When I think about it, I really didn't have any friends before. Just Fess. He's not really a friend, but he's the only one who hasn't treated me like a nobody. Fess comes in my room to be with me. He's okay. He's not mean like the others. He plays chess with Grunt once in a while. He said if I learned he would play chess with me too.

But I don't really want to play chess. I only want to do one thing. It's all I can think about. I want to hurt Grizz worse than he hurt me. I want him to pay for what he did to me—and one day he will!

# Chapter Twelve
## 1970

MAVIS USED HER key to let herself in the back door of The Red Crab. She managed to get her keys put away while she juggled her armful of paperwork and a large Styrofoam cup of sweet tea. She loved her sweet tea and it was one drink that wasn't on the bar's menu. She made her way down the short hallway to her office. It was still early, but she could hear some regulars out in the bar. She opened her office door, which she never kept locked, and stopped short.

"Excuse me! I didn't realize my office was being used as a brothel!" Mavis exclaimed in disgust as she surveyed the scene before her. The couple scrambled to adjust their clothes. "I'm going to have to disinfect my desk before I can use it again. And you should know better, Pauline." Mavis eyed her watch. "You're already on the clock!"

"You shouldn't walk into a room without knocking, Mavis!" Pauline huffed from where she'd been leaning over the desk, Grizz behind her. They'd been enjoying a quickie before the bar got busy. Grizz was hung like a horse and Pauline was more than a little miffed that Mavis had to go and interrupt it. Damn her. "And a brothel? When were you born, Mavis? The 1800s?"

"It's my office! Get out!" Mavis looked away in embarrassment and pointed to the hallway that led to the bar.

Grizz had removed himself and was zipping up his jeans. "I was finished anyway," he added nonchalantly.

"Oh, well then, as long as *you* were finished," Mavis retorted.

"I wasn't finished." Pauline whined as she pulled up her panties and skimpy shorts.

"Yeah, like I give a shit," Grizz shrugged.

Pauline walked past Mavis, and Grizz started to follow. He needed to get back to the motel for a meeting.

But Mavis stepped in front of him and shut her office door, yelling after Pauline, "And for your information, Miss Bitchy Britches, I *was* born in the 1800s!" Mavis looked at Grizz. "You stay. I want to talk to you."

He gestured toward her chair behind the desk. He took the one in front of it. "The 1800s? Really, Mavis?"

"I'm seventy-five. It's 1970. Do the math."

He smiled at her. "So, what's up?"

She made a face as she sat down. She laid her paperwork and sweet tea on the corner of the desk and stowed her purse in one of the drawers. She started to rest her arms on the desktop, when she made a face and stopped herself.

"How often do you use my office?" she asked, squinting at him.

"All the time."

"I hope you're careful." She frowned. "I know these waitresses aren't your working girls, but they get around. You better hope your private parts don't fall off!"

"Not that it's any of your business, but I always wear a raincoat, Mavis."

"A raincoat? Who gives a crap about the weather? I'm talking about protection!"

Grizz rolled his eyes. "You really were born in the 1800s. I can't believe I was actually trying to be polite for your sake. A rubber, Mavis. It's another term for a rubber. A condom! Have you ever taken a peek at your wastebasket?"

This stunned Mavis. Actually, no, she never paid any attention to her trash can. It was neatly stowed beneath her desk so she rarely looked inside. Why would she? It was emptied every morning by the cleaning girl. Now, she reached beneath the desk and pulled it out. Her eyes widened when she saw the discarded condom.

"I'm going to throw up!" she cried.

"Yeah, yeah. Just make sure you do it in there," he said as he nodded at the wastebasket she was holding. "What else do you need to talk to me about?"

Mavis carried the basket outside her office and set it in the hallway. She quietly closed the door and headed back to her desk. She sat back down, gave Grizz a level look and said, "Grunt."

"Talk to Blue," he said as he started to get up.

"I did and he told me to talk to you. So sit back down."

He sat back down. "I'm listening."

"The fifth grade is going on a field trip to the local Seaquarium. I'm a chaperone. I want to bring him along."

"No."

"That's it? Just no?"

"Of course the answer is no. He can't go along with you on a school field trip. How would you even explain him being there, anyway?"

"I already did. I told them that my friend's grandson was in town and was bored to tears. I asked if I could have permission to bring him when I chaperone the fifth grade trip. They said yes. It'll be good for him. Get him around some other kids."

"You and your imaginary friends and their imaginary grandchildren." He blew out a long breath and looked hard at her. "You know Blue kidnapped him, right? You know he might be recognized? No way, Mavis."

"I think you're being paranoid. I don't see any reason why he can't come along!"

"Mavis. How can you say that? There is no way you can bring him on a school field trip. It's not going to happen!"

"Look. He won't be recognized. You told me he was from somewhere in North Lauderdale up toward Pompano, right? It's not the same school district and even if it was, he would be in sixth grade, right? Not fifth?"

"It doesn't matter. He was in and out of foster care and was placed in different districts. It would be too risky. No."

"Grizz, he needs to have some interaction with other kids. He's cooped up at that motel with no friends. He's a smart child and I know he loves his books, but kids need to have some kind of activity. It's just an afternoon at the Seaquarium. It'll be good for him." Before Grizz could say anything, she continued, "And he doesn't even look like the same child. He's filled out. He's getting big. He doesn't have that long, scraggly, lice-infested head of hair. That would be the child that someone would remember. Not the child he is now."

He didn't answer her right away, and she knew she'd won him

over. She also knew that if anyone else spoke to Grizz the way she did, they wouldn't have any teeth left in their mouth. Mavis didn't know why he let her get away with what she did, but she was glad. She actually liked Grizz very much. She didn't know if she would go so far as to say he was the son she never had, but she cared for him. And she was pretty certain he had a soft spot for her, too.

"I guess you're chaperoning Gwinny's class?" he asked finally.

"Ginny's class."

"Who?" Grizz asked.

"She's calling herself Ginny now. She told me she thought Gwinny sounded too babyish. I love this girl's spirit, and to answer your question, yes. I'm chaperoning her class. And I will keep him away from her. I know you don't want them to interact. The whole fifth grade is going. There will be parents and teachers escorting them. We'll each get a group of about seven children. They'll be divided up by boys and girls. I'll have him in my boy group. Chances are he won't even come into contact with her."

"No, Mavis, you *make sure* he doesn't come into contact with her. It'll make it harder for us to keep an eye on her family if Grunt is ever noticed. She might remember him from the field trip, then make the connection to you. Aw, hell. No! What am I thinking? He can't go."

"Grizz, I'll make sure they don't come into contact. I promise. You can trust me. You know you can."

He didn't say anything, just looked at her and nodded okay.

She smiled at him. "So, how is the new neighbor working out?"

"Guido? Yeah, he's an asshole, but he's okay."

Guido was one of Grizz's guys. Mavis thought he had something to do with drugs, but she never asked. She remembered how concerned Grizz had been last year when she told him Gwinny hadn't made her way down to the convenience store to buy her mom's cigarettes for three days in a row. Grizz went ballistic and was on the verge of hiring someone to find them when they showed back up. Apparently, the family had made a trip to Woodstock.

"How do you know she didn't go three days in a row? Thought you only worked on Mondays and Thursdays?" he'd asked her.

"The owners have been giving me more hours. They can't keep

anyone full time so I've been going in. But your accounting work hasn't suffered. I've been taking a lot of it home with me at night."

"Is that why you always look so damned tired? You're working full time at Mindy's?" he'd yelled.

"Yes. They really need me," she'd said sheepishly.

"Of course they need you, Mavis. You're reliable. They're taking advantage. You're going to quit anyway, right? School is starting up and you'll get your cafeteria job back?"

"Yes, it's just another week or two. I'll put my notice in."

Grizz had never concerned himself with how someone was feeling. But Mavis was different. The old woman was growing on him. Maybe he put too much pressure on her to watch out for the little girl.

So right after that conversation last summer, he bought the next house that came up for sale near Gwinny's. It happened to be right next door. He planted Guido there and told him that in addition to his other duties, he would be keeping an eye on his next-door neighbors. He didn't let on that he was concerned about the child's welfare. He just told Guido to watch them all and report anything unusual to him.

He hoped Guido would have enough common sense to notice if the little girl, who was often overlooked, was suddenly being abused, malnourished, or further neglected. She had looked okay that day he'd taken Grunt to check out the lawn service, but he was still concerned about her. Her parents were alcoholic, drug-using hippies. He was actually impressed they both had jobs. But he was certain Gwinny was essentially taking care of herself.

He just wanted to make sure she wasn't being abused. He knew from experience how easy it was for families to hide the abuse they inflicted on their children. He shook off the memory and told himself that planting Guido next door last year was the right thing to do.

********** 

"Okay, Grunt, we need a new name for you today. Remember, you're my friend's grandson. You're visiting from Akron, Ohio."

"I know, Mavis. I've been working on my story ever since you told me this last week. I know everything there is to know about Akron. I even made up my grandmother's name and everything!"

"Oh! I guess that's a good thing. Maybe you should tell me what her name is," Mavis replied with amusement.

"It's Ethel. That sounds like a good name for a grandmother, don't you think? Simple and easy to remember."

She looked over at him. "Grunt, honey, you know I want to bring you along so you can be around some kids your own age, but you're older and smarter than these fifth graders. I don't need to tell you why you can just be friendly, but you can't actually make friends, right?"

"No, I get it," he answered sadly. "Especially Ginny. Grizz told me already, and I know why. And he told me I'm supposed to tell you if I recognize anybody. If I do, we'll need to leave."

"That's right. And don't be sad. We'll have some fun. Oh, what's your name going to be?"

He then sat up straight in the passenger seat of her car and with his head held high, he announced, "Bartholomew. It's Bartholomew Edward Kensington!"

"Bartholomew Edward Kensington?"

"The sixth," he replied. "Bartholomew Edward Kensington the Sixth."

"Who do you think you are? A member of British Parliament?" Mavis shook with laughter.

"What?" he asked. "What's so funny, Mavis? I think it makes me sound important."

"It's not funny. It's just a really big name. Can we shorten it to Bart?"

"Yeah, I can be Bart."

They arrived at the Seaquarium and parked as they watched the buses unloading. The school knew Mavis would be driving herself. She'd found someone to cover her cafeteria shift and told the other chaperones she would be meeting them with her friend's grandson. It wasn't an issue. There were plenty of adults to supervise on the buses.

Grunt put on the baseball cap Grizz had insisted he wear today.

He leaned up to look over the dashboard. Mavis knew who he was looking for. They spotted her immediately. Ginny. She was walking with another girl toward a larger group of kids. She was wearing a pink shirt, a long flowery skirt with sandals, and a big floppy hat. It wasn't just the outfit that caused her to stand out among the other girls. It was the way she carried herself. *She's had to grow up awfully fast and it shows.* Mavis recognized the outfit as one she'd passed on to Ginny from her fictional neighbor's granddaughter. *Poor kid. I haven't seen her wearing anything except the clothes I've been giving her.* And yes, Mavis had to agree. She looked more like a Ginny now than a Gwinny.

Mavis looked over at Grunt, then back at the kids who were now pouring out of the buses. He'd had a growth spurt and was much bigger than them. She hoped he didn't stand out too much. *Dear Heaven, please don't let this be a huge mistake.*

Thirty minutes later, they were divided into groups and following their chaperones as they headed into the venue. Mavis made sure she stayed as far back from Ginny's group as possible.

The visit proceeded without incident. She had a total of six boys in her brood: Grunt, who was introduced as Bart from Ohio, plus five boys from school. She was glad she didn't get stuck with troublemakers. This was a nice group and they tried to include Grunt. He remained friendly and polite, but distant. He was following Grizz's orders. Smart kid.

They were about an hour into their visit, had just finished watching the trained porpoise act, and were walking down the steps when Mavis felt her first stab of panic. Before, they'd been sitting up high in the grandstand and could see Ginny way down in the front with her group. She was easily recognizable with her big, floppy hat. But as Mavis and her troop now made their way down the cement stairs, she noticed Ginny had stopped at the end of her row and was engaging one of the teachers in conversation. She was standing right next to the steps they would be passing. Mavis gave a quick look in Grunt's direction and saw he'd noticed, too.

Okay, no big deal—they would simply walk past her, Mavis

determined. Grunt knew not to make eye contact. Ginny was so involved in her discussion that Mavis doubted she would even see Grunt. As they got closer they could hear her talking.

"Mrs. Davis, I just think someone really does need to do something. The little pool pens they're kept in are not good for them. God made porpoises to swim in the ocean. I just don't think He would like what's going on here."

Mavis smiled to herself. That was Ginny. Championing the little guy. Before anyone realized what was happening, a hand had reached out and swiped the girl's hat right off of her head. A voice could be heard above the chattering of the other students. Curtis Armstrong.

"Yeah, Gwinny or Ginny or whatever your name is now, and God made your hippie-whore mother to suck wieners all day long."

Instinct told Mavis to grab Grunt. He may have seemed a little naïve, like when he didn't know that Bartholomew wasn't the coolest name he could've made up. But he was tough. He had been living at the motel for over a year. If that wasn't going to make a man out of him, nothing would. She knew he'd want to pounce on Curtis without hesitation.

She was right.

She gripped him tightly and could feel the muscles in his upper arm tightening. "Ignore it," she whispered. "Let the teachers take care of it. You have to ignore it."

Before Curtis could run off with the hat, another teacher, Mr. Rayburn, grabbed Curtis by the scruff of his neck and yanked Ginny's hat from his hand. He handed it back to her and told Mrs. Davis, "I'll handle this."

He roughly shoved Curtis toward Ginny and told him, "Apologize. Apologize now, son, or you will spend the rest of this trip on the bus with me. I'll sit there with you the entire time."

"Sorry," Curtis sneered.

It was clear he didn't mean it. It was just a way to get out of being stuck on a hot bus with Mr. Rayburn.

"And you will spend one hour every day after school for two weeks cleaning blackboards and emptying garbage cans," Mr. Rayburn added. "Now get back to your group."

Grunt wouldn't let himself look at her. He knew if she looked hurt, he would lose it. The group was heading toward another exhibit now, and then there would be a lunch break.

"Mavis, I need to use the bathroom, Grunt said quickly. "I can meet you at the seal tank."

Mavis looked around and spotted Curtis. He was on the opposite side of where she knew the bathrooms were. Grunt was watching her and knew what she was thinking.

"Really, Mavis." He gave her a look. "I just need to go to the bathroom."

She nodded. "Okay, use the bathroom and then come straight over to meet up with me."

Grunt made his way through the crowd and went into the restroom. Surprisingly enough, it was empty. He walked over to one of the sinks and splashed cold water on his face. What had Ginny ever done to that Curtis Armstrong to make him hate her so much? He didn't know when or how, but he knew that one day he would make Curtis pay. He went over to the paper towel dispenser and dried his face. He then entered a stall. He was just about to flush the toilet when he heard them.

"Wow, Curtis. Two weeks staying after school. Maybe you should just leave Ginny alone."

"Yeah, Curtis. Why do you hate her so much anyway? I ain't ever seen her do anything to you. Except the lemonade thing, but that was only because you dumped dirt in it."

There was a round of laughter.

"I'm gonna get that little bitch," Curtis snarled.

Grunt stayed where he was. The rest of the conversation was hard to hear over the sound of urine streams and flushing toilets. Grunt peeked through the crack of his stall. Curtis's two friends had finished their business and left the bathroom. Good. He and Curtis were there alone.

Grunt sprinted out of the stall and toward the bathroom door. He kicked the door stop away and the door swung shut. No inside lock. He would have to work fast and hope nobody else came in. He could hear the crowd in the distance clapping at the seal tank.

Just then, Curtis came out of his stall. Before Curtis knew what was happening, Grunt grabbed him by the shoulders, flung him around to face the stall he had just come out of, and kicked the back of his legs. Curtis was on his knees before he could do anything. Grunt had him by the back of his hair.

"You—" He thrust Curtis' head into the toilet and then yanked it back.

"Will never—" Another dunk. "Bother—" Dunk. "Ginny—" Dunk. "Ever, ever again!"

With that he yanked Curtis to his feet and shoved him against the door of the stall. Reaching into his back pocket, he pulled out a switchblade. This wasn't the little pocket knife he'd used a year ago to puncture Curtis's bicycle tires. This was the real deal and he'd seen more than enough at the motel to know how it was used. He held the knife to Curtis's throat.

"You listen to me, you little dick sucker. You will stay away from Ginny forever. Do you understand?" Curtis was still trying to catch his breath.

Grunt pressed his knee up against Curtis's groin. "Do you understand?"

"Yes, yes!" Curtis shrieked.

"I know who you are and I know where you live. You think about telling anybody about our talk and I'll come get you. I swear I'll come for you."

"I won't tell. I swear!"

"And you'll stay away from Ginny." It was an order, not a question.

"Yes, I promise I'll leave Gwinny, uh, Ginny, alone," he managed to say while sucking in large gulps of air.

With that, Grunt closed his switchblade and kneed Curtis between the legs. As he was walking out of the bathroom a couple of boys were approaching.

"You might not want to go in there," he offered. "Some kid is barfing all over the place."

# Chapter Thirteen
2000


GINNY LOOKED AT her son in horror. "Corbin said *what*?"

Jason shrugged. "Corbin said you and Dad used to be part of some motorcycle gang and the guy that owned the gang was getting the electric chair. Is it true?"

Ginny willed herself to stay calm. Corbin was in Jason's grade at school. He was a troublemaker. They'd had the same teacher last year. Hopefully they wouldn't be in the same class when school started again. Corbin also lived on the same block as the Reynolds', so it wasn't unusual that the three boys would have played together over the last couple of days.

She inhaled deeply.

"Nobody can own a motorcycle gang, honey, and the State of Florida doesn't use the electric chair anymore." She knew her reply sounded lame even to her own ears, but she was so unprepared for Jason's question that she didn't know how to respond.

Maybe it would be better if she and Tommy sat Jason down for a talk. Did they really think they could keep this secret from their son after it was resurrected in the media last year when Moe's remains were found, and again a few days ago with Grizz's execution?

It wasn't a media circus like it had been fifteen years ago when Grizz was first arrested, but Moe's story had been picked up by a few reporters last year. It was briefly featured on the local news and she and Tommy were each discreetly interviewed by the police.

Moe's family had eventually given up their horses and sold their land. Moe's remains were found by an excavating company as they were prepping the site for new construction. The remains were unidentifiable; but experts were able to extract some DNA from the roots in the skeleton's teeth, as well as partial DNA from some human flesh found in a plastic food container. After comparing it to that of one of Moe's half-sisters, it was determined that the body belonged to Miriam Parker, missing since 1969. Fingerprints were found on the container as well – fingerprints that belonged to another young woman, a fifteen-year old who'd gone missing in 1975 and was later discovered married to her captor.

Ginny's fingerprints were on file with the police thanks to Sister Mary Katherine, who had insisted after Ginny had gone missing that someone go to the house and at least get a record of her prints in case she was ever located. This was long before DNA evidence was used, yet the elderly nun knew that having them might someday be valuable. Surprisingly, the police complied. As technology advanced, the prints were eventually scanned and entered into a national database.

When she'd first learned this, Ginny remembered being grateful to the holy sister. Someone at least had cared enough about her to try to push for authorities to search for her. But, truth be told, she was sorry now that it had gone that far.

Ginny recalled how she'd sat calmly with Tommy that day in the detective's office as they explained once again how Moe had died of an overdose. She'd told them the same story years before, so it was nothing new, but it was still painful to relive. The detective took down the information and thanked them. The whole process took less than thirty minutes.

They'd decided on the way home that they would tell Mimi. A chill came over Ginny as she remembered that conversation.

"So you and Dad didn't meet at school?" Mimi had asked matter-of-factly.

"No. Your mother and I met when we ran with a rough crowd," Tommy said.

Mimi had looked first at Ginny, then at Tommy. "*You two* ran with a rough crowd? Yeah, right," she said a little too mockingly.

"Tell her, Tommy. Just tell her the truth. She's a smart, mature girl. She can handle it."

So they'd told her. Mimi didn't interrupt once as they took turns filling in the story. They left out a lot of details, including Grizz being her father.

"So where is this Grizz guy? Did they execute him or is he still in prison?"

Ginny shifted uncomfortably in her chair. "He's still on death row. We wanted to tell you because if it catches the media's attention, we might all lose some friends. I honestly don't know. But we do know that we want to keep it from Jason if we can. He's still too young."

Tommy had looked at the girl. "Are you okay with this, Mimi? We know it must be a shock, but we're a family. Families have to trust each other, even with secrets."

"Am I okay with this?" Mimi asked, an odd smile lighting her face. "It's the coolest thing I've ever heard."

"Cool?" Tommy had blinked. "No, Mimi, it's not cool. It's a part of our past that we have done our best to leave behind. It's not something we're proud of. We're only telling you because there's a chance you'll hear it somewhere else and we want to set the record straight up front. It's—"

Mimi cut Tommy off before he could continue. She stood and slung her backpack over her shoulder. "I get it. It's a big, bad family secret that people may or may not find out about. Whatever."

And with that she'd left the den without giving her parents a backward glance.

Ginny had always imagined that she would be close to her daughter. Up until a couple of years ago, she thought she had been. She had warm and heartfelt memories of that younger Mimi. How they had giggled together one day after they'd come home from piano lessons to find a bouquet of handpicked roses wrapped in tinfoil on their front step. Ginny had smiled as Mimi had read the awkwardly written note attached to it declaring a young admirer's undying love and his willingness to save Mimi a seat at his lunch table. That was the daughter she'd taken shopping. Who'd held her mother's hand nervously as the doctor pierced her ears. Who'd flung herself into her father's arms when he got home from work every night.

That Mimi was gone. That Mimi no longer existed.

Maybe she should just count herself lucky to have had some semblance of a mother-daughter relationship for a little while. She certainly hadn't experienced that with her own mother, Delia. And she knew Tommy had never experienced any kind of decent home life. What would they know? What would they have to compare it to?

Nothing.

She sighed loudly as she thought about the cold shoulder she would get from Mimi when she asked too many questions. The nasty attitude when she enforced the house rules, curfews, and insistence that Mimi check in regularly when spending time with friends. She'd thought maybe they'd bonded a little bit when Mimi encouraged her to give Leslie the interview. Apparently, she'd been eavesdropping on her parents discussing it and was only too willing to offer her support. Ginny had agreed to the interview, thinking it would be a good way to fix whatever had been missing between her and Mimi the last few years. It seemed to be helping a little, but Ginny wasn't certain.

She put her memories of last year and Mimi's recent support of Leslie's interview on hold as she pulled into the driveway and noticed Tommy's car was still in the open garage. A car she didn't recognize was also parked in front of the house. So he hadn't left and he had a visitor.

Maybe it was better that he was home.

Maybe Corbin's comment was something they could talk to Jason about together.

She steeled herself and followed Jason into the house. As soon as they got rid of the visitor, she told herself, they would sit down and talk to Jason together.

Then, if he hadn't already done so, she would help Tommy pack his bags.

# Chapter Fourteen
2000

TOMMY DIDN'T KNOW what to say to Louise about the journal. He never knew Moe had kept one. Before he could reply, the front door swung open and Jason came barreling in.

"Dad!" He dropped his bag on the floor and ran to Tommy in the living room, grabbing him around the waist. "I missed you, Dad. I'm glad you're back from your trip. Is my helmet fixed? Are we gonna ride today?"

Tommy hugged him back as he gently laid the notebook on the seat he had just vacated. He looked over Jason's head and saw Ginny calmly walk into the house. She laid her purse and keys on the small table and strode into the living room. Their eyes met.

"I missed you too, buddy." Tommy said without breaking eye contact. "Yes, your helmet is fixed and I'll take you for a ride this evening, when it's cooler out."

Jason looked up at him and Tommy patted his back. "Your mom and I have a guest and we don't want to be rude. Can you take your bag upstairs and get yourself unpacked?"

"Sure, Dad." Jason glanced at Louise.

Before his son could fire off a round of questions, Tommy quickly added, "Jason, this is Miss Bailey. She's the daughter of an old friend. She came to see me and Mom today, so I'd really like to have some time with your mom and her so the three of us can visit."

Louise smiled at Jason. "Louise. It's just Louise. Nice to meet you, Jason."

Her expression told Tommy she knew after whom he'd been named.

"Nice to meet you, too. See you later," Jason called over his shoulder as he passed his mother, grabbed his overnight bag off the floor and bounded up the stairs with the unlimited energy of a ten-year-old.

Ginny's curiosity was aroused. She had been eyeing the woman during Tommy's introduction. A friend's daughter? She doubted it. It was probably a reporter telling another lie to get in the door. Would Tommy actually let another one in their home after the debacle with Leslie? But this woman seemed familiar.

"This is Chicky's daughter, Ginny," Tommy said quietly. "Louise Bailey."

No wonder she looked familiar. Ginny smiled and breathed a sigh of relief. "Oh, Chicky! Oh, dear Chicky. How is she?"

Louise explained about Chicky's battle with cancer and subsequent death, then circled back to her main reason for being there: the journal.

Tommy nodded toward the notebook on the chair. "Louise was delivering this."

Ginny looked at the notebook, then at Tommy. Before she could ask, he added, "It's a journal. It was Moe's."

"Her journal? I didn't know Moe kept a journal," Ginny said, the shock evident in her voice. "How did Chicky have a journal that belonged to Moe?"

"She found it," Louise replied.

"Where? When?" Ginny asked as she distractedly sat down on the piano bench. She looked at Louise and then at Tommy, bewildered. "Did *you* know Moe kept a journal?" she asked him, an edge to her voice.

"No, Gin. I didn't know," Tommy said simply.

Louise looked from one to the other. "Mom found it after Moe died. She told me Moe's room hadn't been used for a while. I guess it was a sad time for you." Louise nodded at Ginny.

Ginny looked down at her lap. "Yes, it was very sad. I couldn't bring myself to go in there for a long time. But," she added, "I looked through her room the day she died. Tommy was with me. We didn't find any journal."

"It was there. Mom said that after a few weeks had passed, you'd asked her if she would clean out Moe's room. You told her you thought Moe would want her things to go to charity, but you couldn't bring yourself to do it yourself."

"Yes, that's true." Ginny remembered it all now, the way the grief and the guilt had held on and on, the way she'd kept picturing Moe, her dark hair and eyes, her small shy smile.

"Mom said she found it under a stack of drawing paper and supplies. Guess it was easy to miss if you thought you were just looking at a pile of art stuff."

Tommy looked over at Ginny and the expression he saw on her face was pure torment. Ginny had already confided in him years before about the horrible guilt she felt after Moe's suicide. How she hadn't noticed Moe's despair. He knew what she was thinking.

"Don't think it, Gin. Don't even think it. You missed a notebook that looked like it belonged with a pile of her drawing stuff. I missed it, too."

"I missed everything that was important," Ginny said a little too loudly, her voice thick with unshed tears.

Louise held up a hand. "I'm sorry. I—I didn't mean to bring bad memories or anything like that to your door. I was just trying to do what Mom wanted." She looked at Ginny directly. "You know, Mom didn't want you to have this until after Grizz died. Maybe it's better that you didn't find it back then." She paused, then added, "That's just my opinion. I've taken enough of your time. I can see myself out."

Tommy and Ginny watched her leave. Then they looked at each other, and then the notebook.

"Moe's journal wasn't the only surprise today," Tommy told her quietly.

"You're telling me? Let's just add it to the pile of garbage that is going to trigger the end of life as we know it." At his curious expression, she gave a short laugh and began to tick off the day's events on her fingers. "Let's see, you're Grizz's son, Moe had a secret journal, Corbin told Jason we went to see some guy get fried, what else? What else could there possibly be, Tommy?"

"We got a delivery today, other than the journal."

"Oh, yeah? What did we get?" she asked bitterly.

"Grizz's chess set."

# Chapter Fifteen
1971


"WHY CAN'T YOU just let Moe drive me? Then I don't have to wait so long in between," Grunt told Blue as they were pulling into the motel.

"I don't know. I never said Moe couldn't drive you. Have you ever asked her?" Blue gave Grunt a sidelong glance. They had just come from the library. Blue was juggling the gang, a wife, and a full-time job, so library visits were few and far between for the twelve-year-old.

"Of course I asked her." Grunt shrugged. "She doesn't have her own car."

"She can take one of Grizz's cars."

"No, she can't. She can't see over the steering wheels of most of them, and he'd never let her take his Mustang." A thought occurred. "Blue, can you talk to him? Can we get her a car of her own that she can drive easily?"

Blue considered it. "Yeah, I'll ask him. We'll come up with something." He parked the car by the motel office, slamming the door hard. "Put your books away and come on out to the pit."

Grunt watched as Blue headed for the fire. He made himself comfortable in one of the chairs and didn't seem to object when one of the girls walked over to him and parked herself in his lap.

Grunt carried his library books to his room, then went to the pit to seek out Grizz. Even though he'd asked Blue to talk to Grizz, it was probably better if he talked to Grizz himself. He noticed the girl on Blue's lap now with her hand down the front of his pants. Blue had his head leaned back, his eyes closed.

Grunt secretly hoped his sister-in-law would never show up at the motel. Jan would probably kill Blue on the spot if she saw what he did with the other women. Sissy in particular. He wondered how Blue managed to juggle two women at once. They were both demanding of his time. He was surprised they'd never actually found out about each other—yet. Grunt remembered hearing Blue explain to Grizz once that he wanted a woman who wasn't connected to the gang. A wife who would take care of their home and future children. He wanted a lady—and according to Blue, Sissy was no lady. They had argued about it, and Grizz had actually warned Blue that he didn't think a woman like Jan would ever be able to accept her husband excluding her from this lifestyle.

"She wants to be excluded," Blue had said. "She doesn't want this lifestyle. I told you, she's a lady. And she's okay with me not bringing her into it."

"She may not want to participate, but she won't like it when she finds out you won't be giving up other women for her," Grizz had told him.

Blue had confidently replied that he could handle Jan.

Now, surveying the scene, Grunt swallowed back a smile. *Blue got his lady all right, and all of the baggage that came with her.*

Grunt spotted Grizz standing near the playground equipment talking to someone. He walked purposefully toward him, giving Moe a little wave as he strode past. She was sitting by the fire, staring into the flames, as was her habit. She waved back, then continued her gaze.

"Grizz, can I ask you something?" the boy said, interrupting Grizz's conversation.

Grizz turned around to look at him. He didn't answer right away. "Yeah, I'm done here." He dismissed the man he'd been talking to with a nod, and the man walked off. "What do you want?"

"I asked Blue if you could get Moe a car so she could drive me places. Can you?"

"Why does she need to drive you? Blue takes you out."

"Blue is always busy." Grunt made a face. "If you get Moe a car, she can grocery shop and everything, and I can go with her. All the cars around here are too big for her to drive herself."

Grizz thought about it for a second. He hadn't really given much thought to Moe. The kid was right. Moe didn't have a car; she always just relied on whoever was available to take her to the store or anywhere else she might need to go. She rarely left the motel. She made sure the rooms were clean, the laundry was done, and the refrigerators were stocked. He hadn't thought about the inconvenience of her having to beg rides to the grocery store and everywhere else.

He also hadn't noticed Grunt wasn't getting out as much.

"It makes sense," came a voice from behind, and Grunt turned to see Blue had walked up behind them and was listening to the conversation. "And it would help me out. Why don't you give her the Caddy? It just sits there. You never use it."

Grunt shook his head. "It's too big. She needs something little, like her. Something she can drive and actually reach the gas pedal."

Grizz stared at the ground for a minute, considering. "You're right. I don't use the Caddy. Maybe we can trade it for something smaller." Blue started to say something, but Grizz knew what he was thinking. "It's legit. Title says Richard O'Connell. Martin couldn't pay up a couple years ago and I took the car. But still, call Axel and see who he knows that will accept the title transfer without any questions."

Axel was one of Grizz's mechanics and Grunt was certain he handled more than tune-ups. He was in charge of all of Grizz's car needs, including planning well-executed car heists and converting the stolen autos in his garages to vehicles that couldn't be traced. Grunt knew that as good as Axel was at his job, Grizz would never risk Moe getting stopped in a stolen vehicle, especially if there was a chance that Grunt was with her. Grizz would make a lawful purchase.

Grunt heard the low rumble of a motorcycle pulling into the motel and grinned, pointing. "You don't even need to call him. He's here!"

Grizz called Axel over and filled him in on the plan. Axel told him about a car dealership off Dixie Highway. Blue was given the order to take Moe to get a car.

"I want to go, too," Grunt quickly added. "It was my idea, so I should help her pick it out."

Grizz looked at Grunt and nodded. Then he turned to Blue. "Make sure they don't get screwed. The Cadillac is in excellent condition. I expect her to drive away with something nice and the title will be made out to Richard O'Connell."

"You got it, Grizz."

"I'll make a call," Axel said. "They'll be taken care of."

"I'll make sure it's handled," Grunt spoke up, standing up a little straighter and puffing his chest out. "I know how to wheel and deal. We won't get screwed. I got ya covered, Grizz."

Grizz and Blue tried not to smile as the kid headed toward the pit to tell Moe.

"Moe, guess what?" Grunt was saying as he approached the fire. She was sitting cross-legged on the ground, staring into the flames. He stopped short when he saw a guy in a lawn chair shove her from behind with his foot, just enough to jostle her a little. Grunt could tell he wasn't hurting her, but she was uncomfortable and clearly trying to ignore him.

Grunt approached slowly now, watching as the guy stood and began to address some of the people sitting in the pit. He was new to the group and went by the name Monk. *Stupidest name ever—probably short for Monkey.* Grunt just watched, keeping a careful distance.

"Guess she thinks if she doesn't answer me, I'll leave her alone," Monk said to no one in particular. Nobody replied. He turned toward her again, this time using his knee to shove her harder, closer to the fire. "I *said* I want some time alone with you, baby. You keep ignoring me and I'll make sure you'll cry tonight. And not in a good way."

Monk laughed to himself, raising his knee again. In a sing-song voice, he began to taunt, "Moe the ho, Moe the ho, I'll screw her ass to and fro—"

Before Monk could say more, Grunt charged him with a head butt to his stomach that knocked the wind out of him, toppling the bigger man onto his back. Grunt jumped on him, pummeling his face with both fists as hard as he could. Moe leaped from her place by the fire and started to drag Grunt away. Unfortunately, this gave Monk the chance he needed to get to his feet. With a roar, he shoved the boy away from him. Grunt quickly jumped up, the momentum causing him to stumble and fall backwards, knocking Moe and himself to the ground.

Monk whipped out a switchblade. "You little shit. Who do you think you're fucking with?"

Blue and Grizz had been approaching the pit. Even though they couldn't hear what was being said, they saw the entire scene play out. When Monk took out the switchblade, Blue started to go after him, but Grizz put out his hand to stop him.

"Wait. Just wait."

Blue looked at Grizz with an "are you kidding me?" expression, but didn't go any further.

The pit had fallen quiet now, and Blue and Grizz could hear them. Blue clenched his fists and watched as Grunt quickly got on his feet.

"You should show more respect." Grunt glared at Monk.

This seemed to amuse Monk. "Respect? To who? That whore?"

Monk absently waved the knife in Moe's direction. She had gotten herself back up and was standing just behind Grunt. She started to grab Grunt again, but this time thought better of it. She was probably the reason he'd lost the upper hand in the first place.

"She's not a whore. She's a person. She's a lady." Grunt said, the muscles in his back tightening. He pictured his own switchblade resting on the nightstand next to his bed. He didn't have a weapon on him. He wouldn't make that mistake again.

"A lady?" Monk snorted. "You little shit. I don't care what you think she is, but I know what you are. You are fucking dead."

He lunged at Grunt, swinging the knife. Grunt managed to duck and avoid it. Monk took two more swipes, narrowly missing Grunt both times. The more the kid evaded the blade, the madder Monk got.

Grunt finally saw his chance. He managed to block the knife-wielding arm while thrusting his right fist up under Monk's chin. This caused Monk to stumble backwards. He was dazed from the blow but didn't lose his footing.

"Stop it now," Grizz told Blue.

As Blue approached, Grunt briefly glanced over. It was just enough time for Monk to make one more lunge for Grunt.

Grunt knew the instant he looked away that he'd made a mistake. The last thing he remembered was white hot pain like he'd never imagined and the look of terror on Monk's face as Blue grabbed him from behind and said, "You got some big ones fucking with *my* brother."

Then everything went black.

Nobody realized Monk had stabbed Grunt. Blue roughly shoved Monk to his knees and wrestled the switchblade easily out of his hand. Blue looked up at Grizz, who gave the nod.

In one swift motion, Blue slit Monk's throat ear to ear.

"Get rid of this piece of shit," Blue muttered to one of the guys standing nearby, wiping off the blade on Monk's shirt. Then he folded Monk's knife and shoved it in his back pocket.

When he looked up again, he was surprised to see Grizz carrying Grunt to one of the motel rooms. Moe was running alongside him trying to keep up with his long, urgent strides.

Grizz yelled back over his shoulder, "Get Doc here, now!"

*********

*Moe's Diary, 1971*

*Dear Elizabeth,*

*It's my fault he was stabbed. If I'd just gotten up and taken Monk to my room, Grunt wouldn't have gotten hurt. He hasn't woken up for two days. Doc said he should be okay. The cut was deep but missed all the important organs. He said not to worry. The pain pills are going to make him sleep a lot. Still, I'm worried.*

*I can't believe he went after Monk like that. Nobody's ever stuck up for me before. Grunt really is my friend. The only reason Blue killed Monk was because he was fighting with Grunt, though I can't believe he didn't try to stop it sooner. Grunt could've been killed. But nobody cared that Monk was kicking me. Nobody cared what he was saying. Just Grunt.*

*I don't think I would ever forgive myself if Monk had killed him.*

*Axel told me that when Grunt gets better I'm going to get my own car. Blue could take me now, but he said that Grunt really wanted to be there. I can't believe Grizz is letting me trade his Cadillac for a car of my own. I haven't had something of my own in a long time. Not for a long, long time.*

*I guess it should make me feel better. But it doesn't. I won't feel better until I know for sure that Grunt is gonna be okay.*

*********

A few weeks after Grunt's recovery from the knife wound, Blue showed up at the motel around eleven one morning. Grunt was still a little sore, but very anxious to go with Blue and Moe to find her a car. Blue banged on the door of number four and went in without waiting to be invited. Grizz was coming out of the bedroom and zipping up his jeans.

"Sorry man. Got company?" Blue asked as he nodded toward the bedroom.

Grizz scoffed. "When do I ever have company in here? Just taking a piss. What do you want?"

"Keys to the Caddy and the papers. I'm gonna take Moe and Grunt today to get her a car."

Grizz disappeared without a word into the bedroom and returned with keys and an envelope. "Title's in here," he said, handing them to Blue.

Less than an hour later, Blue, Moe, and Grunt pulled up to the car dealership Axel had recommended. Al's Auto wasn't as bad as Blue had thought it would be. From the looks of it, they offered a pretty decent variety. He breathed a sigh of relief. He was worried the selection wouldn't be up to Grizz's standards, so he'd anticipated a day of hopping from one dealership to the next. Axel had made several backup recommendations in the event Al's didn't work out.

A man in a light blue polyester suit and slicked-back hair approached them as they got out of the Cadillac.

"Here to make a fair trade." Blue said, nodded at the Cadillac. "Axel sent us."

The man stopped short and smiled wide. "Yes, Axel told me you'd be coming. Expected you a few weeks ago. I'm Al." He smelled like cheap hair tonic and fried chicken. They must've interrupted his lunch.

"Got held up. Can I use your phone?" Blue asked.

"Yeah. Right inside the door," Al said, waving his hand in the right direction.

Blue went inside to make a call. When he came out he spotted

Grunt and Al standing next to a convertible Mercedes. Moe was sitting in the driver's seat. Blue smiled. *Grizz said a fair trade. I think this will work out just fine.*

Grunt looked over at Blue, who nodded. Grunt smiled and listened as Al did his best to enlighten them on the many advantages of owning a high-end foreign auto.

Blue leaned up against one of the cars and waited. Less than fifteen minutes later, a car pulled into the lot. A pretty brunette was behind the wheel.

Grunt noticed the approaching vehicle and squinted in the sunlight to see who was driving. It was Pauline, one of the girls from The Red Crab. She wasn't with the gang, but after realizing she wouldn't be anything more than a lay to Grizz, she'd clearly set her sights on Blue. She didn't care that he was married. She wanted a man of her own and if luring one away from his wife was her ticket, then so be it.

Blue walked over toward the threesome now standing next to another expensive foreign car. He looked at Al. "I've got business. Give them what they want." Before Al could respond, Blue said to Grunt, "You can take care of this. You're looking at the right kinds of cars. Grizz will be happy. Moe can drive you back to the motel. Title's in the Caddy." He looked at Moe. "You have your license?"

She nodded her reply, and without waiting for any kind of acknowledgment from Grunt, Blue headed toward Pauline's car.

"I'll drive. I could use some 'servicing' while we're on the road," he said as he approached the driver's side.

Pauline put the car in park and slid over. Blue jumped in the driver's seat and did a sharp U-turn in the lot. As they pulled out of the dealership and onto Dixie Highway, Grunt noticed Pauline was no longer visible next to Blue. He slowly shook his head. *One day Jan is going to kill him.*

Less than two hours later, Moe and Grunt had finalized their purchase with Al. Moe was adamant about the car she wanted. It was a little noisy, but Grunt was certain it was something Axel could fix. He was happy for her. He hadn't seen her smile in a long time.

When they got back to the motel, Grizz was bent over with his head in the refrigerator. He was hungry and didn't feel like driving to get food. "Damn," he said to no one. He had to admit Grunt made a good call where the car was concerned. It would be better for Moe to have her own transportation. It was obvious nobody, himself included, had taken her shopping recently. Not that he ever took her shopping. He ordered the others to do it, but from the lack of food, it seemed everyone had somehow avoided it this week.

He decided he would take a ride over to Razor's, another one of his bars, and grab something to eat there. He shut the refrigerator door and was reaching for his car keys on the kitchen counter when he was distracted by a noise from outside. *Motorcycle? Hmmm, that ain't like no motorcycle I ever heard before. What the fuck is causing all that racket?*

He swung open the door and walked outside. He squinted as he saw a black Volkswagen Bug circle the pit and make its way back toward him. His jaw dropped as he recognized who was in the car. Moe was driving and Grunt was waving excitedly at him.

"Stop." Grizz held up a hand as he strode toward the car. "Stop right now. Stop right here." He walked to the passenger side and asked Grunt through the open window, "Where's Blue?"

"He had to go somewhere," Grunt replied matter-of-factly.

Grizz crossed his arms in front of his chest and stood back. He looked at the car slowly from one end to the other. "You traded my Cadillac for this piece of shit?" His face was red with anger. "Moe, turn it off! I can't hear myself talk."

Moe turned the key. It sputtered for almost thirty seconds before finally turning off completely. As if on cue, a giant cloud of black smoke appeared from the exhaust pipe.

Grunt got out of the car and looked up at Grizz. "It's the one she wanted. I know it's making a lot of noise, but Axel can fix it." He paused. "It's perfect for her."

Grizz was actually at a loss for words. He gained his composure and asked calmly, "Where is he? What's her name?"

"He left with Pauline." After a short pause, Grunt added, "You shouldn't be upset. I got you a deal. I told you I would handle it."

"This is a deal?" Grizz growled.

"Yeah, it's a deal," Grunt replied, reaching into his pocket. "It's the one Moe wanted and I wanted her to be happy. And now she's happy. And you shouldn't be so mad."

He handed over something to Grizz. It was an envelope.

Grizz opened it and took out a piece of paper. He carelessly tossed the envelope on the ground and opened the folded document. It was a car title in the name of Richard O'Connell and stapled to it was a check from Al's Auto.

Grizz's eyes widened when he saw the amount of the check that was made out to his alias.

"Told you I'd get you a deal," Grunt said as he strolled back to his room.

# Chapter Sixteen

2000

"GRIZZ'S CHESS SET?" Ginny asked.

"Yeah." Tommy crossed his arms, a line creasing his brow. "Grizz didn't mention it. Someone must've packed it up from the prison and sent it here. I guess it's something that should really be saved for Mimi."

"I don't think we could give it to Mimi without explaining why it would rightfully be hers," she answered him coolly.

"I didn't say we should give it to her today or even tomorrow, Gin. I just said we should save it for her."

"Fine. Then it's agreed. I say we stick it in a closet until we can figure it out." She put her hand to her forehead and, lightly shaking her head, said, "I can't think about this now, Tommy."

She didn't look angry anymore. She looked sad.

"What *are* you thinking about, sweetheart?" His voice was quiet.

She stiffened at the "sweetheart," but her desire to talk prevailed. "I was just remembering when I got it for him," she whispered. "I don't know what I was thinking. I was so into saving the animals when I was a kid. I'd started this petition to free the porpoises from the Seaquarium when I was ten." She gave a rueful smile, thinking back at the girl she'd once been. "I'd spend hours walking down my block with a laundry basket, wearing oven mitts. I couldn't stand the thought of the land crabs getting run over so I relocated them."

Tommy already knew this because he had witnessed some of it. But he didn't interrupt.

"But I never realized what that chess set cost the animals that had to die for it. I mean, ivory pieces?" She shook her head. "What an idiot. Never once did it occur to me to wonder where ivory came from. Maybe we should donate Grizz's set to charity. Maybe it could be used in some way to put an end to the illegal ivory trade."

"Ginny, will you ever stop beating yourself up about everything? I'm not an expert and neither were you when you got it for him. You were only fifteen. We didn't even have the internet back then for you to look into it. How would you have known if the ivory trade was illegal or not?"

"It should've been."

"Yes, Gin, it should have been." He walked over to where she was still sitting on the piano bench, taking her hand. She pulled it away. "We have to talk, Ginny, and we can't do it now. We don't have time. Jason is expecting a ride later and you and I have too much to discuss. What you said before, about his friend asking if we'd gone to see someone get fried? And now this journal?"

She stood and looked at him sadly. "You still have to leave, Tommy. I honestly don't think I can have you living here. Not after knowing you kept this—this huge secret from me for so long. I have things to settle in my head. I have thinking to do."

He started to speak, but she held up her hand. "I don't care how you look at it. You deceived me. I am a fool for never having seen it, but still, you should have told me."

She sized him up now with fresh eyes. Tommy didn't look like Grizz, didn't have the same features, but he was big and imposing. He had matured into a man with the same build as his father. How had she never noticed? Or had she noticed and never let herself pursue the thought?

No. She wouldn't do that to herself. Tommy didn't resemble Grizz in the least. She'd never had a clue.

He'd deceived her. They'd all deceived her.

Her life was a lie.

Tommy touched her arm. "Gin, I can't leave. Mimi and Jason would want to know why. No." He shook his head, his voice firm. "I'm not leaving."

She wrenched away from his touch. "Well, then, I guess I will."

"Ginny, wait. Moe's journal. I never knew about it. Don't you think we should read it? Together?"

"Maybe, but not now. I need to pack. I'm going to Carter's."

"You can't leave, Ginny. What do you want me to tell our children?" His eyes were red. "And—and do you really think Carter's house is the best place for you to be after today?"

If she was weakening before, that question bolstered her resolve. Carter and her husband lived in the house Grizz had built for Ginny in Shady Ranches. Ginny straightened her shoulders.

"I've been to that house a hundred times since I moved out. And so have you. I can be there. It doesn't bother me." She started for the bedroom, then turned back. "And as far as the kids are concerned, make something up. You seem like you're really good at that."

Tommy just stared after her.

He looked down and realized he was still holding the journal. Maybe they shouldn't read it together after all. Maybe there was something in it that could hurt her more. Maybe there was something in it that could hurt him, too.

He headed for the kitchen and roughly sat at the table, staring at the closed notebook.

Did he even want to know what was in it?

# Chapter Seventeen
1972

GRIZZ STIFLED A laugh as he watched Grunt quickly grab his glass and suck down the water in one long chug.

"My mouth is on fire!" Grunt cried.

"I told you they were hot. You wanted to try them. Now you know." Grizz smirked. "You want me to get you the mild ones now?"

"Here, kid. You can have some of mine. I don't like 'em hot either," Axel said as he slid his basket of chicken wings toward Grunt. "Mine won't burn your mouth. Go ahead. Try 'em."

Grizz signaled the waitress, Rhonda. She was an attractive woman, well-liked by her regulars at the restaurant. It was a little hole-in-the-wall dive, known mostly for the best hot wings in South Florida.

Grizz had business to discuss with Axel but decided to bring the kid along. Grunt didn't get out much and Grizz knew this would be a treat for him. He even allowed himself to give in when Grunt insisted that they take a quick drive by Ginny's house. He didn't like to drive by her place because he knew he'd have to turn around at the end. But he also knew Grunt was never around any kids his own age. Who knows, maybe checking on the girl made him feel like he had a silent friend.

Grizz was actually quite amused by what they'd seen that day. The girl was wearing oven mitts and carrying a laundry basket full of crabs. The crabs were trying to crawl out of it, and she was so engrossed in keeping them inside that she never noticed the same car passed her twice. It was a comical picture, a determined girl in oven mitts and a ponytail carrying a basket of crabs, and Grizz found himself smiling as he remembered.

Rhonda saw Grizz signal her out of the corner of her eye. She was always on the lookout for Grizz. She didn't want to chance him not getting her attention and having one of the other waitresses go to his table. She left the drink order she'd been filling for another customer and rushed over.

Rhonda had only been working at the restaurant a month or two when the biker had first come in. She was immediately attracted to him. He was younger than her, but boy, was he hot. Big, tough, handsome in a rugged sort of way. A real bad boy, and Rhonda was always drawn to the bad boys. She'd tried to warm up to him, but he wasn't really friendly. Today was the first time he'd come in with the kid. She wondered if the kid was his or just another up-and-comer in the gang.

"What can I get ya, Grizz?" she grinned at him after she'd hastily made her way to the table, ignoring the other customers trying to get her attention.

"Another order of wings. Mild this time," Grizz said and nodded toward Grunt.

"A little too hot for you, honey?" She smiled kindly at Grunt.

"A lot too hot. Can I have some more water too, please?" Grunt motioned to his empty glass.

"Yeah, sure," she answered him. She then looked quickly at Grizz and Axel. "You boys need anything else?"

"I'm good," Grizz answered.

Axel had a mouth full of food and shook his head. She walked away.

"She's nice," Grunt told Grizz. "She likes you."

Grizz looked up from his food. "What do you mean she likes me?"

"She keeps watching our table to see if you need anything. She doesn't watch anybody else's table." Grunt crunched on some celery, adding, "I think she wants you to notice her chest. She seems like she's always making sure her tits are right in your face when she's over here."

Grizz looked at Grunt and then at Axel. Axel just nodded and smiled. Grizz hadn't noticed. She was a nice lady. Older than him, he suspected, but well kept. He looked around the restaurant and noticed some of the other customers glancing appreciatively in Rhonda's direction. She did have a nice rack. And she seemed to get along with everybody. He'd just lost two girls at The Red Crab and one at Razor's. He wondered if she'd work topless. Couldn't hurt to ask.

Less than a week later, Rhonda was behind the bar at The Red Crab. The place was packed and the bartender couldn't keep up with the drink orders. She was grabbing a couple of beers so she didn't have to keep her customers waiting. She was placing the beers on her tray when she sensed him. Grizz had come into the bar. She stopped what she was doing and just stared. He'd been walking toward the bar, but was stopped by a regular at one of the tables. She couldn't take her eyes off of him.

"Don't bother. We've all tried. He'll bend you over the desk, but that's all you get."

Rhonda turned to look at the waitress who'd just come up to the bar to get her drink order. Pauline. Rhonda hadn't been working at the bar long enough to really decide whether or not she liked Pauline.

"Maybe you haven't tried hard enough." Rhonda shrugged. "Maybe he hasn't met the right woman yet."

"And you think *you're* that woman? Ha! I'm telling you, it's a waste of your time unless you're into quickies. He's not that kind of guy. No hand holding or kissing. You'll never be more than a lay."

Rhonda raised an eyebrow.

"I know from experience," Pauline continued. "He has a humungous dick, so it'll definitely be worth it. But if you have fantasies of waking up in his bed one morning, you can squelch them now. I don't know of any woman who's actually been in his bed, and I ain't tryin' to insult you darlin', but I don't see anything special about you. You'll just be another chicky in his hen house." She looked away from Rhonda then, yelling at the bartender. "Mike, my order? C'mon, man, you're costing me tips!"

A month later, Rhonda asked one of the guys for a ride to the motel after her shift was over. It was Friday night and her daughter, Louise, was staying at a friend's house. She was going to make her move on Grizz.

She knew about the gang. Or did they call themselves a club? She didn't remember and she didn't care. She just knew that if she wanted to get into Grizz's bed, she would have to be at the motel. She didn't know a whole lot about gangs, but how bad could it be?

She'd done her best the past month to play it cool with Grizz. Flirted with him, but always backed off before it went too far. She knew she had his interest. Just how much interest, she couldn't tell. Grizz wasn't an easy man to read.

They pulled up to the motel and the guy she was riding with cut the engine. His name was Chip. He seemed like an okay guy. She got off the back of the bike and started looking around the motel. It was late and very dark out. A big fire was roaring and she could see some people sitting around it. She spotted Grizz immediately and started walking toward him. Whistling and lewd comments surrounded her as she approached the fire.

Grizz had noticed Rhonda when she first got off Chip's bike. What was she doing here? She was okay, but he didn't think she was gang material. He thought she had a kid. Maybe he was wrong.

He took a swig of beer and watched as she sashayed toward him. Without looking at anyone else around the fire, Rhonda walked straight up to Grizz. Cocking a hip and standing over him, she pasted on her coyest smile and said, "Hi, Grizz. What are you doing here?"

Grizz looked at her. "You know damn well I live here. What are *you* doing here?"

"Oh, just wanted to take a ride with Chip and this is where we ended up. Think you can bring me home later?" Even in the hazy firelight, he could see her flutter her eyelashes.

Grizz stood and grabbed her by the arm, almost pushing her toward the motel. When they were out of earshot from the others, he stopped and looked down at her.

"Rhonda, I thought you were a smart lady," he growled. "You know what coming here means, right?"

She didn't know what to say. He seemed mad. She started to answer him, but he cut her off.

"It means you have just made yourself available to any man sitting around that pit." He leveled a look at her. "If that's what you want, fine by me. But if not, you'd better find yourself a ride back and we'll pretend you never came out here."

He started to walk away from her, striding toward one of the motel units. She was stunned. He seemed so cold and hard. She knew he could be like that, but he'd always been so nice to her at the bar.

She ran to catch up with him. "Grizz, stop! Grizz, wait. Please, just listen."

He stopped and turned around. "What?"

"Fine. I'll be honest. I wanted to be with you. I didn't want it to be at the bar, like the other women. Is that so wrong to admit? That I want to sleep with you?"

There, she said it. It was out. She almost felt relief. She would ask for a ride back to the bar so she could get her car and go home. Maybe Pauline was right.

But before she could blink, Grizz grabbed her hand and started pulling her toward the motel. They went into number seven and he shut the door behind them.

Grizz flipped on the light. It went from pitch black to dim.

"Is this your room?" Rhonda asked as she looked around the clean but old space.

"No. It's not my room." Grizz walked over to an old dresser and reached into one of the drawers. He took out a condom and tossed it on the bed, then stared at her matter-of-factly. "You want to give me a reason to want to put that on?"

Rhonda decided to pull out all the stops to try and arouse Grizz. It didn't take long. She was worried that because he'd already seen her breasts, there would be no anticipation for him there. But that didn't seem to matter. She breathed a sigh of relief when he got an erection almost immediately. Her eyes widened in disbelief when she saw Pauline had been right about his size. Time to spin her magic.

But as hard as she tried, she couldn't get him to kiss her. It was the craziest thing. She'd never thought about kissing in the past with any guy, but the fact that Grizz seemed to purposely avoid it nagged at her.

A little while later, she was under the covers, eyes closed. He was finished but still inside her. She sighed; it had been the most fantastic sex she'd ever experienced. As far as she knew, she'd gotten even further than Pauline had. This wasn't a quickie bent over the desk at the office of The Red Crab. She wasn't in *his* bed per se, but she'd managed to get him into some kind of bed, at least.

She started to say something when he lifted himself off her and headed straight for the bathroom. A few minutes later, he came out and sat on the edge of the bed, pulling his clothes back on.

"You know, Grizz," she cooed, "next time we make love, you don't have to wear one of those nasty rubbers. I hate those things. I'm not like your other girls. You're not going to catch something from me."

Grizz didn't look at her. After putting on his jeans and boots, he stood and pulled his pants up all the way, then buckled his belt.

He tossed a glance at her. "If you're going to be coming out here regularly, you need to come up with a name. I don't like anybody that comes to the motel to go by their real names."

Regularly? Of course she would be here regularly now that she knew she was making progress. She knew she would eventually work her way into his personal bed. And as far as the kissing was concerned, she just needed a little time.

"How about Chicky?" she purred. She couldn't wait to see the look on Pauline's face the first time Grizz referred to her by the name—the very name Pauline had suggested so sarcastically last month. That would show Pauline and her sorry ass.

"Fine," he said without looking at her.

She sat up and leaned toward him, giving him a sleepy smile. "Think you can give me a ride back to the bar?" She reached out to gently move her hand up and down his arm. It was so big and muscular, and covered entirely in tattoos.

He headed toward the door. "You can sleep here tonight if you want. Get someone to take you back in the morning. I'm going to bed."

"Grizz, why don't you come back over here. You can sleep here right next to me," she said, patting the spot next to her. "And when we wake up tomorrow morning, we can make love again and it'll be so much better without the rubber. You're so big they can't be comfortable on you, honey."

His hand was on the doorknob, but he stopped and looked back at her.

"Let's get a few things straight, Chicky." The name, when he used it, sounded more like a taunt than a tease, and she shivered. "I will *never* screw you without a rubber. I will never invite you or any woman into *my* bed. And I will never make love to you. I don't make love to women. I fuck them. It's that simple. Don't try to make it into anything more."

And with that, he walked out the door, closing it behind him.

# Chapter Eighteen
2000

GINNY CAREFULLY TOOK her small suitcase down from the top shelf of the closet she shared with Tommy.

She harrumphed to herself as she thought of Tommy's concern about her going to her old house. The one she'd shared with Grizz for five years. She'd been there many times to visit Carter. Okay, maybe it wasn't so easy in the beginning. But after she'd settled into her happy marriage with Tommy, it really wasn't difficult at all. She'd gotten to the point where she could go without remembering the nightmare of Grizz's arrest. Ever since she was a kid she'd been very strong-minded, always able to block out something unpleasant.

She carried the suitcase to the bed and laid it down. She unzipped it and went to her dresser to get some things. Besides, she told herself, it wasn't the bad memories she had a hard time forgetting. It was the good ones.

Her mind drifted back to a time when she had been happy. Really happy. She'd been living in her new home with Grizz and hadn't returned to the motel even once.

"So Grizz, I have at least four options picked out for us." She had just walked into the bathroom. He was standing at the sink shaving. He gave her a sidelong glance.

"Four options for what, Kit? What are you talking about?"

"The summer concerts. Remember you told me you would take me to a concert? You promised me after I went to Black Sabbath with you that you would go to one that I liked."

He tapped his razor on the side of the sink and flashed a guilty look. "Uh, yeah. Guess I forgot about that. But you liked Black Sabbath, right? You wanted to go with me?"

"Yeah, I like them, but that wasn't the deal. They're *your* group, not mine. I went to keep you company." She grinned at him in the mirror, then wrapped her arms around his waist from behind.

"And sitting on my shoulders for two hours so you could see the whole show wasn't a little perk for you?"

She let go and went to sit on the edge of the bathtub. "Of course it was a perk and I've never heard you complain about me having my legs wrapped around your head before."

He had just rinsed off his face and was reaching for a towel when he started laughing and looked at her. "Sorry, Kitten, I didn't mind having you up there, but you were facing the wrong way."

She grabbed the towel out of his hand and snapped it at him. "You always turn everything back to sex."

"You're the one who mentioned having your legs wrapped around my head." He pulled her close. "Let's go back to bed. We don't have to be anywhere this early. C'mon."

She got serious then. "No. I have school and I want to get there early to spend some time with Carter. I'm sure it hasn't crossed your mind, but she said the guy who's been bothering her seems to have disappeared or found someone else to stalk. Still, I know she's been worried."

Ginny had told Grizz about a man who was causing her college friend some agony. Carter had gone on one date with him, and when she was busy the following weekend, he'd taken it personally and started harassing her. The last straw for Carter was when she'd found a dead animal on the driver's seat of her car. The sicko had actually killed a raccoon and broken in to leave it for her. Actually, they never did figure out if he killed it on purpose or accidentally ran over it and saw it as an opportunity to mess with Carter. Regardless, it prompted her to go to the police and take out a restraining order on him. Ginny guessed it had finally scared him off.

"Good for Carson," Grizz said.

"Carter." Ginny elbowed him. "For goodness sake, you can't even remember her name!"

He gave her a half smile and leaned back against the bathroom sink. He crossed his arms in front of him and said, "Okay, let's hear your concert list. And there better not be any Bee Bees on there."

She shook her head and bit her lip in exasperation. "They're the Bee Gees, and believe me, I know better than to ask you to take me to see them. Okay, so, the first one is at the end of May. Blondie."

He shook his head no.

She looked back at her list. "Okay, there are two in June. We can see Boston, and you know how much I love them, or we can see Styx."

"No. I don't want to see them. What else you got?"

"Journey is playing in July." She looked up at him hopefully. "I know these aren't your favorites, but I listen to them, and I know you like them a little bit."

"Keep going, honey. How about the fifth option?" he pointed to her paper.

She looked down at it, then back up at him. "I didn't write down a fifth option. There wasn't anybody else I wanted to see."

He leaned over her and pointed to the paper. "Sure it's there. See? Option five."

"Grizz, there is no option five. Stop being ornery."

"I see it clear as day from here and it's the one I want."

She laid her list on the bathroom counter and put her hands on her hips. "Okay, let's hear it. What is option five?" She knew he was going to rattle off a string of his favorite bands.

"Option five is the one where I stick an ice pick in my eye instead of going to one of your concerts."

She swiped the paper, scrunched it up, and threw it at him. "You are not funny! And I think risking certain blindness and possible death instead of taking your wife to a concert is telling me something, and I don't appreciate it!"

She started to walk out of the bathroom, but he caught her in his arms and held on to her. She struggled to get free. "Let me go. You make my blood boil and I hate it when you do it on purpose. I said to let me go!"

"I'm teasing with you, baby," he said, his voice soothing and kind. "I'll take you to any concert you want to go to."

She calmed down then. "What's the catch?"

"Why does there have to be a catch?" he asked, inhaling her scent as he nuzzled her neck. He never seemed to tire of it. As a matter of fact, he always had the opposite reaction, seemed to crave it more and more.

"What's the catch?" she asked again, a more serious tone in her voice.

"I just thought that maybe you could come to one of my meetings. A lot of old ladies will be there."

"I'm not an old lady."

"You're *my* old lady and you know it. C'mon, honey, you don't come with me enough."

"I hate going. I don't fit in with the other 'old ladies.'" She had freed her hands and made the last comment with air quotes.

"Everyone is nice to you."

*As if they had a choice.* "I know that. It's just that this—this life has never been right for me and you know that. I thought moving away from the motel would be the end of it for me. I know you have to go there still and go to your different meetings. But I don't."

She bit her lip and looked up at him. "You really won't go to a concert with me if I don't go to a meeting with you?"

"I'll take you to your concert. I really just needed a favor. Actually, Anthony needs the favor."

He knew the minute she realized what he was asking. "Christy. He still doesn't have a handle on Christy?" She let out a breath. "We've seen them this past year. She seems fine. They seem fine."

"Hell, I don't know. Maybe she's having a change of heart."

"I don't see how I can change her heart. They've been together for a while now. I can't picture him making her stay."

"Exactly, Kit. He won't *make* her stay, but something's up, and he's afraid she's going to leave. He doesn't know what's going on and wants you to talk to her. That's all. See if there's something she's not telling him."

Ginny remembered that meeting now, as she threw the final items into her suitcase, and how she did talk to Christy. And boy, something had been up, all right. But Christy and Anthony moved on from there. They'd been happily married ever since, had gone on to have two sons and a daughter. Slade was their oldest. He was three years older than Mimi. Their middle son, Christian, was Mimi's age. And their little girl, Daisy, was five years younger than Jason. As far as Ginny knew, they had a more than stable marriage now, but things were pretty rough for them back then.

With a hint of a smile, she also remembered how Grizz took her to see Boston.

And she'd had the best seat in the house.

Her packing was finished. It was time to go downstairs.

Time to say goodbye to Tommy.

# Chapter Nineteen
1973

GRIZZ WAS LYING on the bed in number seven, Willow on top of him, when Chowder banged on the door and finally just walked in.

"I kept walking by number four and hearing your phone ring," Chowder said, hands up in apology. "I finally went in and answered it. Guido needs to talk to you."

He left the room and Grizz flung Willow off of him. If Guido was calling the motel, it was because of Ginny.

He pulled his jeans on and quickly but calmly walked back to his room and picked up the telephone receiver lying on the kitchen counter.

"What?"

"Just thought you might want to know there's a cop car parked in front of the house next door. Two cops went in."

"Is it the parents? They fighting or something?"

"Don't know. Haven't heard them or anything. Never seemed to have that kind of problem before."

"You think they caught whiff of the mom's side business?"

"Can't say, boss. All seems quiet. They didn't show up with sirens on or guns drawn or anything like that."

"Watch the house. Call me when they leave."

"You got it, Grizz."

They hung up. Grizz stood next to the phone for a minute, lost in thought. He felt arms tighten around his waist from behind.

"C'mon back to number seven, darlin'. Or let's go in *your* bedroom and finish what we started." Willow was trying to unzip his jeans.

He couldn't think. He couldn't concentrate. He certainly was no longer in the mood to get it on with Willow. He yanked her roughly around to face him.

"Get the fuck out."

She pouted. "C'mon baby. I don't know what upset you so bad, but I know I can get your mind off it."

He stared at her for a few seconds and relented. He grabbed her by the shoulders and roughly shoved her to her knees in front of him. She started to object as he unzipped his jeans all the way, then forced her face between his legs, but something in his expression stopped her.

He leaned back against the kitchen counter and closed his eyes, letting it happen. When she'd finished, Willow stood up to lean into him, hoping for a kiss, especially a kiss, or any type of gesture.

What she got was a snub. "Now you can get the fuck out."

Ten minutes later, his phone rang. He listened to Guido, hung up without comment, and dialed another number.

"It's me. There was a call to an address on Southwest 23rd Avenue. Cops were there about twenty, maybe thirty minutes ago. What do you know?" He listened as the person on the other end of the line talked.

He hung up. *Fuck, man. What had Ginny gotten herself involved in?*

Two months passed. Late one night, a small group was sitting around the pit. It was almost midnight and Grunt was getting ready to go inside. A car pulled into the motel and parked in front of the units. Before the owner had cut the engine, Grizz stood and started walking towards the car.

Grunt knew the car, too—it belonged to Ginny's neighbor, Guido.

Grunt could never remember one instance of Guido being at the motel. Why was he here now? Grunt jumped up and followed Grizz at a distance.

"Why are you here?" Grizz demanded, fists clenched. "Is she okay?"

"Calm down, big guy, she's—" Before Guido could finish his sentence, Grizz had instinctively grabbed him by the throat, his anxiety at Guido's presence evident.

So this was about Ginny. Grunt felt an immediate stab of fear, but he quickly steadied himself. He also knew they wouldn't learn anything if Grizz continued to hold Guido by the throat.

"Grizz, let him go," Grunt calmly said. "Let him tell you what's going on."

Grizz let go of him as quickly as he'd grabbed him.

"She's fine," Guido gulped. "But it's a good thing I got to her when I did."

Then he explained everything: how he'd been sitting on his front porch smoking a joint when some guy pulled up and parked partially on his lawn. Walked right up to Ginny's house and knocked on the door. Guido had been shocked when she'd let him in the house. She was a smart girl and he knew her parents weren't there. Something wasn't right.

Guido walked over to the front of her house and peered inside one of the windows that flanked the front door. Good thing he did. The guy had Ginny pinned to the floor. He was holding her hands over her head with one hand and was using his other hand to alternately try and cover her mouth while trying to undo his jeans. Guido tried the doorknob. The deadbolt was in place. That bastard must have locked it behind him when Ginny let him in. That's when Guido started beating on the door, threatening to call the police. The man jumped off of her and went out the back sliding glass doors. Ginny got herself up and ran to let Guido in. He started to chase the guy out the back doors, but stopped when he noticed the kitchen wall that used to have a phone mounted on it. The guy must have yanked it off on his way out. Guido told Ginny to use the phone at his house to call the police. That's when they heard the truck engine start and the guy take off.

"She wouldn't leave the house to call the police," Guido sputtered, keeping a safe distance from Grizz. "Kept insisting she had to wait for her parents to get home. So I hightailed it back to my place, called Smitty's, and told them to get their asses home. I've been calling you, too. Figured it was important enough for me to drive out here."

"I want to know who this guy is and I want to know before dawn," Grizz growled.

"Already know who he is," Guido replied. "Johnny Tillman. Knew the girl's parents from Smitty's."

Grizz squinted in concentration. He'd never heard the name

before.

"Did the police show up and make a report?"

Guido nodded.

"Come inside."

Guido and Grunt followed Grizz into number four. He picked up the phone and dialed a number.

"It's me. An assault or attempted rape report was made in the last few hours. What do you know?" After a few minutes Grizz said, "You will find him and bring him to me." Another pause. "I don't care if someone else picks him up. You figure out a fucking way to intervene and get him. You can say later that he got away from you." Another pause. "Are you questioning me? What the fuck do I care about your reputation? You will find this bastard and you will make sure he is delivered to me. I'll let you know if my guys find him first."

Without waiting for a reply, Grizz hung up.

They wordlessly followed him back out to the pit. There were about five or six guys lounging in flimsy lawn chairs around a dying fire. It was getting late and people were getting ready to go home or crash in one of the old rooms. A plump blonde was sitting on Blue's lap and whispering something in his ear.

"Listen up," Grizz announced, his voice loud in the quiet night. "There is a man out there I want brought to me. Guido will tell you what he looks like and what he's driving." He nodded at Blue. "Blue will organize it so that you cover every possible street. Start with a two-mile grid beginning with Smitty's on Davie Boulevard."

Blue jumped up and the blonde fell to the ground giggling.

Grizz looked at the girl directly. "Tiny, make yourself useful for once. Use Chowder's phone and make some calls. Tell them what I just told everyone."

Without waiting for a reply he turned and walked back toward the motel, calling over his shoulder, "No one comes back here unless that fucker is on the back of someone's bike."

# Chapter Twenty
1975, Federal Bureau of Investigation Headquarters, Washington, D.C.

SPECIAL DIRECTOR MICHAEL Spiro had just hung up his telephone when his secretary buzzed him on the intercom.

"Yes?"

"Agent Pinelli is here to see you, sir."

Director Spiro sighed and shook his head. "Send him in."

He took a long draw on his cigarette and leaned back in his chair as the agent entered. Pinelli stood before his desk, hands gripping a folder, waiting.

"What can I do for you, Pinelli?"

Pinelli was the newest agent assigned to him. He was young but came with high references. Spiro had been impressed by the recommendations and thought that adding someone new might bring some fresh insight to the cases they were assigned.

Unfortunately, Pinelli wasn't quite grasping the intricacy of the operations they dealt with. He wasn't able to keep his personal feelings and emotions in check. Especially when it came to dealing with one operation in particular. He noticed it early on and immediately pulled him from that case. He quickly reassigned him to a legitimate FBI operation.

"Thought you might want to know this, sir," Pinelli said, tossing a manila folder on the director's desk. He took a seat and waited for Spiro to pick up the folder.

"I don't have time to read a report. What do I need to know?"

"He's at it again. Only this time, he's gone too far."

Spiro knew exactly who Pinelli was referring to.

"He's kidnapped a girl," Pinelli continued. "Well, he didn't do it himself. He had someone else do it."

"I know," Spiro replied calmly. "Drop it and keep working on the Giamanni case.

"But, sir, she is fifteen. She's only fifteen!" Pinelli answered, the bewilderment in his tone evident.

"I know who she is. I know she's fifteen and I'm telling you to leave it alone. What the hell are you doing looking at it, anyway? You're not running point on this one and you were specifically assigned to another operation. I can write you up for this, Pinelli. Shit, I can have you fired!"

Pinelli ignored the question and the reprimand. "He probably noticed her after he bought the house next to hers and put his guy there. I checked into her. Not really much of an investigation. Nothing remarkable about her. No gang connection. Her mother and stepfather are drunks. She's a straight-A student. Babysits for spending money. Tried to report the father of one of the kids she was watching. She seems like a nice girl. I just don't know why—"

This wasn't news to Spiro. He'd already run a basic background check on the teenager and her family, and he had to agree with Pinelli. They'd found nothing special and didn't feel she required further investigation. Pinelli jumped when Spiro slammed his fist hard on the desk. "I told you to fucking leave this alone and move on to the Giamanni case. You were directed to do that three months ago. Why are you disobeying a direct order, agent?"

"Because I have a fourteen-year-old sister, sir." Pinelli sat up straighter in the low chair. "And while you may overlook his murdering and maiming tendencies, this one is too close to home for me. He has to be stopped."

Pinelli wasn't going to let this drop. Spiro had to play it right. He took a slow, centering breath and leaned back in his chair.

"You know what? I think you may be right on this one, Pinelli," Spiro said, nodding his head as if in agreement. "I have a daughter and two granddaughters. Yes. Now that I think about it, you've made a good call here, agent. I'll get some paperwork started. Get back over to the Giamanni case. I don't want anything that we're going to do linked back to you. Got it?"

Pinelli seemed satisfied. His posture changed as he stood up.

"Yes, sir," Pinelli said. "And thank you for taking the time to listen to my recommendation."

He reached for the file he had laid before the director. Before he could pick it up, Spiro grabbed it and pretended to look it over.

"Is this everything? Anything else in your files that I'll need?"

"No, sir. Everything is in there" Pinelli replied, nodding at the folder.

"Good work, Pinelli."

"Thank you, sir."

Pinelli left the office.

Spiro looked at the cigarette that had burned itself out in his ashtray. He reached for another one and lit it, inhaling deeply. He picked up his phone and dialed a number.

"It's me. Pinelli's become a problem." He paused while he listened to the other person on the phone. Without saying anything else, he hung up.

He took another drag on his cigarette. Stupid fucking kid. Trying to be a hero.

Spiro found little consolation in the fact that Pinelli wouldn't be leaving a wife and child behind.

**********

*Moe's Diary, 1975*

*Dear Elizabeth,*

*I took Kit shopping yesterday. It wasn't so bad. She really is a nice girl. I think I'm starting to see why Grizz seems to love her. She's different than the women that he's used to being around. She offered to buy me some clothes. Nobody has offered to buy me something since Grunt helped me get my car.*

*Seems like Grunt has forgotten about me. I thought it was school, but I know in my heart it's her. I think I knew it the night he asked me to keep her wallet. I have it hidden in my room. I don't care that Grizz told me to burn it. I hate him! She's too good for him, anyway.*

*I took her to the post office. I forgot about the stupid Missing Persons poster. Back when my parents thought there was a sighting of me, they started putting their posters up again, but I could never go home. I wouldn't be able to stand being around my sisters. I'm sure they're beautiful and have everything I used to have. Including their tongues.*

*I forgot about that poster. It was covered up with other stuff for a while. I know they stopped looking for me years ago. Next time I go there, I need to take it down.*

*I'm going to have spaghetti with Kit and Chowder. I'll write more later…*

*Dinner was actually nice, Elizabeth. It was fun. I was laughing at Chowder. He doesn't say a lot, but when he does, it's funny. Then Grizz came home. He always ruins everything. He sat there and ate with us, and it didn't seem as much fun.*

*I was right about Grunt having feelings for her. I was sitting in the pit when he came home. I think he'd spent the day with Sarah Jo at the beach. I know they're just friends. You'd think that since we both care for Grunt, we'd be friends, too, but Sarah Jo doesn't come around here practically ever, and when she does, she certainly doesn't try to be my friend. Anyway, I saw Grunt walk to unit four, and when he noticed the outside light was off, which means Grizz doesn't want company, he leaned against the door like he was trying to hear if something was going on inside.*

*I have a feeling Grizz hasn't slept with her yet, but I know he will tonight. After I had dinner with them and went back to my room, I realized later I was out of dog treats. When I went back to number four to get some, I heard music that wasn't Grizz's kind of music.*

*I knew what they were doing, and I think Grunt heard it and he knew, too.*

**********

"You are not going to fucking believe this."

Spiro looked up from his desk. Agent Marcus had walked in without being announced and closed the door behind him. His secretary must have been away from her desk, because she was very good about announcing that someone was there to see him. Spiro pinched the bridge of his nose. He had an excruciating headache.

"What is it, Marcus?" He looked at the agent resignedly. "What am I not going to believe?"

Marcus plopped himself down in front of Spiro. "He married her. He fucking married her."

This caused Spiro to sit up straight. He knew exactly who Marcus was talking about.

"Has this been confirmed?"

"It has, sir. He married her. Under his alias, Rick O'Connell, of course, and the alias he created for her," Marcus said, his tone incredulous. "He really fucked up this time."

Spiro squinted in concentration and stared at his agent. "No. He doesn't fuck up. He's never fucked up. There must be a reason."

"Maybe he loves her."

"Loves her?" Spiro said as he leaned back in his chair. "He doesn't love anybody. He is the most brutal bastard I've ever come across. No fucking way."

"You see, though, sir. We have him. If he loves her we can rein him back in. Back where he belongs."

"No, there has to be something else. Something we're missing. He doesn't do anything without a reason; and I can guaran-damn-tee you he didn't marry her for love. You sure there's nothing else on her?"

"There's nothing there, sir. She's just some girl. Other than reporting some child abuse incident—which went nowhere, by the way—she's clean. Parents are drunks, but clean. Except the mom sells weed from a store she works at."

"Could he be involved with that and we missed it?"

"No, sir. Small potatoes. No connection. We have him, sir. He's vulnerable now. He has a wife to protect. His ass belongs to us. Like I said. Time to rein his sorry ass in."

"He doesn't do anything without a reason." Spiro gritted his teeth. "And are you forgetting that he let a kid, who may or may not even be his, get stabbed? He is a first-class son-of-a-bitch who cares about nobody but himself. We sit on this for a while until we figure it out. And rein him in?" Spiro raised a brow. "Exactly who do you think he is? This fucker goes back almost twenty years and we've never been able to completely confirm his identity."

"I was just saying, sir—"

"You were talking out your ass is what you were doing. Go fucking do your job, agent, and leave your sixth-grade excitement and speculations at the door."

The agent left. Spiro's head was really pounding now. This particular operation had been ongoing since the fifties. He was the second person assigned to this top-secret task force. The last one had retired. He had a feeling he would be retiring, too, before this operation came to fruition.

Of course, nobody, including his secretary, knew his real title or job. Nobody knew he and his operatives didn't work for the FBI. They worked for the U.S. Government, and while Spiro did act as director for the other legitimate FBI agents on his team, he had been planted at the bureau to manage one case and one case only. He had two office agents, who he had to occasionally assign to real bureau cases to avoid notice, and one operative in the field. One operative who risked his life daily for the sake of this one assignment.

One he was no longer even sure of himself.

Spiro knew with perfect certainty this case was being overseen as high as the Oval Office. He didn't know why; he just knew what he was assigned to do.

And he was having second thoughts about Marcus now. Too excitable and rambunctious. This was a waiting game and he knew it killed his agents to let this one man get away with so much. But they had to. Their hands were tied thanks to someone at the top.

If anyone needed reigning in now, it was his own agent.

*Dammit.* He picked up his phone and dialed a number.

This was the most cryptic case he'd ever been assigned, and he was afraid it would be the death of him.

# Chapter Twenty-One
2000


MOMENTS LATER, GINNY was standing in the entranceway to their kitchen.

"Thought you wanted to read it together," she said flatly.

Tommy closed the journal and flashed a sheepish smile. "Curious."

"Anything interesting so far?"

He was getting ready to tell her how Moe had written about how much she'd hated Grizz, how responsible she'd felt the night he, Grunt, was stabbed by Monk. He was trying to remember if he'd ever told Ginny how he got that scar. Sometimes he couldn't remember what he'd told her and what he hadn't. It was all a blur. But before he could answer her question, her face changed.

"You know what?" She held up a hand, her expression bitter. "Don't answer that. I don't want to know."

Something in Tommy snapped. It took a lot for him to get angry, but he suddenly couldn't help himself. He stood and slammed the notebook on the table.

"What else is new?" he asked her, voice full of attitude.

"What is that supposed to mean?" She set her suitcase down on the floor, then walked to face him.

"It means that you are the best person I know for putting your head in the sand and pretending something doesn't exist. You did it for ten years with Grizz, and you're still doing it!" His face was red and his hands were clenched. "If Ginny doesn't know about it or let herself think about it, then it didn't happen. It was your coping mechanism. It was then and it is now."

He didn't want to do this, didn't want to be mean to her, but dammit! He'd had enough. Yes, he admitted to himself. Yes, all those years ago, he had come up with a plan. The perfect plan. He remembered the day he'd realized he wouldn't have to lure her away after all. Grizz would handle that—push her away with his ruthlessness. He remembered likening his quest for Ginny's love to a chess game. He was going to outsmart Grizz.

The only problem with the plan was that he found it actually hurt him more to see her hurting. So he'd protected her from certain things Grizz did. It went against everything he'd started out to do, but he loved her so much, he couldn't stand to see her suffer.

He was the fool.

"How dare you." Her eyes flashed and her voice grew quiet. Deadly quiet. "How dare you accuse me of sticking my head in the sand? You are Grizz's son! You are Mimi's brother! Do you think it might've been important enough to tell me? Don't you think I deserved to know I married my ex-husband's own son?"

"Why?" Tommy wanted to hit something. Anything. "Why would I tell you, Gin? It would just be another thing you wouldn't want to know."

"Really, what else is there, Tommy? What else wouldn't I want to know about? For goodness sake, I lived at the motel. I knew what he did. I left after Chico had his guy kill those kids. *You're* the one who convinced me to go back. Do you remember that? Do you remember the day you found me and talked me into going back?"

"Yeah, Ginny. I remember."

# Chapter Twenty-Two
1976

GRUNT LEANED HIS head back against the wall and sighed. He'd been sitting on his bed trying to concentrate on his homework, but he just couldn't do it.

He closed his eyes and immediately saw her. Kit. She was laughing at something he'd said over one of their many chess lessons. They used to be lessons, but now they were just matches, really. She was smart and at this point could almost beat him. He'd thought more than once about letting her win, but that wasn't Kit's way. The girl would have to beat him fair and square. Maybe one day she would.

Now that he thought about it, he couldn't call her a girl. She'd been living with the gang since she'd been abducted last year and was married to their leader. She was now sixteen and had experienced more in the last year than some grown women would in a lifetime.

No, Kit was definitely no longer a girl. She was a woman. And she was the woman Grunt had been in love with for a very long time.

Even before she came to the motel.

Over the years, he'd accompanied Grizz to keep an eye on the young girl then called Gwinny, later just Ginny. Sometimes, he was the one that suggested it—that they go take a drive by her house, check up on things. Grizz didn't seem to have a problem taking him along. Maybe people were less suspicious of a man who had a kid with him. He was sure they assumed he was Grizz's kid.

It didn't matter. He always looked forward to the times he would be able to watch her. He didn't remember the exact moment it became love. There had been too many times to count how often he'd observed her doing something that melted his heart.

He remembered her first night at the motel. It was last May. He didn't know then that Grizz was going to have her brought here. He'd secretly hoped that maybe Grizz would step aside, let her find her own destiny. If that was the case, Grunt was certain he could insert himself into her life.

He'd imagined it a thousand times. Casually running into her somewhere. Making small talk. Making her laugh. He'd even thought about enrolling in her school, but that charade would be too difficult to maintain. Especially since he was already in college and he had no doubt that Grizz wouldn't have allowed it. He laughed to himself at the memory. People in love are willing to do desperate things.

He'd never imagined Grizz was falling for her, too. He knew about the obsession, but somehow he believed the story, believed that Grizz truly was looking out for the girl. A favor to an old friend, he'd said. Maybe Grunt was just too busy wrapping himself in his own fantasies of a life with her. A future.

Unfortunately, as long as Grizz was around, no other man would ever have a chance with Kit, let alone a future.

Her first night at the motel was seared in his memory. He'd been leaning back in a lawn chair, staring into the fire. Willow and Chicky were arguing about something. Monster pulled up on his motorcycle. He could tell there was a female on the back.

He's certain he gasped when he noticed it was her and Monster was walking her towards the pit. *What the fuck?*

He half listened as Willow started arguing with Monster about the "thank you gift." Bullshit. Grunt knew better. Ginny—Kit, she called herself now—was only fifteen and probably scared to death.

But if she was scared, she certainly wasn't showing it. He watched as she calmly observed the exchange between Willow and Monster. He knew she hadn't noticed Grizz when he walked up next to her. What would her reaction be? He wondered, watching her as she noticed Grizz for the first time and her eyes slowly moved up his body until they reached his face. She showed no emotion that he could detect. And when Willow lunged at her and Grizz intervened, the girl never even flinched.

He couldn't believe how brave she was that night. The dying campfire cast an almost angelic glow on her face. The face he had loved for a long time.

And now, she was here.

And she belonged to Grizz.

He'd watched that night as Moe led her to number four. He only half listened as Grizz told the gang they were never to discuss her. They weren't to look at her, speak to her, or address her presence at the motel. Ever. He then watched Grizz turn around and go inside.

It was only a few minutes before Moe came out. She walked toward the pit, her head down. Grunt jumped up when he saw her, gently took her arm and led her to his unit. He heard some laughter from the pit. Who cares—let them think what they wanted.

"Is she okay?" he asked once they were inside. "Was she crying or anything?"

Moe looked up at him with an odd expression on her face and nodded. Shit. Which question was she answering? He grabbed a piece of notebook paper and a pencil, handing it to Moe.

"Let's start over. Is she okay?"

Moe nodded yes.

"Please don't make me ask you, Moe. Just tell me what's going on inside number four."

Moe wrote, "Seems okay. Not crying. Not afraid of him."

He was relieved. "Good. What else?"

Moe retrieved something from her pocket. It was a wallet. She laid it on his bed and wrote something else on the paper. "Have to burn it."

He looked at her without saying anything for almost a full minute. "Will you keep it? Will you hide it? Will you do that for me, Moe?"

She nodded again.

He took the paper she had been writing on and crumpled it up. He would take it out to the pit and toss it in the fire.

He left Moe standing in his room. He ignored the whistles and lewd catcalls concerning his and Moe's time together. *Assholes*.

If he'd taken even a moment to stop and look back at Moe before he left the room, he would have seen an expression on her face he'd never seen before. The look of a woman who loved someone that could never be hers. Moe had the look of a woman who had just realized the man she loved was in love with someone else.

It was the look of despair.

Grunt was jolted back to the present by a loud commotion outside. He got up and went to his window. He shook his head as he watched the scene. Typical. Looked like some guys had lured a young couple back to the motel and were tormenting them. Grizz commanded the dogs to be quiet but was ignoring what was going on just a few feet away from him. He was talking to Chico, who was probably setting up some kind of delivery. It didn't matter. Whatever it was, it was certainly illegal.

Just then, Grunt noticed movement to the left. Kit. She was walking purposefully toward Grizz. She said something to him, which Grunt couldn't hear. Grizz replied to her, but apparently it didn't satisfy her because she didn't go away. He saw Grizz nod to Chico, and Chico said something to one of the other guys.

Grunt saw her flinch when the couple was executed. She turned around and started back toward number four. He could see her face clearly. She was upset, but trying to control it.

Good. This would work out for him. He wouldn't have to come up with a plan to lure Kit away from Grizz. Grizz's ruthlessness would push her away. He would wait.

He needed some time, anyway. He would graduate college. He would make something of himself and be able to offer her a life away from this band of criminals. It would just take some time.

He had time. He would let Grizz continue to show her what a bastard he truly was.

Chess was Grunt's game, and he was the best. This wasn't chess, but it would be the most serious game he'd ever played in his life. Each move would have to be painstakingly calculated.

He smiled as he watched Grizz striding towards number four. The game was on, and Grunt hadn't lost one yet.

He remembered how he'd almost messed up last year. It was the night he took Kit to Jan and Blue's for Thanksgiving. He'd fucked up and told her how he felt about her. There was a pause in their conversation and he quickly reminded himself that he needed to be patient. Having a relationship with her then would've been impossible. He had to keep following Sarah Jo's advice. Jo had told him to wait and that's what he'd been doing. He didn't have a plan then, but he really wouldn't have needed one, anyway. He would just make sure Grizz always looked like a rat bastard in front of Kit. She would see the horrible things that Grizz did, and Grunt would make sure that he was there to comfort her.

He was so lost in thought he hadn't realized Kit had just walked right past his window. She hadn't seen him because she was looking straight ahead, as if on a mission.

Grunt watched her walk around the side of the motel. Maybe she was getting ready to jog, maybe blow off some steam. She had her purse with her, though. She wouldn't need her purse to jog around the motel.

A minute later, he saw her Trans-Am emerge from the right side of the motel and peel out as she gunned it at the entrance to State Road 84. What was she doing? She wasn't supposed to go anywhere alone.

There was no way Grizz knew about her leaving. He had given her strict driving rules when he'd presented her with a brand new car for her sixteenth birthday. She was without a doubt defying a direct order. Grunt's brain went into overdrive. Was she going to the police? Was she taking a drive to calm down? Would she seek out Sarah Jo? She had just seen something horrible. What would a girl like her do after seeing two people get murdered? Should he go after her?

No, not yet. He took a calming breath as it dawned on him. He didn't need to go after her. Yes. He knew exactly where she was going. He wanted to see how Grizz would react when he realized she'd left. He would wait.

**********

For his part, Grizz had left Kit standing in the small living room after she'd confronted him about what Chico's guy did to the couple that had been lured back to the motel.

"I'm taking a shower," he called out over his shoulder as he headed for the bathroom.

He stripped off his clothes and climbed in, letting the hot water soak into his shoulders as he closed his eyes and thought about Kit. Thought about what she'd just seen. *Dammit.* Why didn't he think before nodding at Chico? He didn't think about it because he didn't care. Not about that couple, anyway.

Kit was the only thing that mattered, and he didn't think far enough ahead to predict how Chico would respond to his nod to "take care of this." He'd never had to worry about it before. Worst of all, he didn't know how to respond to her when she confronted him. He was a cold, heartless bastard. He wasn't used to caring what someone thought.

But he cared what Kit thought. He would talk to her. He would be kinder, gentler. Maybe he should get her away from the motel. Set her up somewhere else. He would think about it.

He got out of the shower and dried off. After wrapping the towel around himself, he headed out to the small living room where he'd left her ten minutes earlier.

But she wasn't there. He peeked out the curtain. She wasn't in the pit and she wasn't jogging around the parking lot as was her habit.

She probably went to find Grunt. He would get dressed and go get her.

He left number four and noticed Grunt was in one of the lawn chairs in the pit, his legs stretched out. Maybe he'd left Kit in his room to listen to records or something. Even though she had her own stereo, she might just be angry enough with Grizz to lock herself in Grunt's room and ignore him. It wouldn't have been the first time she'd stayed away. He smiled when he remembered how mad she'd been when he gave her a new car for her birthday, how she'd stayed away from him for a few days when he'd refused to let her and Sarah Jo drive around in it together.

He adored her. He didn't want her to be hurt by the things she saw at the motel, and it dawned on him that he hadn't really done a good job of shielding her from this lifestyle. What had he told her earlier? If you don't like what goes on out there, then stay inside.

He was a bastard. She was not a typical "old lady" and never would be. And truthfully, that's what he liked about her. No. That wasn't entirely accurate. That's what he loved about her. He knew he could have avoided having her see the executions earlier that day, but even after a year at the motel, he still wasn't used to having her around. He wasn't used to caring so damn much.

He banged on Grunt's door once before flinging it open. But it was empty. He was surprised that she wasn't there.

His mouth was still open to say something when another thought occurred to him. It sent a wave of heat up his spine.

No way. She wouldn't leave. She wouldn't defy him.

He found himself striding quickly to the office side of the motel. He was getting ready to break into a run when Chicky came out of one of the units. He almost mowed her down. She was talking to him, but he didn't hear her. He was on the other side of the office now and stopped dead in his tracks.

Kit's car was gone.

Grunt watched from the pit. He saw Grizz brush past Chicky so quickly it almost knocked her over. He had only seen Grizz lose his cool one time, and that was the night that Guido came to the motel to tell them Johnny Tillman had tried to rape Ginny. Grunt could tell by Grizz's stride that he was more than a little upset. Maybe even panicked. Grunt knew it would be worse when Grizz discovered that Kit's car was gone.

He waited.

A split second later, Grizz came barreling back around the side of the office. He got to the pit; only Grunt and a few other people remained. Chico and his men had already left.

"Did you see Kit leave?" Grizz looked at each face, including Grunt's. Everyone shook their head no, including Grunt.

Grunt couldn't help himself. "Leave? Why would Kit leave?"

Grizz didn't answer. His jaw tightened, and his fists were clenched as his arms dangled at his side. He was trying to control his emotions.

"Everyone rides. Find her."

"What do we do when we find her?" Monster asked. "You want us to bring her back? I don't know if we could get her back here without causing attention, you know?"

"No, don't go near her." Grizz's face was shadowed. "Page me from a pay phone and wait. I'll call you and you can tell me where you last saw her."

"Should we go east or head west towards the Alley?" another person asked.

This question caught Grizz by surprise. It hadn't occurred to him that Kit might head over the Alley. But why would she? She didn't know anyone over there. Kit hadn't made any friends that he knew of at the little church he took her to every week. Then again, he never went inside with her, so how would he know?

Just to be sure, Grizz would call his friend, Anthony, and have him post one of his guys at the Alligator Alley exit.

"What the fuck are you all waiting for? Go! Now!" he yelled.

The men who were still sitting jumped to attention and everyone started heading for their bikes.

"I'll take my car," Grunt said as he casually walked past Grizz.

Yep, he knew exactly where she would be, and if Grizz cared half as much for her as Grunt did, he would know too.

# Chapter Twenty-Three
## 1950s, Fort Lauderdale, Florida

IT HAD BEEN four days since that rotten bastard had taken off with everything he owned.

Somehow, he'd made his way to the downtown area, had been sleeping behind businesses and eating out of dumpsters. He had been racking his brain trying to figure out how he was going to survive with only the clothes on his back. He was big for his age and could try to get a job, but it wasn't likely that he'd be hired looking and smelling like he did. He just needed to figure out a way to get his hands on some cash so he could get himself cleaned up and have a decent meal. Maybe then he could think clearer.

He thought about stealing the money. He could mug someone or even break into a business at night and raid the register, but he realized that the fear of getting caught and being connected to his family's disappearance scared him more than being hungry. He'd been hungry before. He'd figure this out.

He was walking along the sidewalk and looking down when he collided with someone.

"Stupid son-of-a-bitch. Why don't you watch where you're going, you stupid ass?"

He realized he'd knocked over an old man who had been carrying his packages out of the post office. He was trying to get himself up and still cussing when the boy extended his hand and pulled him to his feet.

"Sorry, mister. Didn't see you. Can I help you carry your stuff to your car?"

"Yeah." The old man dusted off the seat of his pants and pointed to a car. "That one's mine."

He watched as the kid effortlessly scooped up the dropped boxes and easily strode to his car. He hobbled over and unlocked the trunk. The boy put the boxes in the trunk and slammed it shut.

"Anything else I can do for you, mister?"

Just then, the old man caught a whiff of him. "Holy shit, you stink, kid. Don't your parents let you take a bath? Maybe you oughta go jump in a fountain or something."

The boy didn't say anything, just looked at the ground.

"What's your story, kid?" the old man asked with a suspicious gleam in his eye.

"No story. Just looking for work to help out my family." The boy looked up and met the old man's gaze.

The old man was startled by the kid's bright green eyes. They were intelligent eyes and the old man knew that they held a secret.

He knew because he had secrets of his own.

**********

Two months earlier: The Glades Motel

The old man had just come out of unit seven. He'd had one visitor to the motel that week and they had just left. He didn't have any employees, so it was up to him to clean up the room. He didn't have to. He had other rooms that were clean, but he considered himself a bit fussy, and having one dirty room would've bothered him.

He didn't get many visitors out here. He'd made a bad business decision on a friend's tip years ago that a highway would be coming through to connect the two Florida coasts. His friend had told him that being the first motel out there would make him a fortune. What it had made him was a lonely and bitter old man who'd wasted his life and savings waiting for a highway that hadn't been built yet. When he did get a visitor, it was usually somebody who'd gotten lost in the middle of the night and would rent a room with the intention of starting fresh in the morning.

He had his back to the open door and was busy vacuuming when a voice startled him. He turned around and noticed a very well dressed man with a suitcase in one hand and a large bag in the other.

"I saw the vacancy sign. Can I get a room?"

The old man hadn't heard the car pull up because of the vacuum.

"Sure can. This one just became ready. How long you staying?" he asked his new guest.

"Don't know, yet. Any place out here to get food?" the smartly dressed man asked.

The old man told him the closest restaurant was miles away and back toward the beach. He quickly added, "I got plenty of food, though. I'd be glad to share my meals with you. You hungry now? I can get you a sandwich. Was fixing to get myself one as soon as I was done here."

He looked at the man hopefully. He'd lost more than one visitor because of the remoteness of his motel. He'd learned to offer a homemade meal as a way to keep them from leaving to look for a more convenient place to stay.

He really didn't mind. He had to feed himself anyway. He was getting old, though, and it was harder to fix a little fancier meal for a guest than he would've fixed for just himself. Hopefully, this guy wouldn't mind a sandwich and a beer.

Truth be told, the old man didn't really need guests. He had no debt and his living expenses were minimal. He had just enough saved to help with the bills when guests were too few and far between.

"Sure. A sandwich sounds good," the man told him.

The old man pulled his vacuum cleaner out on to the sidewalk and told the new guest to make himself comfortable.

"I'll get you some clean towels and some food. You can come sign the register later."

"Can you bring me the towels now? I could use a shower and I'll come find you so I can register and take you up on that sandwich."

He had already delivered the towels and was now making his new guest a sandwich. The guy seemed nice. He hoped he would stay longer than one night, but it was doubtful. They'd made some small talk when he brought back the fresh towels. He was an insurance salesman and spent most of his days on the road. Had a wife and two daughters. He didn't get to spend much time with them because his job kept him on the road, but the more insurance he sold, the bigger his commissions.

He decided to surprise his guest by having a cold beer and the sandwich waiting for him when he got out of the shower. He grabbed his ring of master keys and made his way down the walkway. He knocked and when there was no answer he figured his guest must still be in the bathroom. Good.

He let himself in the room and set the food and beer down on the dresser. He started to walk out when the large bag on the bed caught his attention. It was one of those big bags that a soldier might use, made of a heavy tan canvas-type material with one long zipper down the middle. Whatever was in it was causing the bag to bulge out as if it had been filled to capacity. He didn't know why, but it struck him as an odd piece of luggage for the insurance salesman to have with him.

His curiosity got the best of him and he found himself unzipping it. His eyes widened when he realized what was inside.

It was filled to the brim with neat stacks of tightly clad money. A gun was laying on top.

"You shouldn't have come back in here."

The old man flinched when he realized his guest had come out of the bathroom. He was standing at the door holding a towel around his waist with one hand. Steam from the bathroom slowly floated out into the air and added an almost sinister effect to the scene.

"What did you do? Rob a bank?"

"You should've minded your own business, old man." He dropped the towel and made a quick lunge toward the bag. He was going for his gun.

With reflexes that he didn't even know he had, the old man reached for the gun, aimed, and fired.

It took him forever to load up the body and all of his guest's personal belongings into the man's car. He was old and had been a chain smoker since he was ten. The task was daunting, and the only thing that drove him to finish the task was the fear of another guest showing up and catching him. That probably wasn't a real fear, but with his luck, it'd be a bunch of coppers getting lost on their way to a convention.

He drove the car as far out into the swamp as he knew he could go and walk himself back safely. Even after the drive he was still winded from all of the work, and he allowed himself to catch his breath as he watched the car slowly sinking. He would carry the gun with him back to the motel. He'd need it in case he came across any gators.

While he walked back, he would try to figure out what to do with all that money.

One thing he knew for certain. He couldn't spend it for a while. He didn't know who, if anybody, would come looking for this guy. He would hide the money and give himself some time to make a plan.

**********

"I can give you some work, but I'm way out in the middle of nowhere. You have a ride?" the old man asked the kid as they stood outside the car.

"No. I can hitch though."

"You ain't gonna be able to hitch a ride to my place. Nobody comes out there. Sorry." He started to walk towards the driver's side of the car to get in.

The boy followed him. "Maybe I can stay with you. I don't need to sleep in your house or anything. I can camp in your yard, if that's okay. I'll work hard for you."

The old man eyed him warily. This kid didn't have a family. He was probably a runaway.

"You in trouble with the law? Someone looking for you?"

"No, sir. Just fallen on hard times. No family, and I probably don't have to tell you that orphanages are worse than living on the street."

"So, you're a liar," the old man added, not unkindly. "You told me you needed a job to help out your family."

He didn't expect the kid to answer. The truth was, he didn't give a shit. And he really could use help at the motel. He was getting old, and even though he rarely had guests, there was still a lot of upkeep. At the rate he was going, he would die before he could spend all that money. He could use some muscle to take care of the shit jobs like keeping up with yard work, repairs, even the pool. Heck, maybe the kid even knew how to cook.

He didn't give the boy a chance to answer his last accusation. "Got a name?"

The boy looked at the ground.

"What should I call you? Boy?"

The kid's head snapped up and his green eyes were cold. "You can call me anything but 'boy,' mister. Don't call me boy."

"Well, how does Ralph work for you? Can I call you Ralph?"

"Ralph will be fine, mister."

"And I don't go by mister. You can call me Pop. Now get in the car and roll down the fucking window. You smell like a dead dog that's been laying in the sun for a week."

# Chapter Twenty-Four
## 1976

GRUNT WAS RIGHT.

He pulled his car into the church parking lot and parked next to her car. It was the only other car there. She was really taking a big risk here, coming to her old church. Did she subconsciously want to be found? Did she want to run into that nun who'd been trying to get authorities to search for her?

Grunt quietly let himself in the unlocked doors. The church was massive and impressive. The smell of incense burned his nostrils. The lights were dim, but not so dim that he couldn't make out a lone figure in the very front row. He could tell she was kneeling. Her head was raised. She was looking up. He looked up, too, and saw a massive cross over what he assumed was the altar. A man was nailed to the cross. This would be Kit's Jesus. He called Him that because he wasn't sure if he could be his Jesus, too. But He was definitely Kit's.

Kit had tried to explain the basics of Christianity to Grunt. He loved to listen to her and was actually quite fascinated with some of the Bible stories she told. But he couldn't fathom how it worked. And he definitely couldn't fathom how it could work for him. No, he would listen to her stories, he would respect her beliefs, but he could not see how someone like him could be loved unconditionally by the man hanging on that cross.

Yet if he was going to be honest, he would have to admit that he admired, maybe even envied, her faith.

He barely noticed the beautiful stained glass windows that flanked each side of the church as he made his way quietly up the long aisle to where Kit was kneeling. He had reached her now and was getting ready to say something to her when, without turning around, she asked, "Will you sit here with me?"

He was shocked. How did she know he was even there? She turned then and looked at him, as she sat back on the bench. He slid in next to her.

"I saw two people murdered today," she whispered. "I don't know where to go from here. I don't know what to do. Tell me what to do, Grunt. Please."

"What is He telling you to do?" Grunt nodded at the cross.

"He's not telling me anything. Or if He is telling me, I'm not hearing it. Or—" She paused, shook her head. "Maybe I don't want to hear it. I'm so torn. Grizz is so good to me. Am I supposed to turn him in? Turn everybody in, possibly causing harm to Vince and Delia? Or should I stay and try to make a difference?"

Grunt thought about this carefully. She couldn't go back home without calling the police. She'd been missing almost a year. People who knew her would be curious. If she said she'd run away, she'd be asked where she'd been all this time. Kit would never lie about it. At least not convincingly. So if she were to go home, she would have to report Grizz, and the gang to the police.

Grunt knew he was being selfish, but this would mess him up big time. Right now, Blue was paying for his college courses with money he earned from his gang activities. Money he earned from Grizz. If Grunt was ever going to make a life for himself and Kit in the future, he would need an education. That would be interrupted. And heck, he was only seventeen. He might even be put back in foster care, but most likely he'd go to a juvenile detention facility. No telling when he would be able to get back on track.

No. He would have to convince her to go back to Grizz.

His stomach dropped. As much as he hated the thought of her being with Grizz, he knew that his motivation was purely selfish at this moment.

"I don't know if he can help who he is, Kit," he told her softly. "I do know that you are the only good thing in his life. The only pure thing. He keeps you close because you're the only light for him. Can you see that?"

Grunt was speaking from experience. Kit was his only light, too.

"But I cannot see what I see, Grunt. I cannot be true to myself, to my God, and live every day as if what he does is okay or acceptable."

"Who says you have to think what he does is okay or acceptable? You don't have to approve or condone his behavior. Maybe you can even get him to change his ways."

Grunt practically choked on his last statement. The last thing he wanted to do was encourage Kit to get Grizz to change his ways. No, he was banking on the fact that Grizz wouldn't change, that Kit would eventually turn her back on him. If he could just get his schooling finished, get a job, move out of the motel – be self-sufficient.

But he needed more time.

"Come back." He whispered. "Come back, Kit. Maybe you can make a difference."

"So you think I belong with Grizz?" She was looking at him now, her dark eyes unreadable.

This caught him off-guard. He didn't want to tell her she belonged with Grizz. She belonged with him.

But he didn't have to answer. She stood and held her hand out to him. He took her soft hand in his and stood with her.

As he walked her down the aisle and out of the church, he took a silent vow that one day, she would walk up this aisle, taking a vow of her own. As his wife. He would make that happen.

When they were in the lobby area, which Grunt would later learn was called a vestibule, she stopped and looked at him once more.

"He's going to be mad thinking you had to bring me back. Do you think maybe I should just show up back at the motel on my own? Maybe tell him that I was just driving around to cool off?"

Grunt nodded. "Yeah, that sounds like a plan." He smiled warmly at her, and she just stared at him with those big brown eyes. He wanted to kiss her so badly, but it would just confuse her. And besides, he was used to waiting.

"I'm going to drive around for a little while," he told her. "You know, pretend I'm still out looking for you. I'll call or page Grizz in an hour. I'll check in. See if you've been found."

He winked at her and she gave him a smile that melted his heart.

Grunt walked her to her car and watched her drive out of the parking lot. Then he walked back into the church and over to a small table set up against one of the walls in the vestibule. The table was filled with all kinds of pamphlets and books.

That wasn't what drew him back, though. It was something he'd noticed when he was walking Kit out.

He reached up to the bulletin board that was hanging above the table. Her smiling face and big, brown eyes were staring right at him. He yanked the missing person poster off the bulletin board and, stuffing it in his pocket, left the church.

**********

Kit tried not to struggle with her emotions on her drive back to the motel. She wouldn't allow herself to think she was going back to a man who did the things Grizz did.

One thing she did know. He would be mad.

Would he hurt her or punish her for leaving?

She raised her chin in a small act of self-defiance. *If he lays a hand on me, I'll know his true colors. I know I could never be with a man who abused me. One act of violence toward me, and I'll leave.*

And then, before she could even stop the thought: *I hope he doesn't get mad. I want to stay with him.*

Twenty minutes later, Kit pulled into the motel. There were only four motorcycles out front. She knew three belonged to Grizz and one belonged to Grunt. Everyone else was gone.

*Where is everybody?* She parked her car, got out, and was slinging her purse over her shoulder when Grizz rounded the corner. He must have seen her pull in off the highway and head for her usual spot behind the office. He had to be watching from their window. He was now jogging toward her.

She resolutely started walking toward him. She opened her mouth to say something, "Grizz, I—" but was immediately caught up in a bear hug that almost crushed her.

His face pressed into the top of her head, he was inhaling her scent and talking fast. "Kit, you're back. You're home. Where did you go? Why did you leave me?"

Before she could answer, he stood back and placed both hands on her shoulders. He looked down at her upturned face. "I cannot believe you fucking left me. You know the rules. You aren't supposed to drive anywhere alone. Anywhere!"

"Are you going to hit me? Punish me?" Her voice was calm, like it belonged to someone else.

"Kitten, I'm pissed that you left me, and I know I have done some awful things to people." He paused. "I'll probably keep doing awful things."

She cringed.

"But," he added, "I will never, ever, *ever* lay a hand on you."

"I saw you hit Willow. Remember when you knocked out her tooth?"

Once again he pulled her to his chest and bent low to bury his face in her neck.

He whispered, "I was never in love with Willow."

# Chapter Twenty-Five
## 1950s, Fort Lauderdale, Florida

HE'D ONLY BEEN working and living at the motel a couple of weeks when it happened.

He'd worked hard for Pop, thought maybe he'd earned the old man's respect, but that wasn't true. Pop was just like everybody else. He wasn't a nice guy trying to help a kid out. He worked him almost harder than his father had. At least he didn't get the beatings. Pop was too old for that.

Pop lived in a unit that was larger than the others. It wasn't just a room with a bath, but more like a little apartment. He told Ralph he could sleep on the couch in the small living room. Good thing he didn't give him his own unit. More than once, the boy caught Pop asleep in his bed with a cigarette dangling from his mouth. It was a miracle he hadn't burned the place down already.

Ralph did everything around the motel. He'd only had to clean two or three guest rooms since he arrived, but he maintained the grounds and the pool, plus did all of the cooking. He even did the laundry. Pop had taken him on a recent trip into Fort Lauderdale. They picked up his mail at the post office and went to a county office to pay his yearly tax bill. He even went with him to pay the water and electric bill a year in advance. Pop didn't need Ralph with him to do those things, but he did like having the kid to carry out all of the beer and the groceries so he could stock up and make less frequent trips into town.

That night, they'd been sitting in number four. Pop had had one too many beers. He was reminiscing about his own family.

Ralph had never once asked him if he'd had a family.

"He had green eyes like yours," Pop said to him in a slurred voice.

Ralph looked over at him and realized Pop was drunk. He was sitting in an overstuffed chair. They'd been watching some TV. *The Honeymooners* was on; it was a favorite of the old man's. Ralph Kramden was the main character. Guess that was where Pop had come up with his new name. Spittle was forming at the corners of Pop's mouth as he struggled to be heard over the volume of the television.

"I don't know how old you are, but I think my boy might be about your age. Maybe older than you. How old are you?"

Ralph just stared and didn't answer.

"Don't look at me like that. What? You think I'm too old to have a kid your age? You think my dick stopped working or something?" Pop asked as his head started to bob to one side. He was fighting to keep it upright.

"Where is he?" the boy asked him.

"His mother took off with him maybe ten years ago. Couldn't handle being out here waiting for a highway that's never going to be built. She was young, anyway. Took her cheating ass and my son and ran off with some drunk that passed himself off as a sailor. Ain't seen or heard from either of them since. Didn't have enough money to track them down. Spent it all on this place." He gestured with his right hand that had been holding a cigarette. Ashes wafted into the air.

"Been alone here ever since. Stop staring at me with those devil eyes. Stop fucking looking at me!"

"You've been alone here since then?"

He was beginning to understand why Pop may have been so harsh. He had lost someone important to him, too. Ruthie. Is this what loss does to a person? Turns them in to sad, mean old drunks? He knew Pop could be nice. He'd been nice to the few people that had stayed here.

But that was an act. He treated Ralph like a slave. Ralph wouldn't complain, though. He was used to hard work, and besides, he was getting fed.

Pop absently waved his other hand toward a small table.

"I wasn't completely alone. Had my babies."

Ralph looked over at the pictures. Yes. Pop's babies. He'd seen the pictures, but never asked. Two separate pictures, each in their own frame. Two German Shepherds.

He'd started to ask Pop their names, but the old man had already fallen asleep. He picked up his own blanket that he'd been using on the couch, gently draping it over the old man. He then removed the cigarette dangling from Pop's right hand and stubbed it out in the ashtray.

Everybody had their demons.

That night wasn't discussed again and Ralph continued to work hard for Pop. One day he decided maybe he would go a little further past the motel grounds, do some hunting. He had a homemade slingshot and he knew he could make a decent turtle soup if he could find one.

He headed out that morning, figuring he could get his hunting done while it was still cool. He'd left Pop sitting in his chair and made his way out to the swamp, walking well beyond what was considered the motel lawn. He stopped cold when he came upon three graves. A chill ran up his spine.

Each grave had a decent-sized headstone made of natural rock with a hand-painted name and year. Jack. Sandy. Benny.

Had he just found Pop's family? He'd never asked him their names, and there were three graves here. Not two. One looked newer than the others. He started to back up when he heard a twig snap.

"What the fuck you doing nosing around out here?"

Ralph turned around, a startled look on his face. Was he facing off against a murderer who had slaughtered his family? Had there been a wife and two kids? His mind was reeling with possibilities.

He wanted to hurl accusations but instead heard himself say, "Was turtle hunting. Figured I'd make a nice stew tonight. My stepmother used to make one." He paused then and stared at Pop. "You buried your family out here?"

He didn't know what Pop was going to say, but he didn't expect what came next.

Pop started laughing hard and slapped his knee. "My family? You think I killed my wife and kid and buried them out here? What kind of low-life rat bastard buries their loved ones in a homemade grave in the middle of nowhere and slaps a rock on top as a headstone?"

He didn't notice the boy stiffen at his last comment.

"It's my babies," Pop continued. "Although they deserve better than this. Jack was my first. Then came Sandy." He paused then, looked from the third grave and met the boy's eyes. "That's Benny. He died right before you came here. Never got around to getting a picture of him. Bought a frame to match the others and everything, but never got to use it. Too bad. He was the prettiest of the three. Had some wolf in him."

He slapped Ralph on the shoulder and started to laugh again, but it turned into fits of coughing. Following Ralph out this far had overexerted him.

"Buried my family in the swamp. You got some imagination, kid. So tell me, am I going to like turtle soup?"

Less than a week later, Ralph was asleep on the couch. He was a light sleeper and knew Pop had gone to bed drunk that night. It was becoming more frequent and he really did need to make sure that the old man didn't burn the place down with his smoking. He was sleeping when the old man's mumbling woke him up.

"Come here, son. Come let me hold you like I used to."

Poor sap. He was remembering his kid. Ralph wondered how old the boy was when Pop's wife took him. He started to get up to walk him back to his room when he realized Pop was standing over him.

Before he realized what was happening, Pop's right hand reached out and grabbed him by the hair.

"Just one kiss. You just need to kiss it one time, okay? You'll do that for daddy, won't you?"

*What the fuck?*

He realized that Pop was using his right hand to pull Ralph's head toward him. It was dark, but not so dark that he couldn't see the outline of the old man's erection pointed at him.

He tried to pull away, but Pop's grasp on his hair was tight. He was a strong motherfucker.

With all of his strength, he reached up and punched the old man right in the stomach. Pop fell backwards and landed hard against the TV and the flimsy stand it was on. There was a loud crash.

Ralph jumped up and turned on the light.

He couldn't believe what he was seeing. It would've been slightly comical if it weren't so awful.

A naked old man, stretched out on the floor with a TV covering his face and chest.

He knew immediately he'd killed him.

He lifted the heavy TV off Pop, looked down into his open eyes. His shoulders sagged under the weight of what had just happened.

He hadn't meant to kill Pop.

"Ran off with a drunken sailor? That's why your wife left you? She left because you were hurting your son. You stupid old man."

He rubbed at his eyes. It was the middle of the night and he was too tired to deal with this.

"I'll bury you tomorrow with your dogs."

He grabbed his blanket from the couch and tossed it over Pop's body. He then walked back to the bedroom and crawled into bed. He was tired of sleeping on the couch.

The next morning, he started out early to avoid the blistering heat of the day. He dragged Pop's body, wrapped in the blanket, all the way out to where he'd found the dog's graves. He reached down and retrieved the shovel he'd tucked in the blanket with Pop so he didn't have to carry it.

He'd just started to dig when he stopped and leaned the shovel up against a tree. He had to take a piss first.

He had his back to Pop's stiff body and was aiming his urine stream at an ant pile when a strange growling caught his attention. He turned around and stumbled backwards. He was still pissing, and urine shot up in the air as he fell on his ass, mouth open.

There before his eyes, not five feet from him, two alligators were fighting over Pop's body. He started to scurry backwards as he watched. It was the most horrible thing he'd ever witnessed as they tore at Pop's gray flesh, ripping chunks of meat as they played tug of war with the body.

After deciding that there was enough to share, they both slunk backwards into the swamp, taking the body with them. The last thing he remembered seeing was Pop's wide eyes open and staring at him as one gator bit down hard on his head before sinking below the surface.

Bile from his stomach came up, burning his throat. He reluctantly swallowed it as he tried to catch his breath.

He was so paralyzed with fear he couldn't move.

He had never considered the gators when he went out hunting for the turtle. And he definitely hadn't thought about them when he'd dragged Pop out here to bury him.

He felt nauseous, but knew he wouldn't vomit. He managed to stand up and zip his pants.

He picked up the shovel and what was left of the tattered blanket and, with a wary eye, headed back for the motel. He had work to do.

# Chapter Twenty-Six
1976

GRIZZ PAGED BLUE, who in turn got the word out that Kit was back. Eventually, bikes started rolling in and people started taking their usual places around the pit.

Kit stood at the window of her unit and watched. Even after rambling off the list of questions after she returned, Grizz never waited for her to reply. He knew why she'd left. He'd already admitted he was an awful person who did awful things and had no intention of stopping.

Maybe Grunt was wrong. Maybe she wouldn't be able to convince Grizz to cease his criminal activities. She wouldn't think about that now. She wouldn't let an unknown tomorrow interfere with today.

Grunt's car pulled in from the highway and headed for the office parking lot. He had someone with him. *Who would he be bringing here?* She caught herself before she allowed herself to even consider she might have had a flash of jealousy. Then she laughed when she thought about how jealous she'd been of Sarah Jo, how that had turned out.

She'd left the window and was rummaging through the refrigerator to make something for dinner when she heard the door to her unit open.

"Grunt thought you might need a friend," she heard the girl's voice say.

"Oh, Jo," she cried, as she ran to her friend and threw herself into her open arms.

Kit and Sarah Jo talked as they made dinner. All of Kit's fears and insecurities about being with Grizz tumbled out. It was the first time she'd really opened up to Sarah Jo since their friendship had begun the previous winter. It was now almost a year since Grizz brought her to the motel, and she'd been close with Jo for about the last five months.

"Kit, if I'm going to be honest with you, the truth is I don't know if I like Grizz. He's scary."

Kit paused from chopping onions and looked at Jo. The fact that her best friend didn't like her husband caught her off-guard. "Has he ever done anything to you?"

"No, no," Jo answered quickly. "Of course he hasn't done anything to me. But I'm not an idiot. I know what he does to other people. I guess I'm just afraid for you. You know, your parents were lame, but you weren't exposed to anything like you've seen living here. Have you ever thought about just going home?"

Ginny didn't want to answer the question, so she ignored it. "Don't be afraid for me, Jo. Grizz would never hurt me or let anyone hurt me."

"Okay. I believe that, but he can't protect you from everything. And he can't give you a normal life. Do you really want to be with a man whose only form of income is from illegal activity?"

Kit looked at Jo questioningly. They both knew Sarah Jo's father, Fess, was paid by Grizz. Fess was a teacher and never participated in actual gang activity, but he was responsible for maintaining Grizz's list of informants. The work was important enough to earn him a decent kickback from Grizz.

"No, I don't want to be with that man, but I want to be with Grizz."

"I guess it really sucks, then, that they're the same person."

Jo had finished helping with the casserole now baking in the oven. She sat on the couch, casually flipping through a magazine while Kit worked on a homemade dessert for later. She thought back to when Kit had first been brought to the motel, when she'd first met her.

Grunt had showed up at Jo's school that day, a Friday afternoon almost a year ago. May 1975. She was heading toward her bus when she heard a horn. Putting her hand up to shield the bright afternoon sun, she caught a flash of blue. *What was Grunt doing here?* She quickly changed her direction, and instead of getting on her bus, made her way to the parking lot in the front of the school. The end of the lot where Grunt was parked was visible from the bus loading area.

"Hey, what brings you to school?" Jo had casually asked, then came a flash of fear. "My dad?"

Grunt had reached for her and caught her in a quick, friendly hug. "No, no, nothing with Fess. I just need to talk, Jo."

She'd stepped back then, looking up into his face. "What's wrong? Are you okay?"

"No. I'm not okay." After a pause, "Grizz had Ginny brought to the motel last night."

"Oh, no!" He held the passenger door open for her, slammed it, and went around to the driver's side. He got in and started the loud engine.

"Why? Why did Grizz bring her to the motel?" Jo knew Grizz had been keeping an eye on Ginny for a long time. She knew about Grunt's occasional outings with Grizz as they went to check on her. She knew that after getting his license, Grunt had watched her a few times on his own, without Grizz. She'd heard stories about Ginny for the last few years.

She also knew Grunt was totally obsessed with Ginny. Ginny was all he ever talked about.

"Did he bring her there for you? Like a gang thing? Like, you know, so he can give her to you?"

"No." Grunt's voice was toneless as he pulled out of the parking lot. "He brought her there for him."

"For him?" Sarah Jo sat ramrod straight and stared at him. "Why would he want her? Isn't she my age?"

"Yes, she's your age. I guess he just felt that she should be with him." He slammed his fist against the steering wheel. "Jo, it caught me off guard. I still haven't figured out his intentions. I just don't know what to do."

Jo was quiet for a minute. "Grunt, don't do anything. You have to wait this out and see where he goes with it. You can't make a decision to act until you know what he's up to."

"Yeah, well, you know Grizz. It's not like he announces his intentions or asks anyone's permission to do whatever the hell he wants. This totally surprised me."

"Hmmmm. Can't imagine Willow is real happy about this."

Grunt gave a short laugh. "You're right about that. She was really pissed. Doesn't matter though. Grizz doesn't care what anyone thinks, especially Willow." He was quiet for a minute. "But I worry about that, you know? I don't want Willow to hurt Ginny or anything. I'll kill her myself if she goes near her."

"Will Grizz let Willow hurt her?" Jo frowned.

"No, I don't think he will. He practically choked the life out of her when she lunged at Ginny last night."

"So he cares," Sarah Jo said quietly.

This was new. Other than making sure Blue got money to cover Grunt's college tuition, Sarah Jo had never heard one story about Grizz that indicated he had a heart. Whether or not he had a soul was still debatable.

"Yeah, he cares. But I don't know if that's good for me or not."

"Just wait, Grunt. Give it some time. Keep an eye on her without letting anybody know what you're doing. It shouldn't be too hard. You've been doing it for years anyway."

That's exactly what Grunt did. He stayed in the background. But it wasn't always easy.

Now, watching Kit make the homemade dessert, Sarah Jo remembered the night Grunt had called her up with a strange request. It was more than a month after her friend had been brought to the motel. After she was given her gang name. Kit.

Grunt's voice had been cold. "Jo, I need you at the motel. I need Kit to think you're my girlfriend."

"Why?"

"Grizz thinks she's spending too much time with me."

"Is she?"

"Yes." Grunt had sighed over the phone line. "But just for the last week or so. She's been seeking me out to play chess and listen to records. And before you say anything, I know I'm wrong to encourage her, but I can't help myself. I want to be with her, Jo."

"You'll never be with her if Grizz suspects you have feelings, Grunt. You'd better figure out a way to make him think you don't care. And if Grizz thinks Kit cares for you, you better make him think you could care less."

The next morning Fess dropped Jo at the motel. She knocked on

Grunt's door and went in without waiting for an invitation. He was sitting on his bed, head in his hands.

"Grizz told me last night I could take her off the motel grounds for the day. He made it clear he thought she might be crushing on me and I was to put a stop to it."

Sarah Jo laid her helmet on the dresser and sat next to him. He started to tell her a little bit about the night Kit lost her virginity. She didn't say anything at first. Finally she'd heard enough.

"I can't believe Grizz let you be her first!" Jo paced the room. "I just can't believe it! How in the world did you convince him to let you do that? I mean, I know being Blue's brother offers you some form of protection. But you told me how protective he is of her, Grunt." She shook her head. "How are you even still alive?"

Grunt then told her the story about his manipulation of Grizz that night. He didn't tell her everything, though. She knew that. He left out some details. She was his best friend, but some things were too intimate to share, even with Jo. When he was finished with his story, neither one of them said anything for a few minutes.

Jo didn't know what to say. Finally, she took a deep breath. "So what's the plan? How does this go down?"

"Let's walk down to Grizz's unit. She's mentioned more than once she thinks Fess is really nice. I'll just act like it would be nice for her to meet his daughter. Remember, don't slip. It's Kit now. Forget you know her name."

"No problem," she said as she slipped into his jacket. She looked up at him and shrugged, "For effect, don't you think?"

"Yeah, it swims on you, but the fact that you're wearing it will mean something." He looked at the ground, his shoulders slumped. She'd never seen him like this.

Jo went to him, wrapped her arms around him. "Patience. Your heart is in the right place. This will work out."

He met her eyes then. "You're a good friend, Jo. C'mon." He handed her helmet to her, then draped his left arm over her shoulders. She wrapped her right arm around his waist.

"You're a good guy. You make being your friend easy. Oh, hey," she elbowed him. "Did I tell you Blue's wife invited my family over for dinner?"

Grunt stiffened.

"I know how much you hate her. Is she still trying to make you believe Kevin is your son?"

"Yeah. She's a crazy bitch. I'll tell you about it later."

"Just so you know, my youngest brother looks exactly like my Uncle Dave. He's my dad's brother. It wouldn't be unusual for one of Blue's kids to look like you."

"Yeah, I know." He sighed. "I just hate her so much, Jo."

"I was thinking if we do go to Blue's for dinner, I could melt a laxative and drop it in whatever she's drinking."

"No, she deserves worse. How about a mini-explosive in her tampon?"

Sarah Jo started to giggle.

An exploding tampon would serve her right, Grunt thought to himself. He started to laugh too.

They were both still laughing when Grunt opened the door. Kit was standing there with her arm raised. She must have just been ready to knock on the door. She had an expression on her face that said she'd just taken a punch to the gut. It broke Grunt's heart.

Grunt spent the day with Sarah Jo at the beach. He did his best not to think about Kit, but she'd consumed him for as long as he could remember. Jo knew when not to say anything. She just listened, and it was all that he needed. She couldn't help herself though. One thing had aroused her curiosity.

"You told me you slept with her against her will, or at least I think that's how it sounded," she said, peering over at him from her bright orange beach towel. They were lying side by side. "But it's a little confusing. She actually *asked* you to personally screw her?"

Grunt pinked a little at that. "I told you I made him think I was going to use the police baton. Well, when she saw it, she asked me to do it myself. I didn't just *screw* Kit, Jo."

Jo flushed. "I didn't mean anything by it, Grunt. I guess what I'm trying to figure out is why she seems to like you after that. I mean, if it was against her will, it was technically rape. But then you said she asked you. I don't know. I just can't understand it, I guess."

"You don't have to understand it, Jo," he snapped.

Jo looked over at him, but he'd already turned his face away. She sighed and closed her eyes. She guessed there were some things she would never understand.

They spent the rest of the day on Fort Lauderdale Beach. They had a late lunch at an outdoor cafe, then spent some time window shopping at some of the stores along the beach.

It was sad how much he loved Kit, but they both knew he had to follow Jo's advice. He waited.

"Jo? Jo, do you want to try it?"

Kit's voice snapped Jo back to the present. She hadn't realized she'd been staring blankly at the same page on the magazine, lost in last year's memories. Kit was standing over her now, holding out a spoon with chocolate on it.

"Here, take a lick. I know how much you love chocolate. It's homemade mousse. What do you think?"

Jo took the spoon from Kit's hand and licked it.

"Heaven," was all she said, giggling, then handed it back.

Kit went to the kitchen while Sarah Jo wandered over to the window and looked out. She was still gazing outside when Kit walked up next to her.

"What are you looking at?"

"Just checking out the women in the pit." Jo gave a shrug.

"What about the women in the pit?"

"I don't see Chicky or Moe, guess they're off somewhere, but it seems to me that every other female out there is trying to get your husband's attention."

Kit looked out to where Sarah Jo was staring. Grizz was standing off to the side, closer to the playground area and well behind the lawn chairs. He looked to be having a serious conversation with Blue and some other guy Kit didn't recognize. The usual crowd was sitting around the pit with some newcomers. Some had women on their laps. There was even one girl crouched between Monster's legs.

"Really, I don't see any women trying to get Grizz to notice them." Kit said.

"Yeah? Then why do you think every woman out there, and I'm counting five, has brown hair and bangs?"

"Ummm, because they have brown hair and bangs?" Kit rolled her eyes at Jo.

"You're wrong. Isn't that Tiny on Axel's lap? Didn't she use to be a blonde? And I know Chili. I've seen her before, know for a fact she's a natural redhead. Always wore her hair parted down the middle. Not anymore."

"Okay, so some girls changed their hair. So what?"

Jo raised a brow at Kit, who was watching Grizz. "You honestly don't know, do you?"

"Know what? What are you talking about?"

"I can see why they love you. Why *he* loves you." Jo caught herself quickly. "I can see why Grizz loves you. You are so innocent about some things. You obviously don't get it."

Kit huffed out a breath. "Don't get *what*, Sarah Jo? What don't I get?"

"That every woman out there is trying to be you."

# Chapter Twenty-Seven
2000

"YES, I CONVINCED you to go back to the motel," Tommy told Ginny. He couldn't meet her eyes. "I admit it. I was being selfish. I knew if you went to the police, I would lose you. I would forfeit my education. I don't know, maybe I shouldn't have convinced you to go back. I mean, I probably would've been able to get back on track after a couple of years, but I didn't think it would take that long to be with you. My plan was for you to see how awful and rotten Grizz was, and then want to leave him. And I did that, Ginny. I'm sorry. I did it just the one time."

"What time?" She studied his face. "What did you do, Tommy?"

"It was a chess game for me, Ginny. I was planning and scheming to make sure you would see Grizz do something awful." He paused, then in the quietest voice he could muster, "That time at the docks."

She gasped and put her hand to her mouth. "The docks—that time I pulled up and saw Grizz and Blue dump two bodies in the water? *You're* the one who made sure I went there? Saw that?"

He blew out a long breath. "Yes, I set it up. I set you up. I knew Grizz and Blue were going there to deal with two punks who'd hijacked a dealer's boat full of cocaine. I knew what would happen to them."

"I cannot believe I'm hearing this. Do you remember how upset I was?" She paced the kitchen now. "I can't even remember now what made me go there, but I never suspected it was you. If Grizz had suspected it, he probably would have hurt you. Maybe even killed you."

"I remember how upset you were because you came to me." He folded his arms, remembering the look on her face then, the shadows beneath her eyes. "When I saw what I had done to you, how badly it hurt you, I stopped all the game-playing. Not to mention, if they'd been caught and you'd have been there, it would've implicated you too. I can't believe I put you in that kind of situation." She just stared at him. She crossed her arms, perched now on a stool at the breakfast bar. "Gin, I could've continued to trick you and him, but I didn't. I realized I couldn't hurt you like that, I couldn't expose you to more danger. I *loved* you."

He stared at her, but she didn't say a word. Just kept looking at him like he was a stranger. His words barreled out now; he couldn't stop them. "I guess after that it became about protecting you. Protecting your heart from knowing the awful things he did, and protecting you physically from being put in those situations. It was the opposite of what I'd started out to do."

"And I guess you want credit for that? You protected me? Gee, not sure how much I should believe." Her tone was laced with sarcasm. "Aren't you the same man who accused me of sticking my head in the sand because I didn't want to know what he did, and yet you're telling me your plan was to make sure I did know about it?" She held up a hand as he started to speak. "And before you jump in and tell me what a rotten person he was, let me remind you that other than tossing Willow on her back and backhanding her, the nod to Chico that time in the pit, dumping those bodies at the docks—thank you for that, by the way—and him beating up those kids who spit on me at the warehouse, I never saw Grizz do anything. I was with him for ten years, Tommy. Ten years. And I never witnessed anything beyond what I've just told you."

His eyes flashed. "And because you didn't see it, it wasn't happening?" His voice was starting to rise now. "Okay, so you don't believe me. Look, Gin, I never thought it would take ten years to finally be with you. I don't know. Maybe you would have left him sooner, but there were still a lot of things I just had to keep from you. Things that would have torn you up inside. I knew you already struggled with guilt over his criminal activities."

She stood and started to walk toward him. Arms crossed and chin raised, she gave him the coldest look possible. "One thing. Tell me one thing you hid from me, other than what I've discovered in the last couple of hours, which might've persuaded me to leave him. Not that I'm even certain leaving Grizz would've ever been an option as far as he was concerned."

"If I thought you wanted to leave him, maybe I would've done something that could've gotten him arrested before Jan blew the whistle. But quite frankly, you seemed happy in your little silver-lined cocoon."

"Are you saying you're the reason Grizz got arrested?" Her voice was practically a scream.

"No!" Tommy was quick to add. "I'm not saying that at all. I had nothing to do with his arrest. But when it finally did happen, I was glad, Gin. I felt like I had run out of time. Have you listened to anything I said? I waited for ten years while you were with him!"

"So answer my question. What things did Grizz do that you hid from me?"

Tommy sighed heavily. "Ginny, for once I'm *telling* you to stick your head in the sand. You don't want to know."

"And I'm telling you that I don't like the accusation that that's what I've done for twenty-five years. Tell me!"

"Fine. If that's how you want it, I'll tell you. Do you remember when you asked me how Willow and Darryl died?"

"Yes, of course I remember. It was horrible. It was torture for them."

"Let me ask you this," he said, looking at her. "Johnny Tillman was slowly cut to pieces for *attempting* to rape you. Do you honestly think Grizz calmly walked Darryl and Willow down into the empty pool and simply let them die of exposure? Keep in mind that Darryl tortured you for over two hours, and Willow is the one who planned it."

"W-well, that's what you told me happened. I never asked Grizz because I asked you. And that's what you said."

"Yes, Ginny. That's what I said. I held it back from you because even though I loved you and wanted to be with you, I couldn't stand the thought of you having the image of what he really did to Darryl and Willow stuck in your head forever. You had enough guilt over their deaths. And yes, they did die in that pool. But not from exposure." He looked down. "I can tell you with certainty they were both begging for death long before they actually died."

They were both quiet a long moment.

"Tell me," she whispered.

"You know he was obsessed with it, right? Grizz never believed it was a lucky coincidence that Darryl came to the motel that night."

Ginny just stared at him.

"Grizz believed for a long time it was an inside job. That someone knew he wouldn't be there that night. Whoever set it up knew Moe habitually let the dogs sleep with her. Someone knew you'd be alone that night, Gin."

He told her almost everything then.

What Tommy didn't tell Ginny was that it wasn't just something Grizz had suspected. It was true. Grizz had gotten a name out of Willow. With her dying breath, Willow swore it was a woman named Wendy who'd tipped her off. The woman had a Southern accent and only communicated with Willow by telephone. Willow said Wendy had a contact at the motel, but Willow swore she didn't know who it was.

There wasn't any Wendy they could connect to the motel.

Worse yet, Darryl hadn't even finished the job. He was supposed to have killed Ginny that night. He thought he had when he'd beaten her unconscious.

No. Ginny didn't have to know all of that.

What she knew was bad enough. Shaking, Ginny made her way to one of the kitchen chairs at the opposite side of the table. She yanked it out and sat down, looking into her hands resting loosely in her lap. She couldn't focus. She was stunned. Her stomach was churning.

"You're right, Tommy," she whispered. "I wouldn't have wanted to know." She paused before adding, "But maybe I should have. I don't know." She buried her face in her hands. "This is all so unexpected."

He jumped up and went to her. Kneeling in front of her, he took her hands in his. "It's okay, sweetheart. I'm so sorry. I'm just so sorry. I never did see how you knowing all of this would matter." He held her close, stroking her back as she sobbed. "It's always been about protecting you, Gin. That's all it's ever been about. Please don't leave me, Ginny. I couldn't bear to be without you. Please don't leave."

What he didn't add was that as much as his need to protect her all these years was true, he also had good reason for talking about it now. He still didn't want to tell her certain things, but he knew he had to.

When she pulled back to look at him, she saw he had tears in his eyes.

With a very real ache in her heart, she gathered her strength. "I love you, Tommy. But I still have to leave. I just need some space. You have to understand that. This is too much of a shock, and the kids will be fine. We'll tell them I'm staying with Carter to keep her company and help with the animals while Bill is out of town. I've done it before. They'll never suspect that I've left for another reason."

She paused. "When we do have some time together—" She trailed off, then collected herself. "Everything. I want to know everything. From the beginning. I want you to tell me every single thing, Tommy. Even if it'll be difficult for me to hear."

"I will, Gin." His voice sounded dead, empty. "I will."

"And I need you tell me what you talked about when you went to see him before the execution."

He had intended on doing just that before he was blindsided by Leslie's comment.

Tommy nodded and started to reply when he was interrupted by Jason's voice.

"Moooommmmm! Daaaaaddd! Can you come here? I have a surprise for you!"

# Chapter Twenty-Eight
## 1978

SHE HAD ALREADY managed to contact Willow. It was a little time-consuming, but she knew the type of place Willow would be staying. After six hotels, she finally hit pay dirt.

"The super skinny blonde with the mouth on her?" asked the guy who answered the phone.

"Yeah, that's her. Is she there? Is she staying there?"

"Nah, kicked her out for not paying. I think she's at a place on 5th or something. I don't know. I know she picks up most of her johns at The Speckled Egg."

"Is that a motel?" She added a seductive tone to her voice, drawing out the Southern accent.

"No. It's a bar. You'll probably find her there, or find someone who knows her. If you do find her sorry ass, tell her she owes Mick fifty-five bucks, the lazy no-good piece of shit."

She got a message to Willow to call a certain pay phone on a specific day at a specific time. The message said it concerned Grizz.

And of course that phone rang at exactly the time she was told to call. Willow was only too eager to help Wendy with her plan.

Moe would be a little more difficult, as she couldn't talk on the phone. But Wendy had a plan for that, too.

She watched as Moe got out of her little black VW and walked into the post office. She approached the car and dropped an envelope through the open window onto the driver's seat. Then she darted to her car, got in and drove away before Moe came back out.

"Dear Moe," the note read. "I know how unhappy you are. I am, too. It seems that ever since Kit got to the motel, nobody ever notices you anymore. Not even Grunt. Yes, I've seen her. I know how much everybody loves her. Maybe we can help each other out. I don't want her to get hurt or anything, but maybe we can use her to get what we want. To get our lives back. If you think you can help me with this, then be at the pay phone on 441 and Taft Street in Hollywood on

Sunday at exactly 4 p.m. Your friend, Wendy."

Two days later, Wendy watched from inside the convenience store as the little black car pulled up across the busy street and parked in front of the telephone booth that was situated between the pharmacy and a beauty salon. Moe had come alone.

She dialed the number. Moe picked up.

"Hi, Moe. I'm so glad you answered. I know you care about Kit and don't want her to get hurt. I don't want her hurt, either. I just really hate Grizz and I think the best way to get back at him is to take something away from him. You know, like how he cut out your tongue. He took something from me, too. It'll be tit for tat. If you think you can help me, if you think we can work together without anybody having to get hurt, then press one of the numbers on the pay phone once."

Wendy watched as Moe hesitated. Then she looked around. Wendy knew she couldn't be seen.

"Nobody will get hurt. I just want Kit to go back home. That's all."

Moe lifted her hand to the face of the telephone. The beep resonated through Wendy's end of the phone.

Wendy's face lit with triumph. It was done. She had her inside person at the motel.

And she knew Willow would take care of the dirty work. There would be nothing to trace it back to her. She would deal with them through pay phones and a pager that she'd borrowed from a friend. He was only too glad to give up one of his father's work beepers for a couple of extra bucks to support his drug habit. When everything was arranged, she would tell him to quietly return it to his father's company. There were so many people who worked there that it would be impossible to make a connection.

And that was only if someone suspected it was a setup.

She had to watch Grizz. He was smart, but so was she. He kicked Willow out because of Kit. He cut out Moe's tongue. He had taken something from her, too. Something she hadn't been prepared to have stolen from her.

Grizz would pay for hurting them. Just like she'd told Moe, it would be tit for tat.

# Chapter Twenty-Nine
2000

TOMMY AND GINNY looked at each other with the same expression: Horror. They'd both thought Jason was still upstairs unpacking his bag. How much, if anything, had the ten-year old actually heard?

"You're gonna like the surprise," Jason called out in a sing-song.

The den. His voice was coming from the den. Exchanging another glance, they headed for the den and stopped short.

There on the coffee table was Grizz's chess set.

"I went in to dad's office to get some paper and saw it on his desk. I wanted to help him unpack it and set it up. Are you surprised?" Jason grinned like he'd won the lottery.

Tommy saw the empty box sitting on one of the couches. "How did you carry that box in here, son? It weighed a ton."

Jason shrugged, looking around at the packing material strewn all over the floor. "I brought the pieces in here a few at a time until the box was light enough to carry." He added sheepishly, "I'll clean up the mess."

Ginny was in too much shock to know what to say. Memories washed over her, causing her to feel a little unsteady on her feet. Tommy detected it and gently took her arm, walking her to the other couch.

When she sat down, Tommy turned to address his son. "Jason, I'm glad you wanted to help. But you shouldn't have touched something that wasn't yours to touch."

The boy looked crestfallen. "But Dad, I wanted to surprise you!"

"That's not the point, Jason, and you know it." Tommy looked angry now. "How many times have I told you that my office is off limits? You know better and you will be punished for this."

Ginny's heart was torn. She could tell Jason really did think he was helping and was confused as to why his parents were reacting this way.

"It's not all there, anyway." Jason kicked at some of the packing material. "Do you want me to pack it back up?"

"What do you mean it's not all there?" Ginny frowned.

"The dark king is gone. Can't play without the king. Right, Dad?" Jason asked, looking up at his father.

Tommy and Ginny looked at each other. They both knew laying down your king meant you resigned the game; you were acknowledging your opponent's win. It was an admission of defeat. Of surrender. Was Grizz sending a message from the grave? Was he admitting defeat?

Or, worse yet, was he issuing a challenge? It's not like he'd laid the king down. He—or someone—had removed it from the game.

Did that mean anything?

*Ridiculous.* Tommy reminded himself he'd seen Grizz a few days before he'd been executed. They'd talked for a long time and settled things. At least he thought they had.

It was probably some idiot at the prison tasked with packing up the chess set, somebody who wanted a souvenir that had belonged to Grizz. That's all. Nothing to worry about.

But Tommy wasn't naive. He still had underground contacts.

He also knew Grizz had loyal members who would do anything for him. Even after the execution.

Tommy would put out some feelers to be sure. But right now, he needed to comfort and reassure his wife.

He sat next to Ginny and started to put his arm around her. Just as Tommy was about to speak, Jason jumped up. He had quickly recovered from his father's reprimand and seemed even more excited than before.

"I almost forgot! Here's the best part of all! Even better than the chess set." Jason reached down and yanked something up that was sitting on the floor beneath the coffee table, hidden by the scattered packaging material. "It was at the bottom of the box."

Ginny gasped when she saw what her son held in the air like a prize.

"This really neat jacket was in there, too! And look—the girl on the back looks just like Mimi!"

# Chapter Thirty
1979

"YOU SHOULD KNOW better than to ask for that, Kit," Grizz said to her one afternoon as they sat in the living room of number four. "You asked me what I wanted for my birthday and I told you. You shouldn't have asked if you didn't want to know."

"C'mon, honey. Don't play these games with me. You know I'm not going to tell you my name. It's not important anyway."

"Okay, you don't have to tell me your name. How about you tell me anything. Anything about you and your life before this motel. Anything, Grizz. I am your wife. Married couples share these kinds of things."

"My life, up until I brought you here, was nothing." Grizz sighed. "What do you want to hear? A list of criminal acts, jail time, what? Believe me when I tell you that my life started after I brought you here, Kitten. Trust me on this."

"Come on, Grizz. We can keep it simple. How about what elementary school you went to? Did you have a pet growing up, and if so, what was its name? Did you have parents who loved you? Did you sit down to Sunday dinner? What was your favorite TV show growing up? What was the color of your first car?" She smiled at him. "Anything, Grizz. I know *nothing* about you. And it hardly seems fair since you know everything about me."

He sighed and ran his hand through his hair. It was his own fault. He'd asked her what she wanted for her birthday and she was telling him.

"Can't I just tell you that my life sucked and I don't want to talk about it?" And before she could answer him, he said, "Green."

"Green what?" she asked, eyes wide. She sat up eagerly on the edge of the couch. "Is that your real last name?"

"No. My first car was green, and before you ask, I stole it."

She stood up and folded her arms across her chest. "Ooooh, you have the most irritating personality. Has anybody ever told you that?"

He raised an eyebrow at her. He was amused by her question, but didn't want to piss her off any more than she already was. His face softened.

"Kitten, please just tell me something else that you might want for your birthday. Please?"

He was getting desperate. It didn't help that he felt enormous guilt over her assault and rape last summer. He was still looking for the person who did it. He actually fantasized about how much he would enjoy torturing the person who'd dared to lay a hand on his wife. But before she could get another word out, he added, "And no, I will not go to church with you, so don't even ask."

She stared at him. Her face was turning red. She was really mad at him. She looked adorable, he thought. He almost smiled, but caught himself.

The phone rang, interrupting their conversation.

"You answer it," she said and started for the door. "I need some air."

Grizz spotted her car keys in their usual spot before heading for the phone. At least he didn't have to worry about her driving off mad.

When his phone conversation ended, he went looking for her. After checking in a few of the vacant motel rooms, he walked around the office side of the motel. He saw her rear end sticking out of the passenger side of her car.

He stopped himself and looked at her ass. It was a beautiful ass. An ass that he never got tired of looking at. He started to get hard as he looked around. *I wonder if I can convince her to pull down her jeans?* He asked himself. Then he dismissed the thought. No. He much preferred having her in his bed.

He got angry when he thought about her rape. There was someone out there who'd not only seen her, but had been inside of her. Yes, he thought to himself. He would find out who'd attacked her and enjoy killing him.

Slowly.

"What are you doing, Kit?" he asked as he approached her

"My necklace," she said from inside the car. "The one Grunt gave me for Christmas. I just remembered I lost it or something."

She perched sideways on the passenger seat now, one leg beneath her and the other on the ground. She threw up her hands in exasperation.

"You think you lost it in the car?"

"Yeah, I think so. The clasp on it broke and I had dropped it off at the jewelers to get repaired a few weeks ago. When I went to pick it up, I'd just had my nails done and realized when I got in the car that I couldn't unfasten it and refasten it with my new manicure. So I draped it over the rearview mirror. I just now remembered it." She frowned. "But it's not here. I can't figure out why. I'm certain I hung it up and left it there."

"The cross? The religious necklace?"

"Yes, my cross," she answered him absentmindedly, fishing now between the console and the seat.

"You want me to get you a new one?"

"No, I want to find the one that I know is here somewhere." She blew out a frustrated breath, and the bangs on her forehead fluffed up and then settled back in place.

"Maybe someone stole it."

"No. I lock my car when I go out. I only leave it unlocked here."

They both knew nobody would dare take something out of Kit's car at the motel.

"Come on back inside. I'll have one of Axel's guys detail the car for you. If it's in there, they'll find it."

She got out of the car and slammed the door shut.

Less than ten minutes later, they were in bed.

"You sure I'm not hurting you, Kitten?" Grizz asked. He was on top of her and inside her, slowly moving his hips while kissing her neck.

"No, you're not hurting me, Grizz. Not at all." She moaned now, arching her back in pleasure. "Just keep doing what you're doing, okay?"

He smiled into her neck. He cupped her breast with his right hand, teased her nipple. Slowly, slowly he started to remove himself from inside of her, his mouth moving to her throat. She resisted his withdrawal, and moaned again as she wrapped her legs tightly around his waist, trying to keep him inside of her. Gently, he suckled her already hard nipple.

Then he felt her stiffen. *Dammit.* She was remembering the rape. The bites.

"It's okay, Kit. It's me, honey." He felt her relax then.

Their eyes met and she could see his anger. She grabbed his face, pulled it close.

"I know you're still mad at Moe because she had the dogs that night," she whispered.

He hadn't expected this. She was right.

"Damn right I'm still mad at Moe." He started to say more, but she interrupted him.

"Like I said, I know you're still mad at Moe, but I know you blame yourself, too."

He looked away from her then, but she pulled his face back to meet her eyes. "Your anger at Moe is because you think you somehow failed me. You're afraid I'll see you differently because of that. Just like you felt when I witnessed what Chico's guy did to that couple in the pit. You were worried I couldn't go back from that. That I wouldn't love you anymore."

He didn't know how to answer her. Again, she was right.

"I hate what you do. I know you know that. And I keep telling myself that one day you'll stop. That my being with you will somehow be a positive influence. I honestly don't know if that's true or if you're capable of stopping."

He looked away from her again, and this time she jerked his face back hard.

"I love you with an intensity that scares me. It's why I stay. It's why I overlook so much. You need to know that I don't blame you for what happened to me. I am and always will be in love with you."

He let out a sigh of relief. "I love you too, Kitten. I love you so much it scares me, too."

She smiled and playfully nipped at his bottom lip. He growled as he kissed her with a passion that pulled the air from his lungs.

A little while later, Grizz sat up, lazily tugging at her hand.

"Come take a shower with me."

She looked over at him. "I should start dinner," she replied. Before he could say anything, she added, "Your nose looks better. Does it still hurt?"

Grizz had had his nose broken a week earlier when he'd tried to break up a fight.

"It's been broken so many times, I've lost count. No, doesn't hurt. Take a shower with me and I'll take you out to dinner."

"Really out to dinner, or a business visit with a dinner in between?"

"Really out to dinner. Your choice."

She smiled. She knew exactly where she wanted to go for dinner. Vincent's was a small restaurant that had been tucked away in a dying strip mall down by the docks. Grizz used to take her there when he was concerned about her being recognized back when he'd first brought her to the motel. Today, she was in the mood for garlic crabs and Vincent's had the best. She was supposed to go with Grunt last week, but he had been called out of town on business. She thought he might have been sent to Vancouver for a few weeks. Unfortunately, she hadn't been able to get the garlic crabs out of her head. She was craving them.

"I'll beat you to the shower," she said, tossing off the covers and racing for the bathroom.

Five minutes later, Grizz panted as he plunged deeper into her, one hand against the slippery shower stall for support.

"I just can't get enough of you, Kitten," Grizz said.

The shower had started out innocently enough—you wash my back and I'll wash yours. But before they knew it, they were once again making love. He was holding her up now and had her pressed against the shower wall. She had her legs wrapped tightly around his waist. They had just made love in the bedroom less than fifteen minutes ago. She moaned as his thrusts became more urgent. He felt her release and immediately followed.

Slowly, tenderly, he let her down, and she looked up at him. He took her face in his hands and kissed her deeply and fully.

She kissed him back. "This last minute shower session may have cost us beating the dinner crowd."

"I don't care, Kitten. Don't stop kissing me."

An hour later, they'd made it into their clothes and were at the restaurant. They had just ordered their meals and the waitress had collected the menus.

"I'll be right back with your drinks," she told them.

Grizz smiled at Kit. "Have you given it any more thought?"

She tilted her head. "About what?"

"Your birthday."

"Oh. I thought for a minute you were talking about where I might have lost my necklace. Hmm. Let me think." She gazed around the restaurant and looked quickly back at Grizz. She gave him a big smile as something came to her.

"Yes! There is something I want for my birthday. Something I really want! I've been thinking about our prom date last year."

"You want another romantic night at Martin's beach house?" He grinned, relieved. A night making love with Kit at the beach house. Ohhhhh yeahhhh.

"No. Not the beach house." She was bouncing in her seat now. "I want you to take me out! Dancing. I want to go to a club and go dancing."

His smile faded and he looked a little deflated. He wasn't going to tell her his name. He wasn't going to go to church with her. How could he tell her no to the third thing she'd asked for?

"Shit, baby. You have to know I'm not a dancer. I barely got by with the slow dancing in Martin's gazebo."

"I want to go dancing, Grizz. Please! The only time I ever get to dance is when I convince Axel to dance with me in number four. And you know that's barely ever. He won't do it if there are a lot of people at the motel. He doesn't want to risk being seen."

Grizz had to smile at this. He'd walked in more than once on Axel and Kit dancing to one of those groups that Kit loved. If you asked him, those guys' voices sounded like someone had their balls in a vice. A high-pitched squeal is all he ever heard and he never stayed around long enough to listen to an entire song.

"Why do you dance to a song about a bald-headed woman?" He'd asked her once.

Axel and Kit had stopped and peered at him strangely. "What do you mean by bald headed woman?" Kit had asked as Grizz turned the stereo down.

"These guys, who sound like women, are singing about a bald-headed woman," Grizz replied.

She'd started laughing. "The Bee Gees are saying 'more than a woman,' Grizz. Not bald-headed woman! The song is called *More Than a Woman* and I happen to love it."

"Whatever it's called, it still sucks. I'm outta here."

Grizz appreciated that Axel danced with his wife. And yes, he knew Axel's other secret, too. He honestly didn't care. He didn't care what any guy decided to do with his dick as long as it was never near his wife. But he also knew he had to keep Axel's secret. As leader, he had final say as to who could be in the gang. Still, he knew not everyone would be tolerant of Axel's lifestyle. It was just easier to let it stay a secret. And besides, he was certain nobody suspected a thing.

"I don't dance, Kit." Grizz said now, shaking his head.

"But I want to go dancing for my birthday." She folded her arms and gave him an accusing look. "You asked!"

He shook his head slightly and looked at her. "Can't I just buy you another car?"

# Chapter Thirty-One
2000

GINNY AND TOMMY managed to compose themselves for Jason's sake. Tommy took the jacket from his son and returned it to the bottom of the box.

"Start packing it back up, Jason."

"But Dad—"

"Do it now, son." He looked at his wife. She was pale.

He knew what she was thinking. She wanted to leave, and she wanted to leave right now. He walked her to where she had left her small suitcase. He held her hand as he carried it out to the car.

"I love you, Ginny. It's because I love you that I know you need some time. I won't fight you on this. I'll handle the kids."

He set her suitcase in the back seat and turned to her.

She willingly leaned into his arms. Being in his embrace, in those arms that had grown into achingly familiar ones, brought her up short. Now that she knew he was Grizz's son, would it be a constant reminder of Grizz? These were the same arms that held her for almost fifteen years. Why was it that, after learning the truth, it all seemed somehow tainted?

She inhaled his scent. At least that was uniquely Tommy's.

Then she remembered the reason she was leaving and hastily removed herself from his loving grip. He tried to reach for her again, but she shrugged him off, got in the car, and started it. She rolled down the window.

"Would you mind giving Carter a call and telling her I'm on my way over?"

Without waiting for his reply, she put the car in reverse and headed for Shady Ranches.

On the drive over to Carter and Bill's, Ginny's mind drifted. With the population growth over the last several years, traffic had become a nightmare. It would take at least forty-five minutes to get to Carter's house. The house she had once shared with Grizz. She knew Carter would be there and that Bill was out of town.

Carter had been with Sarah Jo outside the execution viewing room just a couple of days ago. She'd told Ginny how badly Casey had wanted to be there too, but she'd been delayed at an airport somewhere in the Middle East. Casey, one of their other college friends, was now a journalist and worked for the foreign press. She was always traveling. She'd tried her hardest to be there for Ginny when Grizz died, but she couldn't get a flight out in time. Ginny wondered if she'd ever even made it to Fort Lauderdale.

She thought back to how she had married Tommy in a quick ceremony, but couldn't bring herself to have him move into the house in Shady Ranches. The very house she was driving to now. She'd been pregnant and emotional. It was hard enough marrying another man—even Tommy, who she'd known almost as long as she'd known Grizz. She remembered how shocked she'd been when Grizz sat her down that day, told her he'd always known Grunt had feelings for her—and that Grizz wanted her to marry him.

She sat at the red light and gulped. *How much of that was true?* She didn't know what to believe anymore.

Yes, she had a lot to discuss with Tommy. But not yet. She needed some breathing space. She needed to think.

The light turned green and she drove on, the past wrapped around her like a blanket. Carter had been the perfect choice to live in their former home in the rural subdivision. She was one of those people who took in every stray animal that needed a home. The house, on a few acres, was just right for Carter and her adopted "children." Her friend hadn't been married when she'd first moved into Shady Ranches, at first to keep Ginny company, and later on her own. She met Bill a few years later at a fundraiser for an animal rescue organization. It had been love at first sight and the pair were married almost immediately. Bill had a career in computer programming and traveled frequently for his job. He made an excellent living, and it enabled them to support Carter's animal rescue activities, but computer programming wasn't his passion. Rather, Bill loved anything and everything that had to do with surveillance—what he called his "spy stuff." He'd even set up a system at Tommy's office to help them catch someone who'd been stealing from the corporate bank accounts. Bill was an electronic wizard.

With Bill gone more than not, it wasn't unusual at all for Ginny to spend time at the house, helping Carter with the animals. Ginny laughed to herself when she remembered how Carter had provided a temporary foster home to a nasty camel named Phil. Phil turned out to be quite the challenge, and she was certain even Carter had breathed a sigh of relief when Phil was finally placed in an animal sanctuary.

Grizz had specifically asked her not to sell the home, so having Carter and Bill there, taking care of it and making good use of the property, worked out for everyone.

Even behind bars and now, beyond the grave, Grizz seemed to have his hands in everything.

She pulled into Shady Ranches and up the long, familiar driveway. Waiting for her, she saw Carter and Casey, both standing on the porch. So Casey had finally gotten a flight. She was glad. And Tommy had called ahead. Ginny had known he would. He was the most dependable human being in the world.

But apparently, just not the most honest.

She felt a stab of pain in her chest.

Her friends approached the car. She couldn't park quickly enough. She practically fell into their outstretched arms. She leaned heavily on Carter, sobbing, while her friend gently guided her into the house. Casey retrieved her small suitcase from the back seat and followed them inside.

# Chapter Thirty-Two
1979

"KIT, AXEL JUST pulled up. Are you ready?" Grizz called from the living room.

"Just a sec," she called back.

She never did convince Grizz to take her dancing for her birthday a couple of months ago. She knew asking him was a stretch, but she figured she'd give it a shot. She was still happy she was getting to go to a dance club. She loved to dance and Axel was only too happy to oblige. Of course, he'd told Grizz if he was coming to the motel to pick up Kit, he didn't want to get hassled by the others. Grizz understood and they put on a pretense in front of some of the regulars. Grizz "ordered" Axel to take Kit dancing, and Axel pretended to stomp off, mad. Kit was actually surprised that Grizz had agreed to play along.

Grizz watched from the window as Axel talked to some of the guys in the pit. He could tell by his body language that Axel was "complaining" about why he was there. Grizz actually smiled.

Then his smile faded as he thought about Kit's rape last year. He still hadn't caught the guy, but he knew he was getting close. And if he was going to be honest with himself, he didn't like her going out dancing.

But he knew he had to let her. She tried to put on a brave face, but he would watch her sometimes, could tell when she was sinking into the horrible memory of that night. He had to let her have some freedom, some kind of recreation that didn't involve him or the motel.

"All ready!" She said from behind him.

Grizz turned around to see his wife standing there, a vision. His mouth actually hung open. He stared at her slowly as his gaze made its way down from the top of her head to her pretty pink toes.

"What's wrong?" she asked, looking down at her dress. Then she brought her hands to her face, patting her cheekbones. "What? Is my makeup smudged or something?"

"You look beautiful," Grizz told her.

"Oh, thank you!" She did a quick twirl, relief evident in her voice. "I bought the dress last week. I love it! I think I'll look great on the dance floor. Don't you?"

"No. Take it off. You're not wearing that dress out."

"What? What do you mean take it off? I'm *not* taking it off. I love it, and it's perfect for dancing."

He pointed. "Your nipples are showing."

She looked down. "My nipples aren't showing."

"I can see your nipples. You're not wearing that dress out, Kit."

"You can't see my nipples, Grizz. This dress isn't see-through. They're hard because it's freezing in here. You keep the temperature as low as possible."

"Then put on a bra."

"I don't have a bra that I can wear with this dress and you know it! Look how the straps are."

"Then put on a sweater."

"No, I'm *not* wearing a sweater to a discotheque! No way. You're being ridiculous."

He marched past her and headed for their bedroom. She could hear him rummaging around. If he thought he was bringing back a sweater for her to wear he was crazy.

He walked back into the small living room. "Here, these'll work. I'll help you put them on," he said, handing her two bandages.

"You want me to put Band Aids on my nipples? You are just too over-the-top! No way, Grizz!" She crossed her arms, refusing to take them. "You have topless women running all over your bars and you don't care who sees *their* nipples!"

"None of them are my wife!" he growled. "I'm telling you now, Kit. You are not leaving here in that dress."

He glanced out the window. Axel was walking toward number four.

He leveled a look at her. "Change or I'll tell Axel you're not going."

She stomped off to their bedroom. She came back out less than five minutes later, this time dressed in a more conservative black number. Axel was inside now, talking to Grizz.

"Better?" she asked Grizz with a hint of an attitude. She stood there stiffly. "Any other rules I need to know about?"

"No. Axel knows what time I want you home."

Axel looked from one to the other. Something was wrong, but he didn't know what it was. He could sense the tension in the room. He decided to lighten the mood. "Is that your new dress, Kit? It's really nice."

"No, it's not my new dress," she answered him, her chin raised just a little too high.

"I thought you told me you bought a new dress just for tonight," he said quietly. Maybe he was getting into something he shouldn't. He looked from Kit to Grizz and back to Kit again.

"I did buy a new dress, but I'm not allowed to wear it." She clutched her oversized purse to her chest and approached the front door. As she swung it open, she called out over her shoulder. "Apparently, if I want to wear my new dress tonight, I need to leave my nipples here with Grizz, and since I can't do that, I changed my dress."

Axel looked at Grizz with an expression of bewilderment.

Grizz just laughed. "Keep an eye on her. Get her home safely."

He stood in the open doorway and watched as Axel escorted her to his car and held the door open as she climbed in.

He smiled to himself. Did she really think he wouldn't notice her bulging purse? He knew he had to let some things go. He knew he had to let her occasionally think she'd won. He would allow her this small victory, but he didn't have to like it. He closed the door and went to make a phone call.

They were about fifteen minutes into their drive when Kit said to Axel, "Do you mind stopping before we get there? I really need to use the bathroom."

"Yeah, sure no problem, Kit," he said and pulled into a fast food restaurant. "Is this okay?"

"It's fine. I'll just be a minute."

Less than five minutes later Kit walked out of the restaurant and headed for the car. She was wearing a different dress.

"Don't say it, Axel," she said as she slid into the passenger seat. "Don't say a word. I'll change back before you bring me home. I could've worn a stupid sweater and taken it off, but it's the principle of the thing. He always has to win. Well, not this time." Then she tossed her large purse and the dress she'd been wearing, along with her bra, in the back of the car. "He can't always get his way, you know. Sometimes he can be such a bully."

"Sometimes?"

Then he smiled and put the car in reverse. Truth was he really liked her. She was a sweet girl. Probably too sweet for Grizz. But he could understand where she was coming from. Grizz was a bully, and even though Axel would never be disloyal to him, he was willing to let some things slide. This would be one of them. He knew that she was still a little upset so he decided to let her know, in his own way, he was okay with the wardrobe change.

Without taking his eyes off the road, he extended his right hand toward her.

"I'm not really into the whole nickname thing. I'm Greg. It's nice to meet you." He glanced over at her with a kind smile.

She smiled back and extended her own hand, then hesitated. Should she? Could she? Then she grabbed his hand, gave it a shake.

"I'm—I'm Ginny. Nice to meet you, Greg."

They talked the rest of the way about anything and everything not related to the motel. Even with the dancing in number four, they'd never really been out together, and they were both glad there seemed to be a real friendship that went beyond the motel and their dance lessons. They both agreed that even though Saturday Night Fever was already two years old, disco would always be around and John Travolta was dreamy.

When they arrived at the club, there was a long line out the door. Axel walked her past the line and, nodding at the bouncer who opened the rope gate, escorted her inside.

It was loud and crowded inside. The dance floor was packed as the crowd swayed and gyrated to Gloria Gaynor's "I Will Survive."

Axel scanned the room. When he saw who he was looking for, he nodded and smiled. Kit noticed the exchange but couldn't see who he was looking at.

He walked her down the hallway toward the restrooms. It was still loud, but here he wouldn't have to yell.

"Kit, there's been a small change of plans. I hope you don't mind." He looked at the ground shyly.

This was new. Axel almost appeared to be blushing. He looked over her shoulder and smiled at someone. She turned around and gave a quick glance. That's when she saw him. He was a short redhead with a boyish grin and freckles. She looked back up at Axel.

"He's cute. Who is he?" She grinned.

"His name is Jonah," and after a pause, "He's younger than me. No gang connections. A really good guy."

He looked at the ground again.

"It's okay, Axel. I understand. If I didn't know better, I'd say you're blushing," she teased.

"It's the real thing, Kit. I think I'm in love."

"Go. Go be with Jonah. Have a special night. Just be back here thirty minutes before you told Grizz you'd have me home."

He looked at her then and broke into a wide grin. "You didn't think I'd leave you here all alone, did you?"

Before she could answer, she felt a breath on her ear and heard a voice ask, "Do you think I'll be a decent substitute for the Saturday Night Fever king?"

She turned and smiled. "Grunt!"

They talked a few more minutes. Axel explained it was a last minute thing. He didn't mean to be deceptive. He had an opportunity to attend some benefit with Jonah. He didn't go into details, but said that it was a rare chance to actually be somewhere with a man he loved. A place where he wouldn't be judged. Kit didn't ask for information. She knew he was loyal to Grizz, and she also knew she didn't want to deprive him of a special night with his new beau.

She looked at them thoughtfully as they made their way down the hallway and out the door. Then she looked up at Grunt, who was smiling down at her. She hadn't seen him since he'd returned from his business trip to Vancouver over a month ago. She realized how much she'd missed him.

"I'm not the best dancer, but I don't think I'll embarrass you," he told her.

She hugged him. When she pulled away from him, he looked down at her, his expression serious.

"You really look beautiful tonight, Kit," he said. And before she could thank him for the compliment, he added, "I can't believe Grizz let you out the door in that dress. Your nipples are showing."

# Chapter Thirty-Three
## 1950's, Fort Lauderdale, Florida

POP HAD BEEN dead for about a month. Ralph had settled into a routine at the motel and was easily able to keep up the charade of having a sick elderly grandfather who spent his days in bed. He explained to the few guests that he was there for the summer helping his grandpa out. He handled the guests with a maturity and expertise that didn't make them question his story.

He'd bum an occasional ride from a guest who was leaving and make his way into the city to handle necessary business, but it wasn't much. He'd check the post office for mail and get some groceries. He couldn't buy beer, but he didn't drink beer anyway, and there was a lot of it left over from Pop's last grocery run. He didn't have to pay the utility bills because he'd been with Pop the day he paid them up for the next year. He did have to pay the phone company, though, but he did that by mail. He forged Pop's signature on any checks that he wrote. After getting a bank statement in the mail and seeing Pop's balance, he knew he didn't need to worry about money. It wasn't a lot, but it was more than he'd ever known in his life. More than once he considered trying to withdraw it all and leave, but why would he? He had nowhere to go and he felt safe here.

He woke up that morning and got himself fed and dressed. He took Ruthie and Razor's picture off the dresser and tucked it in his back pocket. He had a habit of keeping it with him. He felt better having them close, even if it was just a picture. It was starting to get worn-looking and he wondered what he could cover it with to protect it.

He was skimming leaves out of the pool when he heard a rumbling. Looking up, he saw three motorcycles pull into the motel. He wondered if they were lost or would be looking for rooms. He hadn't had a guest in about six days.

He laid down the skimming net and watched as they made their way around the pool and playground area, parking their bikes in front of the motel. All three got off and started walking toward him.

They looked like trouble. They looked like serious trouble.

He didn't say anything. He would let them talk first. The one who appeared to be the leader spoke first.

"You work here?" he asked the boy.

"Yes, sir. I help my grandpa out. He's the owner."

All three stopped in front of him. The leader spoke again. "Doesn't look like you get much business out here, do you?"

Ralph started to get nervous. Why would the guy want to know how much business they got? He felt uncomfortable. With a calmness he wasn't sure he felt, he answered, "Not much."

He met the man's gaze. Ralph was big for his age and hoped he gave the impression of being a little older than he actually was.

The leader nodded his head, slowly looking around. The two guys behind him were doing the same thing.

Before the guy could say anything else, Ralph asked, "You guys looking for a room?"

There was a round of laughter. "Nah, don't think we'll need a room. Just looking for a place to rest our asses for the day. You got anything to drink?"

"What do you want? Got water, soda pop, maybe some iced tea."

"How about a beer? Does your grandpa drink beer by any chance?"

"Yeah, I think I can give you some of his beer."

"Is he here?" the leader asked. "Should I ask him for permission?"

Another round of laughter. Ralph knew they were playing with him, but he didn't know why or to what end.

This could turn out bad.

"You can meet him if you want. I'll have to take you into our room, though." He nodded at number four. "He's real sick. Doesn't get out of the bed except to use the bathroom. Has a hard time breathing. I help him out."

He knew he could get caught in this lie, but he was counting on the fact that they really didn't care. They were just feeling him out. He was right.

"Nah, don't need to meet him as long as he's willing to share his beer."

Ralph brought them their beer and watched them from the corner of his eye as he continued with his chores. They grabbed some chairs from the pool area and set themselves up between the playground equipment and the pool. He noticed when they were finished with their beers so he made a few more deliveries without being asked. They seemed to like that.

They only bothered him once when it started to get dark. He'd made them some sandwiches and was bringing them out when he stopped short. There was a blazing fire going and they were sitting around it. They'd made a fire right between the pool and playground. What the hell! He'd been taking care of the grass and now there would be a gigantic burn mark right in the center of it.

He slowly approached them, and when the leader saw him he stood up.

"Hope your grandpa don't mind. We won't be needing any rooms, but we've decided we're going to stay and maybe have a little campout right here."

"Hope he didn't need that picnic table," one of the other guys said.

This brought some chuckles. They'd used one of the tables to make their fire. His first reaction was to get angry, but then he realized he really didn't care about a picnic table.

"He won't care. Here's your sandwiches and more beer. It's the last of it, though." It was true and he looked the leader straight in the eye as he said it.

"Thanks, kid. What's your name?"

"Ralph."

"Well, Ralph, I'm Red and this is Chops and Dusty."

The boy nodded and walked the food over to the two men. He had the beers tucked into his pants and there was another round of laughter when he pulled them out.

He handed Red his beer and sandwich. Red set them on the chair he'd been sitting in and, draping his arm around Ralph's shoulder, slowly walked him toward number four. When he was out of earshot of Chops and Dusty, he asked the boy, "How long you been here with your grandpa?"

Ralph didn't expect the question and couldn't think straight to tell the truth. "Since I was little," he answered.

Red seemed to like this answer. He nodded. "You take care of all the business? All the guests?"

"Yes, sir. I have to take care of them."

"Your grandpa ever help out?"

"Pops doesn't get out of bed barely at all. Just to use the bathroom, like I said before. So, no, he can't help out."

"Good. Good. Do you remember a guy who might have stopped here three, maybe four months back? Nice-looking guy. Clean cut. Probably wearing a suit and driving a nice car. He was an insurance salesman. You remember anybody like that?"

Ralph could answer honestly. "No. Nobody like that comes to mind. I'd remember. We don't get many people here."

"Thanks, kid. I appreciate the hospitality." He reached into his pants and pulled out a wad of cash. He took some money out and handed it to Ralph. "Tell your grandpa to let you keep some of this. I watched you working around here all day. You earned it."

Ralph just stared at the money. He couldn't remember anybody ever paying him for anything. Pop had never paid him. He gave him food and shelter, but nothing else. Before he could say anything, Red told him, "Go to bed. You worked hard today."

He slapped Ralph on the back and turned around, heading back to his friends and the fire. Ralph let himself into number four and locked the door behind him.

The rest of the night was uneventful. He was grateful the television hadn't broken when Pop fell into it. He fell asleep watching it and woke up sometime after midnight. He shut off the TV and started to head back to the bedroom when he stopped to peek out the window. The fire was just a soft glow and he could see the three men sleeping around it. They must've brought bedrolls, he thought. He glanced at the door. He'd remembered locking it behind him when he came in earlier. He double-checked to be sure. He headed for the bedroom, and without taking off his clothes, plopped on top of the covers and fell asleep.

He wasn't sure what time it was or what woke him. He stared around the bedroom, trying to adjust his eyes. The previous day's events invaded his senses. Bikers, sandwiches, beer, a fire. His eyes flew open and he bolted upright when he realized the pitch-dark room had a soft red glow. Was there fire in here?

He looked to his right and noticed the cause. The phone on the bedside table was lit up. The motel had two phones. One in the office and one in Pop's room. The one in Pop's room shared the same line as the office phone and Pop had shown him early on how to press down the red button, lift the receiver and listen in on guests' phone calls.

Pop was a nosy old man. Maybe he was just lonely, and listening to other people's conversations gave him a small thrill. Whatever the cause, it didn't happen a lot because there were very few visitors, and Ralph hadn't remembered one since Pop died that had asked to use the office phone.

Someone was using it now. Whoever it was had to have broken into the office. It was locked and the only key was on a peg out in the living room.

Using the technique he'd seen Pop do only twice, he slowly pressed down the red button while lifting the receiver. He didn't hear a click and hoped the person using the office phone didn't hear it either. He held his breath as he listened. He recognized Red's voice.

"I've already confirmed he hasn't been here."

"Exactly how did you confirm this?"

"It's just a kid and an old man. The old man can't get out of his bed. His grandson runs the place. Asked if he was here. The kid wasn't lying. I know when someone is lying. He wasn't here. Plus, his name's not in the register."

"He wouldn't have used his real name."

"I fucking know that. I know his handwriting. I even know how he would disguise his handwriting. Only a few signatures and I can guarantee none of them are his. He hasn't been here."

"You keep looking for him. You find him and you bring him in. And you make sure he has the fucking bag with him."

"Don't worry. I'll find him and you'll get your money back."

"This is not about the fucking money. I want that bag."

Just then, a wild animal gave a piercing cry from behind the motel. Ralph clasped his hand over the mouthpiece. Would Red hear that through the phone? Or would he hear it just like Ralph was hearing it coming from behind the motel? He froze.

"Is this a secure line, agent?"

There was a pause before Red answered. "Yes, it's secure."

"Find that bag."

There was a click. Ralph knew without a doubt Red knew someone was listening.

He jumped up and ran to the living room. He peeked out the window. He saw Red come out of the office, and he could tell that he was carrying the ring that held all the motel keys on it.

Red approached the first door, Unit 15. He jiggled the door handle. Of course it was locked. He used one of the keys to unlock it and let himself inside. Ralph knew there were no phones in any of the rooms except for this one. If Red was going to check each one to be sure, he'd have to work fast.

He unplugged the phone from the wall and walked to the small laundry basket that held some dirty clothes. He stuffed the phone down into the pile. He almost laughed at himself at the absurdity of hiding the phone. If Red made his way back to the bedroom and discovered there was no old man back here, he'd have a lot of explaining to do. Fuck!

Think, think, think. He had one shot.

He went to the dresser and pulled out Pop's cigarettes. Thank goodness he'd never thrown them away. He lit one up and started puffing on it as he grabbed a blanket and pillow from the closet and carried them out to the couch. He grabbed an ashtray off the kitchen counter. He had to fumble around for it because he refused to turn on the lights. He dashed back to the bedroom and placed the ashtray on the nightstand. He put the cigarette in it. He pulled back the bedspread he'd been laying on and mussed up the bed some more.

Then he went into the bathroom. He turned on the shower and turned the hot water up as high as it would go. He left the light on and locked the door from the inside. He pulled it shut.

He ran out to the living room and peeked out the curtain. Red was at number six. One more unit to check before he got to four. He hesitated for a second and then came to a decision. He unlocked the door and jumped on the couch. He stood up again and yanked off his pants, leaving them on the floor. He laid back down on the couch and pulled the blanket up.

He had just closed his eyes when the door opened. Red stood in the doorway, the moon casting a shadow that spilled into unit four. Ralph knew that Red hadn't expected the door to be open. He watched through slitted eyes as Red tossed the master keys off to the side. They must've landed in the grass because they didn't make a sound.

Red reached around the wall and turned on the light.

Ralph sat up on the couch and used his hand to shield his eyes. He knew he gave the impression of having been startled out of a dead sleep.

"Sorry, kid. Didn't mean to wake you. Need to use the phone. You have a phone in here I can use?" Red was slurring his words and pretended to stagger. Ralph knew he wasn't drunk. He'd heard him on the phone. He was stone cold sober. He also knew Red had thrown the master keys aside because he didn't want to get caught with them.

Ralph rubbed his eyes like he was trying to make sense of the scene that was before him. He sat up and reached down to pull his pants on. He stood up, and while zipping them, answered Red, "No phone in here. Sorry. I can take you down to the office and let you use the one in there."

He walked toward Red and started to take the office key off a peg by the door. He could see through his peripheral vision that Red was scanning the room. He was looking for a phone.

He walked in and brushed past Ralph as he headed back toward the bedroom.

"You sure, kid? Maybe your grandpa has one I can use." He headed back to the bedroom and fumbled for the light switch. Ralph was right behind him and could tell he was taking in the room slowly.

No phone. No old man, either.

Still feigning sleepiness, Ralph answered, "No. No phone back here, either." He brushed past Red and walked to the nightstand. He took the lit cigarette and quickly stubbed it out. He then looked toward the bathroom door. The light was on and steam was coming out from underneath the door.

"Your grandpa always take showers in the middle of the night?" he asked nodding at the bathroom door. He didn't sound as drunk.

"Yeah. Said the steam helps his lungs. Makes it easier to breathe. He'd probably breathe easier if he'd quit smoking."

Ralph shook his head and started to walk back to the living room, leaving Red in the bedroom doorway.

Red took one look around the room. There was no phone here and he was certain there wasn't a phone in the bathroom. He fake staggered back out to the living room. Ralph had already laid back down on the couch.

"Sorry to bother you, kid. I'll just use it in the morning. If I can remember by then who I wanted to call." He switched off the light and closed the door behind him.

Ralph jumped up and peeked out the window. He watched as Red retrieved the motel's master key ring from the grass and made his way back to the office to return it. He wasn't staggering.

The next morning, the three bikers asked for a skillet, some eggs, and any kind of meat. Ralph brought them what he had and noticed they'd restarted the fire and placed a grill from one of the barbecues on it. A coffee pot was sitting on top of that. They had what looked like army mess kits, so he didn't need to provide them with any cups, plates, or cutlery. He was glad.

He went about his chores and acted like nothing unusual had happened the previous night. They finally finished their breakfast and used the motel hose to clean up their mess kits. Red announced they were leaving. They had packed up their bikes and were standing around the fire talking. Ralph walked over to them and started to pick up a chair. He was going to return it to the pool area. He had his back to them as he started to walk away.

"Hey, kid, what's this? You dropped something."

He turned around and noticed the guy that had been introduced as Dusty was holding something. He dropped the chair when he realized it was the picture of Ruthie and Razor. It must've come out of his back pocket. He considered it his good luck talisman and had never considered what he'd do if he lost it.

He lunged for Dusty to grab it away from him, but Dusty had anticipated it and took a step back.

"Whoa, whoa, kid. Give me a second to look at it. Don't have to get your balls all twisted."

Ralph reached for it again and Dusty took another step back and held the picture up high.

"Quit fucking with the kid. Give him his picture," Red growled.

"I will. Just don't see what all the excitement's about. Just some girl and her mutt."

He started to hand it to Ralph and when Ralph reached for it, Dusty swiped it away before he could grab it. The quick movement caused him to lose his grip on the picture and, as if in slow motion, it softly floated over the fire pit and landed in the burning embers. It quickly caught fire, and before Ralph could reach for it, it was gone. He stood there and stared.

They were gone. He would never see Ruthie's smiling face again. He would never see her curls. He would never see Razor's intelligent eyes.

Never.

"Gee, kid. Didn't mean for that to happen." Dusty was being sincere.

The three men shook their heads and started walking away, single file, toward their motorcycles. Dusty was bringing up the rear.

There was a loud cry, almost guttural, and before they could turn around, Dusty was on the ground and Ralph was on top of him. Ralph had picked up one of the pieces of wood from the fire and clobbered Dusty as hard as he could as the man turned to see where the sound was coming from. Dusty was now on his back. He hadn't been knocked out by the blow, but he was too dazed to fight back. Ralph was sitting on his chest and bloodying his face. It took both Red and Chops to pull him off.

Red hoisted Ralph up by grabbing him beneath each armpit and pulling him to his feet. Then in a common wrestling move, he clasped his hands together behind Ralph's neck, making it hard for him to break free. He was breathing heavy. Red held him back while Chops tried to help Dusty.

"Calm down, kid. Take it easy and catch your breath. I know why you got mad. Dusty is an ass, but I know he didn't mean it. Calm down."

Ralph's breathing slowed as they watched Chops help Dusty into a sitting position. He took a bandana from his pocket and gave it to Dusty to wipe his bloodied face.

Dusty looked up at Ralph. "I should fucking kill you, you little bastard. You fucking broke my nose."

"Shut up, Dusty. You pulled your shit on him. You had it coming. You two. Get on your bikes. Get outta here. I'll catch up."

He never relaxed his grip on Ralph as they watched Dusty and Chops get on their motorcycles and take off. Dusty had staggered a little bit. That hit to the head was pretty rough. Apparently, he had a hard skull.

When they drove away, Red let go of Ralph. Ralph turned around to face him.

"He had it coming."

"I know he did. You didn't do anything wrong."

They stood there and stared at each other. Red sized him up. Red was an intimidating man. He was large and rough in appearance. He was covered in tattoos and had a deep voice that resonated long after he spoke. Ralph broke the stare first and looked at the tattoo that was showing just above the neckline of Red's shirt. Without being asked, Red answered him.

"It's a devil. You're seeing its red tail."

Ralph didn't say anything, just looked back up at Red. There was something in the glance Red recognized. This kid knew something. He never found a phone, but he knew this kid had been listening. This kid had a secret, too, and even though Red didn't know what it was, he intended to find out. He could beat it out of him, but something told him this kid wouldn't crack.

Red looked over at number four. There was no old man in number four. This kid was smart enough to be living here by himself. He glanced back at Ralph and the boy's cold, green eyes told Red he was right.

He gave a half smile and nodded. He needed to get this kid to come to him. To trust him.

"Look, kid. If anything ever happens with your grandpa," he paused. "You know what I'm talking about?"

Ralph didn't answer so Red continued.

"You know, with his health? Anything ever happens and you don't want to be out here by yourself, you come find me. I'm in Fort Lauderdale. I'll give you a job."

Ralph didn't say anything at first. He just stared with those intense green eyes. He finally asked, "How will I find you?"

"You find my bar down by the beach and you'll find me." He started walking toward his  bike and called out over his shoulder. "It's called The Red Crab."

# Chapter Thirty-Four
2000

THE THREE FRIENDS had had so much to talk about, they hadn't even realized the sun was coming up until Carter's rescued rooster, Victor, began to crow.

Ginny was exhausted, but she felt immensely relieved. She'd told the girls everything and they never interrupted. They knew she had to get some things off her chest. The journalist in Casey found it very difficult not to jump in and ask questions. But, Casey had reminded herself, this wasn't a news story. This was a dear friend, a friend who just needed them to listen. And that's what they both did.

They'd even had some good laughs.

"I remember when that guy came for Grizz's chess set," Carter said after hearing the story about how it had shown up at Tommy and Ginny's house, how Jason set it up as a surprise.

Ginny couldn't help herself. She smiled. She knew the story Carter was getting ready to tell.

"What?" Casey asked. "I'm sensing a story. Did I miss something?"

"Yeah, you were out of the country," Carter answered her. She took a sip of her wine before continuing. "The chess set was here when I first moved in," motioning with her hand. "You'd just left for Africa and Ginny had moved back here after staying at Stephen and April's a while. I noticed she kept avoiding this room."

"Some things were just so hard," Ginny said in a small voice.

"I know, sweetie. That's why I had Tommy come over one day and pack it up and put it in the guest house over the garage. I had taken you to one of your doctor's appointments so you wouldn't be here. I didn't know if you ever realized I moved it." Carter looked thoughtfully at Ginny.

"I don't really remember what I thought," Ginny answered honestly. "Getting through each day was such a struggle."

"Okay." Casey looked from one to the other. "So, what was so funny?"

"Yeah, that part," Carter continued. "It was about two years later. After Grizz was sentenced to prison. I was home one day and there was a knock at my door. I was expecting someone from an animal sanctuary. They were supposed to be picking up Phil."

"Phil?" Casey asked.

"Yeah, that damn camel that gave me such a hard time. Anyway, Tommy left a message saying someone would be coming by to get the chess set. But I hadn't listened to my messages."

"And—" Casey used her hand to urge Carter to continue.

"And, I swung the door open and the most handsome man I have ever laid my eyes on was standing there. A big, gigantic Native American! I know I just stood there and gaped at him."

"Anthony Bear," Ginny explained to Casey. "One of Grizz's friends. I don't think either one of you met him. He came over with his wife, Christy, a few times, but I'm not sure you were ever at my house at the same time as them."

"I think I would have remembered a big, handsome Indian." Casey wiggled her eyebrows.

"Especially this one!" Carter added. "Anyway, it was just awkward, because I thought he was there to pick up Phil. He knew he was getting something to deliver to Grizz, but nobody told him what it was. We weren't communicating and it didn't help that I was totally tongue-tied. I swear, I turned into a giggling eighth-grader!" Carter grinned. "I walked him to the back of the house and pointed to Phil. The look on his face was comical. That's all. It was just funny."

Casey just shook her head, a bemused expression on her face.

"You'd think it was funnier, Casey, if you'd ever met Anthony. For starters, he's bigger than Grizz and I think even more serious." Ginny paused, looked at her lap. "If that's even possible."

There was a lull in the conversation.

"Carter, do you have any aspirin?" Ginny asked.

Carter started to get up, but Ginny beat her to it. "I can get it myself. Still keep some in the kitchen?"

"Medicine cabinet in my bathroom."

Ginny walked toward the back of the house. Carter's bathroom would be the master bath. The one she'd shared with Grizz.

She remembered when they were having the home built all those years ago. Grizz had insisted on a gigantic tub.

"Why in the world would I need a tub this big?" Ginny had asked him as she'd stood over it, hands on her hips. The bathroom wasn't finished yet. She'd been there to talk to the contractor about tile selections.

Grizz had come up behind her and put his arms around her waist. Pulling her to him, he bent down to nuzzle her neck. "It has to be big enough for me to fit in it with you."

"You're going to take a bath with me?" she'd asked, surprised.

"Yep. And I'm going to make love to you in this tub. I'm going to make love to you in every room of this house, Kitten. The tub, the kitchen, in front of the fire. Everywhere."

He'd turned her around then and gently kissed her. The kiss deepened and she could feel his arousal press against her stomach.

She'd broken the kiss and looked up at him. "Grizz, not here! The builder is going to be here in a minute."

"I could kiss you all day, Kitten," he said, taking her face in his hands. "Nothing's going to happen, honey. Just let me enjoy you for a few minutes." And he'd lowered his mouth back to hers.

Ginny felt the tears start as memories of Grizz washed over her. She sat down on Carter's bed. What was wrong with her? She'd been in this house many times since Grizz's arrest. Why was she reacting this way now?

Maybe it was the fact that he was gone. For good. Maybe she'd never gotten to properly mourn him. She moved her wide wedding band forward on her knuckle as she rubbed the spot where Grizz's name had been tattooed almost twenty-five years ago. Long before ring tattoos had become popular. There was still a slight burning sensation from the visit to Eddie's Tattoo Parlor on Saturday. She finished rubbing it and moved her wedding band back in place.

She didn't know what she was feeling and she didn't want her friends to come looking for her. She stood up and wiped her eyes with her hands. *Deep breath. Brave face, Ginny. You can go in there and get the aspirin.*

Carter and Casey whispered, head to head, after Ginny left the room. They were worried about their friend, but they knew she would get through this.

"Do you think it's up to us to tell her some things Tommy told us?" Carter asked softly.

"Maybe." Casey frowned. "I just can't believe Tommy was deceitful for any other reason than to protect her all these years. He needs allies. I think he's a good guy, Carter. I've never seen anything to make me believe otherwise."

"Do you think he ever told her the prom story? Or maybe Sarah Jo told her."

"I really don't know. When Tommy told us I never thought to ask if Ginny knew. And the fact that Gin has never mentioned it makes me wonder what she has or hasn't known about all these years. You know, other than Tommy being Grizz's son."

Their conversation was interrupted by a bloodcurdling scream coming from the master bathroom.

"Carterrrrrr!!!!!"

"Uh oh," Carter said, jumping to her feet and heading toward the bathroom. "I guess Gin just met Richard Pepperbloom. I forgot to tell her about him."

"Who the heck is Richard Pepperbloom?" Casey followed at her heels. "You didn't mention him to me either."

"I'm keeping him in my tub until someone comes for him tomorrow." Before Casey could comment further, Carter added nonchalantly, "He's an alligator."

# Chapter Thirty-Five
1979

GRIZZ AND AXEL were sitting in number four. Grizz had called Axel inside for a meeting. Grizz was in his recliner, Axel on the couch. He kept glancing over Grizz's shoulder toward the small kitchen.

"Axel, what the fuck is so interesting that you keep staring past me into the kitchen?"

"Uh, what is Kit making for dinner?"

Grizz gave him a look. "I called you in here to talk about business and you want to know what Kit is making for dinner?"

Axel actually licked his lips.

"Some kind of roast, and before you ask, yes. You can have dinner with us. But," Grizz added, "Not if we don't finish this conversation before she comes back inside."

"Your wife is the best cook I've ever met," Axel said dreamily. Before he could say any more, Grizz slammed his fist on the small side table.

"Axel!"

"Yeah, got it right here, boss." Axel put on his business face, stood up and handed Grizz an oversized envelope. He perched on the sofa, watching Grizz open it.

Grizz had confided in Axel that Kit was having some serious depression over Moe's suicide. She really wanted to go to college. If there was anything Grizz had a difficult time with, it was saying no to Kit. He would move the earth for her if it was within his power. Grizz knew she would do her best to stay under the radar of any old classmates that she risked running into. He was hoping that allowing her to spend more time with Grunt was helping, but she needed more, and he knew that.

He sifted through the contents of the envelope and read what he was holding, then looked up at Axel, one eyebrow raised.

"You are fucking kidding me," was all he said.

"Nope, Grizz, not kidding you," Axel replied. And then after a pause, he added, "You can't make this shit up."

"Denmark?" Grizz asked incredulously. "They do this shit in Denmark?"

Axel nodded at what Grizz was holding. "Says it in there so, yeah, I guess that's where they do it."

Just then, Kit walked in. She had been outside taking care of her garden. She was growing vegetables in the back of the motel. Grizz insisted she keep one of the dogs with her at all times. He'd recently noticed more alligator activity around there than usual, and he knew Damien or Lucifer would alert her if they detected an intruder of any kind.

Grizz had taken some lighthearted ribbing about how pretty the front of the motel was becoming. He'd encouraged his young wife to spruce up the place a bit. In addition to her vegetable garden, she'd planted flowers along the motel sidewalk, and she recently added hanging plants outside their unit. He thought it might have been helping with her depression a little bit, but he knew in his gut it wasn't enough. He needed to figure out a way to let her go to college. That was why Axel was there.

"Hi, Axel, I didn't know you were here." Kit walked over to the smaller man, planting a light kiss on his cheek. "Do you want to stay for dinner? I made a roast. There's plenty."

Axel looked at her innocently. "Sure, if you think you'll have enough."

"I'll definitely have enough." She kissed Grizz on the top of his head before moving to the kitchen to check her roast.

"Okay, Kit. If you insist."

Grizz pinched the bridge of his nose. He was getting impatient.

"I need fifteen minutes to get it all together," she told them as they stood.

"We'll be in the pit," Grizz told her. "Just yell."

"Okay," was all she said.

There was a small dinette table with two chairs where she and Grizz ate their meals. It was so small that Kit set up dinner buffet-style on the kitchen counter, since it was very rare that someone was invited into number four to eat with them. The three of them could serve themselves before sitting down. She carried Grizz's desk chair over to the little table.

"She's not limping as much. She seems stronger," Axel commented to Grizz as they headed for the pit.

Axel remembered a few weeks earlier when he'd visited, standing outside of number four. He'd been deep in conversation with Grizz and Chowder when they heard a small cry. Kit had been jogging around the front of the motel on the old and crumbling asphalt. She must have landed wrong and lost her footing. Grizz was immediately at her side and effortlessly picked her up, cradling her closely.

"I'm okay, Grizz. I just stepped funny," she'd said wincing.

"You're not okay. Your ankle is already swelling. We need to get you inside and get some ice on it." Before she could reply he shouted at Chowder, "Get this fucking road paved. She could've broken her ankle!"

Chowder watched as he carried Kit into number four. "I've been asking you for five years to let me get it paved," he said quietly. "It wreaks havoc on the bikes and cars, too."

"Just do it!" Grizz barked as he entered the unit.

Now, Grizz just shrugged as they got to the pit and took a seat. "Yeah, it was just a sprain. She seems fine."

Less than fifteen minutes later, Kit stuck her head out. "Dinner's ready, guys!"

She ran into the bedroom to change her top before dinner. She had somehow managed to spill gravy down the front of it while she was setting the food out. She was running some cold water from the bathroom sink over the blouse when she heard a small commotion. Leaving it in the sink, she headed out through the bedroom and into the kitchen and living room area.

There she stopped dead in her tracks. A wave of nausea passed over her, then panic.

Grizz and Axel were in the kitchen. Blood was everywhere.

"We need to call Grunt or Doc. You definitely need stitches," Axel exclaimed to Grizz while he was reaching for the dish towel that Kit kept hung on the oven door.

"I don't need stitches." Grizz glared at him, one hand clamped against his forehead.

"Oh, my God!" Kit rushed to them. "What happened? Oh, no! Oh, Grizz, did you get in another fight? Who hit you? Let me see it!"

"Kit, I didn't get in a fight and you can't see it. There's nothing to see."

"Yes, there is," Axel's voice was firm as he moved Grizz's hand aside and pressed the towel to his forehead. "It's bad, Grizz. Looks real deep. You definitely need stitches."

"Shut up, Axel. I don't need stitches."

"Let me see it." Kit stood on her tiptoes, peering at his head. Blood was all over his face by now and running down the right side of his neck. Another wave of nausea threatened.

"Nothing to see, Kit," Grizz huffed. "Axel can help me put a bandage on it. Why don't you help with that, honey? Go back into the bathroom and get some bandages and alcohol or something. Go on. Get me some stuff to clean it up with."

Kit reluctantly headed back through the bedroom. They could hear her digging around in the medicine cabinet.

"You definitely are going to need stitches. I'm telling you, Grizz. It's really deep. I got a good look before you covered it up with the towel. Fuck, man, you already need another towel." Axel looked worried.

"Fine. Give Grunt a call; he can stitch it up. I just didn't want Kit to see it." Grizz gave him a look. "Blood makes her as woozy as needles. Hurry up. Call him."

"Blood, too? Really? Boy, did she ever marry the wrong guy," Axel muttered under his breath as he picked up the phone.

Kit came back out carrying antiseptic, bandages, and medical tape. She also had a pile of washcloths. Grizz grabbed a washcloth from her and swapped it for the bloody dish towel before she could take a good look.

"Oh, Grizz, what happened?" She tentatively rested a hand on his arm, then moved it away, afraid of hurting him worse. "If you're this bloody and messed up, I don't know if I even want to know what happened to the other guy."

"Nobody else got hurt, Kit, and you don't need to worry." He managed to take a seat at the small kitchen table, trying his best to avoid dripping blood on the floor. "Head wounds bleed a lot. It's not a big deal. Doesn't even hurt."

"You're a bloody mess and have a cut that needs stitches and you don't think I should be worried about the other guy? C'mon, Grizz. I'm not stupid. Is there someone else out there that needs help?"

"Kit, I did not get in a fight. I did not hurt anyone. Okay?"

"Really?" She stood in front of him, hands on hips. "You come in here looking like you do and expect me to believe the other guy is walking away?"

She'd been down this road many times before. She didn't even want to think about the time a year or so ago when Grizz had come home with a bullet wound. Her eyes wandered to the door and Grizz knew she was debating whether or not to go outside and check for herself.

"There is no other guy, Kitten." Before she could challenge him, he added, "I cracked my head on one of your hanging planters."

\*\*\*\*\*\*\*\*\*

Two days later Grizz sat in the passenger seat of the car and waited. He didn't have to break into the car. It was unlocked. It was an older model but clean and he rolled down the window to let some air in.

"Good thing it doesn't have automatic windows," he muttered to himself as he reached over and rolled down the driver's window, too. He didn't feel like hotwiring a car just to put down electric windows. On second thought, he might hotwire it just to get the air conditioning running. Fuck, it was hot.

He looked at his watch and glanced back over to the doors just as the person he was waiting for came out. The guy walked with a bounce to his step, not even bothering to check his surroundings. Trusting fool. Grizz could hear him whistling to himself as he approached the car. He didn't even notice the windows to his car had been rolled down. He climbed into the driver's seat and almost choked after he saw Grizz.

"I'm not here to hurt you," Grizz stated, a warning hand on his arm. "I just want to talk."

By now the guy, Sam, was shaking. He remembered Grizz from a few years ago—who could forget a man that big? He'd watched that day from his living room as the biker rolled up to Sarah Jo's house and effortlessly handled Neal. Neal had been harassing Sam and his mother, Vanessa. Neal never bothered Sam or his mom again.

"Does the A/C in this thing work?" Grizz asked him.

Sam nodded, trying his best to calm the shaking.

"We're gonna take a ride. Shut the door and start the engine."

Sam's hands shook so badly now that he couldn't get the key in the ignition.

"I'm not going to hurt you," Grizz said softly. "Okay? I just want to talk to you and it's too fucking hot to sit here and do it. Just drive and don't fucking get us killed. If I'd wanted to hurt you, I'd have done it. Got it?"

Sam nodded, somehow getting the car started. He rolled up his window and turned on the air conditioner. He slowly backed out of the parking spot and made a right onto University Drive.

"Where are we going? Where do you want me to take you?" Sam's voice was calmer than he actually felt.

"Just head up to Commercial Boulevard and make a right. We'll make a circle and you can bring me back here."

Sam did as he was told.

After a minute, Grizz gave him a sidelong look. "You remember Kit?"

This caught Sam off guard. "Yes, I remember her. She's the one who called you the day Neal was trying to steal Fess's bike. She's your girlfriend. Right?" He shot Grizz a glance, then quickly flicked his eyes back to the road.

"She's my wife. She wants to go to college. I'm thinking about letting her go, but I want someone who can keep an eye on her for me. I think that someone is you."

"Me?" Sam breathed slowly through his nose. "Why me?"

"Because she knows you. You're Fess's neighbor. I think she'd trust you."

"I attend night classes at the community college. Will she be enrolling there?"

"No. She wants to go to Cole."

"I don't think I can help you out, then. I can't afford Cole. And even if I could, I work full-time just to pay for my night classes."

"What if I paid your tuition?" Grizz crossed his arms in the small car. "And I don't expect you to be in all of her classes. Just a couple if you can. But I would expect you to try and line up your other classes so you're there on the same days and stuff. Run into her between classes. Be her friend."

"You would pay my tuition just so I could be your wife's friend?"

"More like her bodyguard friend. But yeah, I would do that. The only thing I'll want to know about is if she makes friends with anybody. Girls, guys, whatever. You know who I am and what I do. I have enemies. I'll want to know if you notice anybody watching her, anything like that."

They were quiet a moment, the low hum of the car's motor barely audible in the South Florida evening.

"I'll expect you to check in with me occasionally," Grizz said finally. "I'll give you my pager number and your own code so I'll know it's you."

Sam considered it—how it'd work, how he'd manage to handle school and report back to Grizz and not be too obvious. Excitement began to build. Cole was a good school, a very good school. This wasn't the sort of opportunity you sneezed at. And Grizz wasn't exactly the kind of man you could say no to.

At last he looked directly at Grizz. "So I'll enroll at Cole for January classes?"

"Yes."

Sam frowned a moment. "I don't know how I'd know what classes she would be taking to even try to be there the same time as her."

"Don't worry about that. I'll find that out and get the information to you, as well as the money to cover it. After you get it, you enroll."

Sam was nodding now. "Yeah. Yeah, I can do that. Um, how do I handle small talk and stuff?" He glanced at Grizz. "I know about your gang a little, and I just don't know what types of things I could talk to her about. I haven't seen her in years." He cleared his throat, not sure if he'd said too much. "You know?"

"If we never had this conversation and you ran in to her, what kind of things would you say?"

"Honestly? I'd probably ask her about you and stuff."

"Then ask her about me. I don't care. You need to be as authentic as possible."

Sam smiled. He remembered Kit well. She was a nice girl, pretty, and even though he didn't really know her he had a feeling this could work out nicely.

"I'll do it. I'll definitely do it. I can't afford Cole University on my own and I want my degree. I'm your guy."

Grizz looked over at him then and scowled. "Yeah, you're my *guy*, Sam." After a brief pause, he added, "I know why you can't afford Cole. I know what your mother spends her money on. All those trips to Denmark have been expensive. Practically turned her into a pauper."

Sam gasped, gripped the steering wheel tighter. He started to shake. He slowed down and looked over at Grizz.

"Your mother was right to ask Fess to help get you out of jail that time. You wouldn't have lasted much longer."

Sam didn't know how to respond so he didn't say anything.

"I obviously know your secret, Sam. You'll do this or you'll be sorry."

Sam gulped and nodded. "Yeah, Grizz. I'll do it."

"I know you will." And after a long pause, Grizz added, "Samantha."

# Chapter Thirty-Six
2000

"HOW COME SHE didn't take me?" Jason asked, crestfallen, after his father had sat him down and explained that Ginny was going to be helping Carter with the animals while her husband was out of town. "I like to help at Aunt Carter's, and besides, it's summer. I don't have school tomorrow."

"Because you and I have to go for a motorcycle ride." Tommy gave him a smile.

Jason's face lit up. "I almost forgot! Can we go for a long ride, Dad? I like when we go on the motorcycle."

"Sure, kiddo. We can go for a long ride."

Tommy knew Mimi wouldn't be coming home until much later, and quite frankly, he wasn't up to the mental challenge needed to spend the next several hours alone with Jason. The boy was a chatterbox, pretty much like he was at his same age. He smiled as he remembered how Grizz would purposely take him places on the motorcycle so he could avoid conversation.

Thirty minutes later, Jason propped up behind him on the motorcycle, the wind in their face and the sun on their arms, Jason leaned up and yelled something into Tommy's ear. Tommy nodded and felt Jason lean back on the bike.

He remembered when Ginny got pregnant with Jason. They'd been married just over four years. Before the trial, they never consummated their marriage. It was more than a year after the trial before she actually let Tommy touch her. When she had, it had been better than they'd both imagined.

One morning, he woke up next to her. It was a bright, sunny morning, he remembered, and she'd had her back to him. He could tell she was having a dream. She woke and rose up a bit, looking over her shoulder.

"Oh, thank goodness it was just a dream!" she said, her hair tangled and messy yet somehow perfect. He caught his breath to look at her. "I was so angry at you, Tommy!"

"Me?" He smiled at her and caressed her back. "What were you mad at me for?"

She rolled onto her back and looked at him. He rested his hand on her stomach. The baby was due in five weeks.

"I was dreaming I was in labor." She closed her eyes, then opened them to glare at him. "It was this long, horrible labor, and you were behind me and encouraging me to push."

"Sounds good to me so far, except for the long and horrible labor part."

She frowned at him then. "It was good, even though it hurt, until the baby came out."

"Was something wrong with him?" He could hear the concern in his own voice.

"There was something wrong, all right. The doctor said, 'Look! Congratulations! You have a brand new spaghetti pot!'"

Tommy burst out laughing, just couldn't help himself. "You gave birth to a spaghetti pot? Your hormones are raging, Ginny!" She huffed and crossed her arms. "I swear you are having the strangest dreams. This is the third weird one this week."

"Yes, it was a gigantic, stupid pot. Must have been in my subconscious because I remember telling you last week I needed a new one."

"But, Gin, in the dream, why were you mad at *me*?"

"Because I was upset and told the doctor I was disappointed and was really looking forward to having a baby!"

"And?"

"And you chimed in, 'It's okay, Gin, we really need a spaghetti pot. We'll try for a baby next time.'"

Harder laughter shook him again. "Oh, Ginny, I'm sure you'll be having a baby. And you know what? I'll run over to the store today and buy you your spaghetti pot so you won't have to dream about it anymore."

He kissed her forehead and she smiled at him, the silly dream forgotten.

"You are so good to me, Tommy," she said, a serious tone to her voice. Then her eyes widened, and she started to sit up.

Tommy's worried expression matched her own. "Gin, are you okay?"

"Tommy, it's too early!" Her voice sounded panicked now. "My water just broke!"

They'd been so worried back then—Jason was five weeks early, and Ginny ended up having a twelve-hour labor, somehow avoiding another C-section. She was sent home after twenty-four hours, but preemie Jason spent a week in the NICU just as a precaution. He was fine, but Tommy remembered the fear like it was yesterday.

Now on the back of the bike, Jason squeezed his dad while he leaned up to yell something in his ear about the scenery.

Tommy smiled as he navigated the two-lane road, the hot sun blazing all around them. Jason had ended up just fine. Maybe he and Ginny would, too.

*********

Neither one of them knew that while Ginny was still in the hospital and they were both visiting their newborn son in the NICU, five hours away in a maximum security prison, someone was handing a note to Grizz.

Grizz had been in the yard lifting weights. "Dreams I'll Never See" by Molly Hatchet, was playing over the prison's outdoor sound system.

One of the guards walked up and handed him the paper. "This is for you."

Grizz took the note and opened it. His posture changed as he read it. Two sentences were written: It's a boy. She's okay.

He crumpled up the note, anger coursing through him. As he left the exercise yard, the lyrics to the song taunted him. He wanted to punch the singer, the prison guard, anybody and everybody who stood in his way.

He'd been even angrier when he first found out she was pregnant. He'd insisted on a face-to-face meeting with Grunt. It took every ounce of willpower not to beat the shit out of him that day.

Grunt was able to talk some sense into him. He told Grizz it was unrealistic to think he wouldn't eventually be sleeping with his own wife, that Grizz had known this was coming and had even given his permission. His orders, actually. But somehow, Grizz had naively held onto the notion that Kit would resist Grunt forever, like she had resisted the idea when Grizz first told her to marry him.

She never let Grunt move into their home in Shady Ranches after the marriage. Even after Mimi was born, Kit had to be convinced to finally move into the home that Grunt had built for her in northern Fort Lauderdale. Grizz stiffened as he remembered the day he had to tell her he didn't want his daughter to know him. That Kit had to stop coming to the prison to see him.

Grizz wanted to believe deep down that no matter how much Grunt had always loved Kit, she didn't and wouldn't ever feel the same way. Of course she loved Grunt. Grizz could admit that and even wanted that for her. But up until the pregnancy, he had stupidly hoped it was in a platonic and sisterly way. He could even allow himself to imagine Kit being in a happy and comfortable marriage. But he didn't want her in a passionate one.

When he'd heard she was pregnant, something inside him died. He knew then that it was not just a comfortable marriage based on convenience. He knew she had given herself over to Grunt.

He wanted to punch Grunt. Punch everybody.

But who could blame her? He was the one who'd told her to marry Grunt. He had to tell her that. It was part of the deal he'd made with *them*.

Grunt's words from that meeting filled his head: "If you really love her, you'll let her have a real life with me. Not the fake one you thought I was giving her because she still loved you. You're on death row, Grizz. You should be relieved to know she is *genuinely* loved and is able to love back." Grunt's words had softened then. "And don't forget—you were there the night your daughter was born. You were able to be part of it. At least you have that, Grizz. A lot of guys in your position wouldn't have been able to have done that."

As much as he'd hated to admit it, Grunt was right. But Grizz was still deeply in love with Kit. And the fact that she gave birth to a son that should have been his—would've been his, if it wasn't for the fucking son-of-a-bitch that hooked up with Blue's slut wife and Froggy— infuriated him beyond reason.

He knew early on that Jan didn't have the brains to pull off his arrest alone. Someone had used her. He was pretty certain he knew who it was, and he was patiently waiting for Blue to find Jan and Froggy so he could confirm it and put all three of them in the ground. He'd given the order to look for Froggy. He didn't have to tell Blue to find Jan. Blue would never stop looking for his boys.

Grizz knew he could ask *them* for help, but he wouldn't. *They* were the real reason he was sitting on death row.

He'd been playing cat and mouse with them for as long as he could remember. They'd insisted they had nothing to do with his arrest and conviction, but Grizz didn't believe them. Not for a minute. Besides, they could've stepped in and stopped it. He'd finally agreed to give them what they wanted. But still they were fucking with him. Making him pay for holding back for so many years.

Motherfuckers.

For now, he would seek out one of the guards and get access to one Robert Raymond Ringer. He smiled darkly as he pictured the guy, his fat neck and his stupid flat-blue eyes. Ringer was in solitary confinement. He wasn't your typical baby killer scum—he'd gotten two for one. A serial killer who got off by preying on pregnant women. Grizz quickened his pace, eager to release his anger. *Pregnant women? What the fuck?* Ringer couldn't be kept with the other prisoners for obvious reasons. Nobody could tolerate a baby killer, he didn't care how bad their crime.

Grizz was in the mood to kill someone with his bare hands and he couldn't think of another prisoner who deserved it more than Bobby Ray Ringer.

# Chapter Thirty-Seven
## 1985

"IT HURTS! AGHHH, Tommy, even with the shots, it hurts!" Ginny writhed on the hospital bed. "It's my back. Can you please rub it some more? I feel like I'm being turned inside out!"

Tommy had never felt so helpless in his entire life. There in the delivery room, he pleaded with the nurse who'd just brought in some ice chips. "Isn't there anything that can be done here? She's been in labor for almost twenty-four hours!"

The nurse looked at him kindly. "She hasn't fully dilated. She can't push until then. The baby's vitals are good and the doctor has allowed just enough pain medication to take the edge off. I'm sorry. It's a waiting game now." She looked at her watch and patted his arm. "He'll be in to see her shortly."

"It's no longer taking the edge off, it's—" He was interrupted by a loud wail as the nurse slipped out.

"Grizz! Tommy, I need Grizz. I can't do this without him. I don't want to do this without him!"

She started sobbing then and for the first time since he married her, Tommy thought that he might've been in over his head. What had he been thinking when Grizz had asked him to marry her? That she would instantly fall in love with him and they would live happily ever after? That she'd be able to remove Grizz from her heart and let another man replace him? She wanted Grizz, not him. He was officially married to her and he was going to be here when the baby, a little girl, was born, but it wasn't his baby. It was Grizz's baby.

He was just the replacement husband.

Tommy absently fingered the tie around his neck. The one he'd loosened after he'd arrived at the hospital. Carter had called him, told him Ginny's water had broken. He'd been at work and dropped everything to rush there at once. She was about three weeks early, but that wasn't so bad.

When he'd arrived at the hospital, he'd called the jail and told

Grizz. Grizz made him promise to keep him updated. He'd been calling every couple of hours from the phone in the empty hospital room next to theirs. But a woman in labor had been admitted an hour ago and he couldn't use that phone any more. He didn't want Ginny to know he was contacting Grizz.

He scratched at his chin, feeling the stubble that had started to form. It was time to make another call. He'd have to find another phone.

"Ginny, I need to use the bathroom. I'll send one of the girls in, okay?"

She looked at him with a dazed expression in her eyes, exhausted. She gave a weak little nod.

He left the hospital room, but instead of making a left to go to the waiting room where her friends were gathered, he made a right. It was almost four in the morning and there was only one nurse who looked up questioningly at him.

"Is there an exit here?"

She nodded her head toward the right. "Second hallway on the left will take you to a stairway. No elevator, though."

He thanked her and headed back the way he had come, going through the doors that led to the small waiting area. Sarah Jo, Carter and Casey were there along with three other people. A man was using the only pay phone. That was okay. He wouldn't have used that phone, anyway.

They all looked up when he entered. He shook his head. "No baby yet, and they said she can't even start pushing. I get the feeling that pushing would make her feel better, but she can't."

Sarah Jo, the only mother in the group, nodded in agreement.

Tommy motioned toward the bathrooms. "I have to use the can. Can one of you go in and rub her back? She's in agony."

Casey jumped up. "My turn!" She headed through the doors that Tommy had just come through. Sarah Jo went back to her magazine. Carter stood up and stretched as she watched Tommy walk away. Right past the restroom and into the stairwell.

He found a pay phone one floor down. He dialed a number and waited while someone went to get Grizz.

"Is Kit okay?" was the first thing Grizz asked when he got to the phone. Before Tommy could answer him, "Is the baby okay?"

"I don't know. She hasn't had the baby yet."

"What? Are you fucking kidding me? What do you mean she hasn't had it?"

"That's why I'm calling. The baby hasn't come yet. She can't push because she's not fully dilated, and before you ask, it means her cervix isn't open enough to let the baby safely come through. She's in a lot of pain and screaming for you." Grunt gritted his teeth. "I don't know how you'd do it, but I think you should be here."

There was silence on the other end of the phone. It seemed like a long time before Grizz replied. "Tell me where to meet you. Give me fifteen minutes. I can see the fucking hospital from the jail yard, so I can make it on foot if I need to. Where can you meet me?"

"She's on the fifth floor." Grunt spoke softly and quickly. "The cafeteria is on the second floor and I know there's a service elevator from the back. I saw it when I was there earlier. I'll take it down and bring you up that way and then sneak you into the maternity area by going up some back stairs I found. We'll have to avoid the waiting room where her friends are. There should be a door on the east side of the hospital. I'm going down now to wait for you."

There was a pause before Tommy added, "And Grizz, just don't kill any guards to get here, okay? Pay them off or use whatever you got, but don't kill anybody. She wouldn't want that."

"What are they gonna do, arrest me for murder?" Grizz asked before hanging up.    Tommy made his way to the back of the building.

Twenty minutes later, Grizz stood in the back stairway that led to the maternity ward. Tommy left him with orders to stay put, then made his way back to the waiting area. He told Carter and Sarah Jo he would go back in to relieve Casey. He knew he couldn't let Grizz inside until he'd sent Casey away.

When he arrived back in Ginny's room, Casey looked relieved, stepping aside as a nurse began to take Ginny's vitals again.

"They're getting her ready for surgery," she whispered to Tommy as she opened the door to leave. "They need to do a C-section. The doctor said the baby's monitor is registering fetal distress. You got back just in time."

Right then, Ginny grabbed Tommy's hand, squeezing hard. "It's the baby, Tommy! The baby's in danger." She choked back a sob. "I want Grizz. Oh God, I want Grizz, Tommy. How could this be happening? How could I be having our baby without him?"

He didn't know what to say. He took her hand and brought it to his lips, softly kissing it. He had tears in his eyes and was ready to tell her Grizz was here when she let out another scream so loud it scared him. Pain was all over her face. He wondered if it was even close to the pain in his heart.

Another nurse slipped into the room and then a third. "We need to get her into surgery now," one of them told Tommy, her brown eyes full of sympathy and concern. "The delivery team is waiting. You'll need to put scrubs on before you can come in. I'll show you where they are."

The other nurses started to wheel Ginny out. She was quiet now, her breaths coming in great heaving gulps that were somehow worse than the screams.

Tommy followed them out and watched as they took Ginny down the hall and into another room. Then he backtracked to the stairwell for Grizz and directed him to the right door.

Tommy rejoined Ginny's friends in the waiting area. "She's been taken in for the C-section. They told me I have to wait out here."

In the room, Ginny was terrified. Where was Tommy? Why couldn't Grizz be there? Was the baby okay?

"Mrs. Dillon, we're going to put this over your mouth and nose and ask you to count backward from a hundred," a nurse with a distinct Boston accent told her firmly but not unkindly. "Okay? When you wake up, you'll have a baby."

Ginny nodded slightly as she tried to catch sight of Tommy in her peripheral vision. Where was he? Didn't he tell her he was coming in here with her?

They had just placed the mask over her face when there was a commotion in the delivery room.

"Who are you?" She heard someone ask.

"I'm her husband."

Grizz. It sounded like Grizz! She shook herself through the pain; she knew she was imagining Grizz's voice. There was more conversation, but it was muddled and she couldn't make sense of it. She thought she heard the doctor say, "You need to get scrubs on. I'm performing a surgery."

The nurse with the Boston accent piped up, "We don't have any big enough to fit him, doctor."

She didn't hear the rest. She was fading. The drugs were already in her system and working fast. Right before she closed her eyes, she looked up and met bright green ones. His eyes. Her Grizz.

"I'm here, Kitten," he said, smiling down at her. "I'm here, baby."

She slipped from consciousness and dreamed the best dream her subconscious could muster: that Grizz had been there with her for the birth of their child.

# Chapter Thirty-Eight

2000

TOMMY AND GINNY had a good marriage. More than just good. He could honestly say he was beyond happy.

At least until this morning and the phone call from Leslie that unraveled everything.

He'd been certain Grizz's death would finally put an end to the past. He didn't feel good about the execution. He even felt remorse. But when Grizz was pronounced dead, Tommy couldn't help but admit to himself he felt a tremendous weight being lifted. Like he'd been holding his breath for twenty-five years and was finally, finally able to let it go and take in a good, healthy dose of air. To have a fresh start.

His mind started to wander again as he steered the motorcycle down Sunrise Boulevard toward the ocean, Jason clinging tightly to his waist. Happy memories invaded his thoughts. He smiled as he thought about Jason's first nickname. Ed.

Jason was about six months old. Both he and Mimi were fast asleep and Tommy was in bed with Ginny. He had kissed his way down Ginny's body and was enjoying the taste of her. She'd grabbed his hair and moaned wildly as he'd brought her to a quick orgasm.

"Now, Tommy!" she panted. "I don't think I can wait. I have to have you inside me now!"

Tommy grinned and crawled up to kiss her. He already had a full-blown erection and was only too happy to comply. He was just ready to plunge into her when they heard it—the unmistakable start of a baby's whimper.

Mid-thrust, they stopped, staring at each other.

"Oh, no." Ginny grimaced. "He's awake and he's going to wake up Mimi. I'll go check on him, see if I can get him back to sleep. He shouldn't be hungry. Maybe he needs a change."

Tommy blew out a sigh and rested his full weight on her, his face in her neck, already losing his erection.

"I'll do it," he said.

She couldn't help but smile. He sounded so deflated. It seemed like every time they were going to make love, Jason needed something.

"You check on him," she said in a coy voice, "and I promise to make it up to you when you get back." She sealed her words with a string of gentle kisses on his ear.

In a flash, he'd jumped off of her and headed to the nursery, not bothering to put on his pants.

She smiled again as she listened to him on the baby monitor. Apparently, Jason really needed to be changed.

"I know you can hear me, Gin. You really lucked out when you accepted my offer to check on him. He has taken a dump that would fill up a bucket. Damn, it's everywhere! Oh, no! He's not finished. There's more coming out. Oh, shit!"

Ginny giggled. She was picturing a completely naked Tommy dealing with an overloaded diaper and apparently more on the way. She knew she should go in and help, but quite honestly, she was enjoying listening to Tommy's commentary entirely too much to move.

"Okay, Ed, you're all cleaned up and ready to go back to sleep. Now be a good boy and let Daddy have some quality Mommy time, okay? I don't know why you seem to know every time Daddy wants to make love to Mommy. You've got some sort of built in radar, Ed."

Minutes later, Tommy was back in their bedroom, headed toward the bathroom. She was still smiling when she saw the look on his face. "I have to wash up, Gin. There was crap everywhere, and don't think I don't know you were in here enjoying that a little too much."

A few minutes later, he came out of the bathroom and gently straddled his wife.

"I do believe there was a promise to make it up to me," he said, smiling down at her.

His face got serious then as he gently caressed her cheek. He stared into her eyes. "Ginny, I love you so much. You have made me the happiest man in the world. When I was putting him back down I couldn't stop looking at him." He brought his lips gently to hers. "To think that our love is what created that baby."

He paused as she started to get tears in her eyes. "You're my soul mate, Ginny. You know I've loved you since I first laid eyes on you. Do you know that?"

She smiled through the tears. "Yes, Tommy, I know. You tell me all the time and I never get tired of hearing it."

He started kissing her in earnest then, and their lovemaking went from tender and sweet to passionate.

Later, wrapped in each other's arms and catching their breath, she leaned up on one elbow, looking down at him.

"I heard you in there before. When you were changing Jason. Why were you calling him Ed?" Her hand was on his chest, caressing it softly.

"That's his new nickname." He grinned, eyes still closed.

"His new nickname? Ed? How'd you come up with that?

"I think he has some kind of built in sensor or something." He cracked an eye. "Every time we want to make love and I get a boner, he screams."

She started laughing then. "You're right, it does seem like that. But why Ed? What does Ed have to do with it?"

"Ed. You know, E.D. It stands for Erection Detector."

They laughed until they made love again and then slept in each other's arms.

Tommy was brought back to the present as Jason tapped him on his shoulder and pointed. Tommy looked in the direction his son was pointing and nodded. Jason's favorite fast food restaurant. They had to eat; might as well make it there.

He made a quick right into the parking lot and stopped the motorcycle.

"Can you take me to Aunt Carter's house tomorrow, dad?" Jason asked when they'd sat down with their food.

"Why do you need to go to Carter's?" Tommy asked, taking a big bite of cheeseburger.

"Because you'll be at work and Mimi's never home." Jason shrugged and snagged a French fry. "I don't want to stay by myself."

Tommy hadn't thought of that. Ginny was a stay-at-home mother during the summers. She did some bookkeeping for a few small businesses, but she was always able to do it from home. What would Jason do all summer, or until Ginny came back? If she came back. Tommy frowned a moment, thinking.

"Your sister will just have to stay home with you when she's not working," Tommy finally said.

Mimi had a part time job at a local floral shop. Even though they didn't need the money, her parents insisted she work a few hours a week. They wanted her to have a taste of real life. A normal education. A part-time job. Regular friends. The kind of life that neither one of them had actually experienced when they were her age.

"She's gonna be mad." Jason's face darkened. "She likes to go to her friend's houses or the beach or something if she's not at work."

"Then she'll have to be mad," Tommy said, trying to keep the aggravated tone out of his voice.

As it was, it was going to be hard enough for him to go into work tomorrow given everything that had happened. He should've taken the week off and he wished he had. What was the matter with him? Did he honestly think he could sit there with Ginny and watch Grizz die on a Friday and go back to work on Monday? What was he thinking?

Or more importantly, why wasn't he thinking?

Maybe he'd call one of his partners when he got home, tell them he needed some time off. He could even do some of his work from home. It wouldn't be a problem.

His thoughts were interrupted when Jason blurted, "Hey, the girl who just went by on the motorcycle looks just like Mimi!"

Tommy looked where Jason was pointing out the window, but he didn't see a motorcycle. Just a long line of cars on a sunny afternoon at the beach.

"You didn't look quick enough," Jason said as he slurped his drink. "She's gone."

# Chapter Thirty-Nine
2000

GINNY SPENT THE next day at Carter's helping feed and care for
Carter's menagerie of animals. She should have been tired; they'd
stayed up all night talking. But for some reason, she wasn't. Her mind
was racing with a million thoughts.

Tommy had called earlier, told her he was taking a week off from
work to take care of Jason and hoped she wouldn't be gone that long,
that he missed her. She told him she was sorry she hadn't thought
about Jason. She had a stab of guilt but quickly reminded herself she
subconsciously knew Tommy would somehow handle it. And, of
course, he had. In typical Tommy fashion, he'd told her not to worry.
He was taking care of it, but she needed to give him some time soon
so they could talk. She promised she would.

Carter and Casey had offered to let Jason stay there with them,
telling her she could go home and have as much time with Tommy as
she needed. But she wasn't sure she wanted to even see Tommy right
now, let alone be under the same roof together. It was all still too raw.

Mimi was a different matter. She was fifteen and would definitely
require an explanation. In spite of the fact that Mimi was spending
most of her free time with her friends, she was an intelligent and
observant teenager. She would notice that her mother was gone.
Ginny would have to talk to Tommy about what to tell Mimi.

Ginny was grateful there was so much to do at Carter's. Keeping
busy was exactly what she needed. She spent the afternoon hauling
food bags and brushing dogs, and was pleasantly sore by the time the
afternoon wore away.

That evening, the three friends worked in companionable silence
making shrimp stir-fry. They were exhausted so tonight's agenda was
simple. Dinner, clean up, and bed.

Casey's voice broke the silence. "So, Gin, did Tommy ever tell you
the details about your prom date?"

Ginny stopped cutting vegetables and looked over at Casey. "The
prom date? You mean the prom date Grizz took me on?"

Carter and Casey glanced at each other, then at Ginny. She didn't know.

"When they took you in for your emergency C-section with Mimi, we spent our time in the waiting room trying to keep Tommy's mind off of you," Carter chimed in. "They didn't let him in there with you. He practically wore a hole in the carpet with all of his pacing. We just kept talking to him to try to distract him. I don't remember how it came up. Maybe Sarah Jo said something. I mean, she was in on it."

"I know Sarah Jo was in on it." Ginny shrugged, starting to slice into an onion. "She helped Grizz set it up."

"No, Ginny." Casey took a breath. "It wasn't Grizz who asked Sarah Jo to set it up."

Ginny stopped what she was doing and turned around to look at her friends. With her back against the counter, she cocked her head. "Who had Sarah Jo set it up?"

In unison they both answered her: "Tommy."

"Tommy and Sarah Jo told us everything in the hospital waiting room," Carter told her.

"Yeah, it sounded like he planned it down to the last detail," Casey added.

Ginny stared at her friends as they took turns filling in the details about her prom night.

**********

"So how did you convince Grizz to let you do this?" Sarah Jo asked Grunt as they sat across from each other at the restaurant.

"I just told him that it was an important part of every girl's high school years and since Kit wouldn't have that experience, maybe you and I could do something to make up for it." Grunt shrugged. "Of course, I told him it was *your* idea. Besides, he trusts me now. I have a girlfriend."

Sarah Jo took a sip of her water and rolled her eyes. "Yeah, I know you have a girlfriend."

"No, really, it's perfect. Between school and work, I rarely get to see Kit. Now that I'm living with Cindy, Grizz doesn't seem to mind when I spend time with her." He looked directly at Jo. "Let's talk about more important things. You're all set for tomorrow, right? You know what to do?"

"Of course I know what to do." Jo stuck her tongue out at him. "Kit already said she'd go with me to pick out a dress. I'll tell her I don't want to try on gowns by myself and I'd feel better if she tried some on, too. She'll do it. She's a girly girl."

"And?"

"And," Sarah Jo rolled her eyes again, "when she tries on one that she really loves, I'll make sure someone puts it away. I'll tell them that you'll be in to pay for it later."

"Perfect." Grunt folded his hands. "And?"

"And I'll make sure she spends the actual prom day with me getting my makeup, nails and hair done. I'll insist that I don't feel right getting all gussied up for prom if she's not. I'll tell her I'm treating her as a thank you for spending the day with me." Sarah Jo picked up her sandwich. "Now how about you? It's less than a month away. Are you all set?"

"Everything's a go. Martin never uses the house and it's perfect."

"What's it like?"

"It's right on the beach. He has a gazebo with stereo speakers and everything. Moe's going to spend the day helping me set up."

"You know, Grunt, I'm not really sure you should be doing this. You might be sending the wrong message. You might confuse her."

"Jo, I'm doing what you suggested three years ago. I'm waiting. And don't think it hasn't been hell on me not seeing her as much as I've wanted to." He clenched his jaw. "Grizz will screw up soon enough and I'll be there, but in the meantime, it's really important to me that she doesn't miss out on certain things."

"Like going to the prom," Sarah Jo said quietly.

"Yeah, like going to the prom. She can't go to a real prom. You know that. This is the only thing I could think of."

Sarah Jo smiled at her childhood friend. "It's the most romantic thing I've ever heard."

"So are *you* getting excited? It's your senior year. It'll be the last prom for you and Stephen."

"Yeah, I'm excited, but worried."

"What are you worried about?" Grunt signaled for the check.

"That new girl, April. I think Stephen might actually like her."

**********

"It was Tommy?" Ginny asked. Slowly she walked to one of the kitchen chairs, sitting down heavily.

Carter took the one next to her, her voice quiet. "Yes, it was all Tommy's doing. I can't believe he never told you. He probably wouldn't let Sarah Jo tell you either. You believed it was Grizz's idea, and Tommy didn't want to hurt you by telling you it wasn't. Yes, Grizz allowed it, but he didn't come up with it. Tommy did."

Ginny remembered that night. She'd spent the entire day with Sarah Jo getting their makeup, hair, and nails done. She'd watched as her friend posed for pictures with Stephen and waved goodbye to them as they left in Stephen's father's fancy car. Fess had asked her to stay to help him with some bank statements or something. She couldn't remember what she helped him with, but it didn't matter. The whole thing had been a ruse.

After about thirty minutes, the phone had rung. It was Sarah Jo, frantic. Said she forgot her little purse with all her makeup. Would Kit mind driving it to her friend's house on the beach? There was a pre-prom party there. Kit got the directions from her and headed that way.

She remembered being surprised when she arrived at the impressive house and saw one of Grizz's motorcycles in the driveway. It was Grizz's, wasn't it? And where were all the cars? She thought there was supposed to be a party here.

She went to the front door and noticed a note taped to it. It said to come around the right side of the house. She let herself through an unlocked gate and made her way along the path. When she got to the back yard, she stopped short.

Before her eyes was a gigantic pool with a gazebo on the other side. The gazebo was decorated with white twinkling lights. As she approached, she could hear the ocean, and its salty aroma filled her nostrils. She heard Van Morrison singing "Into the Mystic" but couldn't figure out where it was coming from.

That's when she saw him. Grizz.

He came out of the shadows and walked down the gazebo steps. He was wearing his usual outfit: Jeans, a T-shirt, and boots, his long hair held back in a ponytail. He had recently started growing a beard, something she wasn't exactly sure she liked, but she had to admit that it suited him. She watched him approach, her heart beginning to pound in anticipation. What was going on?

He took her hand and led her back up the stairs. She noticed a coral-colored gown hanging from one of the low beams. She stared at it in amazement. Wasn't that the gown she had tried on a few weeks ago when she was shopping with Sarah Jo? It wasn't as elegant as the one Jo picked out—understated and very simple. Her high-heeled sandals rested on a bench next to the dress, along with a beautiful wrist corsage made of tiny white roses and baby's breath.

She looked down at her fingernails and toes, smiling now as it all sank in. Sarah Jo had insisted on the color. Now she knew why. They matched her dress.

"Grizz?" She said, waiting for the explanation.

Grizz suddenly looked shy. "Thought you might like a romantic night with me on the beach. I know Jo has her dance tonight. I—I didn't want you to feel left out."

He didn't look away from her as he took the dress down from the beam, handing it to her. "I would really love to see you in this, Kitten," he murmured, pulling her into his arms.

They'd spent the night slow dancing, making love on the beach and just talking. The house belonged to a friend of his, Martin. She remembered fantasizing that it was their home. They even got to sleep there. It was one of the most romantic nights she'd ever had.

And now, she thought, looking at her friends incredulously, she was being told it was all Tommy's idea?

Ginny bit her lip. "*Tommy* set up a romantic night on the beach for me and Grizz? Why would he do that?"

"Actually, Gin, he set it up for you and *him*," Casey said softly. "To look like an after-prom party. Tommy had been there all day, waiting for you. Grizz showed up fifteen minutes before you did. Told Tommy he thought you would be disappointed if he wasn't there. He didn't want to let you down or hurt you. He told Tommy that he would take over." She took Ginny's hand and gave her a gentle look. "He sent Tommy, Sarah Jo, and the few friends that were there back home."

**\*\*\*\*\*\*\*\*\***

*Moe's Diary, 1978*

*Dear Elizabeth,*

*I know it was a mean thing to do, but I couldn't help it. I did it before I could stop myself. I was just so jealous.*

*I'm his friend. It seems like he's forgotten about me. Unless he needs something. Like help setting up a romantic date for someone else. For* her.

*I want to hate her, but I don't. She's nice to me. And besides, she's with Grizz. I never see her act like she wants to be with Grunt. But, still. I couldn't stand the thought of him holding her while they danced. The dress was so pretty. I used to wear pretty things like that. You remember, don't you, Elizabeth?*

*Grizz was okay with letting them have their dance. But I had to ruin it. I had to write him a note telling him Kit would really be hurt and disappointed if he wasn't there.*

*He gives Kit whatever she wants. He couldn't stand how the thought of him not being there could hurt her. He hates stuff like that, dancing and dressing up, but he would do it for her. They all seem to do everything for her. Kit, Kit, Kit.*

*Sometimes, I wish she would just leave. Go back to wherever Monster found her.*

# Chapter Forty
2000

BEHIND CARTER'S HOUSE, Ginny leaned against the deck railing and inhaled deeply. Did she smell orange blossoms or jasmine or both? Memories invaded her senses. For a moment, she felt dizzy.

Ginny couldn't believe what her friends had told her. Why hadn't Tommy and Sarah Jo ever mentioned it? More secrets. It was like her life had been built on one big lie. She didn't know what to believe anymore. Or who to believe.

She looked around, trying to breathe, to center herself, and her eyes fell upon the garage. She hadn't stepped foot in that garage in fifteen years. It was a large, three-car unit, separate from the house, with a small guest room on the second floor.

She slowly walked toward it, remembering the bad times along with the good. When she reached the side door under the guest stairs, she knelt and lifted a ceramic frog. The keys were still there. Just as Carter had promised, the garage had never been used. That was one of the only conditions Grizz had insisted on when Ginny told him that Carter would be living there. No one in the garage. Ever.

Ginny had a little trouble with the dead bolt. It obviously hadn't been opened in years. She went inside and flicked on the light. She expected the air inside to smell bad, but she was surprised that it didn't. It was just a little stale.

She stared at the two automobiles covered with big cloth tarps. She knew under each cover was a black vehicle—his and hers. Grizz bought a new black Corvette every year. He tried to buy her a new car, too, every year, but she wouldn't let him. She loved her birthday Trans Am. She wondered if it would now be considered vintage.

She walked past to the three motorcycles lined up in a neat row. She noticed one with a blue bandana hanging on the handlebar. It had been Grizz's favorite bike. The one he had taken her on for her first ride with him. She approached it now and took the bandana off the handlebar. Her hands shook slightly, but she paid them no mind. Holding the bandana gently, she sat on the hard garage floor, lifting the cloth to her face. Could she still smell him?

No, she couldn't. It had been too long.

After a few minutes, she noticed the back wheel of her Trans Am peeking out beneath the cover. She frowned, remembering what it felt like to be inside the car, the smell of the seats and feel of the motor rumbling beneath her. She narrowed her eyes, inspecting the wheel cap. *That* wheel cap.

They'd been married for a couple of years. She didn't remember why they were in her car. Maybe his was in the shop at the time. He was driving and she reminded him that she needed a part.

"Did you remember to ask Axel about my wheel cap?" she asked as they navigated the mall parking lot.

"He didn't get it for you yet?" Grizz raised his eyebrows.

"No, it's just a stupid little cap. I don't know if it fell off or if someone stole it. I don't know why someone would steal it, but my tire looks funny without it. Will you remind him?"

Grizz began to gaze out over the parking lot, like he was assessing the cars, driving slowly. He gassed it suddenly, then took a quick right that was so sharp she grabbed her door handle.

"What the—?"

"Looks like it might be the same year," he said to himself as he jammed the car in park. He reached into the console and took out a screwdriver. Before she could say anything, he was out of the car and walking away.

She turned around in her seat and saw him approach a car that looked similar to hers, then disappear. Two minutes later, he reappeared and jumped into the driver's seat. He tossed the screwdriver and newly acquired wheel cap into her lap and drove off.

Her mouth hung open as she looked over at him. He had a smug little smile on his face.

"Grizz!" She moved her sunglasses on top of her head so she could look him in the eye. "Did you just steal this wheel cap from someone else's car?"

He glanced over at her. "Of course I did. Where do you think I got it from?"

"Why did you have to steal it?" Her temper flared. "Axel could've gotten me one. I can't believe you just stole it!"

He rolled his eyes. "Kit, you were complaining that you needed one. I saw an opportunity to handle it and I did. Now you don't have to remind Axel. What's the big deal?"

"The big deal is that you stole it." She crossed her arms. "I don't know, Grizz. I don't think I can drive my car knowing you stole the wheel cap. It would bother me."

He looked at her then and she immediately knew what he was thinking. She could read his face like a book.

"Oh no, Grizz." She shook her head. "No way. Don't even tell me my car is stolen. Please don't tell me that, Grizz."

"Then I won't tell you," he answered her matter-of-factly.

She jutted her chin and stared out over the dashboard, refusing to look at him. Already her face was getting flushed. She was mad.

He'd confessed later how he loved when she got mad, even if it was at him. He told her the truth, how he would never let her drive around in a stolen car. He had made the purchase legitimately, but sometimes he liked riling her up. And right then she was exactly that: riled up.

"I just don't know who you think you are taking things that don't belong to you!" Her chest began to flush. "I mean, really, Grizz! I suppose you think that whatever's out there is yours for the taking."

He didn't answer her.

"Answer me. You think you can just take whatever you want?"

He looked over at her and smiled. "I took you, Kitten."

Sitting on the garage floor, she stared at the wheel cap now and struggled with the memory of how immature she had been. How enraged she had become over a stolen wheel cap yet she'd been willing to ignore the knowledge of the other awful things he did. Her love for Grizz made her compromise her values. Who had she been back then? Who was she now?

Clutching the blue bandana to her chest like a security blanket, she realized she was crying. Sniffling loudly, she used the bandana to wipe her tears. *Get it together, Gin.* Then she stared at the bandana.

The blue bandana. She had forgotten about the bandana.

# Chapter Forty-One
1985

"I CAN'T, GRIZZ! I can't do it without you. I don't want to!"

Kit had been visiting him in the county jail. She was about six months pregnant with Mimi and the counter behind the glass petition dividing them jutted uncomfortably against her ripe belly.

"Kitten, you can't do what?" he'd asked her through the glass partition, his face a mask of concern. "What can't you do without me?"

Damn, he wanted to touch her skin. Just one gentle caress of her cheek. He wanted to wipe away her tears.

"Anything, Grizz." She was sobbing heavily now. "I don't want to do anything without you. I don't want to have our baby without you. I don't want to fall asleep at night without you." She stopped herself and took a deep breath. "I don't feel safe without you, Grizz. I'm not used to you not being there."

"You have Grunt, Kit. Grunt will be there for you. He would protect you with his life. You know that, don't you?"

"I don't care!" Her eyes flashed. "He's not you, Grizz! Yes, he is wonderful, and I know his feelings are hurt because I've refused to move out of our home or let him live there with me. I'm just not ready to leave it, to be with him." She shook her head, tried to make him understand. "There is too much of 'us' in that home, Grizz, and I just can't leave it. Not yet. You may have moved on from me already, but I cannot imagine a day when I will be over you."

"Oh fuck, honey. Is that what you think? That I've moved on from you?" He never once thought that she would see his insistence that she marry Grunt as rejection. He thought he was protecting her and he assumed she knew that. He'd never been good about expressing his feelings. Even with Kit. Not to mention he'd never been used to telling anyone his reasons for doing the things he did.

"What am I supposed to think?" She'd started to hiccup.

"Kit, is that the life you want? Packing up our baby and bringing it to visit its father in jail every weekend? Is that the life you want for you and our child?"

"If I knew you were going to get out of this place, yes! But you don't even seem like you want to. You seem so resolved that you're going to trial, that a jury will convict you, and I don't know who this Carey Lewis is that Matthew recommended, but I'm sorry I ever suggested Matthew." Her voice started rising again, and she willed herself to tamp down her emotions, to breathe.

Grizz leaned back in his chair and sighed. He felt bad that she thought he was still here because of her suggestion to use Matthew Rockman. And that Rockman had somehow failed them by suggesting Carey Lewis. He'd played dumb that day when he was arrested. He knew that she would suggest her old friend Matthew and he'd gone along with it to appease her. He'd never had any intention of letting Rockman represent him and had put a plan in place long before, in the event that it ever came to this.

He signaled for a guard and when the guard walked over, Grizz whispered something in his ear. The guard nodded.

She was blowing her nose when the guard let himself out of the holding area and approached her.

"Please come with me, miss," the guard said quietly but firmly.

She looked at Grizz and he nodded at her. This? This was it? *This* was his way of saying goodbye? She couldn't believe it. Emotions swirled as she allowed the guard to gently take her by the elbow, leading her out of the room.

She looked back at Grizz and couldn't read his expression. She started sobbing uncontrollably then and didn't even notice that she was brought into a room with no windows. A small table with two chairs was in it. The guard guided her to one of the chairs and left the room. He quickly returned with a box of tissues. She was blowing her nose when she heard him say on his way out, "Five minutes. Five minutes or I lose my job."

She bolted upright. And saw Grizz coming into the room.

Suddenly she jumped up and threw herself into his arms. He held her tightly and walked her to the chair. He sat down and pulled her down onto his lap. Then, placing his hand on her stomach, he looked into her eyes.

"Kitten, listen to me."

She started crying again and wrapped her arms around his neck like a child. He let her sit there like that as he breathed in her scent. Mentally kicking his own ass for letting it go this far. For not making a deal with them sooner.

But even if he'd made a deal, there would've been no guarantees. There still weren't, but he was convinced he was doing what was best for her. For their child. When she seemed to calm down, he gently removed her arms from around his neck and pulled back so he could look straight at her.

He'd been beaten as a child. He'd been shot and stabbed. He'd had bones broken. He'd even been tortured. Nothing. Absolutely nothing compared to the pain he felt as he gazed into her chocolate eyes. He felt as if his heart had been ripped from his chest.

"Kitten, I don't need to tell you the things I've done." She started to interrupt him, but he held up a hand. "No, listen to me, Kit. I am getting what I deserve. Do you understand me? You don't deserve it. You need to have the life you would've had, could've had, if I didn't kidnap you. I was selfish. I took what I wanted."

"What life would I have had?" She sniffled. "Being Delia and Vince's housemaid?"

"Stop acting naïve. We both know you're not. You're smart. You would've gone to college on a scholarship and moved as far away as possible from them. Don't act like I saved you."

"But you did," she whispered. "I was meant to be with you."

He didn't say anything and something in her expression changed. Her eyes narrowed, like she finally understood. She awkwardly got off his lap and stood in front of him. She rested her hands on her pregnant stomach. With swollen eyes and a red nose, she added, "And we both know how smart you are too, Grizz."

He looked away from her.

"You're too smart to get caught like this." She took a ragged breath. "What is it you aren't telling me? Oh, wait, your name? Yeah, that was the big secret forever." Her voice dripped with sarcasm.

"That cat's been let out of the bag. I think I've earned your trust by now, don't you? Don't I deserve some truth about *anything*?"

He stood then, grabbed her and pulled her to him, and she let him. She wrapped her arms tightly around his waist. With a shuddering breath, he took her face in his hands and looked deep into her eyes.

"The only truth you ever need to know is that my love for you is real and will never go away. And everything I've done, no matter how it looks, is so you could be protected. I never wanted to be without you, but it's not my choice now."

Before she could respond, the door flew open and the guard reappeared. "Time's up. Gotta go now."

"Wait." She grabbed both of his wrists and held his hands to her face.

"Kitten." He gave her a serious look. "If you ever need anything. If you are ever in trouble. If you are ever scared—you know that Grunt will be there."

She started to cry again. "But what if he's not, Grizz? I married him, but what if I can never accept him? What if it's just me and the baby? I'm so confused, I just don't know what—"

"Kit, my bike," Grizz whispered into her ear. "My favorite bike in our garage. I keep my blue bandana on it. You know the one, right?"

She nodded.

"If you ever need anything. I mean fucking anything, and Grunt can't be there for you, you put your hair up in one of those high ponytails you like to wear and you wrap my bandana around it. You hear me? You wear my bandana, and it might take a day or two, but you'll get whatever help you need. You understand me?"

She looked at him quizzically, tried to fathom how a blue bandana in the garage was going to help her if she ever needed him.

Before the guard escorted him out, Grizz called out, "Kitten, have you picked out any names yet? Do you know what you want to name the baby?"

"Jason if it's a boy. Miriam if it's a girl."

He raised a questioning eyebrow.

"It was Moe's name."

His expression softened and he gave a quick nod. "Ruth. What about Miriam Ruth?"

"You like the name Ruth? Is it from someone you know?" Her voice sounded hopeful, like she was desperate for one more nugget of truth from his past.

But he merely smiled. "No. I just like it. Better than Miriam Guinevere."

Kit mulled the name and decided she liked it too. "Ruth is biblical. Miriam is, too, but Ruth was an amazing woman. Amazing enough to have her own book in the Bible. If it's a girl, we'll name her Miriam Ruth," she promised.

He kissed her gently on the lips and was gone.

**********

Now, in the garage, she cried and cried as she held the bandana, remembering the way it had looked on him. She'd never had to wear the blue bandana over the years, but she remembered lying in bed late at night and finding comfort in knowing it was out there on his bike. Out there, just in case she ever needed it.

In the jail house visits that followed, her questions to him still went unanswered. And eventually, she mused, she did make the slow transition into a life with Tommy. A life she now cherished. As the old saying goes, life goes on. Time heals.

At least up until yesterday.

She cried harder now into the bandana. And when it couldn't hold any more tears, she clutched it to her chest, laid down on the cold cement, and fell asleep.

# Chapter Forty-Two
## 1950s, Fort Lauderdale, Florida

HE'D TURNED THE motel upside down looking for that bag of money. It'd been weeks since Red and his shitty friends had left and Ralph was convinced by now that there was no money. Whoever the guy was that Red was looking for never stopped here.

He had just come back to number four to have some lunch. Sitting down on the couch with a sandwich, he stared at the TV. It wasn't on, but he stared hard, trying to think of some of the recent television shows he'd been watching. There were some clever ones about spies and crime-solving. Where would someone on one of those shows hide a bag of money?

Taking another bite of his sandwich, he washed it down with some soda pop. He was running low. He hoped a guest would be stopping by soon, maybe someone he could hitch a ride from to go get groceries. He'd take a taxi back if he had to. He'd done it once and it didn't cost too much.

The table next to the television caught his eye. Pop's dogs, Jack and Sandy. Their images were protected forever in those frames. He'd wished he'd thought to put Ruthie and Razor's picture in a frame, but he'd preferred having it with him, so he could pull it out when he needed to. He hated himself for being so careless with that photo.

What was the last dog's name? The one Pop didn't have a picture of? He couldn't think of it. He just remembered the dog had died recently because the grave was obviously newer than the others. He sat back and gazed at the blank television again. He didn't have time to think about Pop's dogs. He had to think like a mastermind. Like the ones he saw on TV. Especially that spy guy. If Pop got his hands on that money, what would he have done with it?

There wasn't much else to do at the motel other than general maintenance. He didn't have to wait on Pop hand and foot anymore, so his days weren't as busy. Some days, he pretended he was someone important, like Red. He could be like Red. Like one of those guys on TV. Was Red undercover? He must've been. The person on the other end of the phone called him "agent."

Lost in a fantasy of beautiful women and fast cars, he suddenly sat straight up on the couch and dropped his soda bottle, the liquid fizzing out on the carpet floor.

He knew where the money was.

By the time he lugged the bag back to the motel, he was panting and filthy. The bag was big and heavy, and it was right where he'd thought. The dog's grave. Only there was no dog.

He couldn't imagine how Pop, in his frail condition, had ever gotten it out there and buried it. As he was digging, he started having doubts. A stab of conscience told him he'd feel awful if he was digging up Pop's dog. Benny. He remembered the name now. That was the last dog that Pop didn't have a picture of. Pop had told him he had a frame for it and everything, but never got around to having a picture taken to put in the frame.

Except when he'd searched the motel from top to bottom looking for the hidden bag, he'd never run across an empty frame. Pop must've lied about it. Still, it could've been true. The frame could've been broken and thrown away. The frame would've been a reminder of the picture that was never taken and maybe Pop had tossed it. Ralph didn't think so.

And he was right.

Now, he spread an old motel sheet across the bed and heaved the heavy bag up on to it. He unzipped it and his breath caught as he gazed upon its contents. There was more money in this bag than he'd ever imagined existed, even in a bank vault. He picked up a neatly bound stack of bills and fanned them.

Then he remembered something. The man on the phone that night said he didn't care about the money. He wanted the bag. Why would he want a crummy old army bag? There must be something else here.

He climbed up on the bed and managed to grab the bag by the bottom, heaving it upside down on the sheet. The money spilled out, some even sliding off the bed and hitting the floor. He shook the bag, making sure it was empty. He didn't see anything fall out with the money. But the bag still felt a little heavy. He jumped down off the bed and stuck his arms in the bag, feeling around. His elbow made contact with something hard and he realized something had been sewn into the lining of the bag.

Quickly, he retrieved a knife from the kitchen and carefully slit open the interior. He reached in and pulled out two heavy metal plates of some kind. He laid them on the bed and knew immediately what he was looking at. This money was counterfeit and these were the plates that were used to make it. Big deal.

He was disappointed. What was he going to do with a bunch of fake money? He couldn't spend it because he'd probably get caught. It would be traced back to the motel and then they'd start looking for Pop. Dammit.

Maybe he should get a phone number for The Red Crab and call Red. Tell him to come get his fake money. He felt totally deflated now; the excitement of seeking and the anticipation of finding the bag was gone. He'd never realized how good the hunt had made him feel. He couldn't explain it; he got a thrill from pretending he was some kind of agent, like Red. Looking for something more important than a big bag of money.

That's what the man had said. He didn't care about the money. Who didn't care about money? He'd remembered how important money was when he was roaming Fort Lauderdale and eating out of garbage cans.

He was sitting on the edge of the bed, wondering what he should do, when something caught his attention. He squinted, looking closer. His eyes weren't lying—something brown was sticking out of the seam he'd ripped when he'd found the plates. Reaching in, he removed a large, oversized envelope. He opened the envelope and pulled out its contents. Some pictures fell out onto his lap. He quickly scanned them, and since he didn't recognize any faces or the names on the back, he turned to the papers he was holding. It was a large document, several pages long. He started to read.

He was young and didn't have a lot of education. But he was smart enough to know what he was reading was important. More important than a bag of counterfeit money. Some names he recognized. Others he didn't. There were specific dates, places, and events. Was he reading this correctly? How could this be?

This was big; he knew it. This kind of information could destroy people. Destroy lives. Maybe it already had.

Pop must have killed the bag's owner. The insurance salesman. He obviously wasn't an insurance salesman. Was he an agent like Red?

He didn't know the extent of what he had read, but he thought he knew someone who might.

Over the next week, he did what was necessary to close the motel. He burned the counterfeit money in the pit—that's what he named the spot where Red and his guys started the fire that first night. He hid the plates and envelope somewhere he was certain they'd never be found. He would relocate them later, but he would need time to plan that. He rummaged up some old chain and crafted a sign that said "closed for renovation," draping it across the motel entrance. He drained the pool and called the telephone company to cancel the phone. He did the same with the water and power companies. He didn't have to worry about the gas pumps. Pop had told him they hadn't been used in years.

He'd already gone through Pop's personal papers. Pop's real name was Gainy J. Talbot. He took Pop's checkbook and some tax documents he might need in the future, plus the deed to the motel and the title to Pop's car. He'd leave the car here. He burned all of Pop's other personal belongings, including some old army pictures and discharge papers. He paused when he came across a document he hadn't noticed before.

It was a birth certificate. The birth date wasn't close to his—Pop's son was older than him—but it would still work. He would save this.

Jason William Talbot was as good a name as any. Besides, he hated the name Ralph.

He packed up everything he could carry and started walking toward the city. He was going to take Red up on that job offer.

# Chapter Forty-Three
2000

CASEY FOUND GINNY asleep in the garage. She gently woke her up and guided her back to the house.

"You should go lock up," Casey told Carter, nodding in the direction of the garage. She turned to Ginny. "We saved you a plate."

"Thanks, but I'm not hungry." Ginny's voice was weary as she padded across the kitchen and made her way to her room. "I'm going to try to get some sleep."

But ten minutes later, Ginny came out of the bedroom with her nightshirt on. She found her friends in the kitchen at the stove, talking quietly.

"I want to go to sleep, but I think my little nap just gave me some unwanted energy." Ginny gave a half-smile and her friends turned to embrace her.

"I thought that might happen," Carter answered soothingly. "That's why I'm making some herbal tea. It should relax you."

"I hope so. I can't stand the thought of being up all night alone with my thoughts."

Carter and Casey exchanged a knowing glance. "Wait for me in the den," Carter said. "I'll bring it in."

Casey and Ginny went into the den and settled themselves into their favorite spots. Carter showed up a minute later with a tray holding three mugs. Steam rose from each one. They sipped their tea in comfortable silence. Finally, Ginny let out a loud yawn.

"Gee, guess I'm more tired than I thought." She looked at her friends' expressions and a memory shook her from twenty-five years ago. A memory just like this. Except this time, she was grateful. This time, an adrenaline high didn't kick in.

She looked at Carter and then at Casey, her words slurring. "You drugged me. I think I should say thank you."

\*\*\*\*\*\*\*\*\*\*

Ginny was dreaming. She was in Grizz's arms. He was holding her. She had her back to him and one of his heavy arms was draped around her waist.

But something was wrong. It was Grizz's arm, but it wasn't Grizz. A familiar scent invaded her senses, brought her out of her deep sleep. Tommy? Why did Grizz smell like Tommy?

She opened her eyes and needed a minute to get her bearings. Carter's guest room. She was in one of Carter's guest rooms. It was the room she had set up to be a nursery for Mimi.

She looked down at the arm wrapped around her. She could see the tattoo clearly. The dangling ribbons that said "Mimi" and "Jason". She knew they were connected to an eagle holding up a heart between its wings. A heart with her name in it.

Tommy. Tommy was in bed with her and holding her.

She turned slightly and saw he was awake. Before she could ask, he murmured, "It wasn't my idea. It was Carter and Casey."

She turned now to face him, filled with unspoken questions.

"They called me last night and told me what they did," Tommy explained quietly. "They knew your power nap in the garage would keep you up all night. You were asleep on the couch when I got here. They went to our house to watch Jason and Mimi. I'm sure the kids will be thrilled to have them there and won't even ask about us. I carried you in from the couch."

She didn't know what to say. She just stared at him, a small smile playing on her lips. He breathed a sigh of relief.

But then her smile faded as she remembered the reason she was at Carter's in the first place.

Her lips pressed together in a thin line. "Coffee," was all she said.

Tommy nodded in agreement. "Uh, they told me you would know what to do with the animals."

"Yeah, I know what to do. I can't believe Victor didn't wake us up at sunrise."

"You mean the rooster?"

"Yeah, he crows like clockwork." She started to get up in a panic. "Oh no, what if something is wrong with him!"

"Don't worry, Ginny. He's okay. He crowed this morning. You just slept through it."

"And you've been awake ever since?"

He didn't answer her. "Your eyes." He peered at her in concern. "What's wrong with your eyes?"

She felt her face, knew they were puffy and raw. "I guess it's from all the crying."

He nodded in understanding. "How about I start the coffee, you get a shower, and then we'll take care of Carter's zoo. Together."

"Okay." She didn't say anything else, but he knew what she was thinking.

"When everybody is settled and happy and fed, we'll talk."

"Yes, we'll talk. I think you have a lot to tell me."

"Yeah, Ginny." His face was serious, sad. "I have a lot to tell you."

He'd wanted to have this conversation in their home, but he wouldn't be able to. This was better than nothing.

A few hours later, chores done, Tommy and Ginny were sitting on the back porch, curled into Adirondack chairs. Ginny was sipping a cold iced tea and Tommy was drinking a big glass of water.

"Where do I even start?" he asked, looking over at his wife. She was wearing denim shorts, a tank top, and cowboy boots. Her hair was piled loosely on top of her head. They had chatted some while they worked together getting the animals fed and exercised. They cleaned out the horses' stalls and used the scooper to clean up where the dogs were allowed to roam in the yard. Tommy hosed down the dog kennels while Ginny administered medicines and vitamins to the different animals. Carter had more dogs than any other animals she fostered and had been very involved in helping to spearhead a prison program, where she and her colleagues went into the penitentiaries and taught some of the most undesirable convicts how to train abused and abandoned canines to be used as service dogs. It was an excellent program where man and beast alike were given a second chance at life through rehabilitation. Ginny and Tommy spent almost a full two hours caring for and playing with the dogs. Carter's animal sanctuary required a lot of work. It was hard work, but physically and mentally fulfilling.

Ginny wrapped her arms around her knees. "It wasn't Blue who killed your sister and her husband that night when you were a kid, was it?"

"Before I start, Ginny, you need to know I had a good talk with Grizz before his execution. I was going to tell you everything. When Leslie hinted there was something I wasn't telling you, it made it look like I was being forced to come clean. Ginny, I was going to do that anyway. I hope you believe that." His expression was sincere. She wanted to believe him.

But something held her back. Ginny realized she wasn't sure if she knew the real Tommy at all. If she'd ever known the real Tommy. She tried to think back over their fifteen-year marriage, but her mind was cluttered and she certainly wasn't going to give too much credence to a facial expression that she'd seen countless times before.

"Please just answer my question," she said quietly. "It wasn't Blue, was it?"

"No, it wasn't Blue."

Then he told her everything: the night Grizz came for him. Moving to the motel. Meeting the gang. His early life there.

"So Moe's gang name was Misty?" she interrupted. "I never once thought about where the nickname Moe came from."

"Yeah, she used to be Misty." He continued with his story.

When he got to the part about Curtis Armstrong, she sat straight up in her chair. "You were there? You saw me dump my lemonade on him?"

Yes, he was there. He was there for a lot of it. There when Mavis approached Grizz about getting some bras. There on the school field trip.

"Mavis?" she interrupted. "You knew Mavis?"

"Yes, Ginny. I knew Mavis. She worked for Grizz. She kept an eye out for you and let Grizz know if you needed anything. You must remember when the food showed up on your doorstep. Or the bicycle you probably thought the neighbors left for you? That was all because of Mavis."

"I haven't thought about Mavis in years," she told Tommy, her face softening. "I stopped running into her after I started going to middle school. I wonder what ever happened to her?"

"She died peacefully in her sleep. She didn't show up at The Red Crab for work one day. Mavis was the most punctual and reliable human being on the planet. Some of the regulars were really fond of her. One of the girls, I think it may even have been Chicky, went to her house after not getting an answer on the phone. She found her in her bed."

Ginny's eyes filled with tears. "She was so nice to me." A laugh escaped suddenly. "She really hated that Curtis Armstrong, though. She never allowed herself to stoop to his level, but she defended all the kids he bullied back then. Not just me."

"She used to say the same thing about you and all your causes. That you were the champion of the little guy." Tommy smiled at her. Then he added, "It's her chess set, by the way. The one I taught you to play on. The one that sits in our bedroom. That chess set belonged to Mavis and her husband. She's the one who suggested I learn to play."

Tears trickled down her cheeks. She didn't know why, but she was moved by the fact that she'd had a secret guardian angel all those years ago. Mavis. Impatiently, she brushed the tears away. She didn't want to start crying again. She wanted, needed, to be strong. She took a gulp of air and changed the subject.

"I knew Chicky was in love with Grizz, you know." Ginny felt a rush of sadness for the woman. "She told me that the day she came to spend with me at the beach over on the west coast. I never knew how she'd come into contact with Grizz, though. She told me she'd finally set her sights on Fess. I guess she never made any headway there. Of course, I'm sure Sarah Jo would've mentioned it if she had."

Sarah Jo never really talked about her father. Fess had retired to Maine years ago.

"Maybe that's why she ended up in South Carolina," Ginny pondered.

"Yeah. I can imagine her running her own bar in South Carolina. Chicky really was an okay lady."

Despite the heat, Ginny shivered a moment. "Grizz told me the day he married me about the first time he saw me. Told me how he'd had me watched. I never asked him any details. I doubt he would've answered them anyway. I just assumed Grizz sent someone to occasionally check up on me. Maybe that neighbor, Guido. I never realized he actually *planted* someone in my life. I never grasped how much he'd actually done for me during those years. I wish I knew some of this before. I can honestly say I would've liked to have thanked him."

She had been staring out over Carter's expansive yard as she said this. She looked over at Tommy. "I also never realized you had been there, too. That you saw me. How could I have never noticed?"

He smiled at her and she could see the love in his eyes. "You were the busiest girl I ever saw," he remembered. "You were always up to something. Involved in everything. Selling lemonade. Rescuing land crabs. Organizing protests. Selling those little potholders you made to try to raise money for some kind of charity you were involved in. When would you have even had the time to notice if you were being watched? Most of the time you were too busy taking care of your house. Your parents really took advantage of you, Gin."

He looked away then. "I heard what you told Leslie in the interview. You painted your mother as a barefoot, happy-go-lucky hippie who loved life and had a carefree and easy nature." He shook his head. "The truth is, you wore rose-colored glasses or your memory has conformed to what it wishes your life was with her. She was a conniving, manipulative bitch who treated you like shit. That's the truth, no matter how you may want to remember it."

This took Ginny aback, but if she was going to be honest—and she was the one who'd been telling Tommy it was time for the truth—he was right. Vince and Delia. She hadn't thought about them in years. She hadn't thought about them at all until a few months ago when Leslie asked her about her childhood.

She let all she'd heard sink in. It hit her then that Tommy could've just told her about Grizz being his father, held back on the other things. But he hadn't. He'd gone further, told her more. So much more. Grizz being Tommy's father was the only secret Leslie had alluded to. Leslie didn't know the other things. About Grizz's real childhood. About Delia knowing where she was all those years. Tommy didn't have to share those things, but he did.

Maybe he really had planned on telling her some things she didn't know. Maybe he was telling the truth.

She pursed her lips. So Delia knew where she was. Knew that Grizz took her. And didn't do a single thing about it. Why would this surprise her?

Actually, it didn't. It was typical Delia.

# Chapter Forty-Four
May 10, 1975
Five Days Before the Abduction

IT HAD BEEN a long day. Grizz leaned on the sink and studied his reflection in the mirror. He'd just shaved off his beard. The skin looked pale beneath it. He would give it a try.

Other than a little sunburn on his nose and forehead, he didn't look as tired as he felt. He'd just gotten back from the west coast of Florida and a meeting with his friend, Anthony. Anthony Bear and Grizz had been friends since their younger days of stealing and selling specialty auto parts. They'd spent some time in jail together, too. Anthony was the leader of his own crew on the west coast. His crowd was housed just past the Alley exit. Grizz and Anthony met regularly to discuss their dealings. Their so-called businesses were managed separately, but they were friends and easily traded stories and experiences that could help the other. Not to mention the occasional business deal.

Grizz hadn't seen Ginny in more than two months. His timing was off each time he'd tried to check up on her. He'd found he was looking after her more now that she was a teenager. He liked watching out for her. He liked taking care of her, too, even if she didn't know he was doing it. He splashed cold water on his face.

Several loud motorcycles were pulling up to the front of the motel, interrupting his thoughts. Running his wet hands through his hair, he walked out to the pit. He checked in with Blue.

Then, without telling anyone where he was going, he left. Less than forty minutes later, he pulled up at Guido's and went inside.

"Hey man, what's up big guy?" Guido asked from his sofa. Guido had been laying down reading the paper when Grizz arrived. A cigarette had burned itself out in an ashtray on the coffee table. Three beer cans, presumably empty, were next to it. Grizz hadn't knocked, just let himself in, but Guido seemed unfazed. Technically, it was Grizz's house.

"Have you seen Ginny? I keep missing her. Is she home now?" Grizz asked.

"She isn't home now, but I'm sure she's okay. She's been tutoring some kid." Guido sat up. "I could hear her telling her mom about it and, of course, all her mother wanted to know was if she was getting paid for it, which I don't think she is."

"What kid?" Grizz stood above him.

"Um, I don't know. He's been coming around. Picked her up for school a couple of days. He's been driving her home, too. He picked her up about eleven this morning. They looked like they were going to the beach." Guido's voice grew small, like he'd realized he'd made a mistake. "Uh, you know, like every other teenager in Fort Lauderdale with a license. He hasn't brought her home yet."

The muscle in Grizz's jaw clenched. It was obvious Guido could tell Grizz didn't like this new development and that Grizz was probably pissed off that Guido hadn't said something earlier. It was a Saturday. Kids do what kids do on Saturdays. What was with this guy and his obsession with the girl next door? The underage girl next door.

Grizz tried to control his temper. He didn't know why he was so mad, but he was. He subconsciously reached for his beard and was caught by surprise when he grabbed his freshly-shaven chin instead. He looked around the small living room. With the exception of some newspapers scattered on the coffee table and the beer cans, the room was tidy. The furniture was minimal but comfortable. The house smelled like cigarettes and perspiration. The windows were open, letting in a warm breeze in the waning afternoon. It was starting to get dark. He'd wait.

He sat in an overstuffed chair that faced the front window and stayed like that for what seemed like forever, but was only about thirty minutes. He made Guido turn off the television and wouldn't let him turn on any lights. They talked in low voices, about business and nonsense, when finally they heard a vehicle pull up.

Grizz stood and went to the window, off to the side. He was certain he couldn't be seen. The hands at his sides clenched into tight fists.

It was a jeep. It had pulled up into Ginny's driveway and parked itself behind Delia's old car in the carport. There were no lights on in the house. Her parents must be getting drunk at Smitty's. He listened as Ginny and the guy got out of the jeep and walked up to her front porch.

"So," the boy was saying, "So...one night this week...do you wanna go out?"

Ginny cocked her head. "Like on a date?"

"Yeah, a date. If that's what you want to call it. We could even go out tonight, if you want to. I can go home and shower and come back for you."

She smiled. "So, a date if that's what I want to call it. So if I don't call it a date, then it's like two friends hanging out?" She walked to her front door and fidgeted in her beach bag for the key. It still wasn't completely dark out, but the waning light was making it difficult to see in her bag. She had to feel around for it.

"Well, no, not like friends."

She found her key and inserted it in the dead bolt, but turned around to look at him. "Not a date. Not friends. You're confusing me, Matthew," she teased, tilting her head to one side as she looked up at him.

"Gin, you have to know that I like you."

"I know I've been tutoring you and spending time with you and your family. They're really great." Ugh. That sounded so stupid, she thought to herself. She looked at the ground shyly. She didn't know what else to say.

Truth be told, she wasn't good at reading signals. And she certainly wasn't good at trading banter with a boy she might be interested in. She'd focused for so long on her grades, getting an education, and getting out of this house that she never let herself have any fun. She'd spent the day at the beach with him without incident. He was a perfect gentleman. They chatted about school as they strolled along the shore. They had come upon a volleyball game in progress and were asked to join in, which they did. When one of the guys she had just met started showing an interest, Matthew interrupted that it was time to get back to their things that they'd left on the beach. That was the first hint that she had that he might like her as more than a friend and tutor.

She enjoyed her time with Matthew. He was a quick learner and probably didn't really even need help. He just had a hard time concentrating. She guessed that was a drawback to being popular. Matthew Rockman was the school's star running back. Football season was obviously over, but he was too busy socializing to focus on the things that really mattered. Like his grades and future.

She couldn't help it, though. She liked him. He made her laugh and laughter was something that was seriously missing from her life.

"Yes. Yes, I would like to go out with you, but not until Friday. I don't go out on school nights and I already have plans for tonight."

What she didn't tell him was that her plans for tonight included vacuuming and laundry. Spending the day at the beach had cost her valuable chore time. And she was a little embarrassed to admit she really didn't go out any nights. She was pretty much a loner and had preferred it that way.

Until now.

"Call it a date, call it a friendship. Call it whatever you want," she said shyly.

Matthew stepped in closer to her and took her face in his hands. He bent lower to kiss her softly on her lips. It was a sweet kiss. No big make-out session, but it had an effect she didn't expect. She liked it. She slipped her arms around his waist and pulled him a little closer to her. The kiss started to deepen when headlights broke the spell. There was a loud noise from somewhere, but it was lost in the sound of the rickety van engine as it pulled onto the swale in front of the house.

"Vince and Delia are home," she said as he pulled back from her.

"Do you want me to ask your father if I can take you out?" Matthew's voice was sincere.

"Not necessary. They won't care."

Guido had started to panic. He'd been watching from behind Grizz as the boy walked Ginny to her door. He was too short to see over Grizz's shoulder, so he looked around the massive biker to see what was happening. Even though Ginny and her friend weren't talking loudly, they could still be heard. The night was quiet, the houses were close together, and Guido's windows were always open. That's how he heard most of the conversations going on in the homes on each side of his own.

He sensed Grizz's body tensing when the boy asked her out. The air was so thick with Grizz's anger it could've be cut with a knife. Guido flinched when the boy kissed her and Grizz punched the wall. He didn't know if Grizz was going to do anything else. He didn't know why Grizz was so angry. Thank goodness Vince and Delia pulled up when they did.

Matthew left. The family next door was now in their home. Lights were turning on and snippets of conversation could be heard. Without saying a word, Grizz let himself out the front door, got in his car and left.

Guido finally turned on a living room light and sighed. There was a gigantic hole punched in the drywall between the front door and the window. Dammit. He would have to get that fixed.

# Chapter Forty-Five
May 12, 1975
Three Days Before the Abduction

GRIZZ PULLED UP to the little store on Andrews Avenue. He could tell by the outside décor that it probably specialized in girly, novelty items. At least that was what the owner thought was being sold. But Grizz knew Ginny's mother was using it as a front to sell her pot. He didn't really give a shit. That's not what he was here for.

Seeing Ginny kiss that boy had really unnerved him. He'd been right in thinking she was maturing. She looked even more like a woman in the arms of a man. Or rather, a boy. His jaw muscles tightened just thinking about how difficult it had been that night at Guido's. If Ginny's parents hadn't pulled in when they did, there was no telling what he might've done. He fell asleep Saturday night dreaming of pounding the kid's face into a shapeless sack and he didn't know why.

He opened the door and had to duck below the tinkling chimes. He immediately was hit with the overpowering scent of incense. It hung in the air like a blanket. He also knew it was burning to mask the smell of weed. So, she was smoking weed on the job. Of course she was. He looked around but didn't see her, so he headed for the counter at the back of the store.

Delia took one last pull on her joint, holding it in for less time than usual. She exhaled and then picked up her cigarette. She had been in the back of the store unpacking some new merchandise. She would go out and see if this new customer needed any help.

She stopped short when she came out of the back room. Standing behind the sales counter was the biggest, scariest looking man she had ever seen, certainly not the type of person who frequented this kind of store. Lulu's sold herbal remedies, macramé jewelry and belts, hanging planters, fragrant homemade candles and soaps. She also had her own specific clientele, but they were more of a casual crowd. This guy looked downright ominous. Maybe he was buying something for his wife.

She casually approached him and laid her cigarette in a homemade pottery ashtray on the counter. She had quit smoking cigarettes a while back and just had them on hand for when she got high at work. They masked the smell of pot in the store and on her breath. This one would eventually burn itself out. "Can I help you?" she asked with almost a touch of arrogance.

He didn't answer. Just stared at her. His eyes were mesmerizing, almost hypnotic. She sized him up without breaking from his gaze. Big and menacing. Criminal? Maybe. She reached below the counter to see if the baseball bat she kept there was within reach. Lulu's wasn't in the safest neighborhood. He noticed her movement.

"You'll leave that where it is," he calmly stated.

"Leave what?"

"Whatever the fuck it is you're reaching for."

She calmly laid both hands on the counter. "Okay, so what can I help you with, Mister—?" She let it hang there, hoping he would offer a name.

He was a little surprised. He knew she was a hippie pothead. But he never expected her to be a brave one. She was stoned. Maybe that made her brave.

"You have a daughter," he began.

"I don't know what you're trying—"

"I'm talking. You will shut up and listen. Got it? Don't answer. Just nod."

She nodded.

"You have a daughter. She's a smart and pretty girl. She doesn't do drugs or sleep around. She makes perfect grades. She does all your banking. Pays all your bills. Cooks, cleans, does your laundry. Even takes care of the animals that run all over your house. She's basically in your employ for food and a room."

This caught Delia off guard.

"You make her sound like a slave," she said, forgetting the rule that she was supposed to just shut up and listen.

"She *is* a slave. I'll make this simple. I want her."

Delia's eyes widened.

"Now, I don't need your permission to take her. I can just take her and I can guarantee you that you will not go to the police. You will tell everyone who asks, including your husband, that she ran away."

Delia didn't know what to say to this. Who *was* this guy and why did he want Gin? She peered at him. "Look. I don't know who you are and I don't know why you want my daughter. But she's not for sale."

"I didn't offer to buy her, but I find it interesting that you mentioned it." He sneered at her.

"I didn't offer to sell her, so—"

"So, since you mentioned it," he spoke over her, "here's the price. I won't tell the cops about your stash and your little side business. I'll even let you and Vince live. How's that for payment?"

She was so shocked by the fact that he knew about her pot business and her husband's name that she couldn't answer right away.

"I—I, I love my girl."

"Yeah, tell that to somebody who'll actually believe it. You use her. You don't love anybody."

"I care about her! And how do I even know you won't do what you said to me and Vince? I still don't even know who the hell you are!"

He cocked his head to one side and looked at her seriously. Interesting, he thought. She's more worried about the threat he made to her and her husband than about her daughter's well-being. Then he remembered the circumstances that led up to the Johnny Tillman incident. Had he actually let himself believe Delia had started to give a shit about Ginny since then? No. She was still a heartless bitch.

"You don't know. But you shouldn't risk it. You shouldn't cross me." He then reached into his right pocket and took out a plastic sandwich bag. He plopped it on the counter.

"Or what?" she asked haughtily. "You'll threaten me with your lunch?"

She squinted at the clear bag now lying on the counter in front of her. It looked like two shriveled and dried up worms.

"Just wanted you to see what happens when someone pisses me off. You remember Johnny Tillman? The fuck that tried to rape her?"

How did this guy know about that? "Yeah, what about him?" she asked, still staring at the sandwich bag. It must have been in the freezer. It looked like there was condensation on the inside of the bag.

Grizz leaned on the counter and got close to her face. "I know what you did that night. And I know why."

This caught Delia off guard. She took a step back and composed herself. She couldn't think of what to say to him so she acted like she didn't hear his last few remarks. "Want me to ask him why I shouldn't piss you off? I can't. He took off."

"You can ask him, but he won't answer," he replied as he picked up the baggie and tossed it at her.

She caught it with one hand. "Really, and why is that?"

"Because you're holding his lips."

She gasped and dropped the baggie. He turned and walked out of Lulu's, calling over his shoulder, "If you need more proof, I keep his balls in my freezer."

Grizz decided to stop by The Red Crab and get something to eat. He had another pressing matter to attend to, but it would be better if he handled that one after dark. He was going to find Matthew Rockman and have a little talk.

**********

Vince met Delia at Smitty's after work and she seemed exceptionally quiet. He asked if everything was okay and she told him everything was fine.

She was relieved when he got up to shoot some pool. She sipped her beer and thought back to earlier that day, when the scary guy came into her shop. She recalled the specific instructions he gave her, somewhere between telling her he wanted Ginny and tossing that disgusting bag at her. It was a blur, but she remembered most of it.

He wouldn't tell her a specific day. He wouldn't tell her when or where, but he was adamant about how it would play out. She recalled his instructions with a shiver.

"One day very soon, she won't come home. You won't panic.

You'll act casual about it with your husband. You'll tell him you had an argument with her and she's probably mad and at a friend's."

"He won't believe it. She never argues. She's an easy kid. Never gives us trouble. And she really doesn't have any friends. Just some acquaintances."

"Then you make up something he will believe."

"I just don't see how—"

"Do it!" He slammed his fist down on the counter, startling her and causing her to shake. "You will do it and you will be convincing. And when Vince isn't around, you'll go into her room and pack up just a few things that she might take with her, and you'll take them down to Miami and toss them in a dumpster. You'll refuse to call the police for a few days because you are certain she's just blowing off steam."

"But it's not like her! Vince will never believe it."

He reached over the counter and grabbed her by the arm, pulling her close to his face. "You'll make him believe it. Maybe it'll be easier for you to come up with something if *your* life depends on it."

He shoved her back just as quickly as he grabbed her and she almost stumbled.

Now, Delia took a sip of her beer and sighed as she remembered what came next. She remembered fighting nausea after she realized the guy knew the reason behind Johnny Tillman's attack on Ginny more than a year earlier. After he walked out, she ran to the restroom and threw up. She tossed the baggie in a dumpster behind Lulu's. She didn't doubt for a second that this guy would make good on his threats.

She was going to have to let him have Ginny.

Downing the rest of her beer, she slapped the bottle back on the bar with more force than she'd intended. Great. This was just great. Not only would she be down a daughter, but she was going to have to start taking care of the house, the cooking, all of it. Dammit.

But Delia did handle it. It wasn't as hard as she'd initially thought. Vince was too drunk to notice the first night that she didn't come home. When he asked if Ginny needed a ride to the bus stop the next morning, Delia made something up about her wanting to get to school early.

"Did she get a ride? Did Matthew pick her up?" Vince asked.

She wasn't sure how to answer. If Matthew was questioned later, she didn't want to get caught in a lie. She didn't have to answer.

"Dammit, Delia! One of your effing cats took a piss in my shoe!"

It wasn't until Sunday night that Vince realized something was off.

"Where is Gin? I haven't seen her all weekend," Vince asked in a drunken stupor. He was inebriated, as was his habit, but not too plastered to realize there was a sink full of dirty dishes, the cats were howling to be fed and he had no clean work shirts for the next day.

It was then that Delia put on the performance of her life. Afterwards, Vince said, "Shouldn't we call the police? Report her as a runaway? Something?"

"What are they going to do?" Delia countered. "She'll come home when she's ready. She's a smart girl. She probably had this planned for a while."

He didn't put up any resistance. *This is easier than I imagined*, Delia told herself. *Maybe she is better off with that guy. Good luck, Ginny, wherever you are.*

She took a drag on her joint, swallowed the last of the warm beer in the can she was holding and decided that she would take the cats to the pound first thing in the morning. She had no interest in caring for them.

# Chapter Forty-Six

2000

TOMMY WATCHED GINNY as she absorbed all he had told her. At least what he knew. He didn't know everything, but he knew enough.

"So you didn't tell me everything Sunday," she said as she looked at her lap.

"No, honey. I didn't get a chance to. You got so mad."

"I mean, when you said Grizz told Delia he was going to take me, I could believe it. You know, that was Grizz. He never asked. He just did what he wanted. But the other stuff." She looked over at him then, her voice very small. "Delia and Vince knew Johnny Tillman would be coming to the house that night? They knew and stayed away on purpose? Why?" Her eyes began to brim with tears.

He took a big breath. He'd promised her he would tell her everything. This was really going to hurt.

"It was connected to that police report, Gin. Do you remember about two months before Johnny Tillman came around? When the police were at your house?"

"Yes, I called them. I called them because of Donny Marcus, that little boy I babysat for. Delia told me to mind my own business, but I couldn't. I just couldn't stand knowing what his father was doing to him and then how he was putting on this face for the public. 'Steven Marcus. The trustworthy and honest face of the city,'" she said in a mocking tone. "He was the lowest form of a human being."

Ginny remembered thinking Mr. Marcus was the perfect husband and father, a true gentleman. He'd always insisted on picking her up and driving her home, even though she'd offered to ride her bike. The Marcuses seemed like a nice family and always paid her well for taking care of their son. Donny was always in his pajamas when Ginny would arrive. She would play with him and read to him. They would make a special dessert together, and after he brushed his teeth, she would tuck him into bed with a kiss on the forehead. She even taught him to say a goodnight prayer. She loved babysitting for him. Donny was part of a family that was the epitome of her dream. She cherished doling out the love and attention she had never received as a child. She wondered more than once if she would be a good mother one day.

She knew something was wrong the night Donny spilled some of his hot chocolate on his pajamas and wouldn't let Ginny change him. He'd started squirming and saying he could sleep in his chocolate-stained PJs and that his mommy would change them when she got home.

It was then Ginny realized she'd never been asked to bathe him or get him ready for bed. He was always in his long-sleeved pajamas when she arrived, regardless of the time. Was he hiding something?

She shouldn't have done it. She should've minded her own business, but her suspicions nagged at her. She knew he was a heavy sleeper since his mother insisted he wear a diaper to bed because he would never wake up, even after wetting himself. So after Donny fell asleep that night , she carefully unbuttoned the front of his pajama shirt. She cringed when she saw the bruises. Some fresh, some older. She slowly pulled his arm out of the sleeve as she rolled his tiny body to one side. She gasped and covered her mouth when she saw his back. There were no bruises there. Rather, there were scars. From lashes. Some faded, some still red. This child was being horribly abused.

She changed his shirt, and when she rolled him back and was buttoning it closed, she looked at his face. His eyes were wide open. He'd been watching her.

"Who hurts you?" she whispered.

He didn't say anything at first, so she repeated the question.

"Daddy," he answered.

"Does Mommy hurt you, too?"

"No. She doesn't like when he does it. One time she cried, so Daddy hurt her, too. She doesn't cry anymore." After a pause, the child added, "He'll get mad if I'm not wearing my same pajamas when he comes home."

She couldn't stand the thought of subjecting the child to another beating. She quickly rinsed his pajamas out where they had been stained and stood in front of the dryer, tapping her foot against the tile floor waiting for them to dry. She had dressed him in his old pajamas ten minutes before his parents walked through the door.

Ginny shivered at the memory. She shook her head.

"Well," Tommy said, "Grizz knew about your call to the police. He checked into this Marcus guy. He was a politician. He must have had some serious dirt on your mother or Vince. He must have made some kind of threats. Your mother and stepfather knew Johnny Tillman from Smitty's. She couldn't get you to stop pushing, so she convinced Johnny to come to the house to teach you a lesson. Guess she figured you'd forget about Marcus if you had your own trauma to deal with. You know how you were back then, Gin. Knowing you, you weren't going to let it drop."

"I didn't let it drop." Her eyes flashed. "I was causing as much trouble as I could. I talked to Donny's teacher. I told the principal at his school. I talked to his neighbors. Nobody would do anything. I kept calling the police to see if anybody checked out my report. Nobody did *anything*, Tommy. Nobody cared!" She looked over at him then. "I even threatened to go to the newspaper."

She sat back in her chair and sighed. "I was going to go to the newspaper and Delia was super mad at me. Told me she was going to kick me out if I stirred up trouble. I never got the chance." She buried her head in her hands, remembering it all now. "Johnny Tillman showed up a day or so later and tried to rape me."

Tommy watched her, his heart aching. "Grizz already knew about your call to the police and that Marcus was abusing his kid. I don't think he knew at that time that Marcus threatened Delia to get you to shut up, and that Delia somehow convinced Tillman to show up at your house. I think she may have promised him some weed. Anyway, Tillman told Grizz everything."

"Delia and Vince didn't just know about it? They actually *sent* him to do that to me?" she asked, her eyes wide with disbelief.

"I don't know how much your stepfather was involved or knew. And I don't know what Marcus had on your mother, but it had to be more than a stupid home-grown pot business."

"I remember the night Vince and Delia showed up after Johnny attacked me. I remember Delia's reluctance to call the police. At first, I thought it was because she didn't want them to snoop around and find her pot. I remember Vince being drunk, but he also pushed Delia to call the cops. I swear she wouldn't have if Vince didn't insist. He's also the one who identified Tillman. Delia was tightlipped." She pinched her brow. "Now I know why. If they found Tillman, he would've probably told them she's the one that sent him."

Ginny didn't say anything for a long time. She just kept staring at her lap. "And Mr. Marcus?" she asked finally. "What did Grizz do to him? I know their family moved away after the Johnny Tillman thing. Did Grizz have him killed or tortured or something? He had to have done something."

Tommy wouldn't look at her. This was one of those things that, even though she'd asked, he knew she wouldn't want details about. "Let's just say Grizz didn't kill him. But I can tell you with certainty that Marcus never hurt his son again. You don't need to know why or how I know that. Trust me on this. Okay, Ginny?"

She gritted her teeth, nodding. "Did Grizz ever find out what it was that Mr. Marcus had on Delia? What was such a big deal that she would set up my rape?"

"If Grizz did know, Gin, he took it to the grave with him."

The conversation was interrupted when they heard a vehicle pulling into the driveway in the front of the house. Ginny went inside and Tommy followed her. They watched as two men approached the front door. Ginny recognized the vehicle.

"What are they doing here?" Tommy asked.

"They're here for Carter's alligator. They were supposed to come yesterday but never made it," she answered him over her shoulder as she approached the front door.

"What alligator?"

"The one in the master bathtub." She opened the front door. "Right this way, gentlemen," she said, as she stepped aside and gestured toward the master bedroom. "Right through there. You'll find him in the tub."

"Gin," Tommy said. "I used Carter's bathroom while you were

taking a shower this morning. I think I would have noticed an alligator in the tub."

"What?" She almost choked. "He's not in the tub? He was there before that! I fed him first thing before I got my shower while you were making coffee."

The two men had made their way through the master bedroom and into the bathroom. They were coming out now, shaking their heads.

"There ain't no gator in the tub, ma'am," the taller one said.

It didn't take too long for the four of them to find the alligator. Richard Pepperbloom had made himself comfortable underneath the hutch in the dining room. Ginny was relieved he hadn't gone after her or Tommy, or escaped into the yard. He probably would have eaten one of Carter's animals.

"Good luck, Richard Pepperbloom," she said as she waved to the two men who left in the unmarked truck. The alligator was actually being relocated to a reptile farm that was privately owned by a couple who cared for them as pets. Ginny didn't know if this was legal or not, and she didn't ask.

"How did Carter end up with an alligator, and where did she come up with that name?" Tommy asked as he followed her back outside and on to the deck.

"You know Carter and her nutty animal names." Ginny shrugged and grinned.

Carter was a collector of both animals and names. She loved giving her animals real people names. There had even been a snooty ostrich that lived at Carter's for a while. Ginny smiled when she remembered telling Carter about her first fake driver's license and how Carter thought Priscilla Celery would be a perfect name for the prissy ostrich.

"Carter told me some lady who lives in Fort Lauderdale found Richard on her back porch. He had broken through the screened room and was under her patio table. Seems he made his way from the Everglades into the intracoastal and then up her canal. How he made it up a seawall is anybody's guess." Ginny took a long sip of her iced tea and settled herself in the Adirondack chair.

"So, Grizz was your father," she said, almost conversationally. "Did you always know?"

Tommy had been drinking his water and paused, setting the glass down on the table between their chairs. He'd been answering her questions as best he could, even though she was jumping around a little bit. This one caught him off guard.

"No, I didn't always know," he answered honestly.

"How did you find out?" she asked, looking over at him. She took another sip of her tea. She wasn't really tasting it. It was warm now. It had been sitting on the back deck during the alligator incident. She just wanted something to do, something to occupy her hands. Something to keep her from going off the deep end.

"I suspected it during the trial," he answered, gazing out over the yard. Before she could ask him, he quickly added, "I'd always thought Grizz might've been my older brother, not Blue. But I never guessed he was my father. Never, Ginny."

He looked over at her then.

"Tell me," was all she said.

# Chapter Forty-Seven
## 1987

TOMMY SAT IN the back of the courtroom and watched the proceedings. Grizz had given him one job. He was adamant about it. Tommy had agreed, and so there was never a problem. It was absolutely imperative that Ginny be kept away from the courtroom. He didn't want her there for any reason.

He and Grizz had been discussing it earlier while on a break. They were alone in one of the conference rooms. It had no windows and no doors. A police officer was stationed right outside as they talked.

"She asks me about the trial every day, Grizz," he told him. "I have to tell her some things."

"That's fine. Tell her some things. But I don't need to tell you what things I don't want her to know about."

"Of course I know that. And I'm doing my best. It's not easy, though. She's tried more than once to find someone to take care of Mimi so she can be here. I've pleaded with every friend we have to not make themselves available to babysit. I've told them it's for Ginny's own good that she isn't here. They've all agreed, and she won't leave Mimi with a stranger, so it hasn't been a problem. But she does grill me when I get home."

He sighed. Truth be told, Ginny seeing the parade of crimes that Grizz was being accused of would've only helped Tommy. But he'd given up that course of action years ago.

They hadn't been intimate, but she was lying next to him every night. At least that was progress. He'd started out sleeping in their guest room. He'd been awakened one night by her screams. She had been having a nightmare, and he went to her and held her all night, promising he would be there to hold and protect her while she slept. That was how he'd started sleeping next to her. He never once made an advance or touched her inappropriately. He would wait. Technically he was sleeping with her. But that was all he was doing.

"So how is it going with her?" Grizz asked finally. "Are you sleeping with her?"

Tommy sat upright at the question. This wasn't an easy subject for Grizz. Tommy could see the vein pulsing in his forehead.

"You know I'm not sleeping with her and you know why." Grizz didn't say anything, and Tommy continued, "She's in love with you. She thinks you're going to get life and maybe get out on a technicality. She's waiting for you. She'll never move on unless you tell her to."

"I told her to fucking marry someone else," Grizz growled.

"Yes, you convinced her to marry me so she wouldn't be alone. So that Mimi would have a father. You convinced her that I love her. That's good, because I do. But she doesn't love me."

"I just want her taken care of until I get this figured out."

This got Tommy's attention. He sat up straighter in his chair. "Figure what out? Are you going to beat this rap?"

"No. I don't think I can beat it, but I can still come up with something."

"So will you change your plea? Are you thinking of pleading guilty for life with no parole?" Tommy was getting confused and wasn't sure if he understood Grizz's motives.

"Doesn't matter what I'm doing. You don't need to know. You need to do what you told me you would do when I first got arrested. You need to take care of her. I'll figure out the rest."

Tommy couldn't fathom what there was to figure out. Grizz had been negotiating with the prosecution for two years. Some people, himself included, were left alone. Others, like Blue and Monster, went to trial.

"Your lead attorney, Carey, told her you'd plead guilty if they would give you the death penalty. Why would he tell her that?" Tommy asked.

"Carey can be a fucking idiot sometimes."

Tommy didn't believe that Grizz thought that for a second. He was hiding something. Then it dawned on him. Pride. It was pride. There was no way Grizz would rot in a prison cell for the rest of his life. And escape would be impossible. Grizz was too noticeable. He'd never blend in. And what would he do, take Ginny and the baby on the lam with him?

Maybe Grizz really was doing all this out of love. He saw there was no way out and he wanted her to have a life. Maybe that was the reason behind his insistence that Mimi never know he was her biological father. But still, what was there to figure out? Was he going to pull a rabbit out of a hat at the eleventh hour and get off? Tommy wouldn't be surprised.

Carey peeked in. "Court's going back in session."

Twenty minutes later, they were watching as a witness was being interrogated. He was a relatively new gang member, so low on the totem pole Tommy didn't even recognize him. William Jackson.

"Then what did you witness the defendant doing?" the prosecuting attorney asked him.

"He was walking her to her car and they were talking."

"Could you hear what they were saying?"

"Just parts. She was saying something about 'giving him a message,' and he was telling her to shut up and not to come back to the motel."

"Did you know who the 'him' was that the woman referred to?"

"No, didn't hear a name. They said some other stuff, but I couldn't hear it all."

"Please, continue, Mr. Jackson."

"It happened so quick I'm not sure if anyone could've stopped it."

"You're not on trial, Mr. Jackson. You're just a witness. What happened?"

"He broke her neck." The man's voice was low, but there was no mistaking what he'd said. "Real quick like. And then he picked her up and flung her over his shoulder. Signaled for me and a couple of the other guys to get rid of the car. I saw him throw her in the swamp."

"So, this woman, who nobody can·identify, was murdered in cold blood by the defendant and disposed of in the swamp?"

"Yeah, that's what happened. He broke her neck and dumped her back behind the motel. And we knew who she was. One of the other guys recognized her."

This caught the prosecutor off-guard. The other two witnesses had long been deceased. They were old members of the gang; one had died of an overdose and the other in a knife fight. The prosecutor didn't remember his witness identifying this woman in the pretrial interview, but he could've been wrong.

"And who was this woman, Mr. Jackson?"

"Don't know her real name, but Chops said her name was Candy."

There was a small cry from the back of the courtroom. Everyone turned around. Tommy almost gasped when his eyes met Ginny's. He looked quickly over at Grizz, who gave him a look that said, "What the fuck is she doing here and you better get her out of here this instant."

Tommy jumped up and quickly walked toward Ginny. He took her by the arm and gently guided her out of the back of the courtroom. When they were in the hallway, he asked, "Ginny, what are you doing here? Where's the baby? Who has Mimi?"

She didn't answer him right away. She was shaking. He led her to a bench in a small alcove, almost hidden from the main hallway. He gave her a minute to compose herself.

"Mrs. Winkle is back from her cruise early. She has Mimi."

Mrs. Winkle was an elderly neighbor who loved to watch Mimi—and who was supposed to be on a three-month cruise to the Mediterranean. A cruise Tommy had anonymously arranged for her. For some reason, she was back early. It didn't matter why. The damage was done.

"How long were you there?" He gripped her hands. "How much did you hear?"

"I just walked in and sat down. I heard that attorney say something about a woman that couldn't be identified was murdered and thrown into the swamp."

Tommy started to say something when Ginny interrupted him.

"Then I heard the guy say it was Candy. Blue's old girlfriend."

This caught Tommy by surprise. "Candy? Did you know Candy?"

"No," Ginny replied, looking at her lap. "But I heard her one night. I was in the bedroom. Grizz didn't know I was there. I had Jo drive me home from the beach. I had a bad headache and was trying to sleep it off. Anyway, Jo drove my car home. Grizz wouldn't have known that I was there. I woke up to them arguing. I guess she wanted to see Blue to apologize for all the bad stuff that had happened. She didn't say what it was, just that she was sorry. Grizz didn't want her to see him. Said that just because she'd cleaned up her act didn't give her the right to insinuate herself back in his life."

Tommy frowned. "Grizz said she was Blue's ex-girlfriend?"

"Not exactly. I assumed it because he'd told me once about her, but didn't tell me her name. I can't believe he killed her. Would he really kill her just to keep her from seeing Blue? Oh, Tommy, this is a nightmare. This is just so awful."

**********

Just then, one of Carter's horses whinnied and interrupted the story Tommy had been telling Ginny. It was almost time to start round two of the care that all of Carter's animals required.

"I remember that day, Tommy. It was the first and last time I was in the courtroom. But I don't see what it has to do with Grizz being your father."

Tommy sighed and, without looking at her, said softly, "Candy was my mother."

# Chapter Forty-Eight
1950s, Fort Lauderdale, Florida

IT DIDN'T TAKE long for Ralph to find The Red Crab. He walked in and laid his bag on a table. He stood still and slowly scanned the room. A jukebox was playing a song he didn't recognize. It was a Saturday afternoon, and there were a few guys at the bar and two more playing pool. He heard some hammering on the other side of the bar and walked around. He smelled fresh paint. It seemed there was some remodeling going on.

"Look who's here. Hey, Red, the kid that beat the shit out of Dusty is here."

Ralph immediately recognized the voice and noticed it came from one of the men sitting at the bar. It was the man they'd called Chops, he remembered. Chops was drinking a beer and eating something. A cigarette smoldered in an ashtray in front of him, a spiral of blue smoke making a halo around his head.

At Chop's words, Red popped up from behind the bar. He caught the boy's eye and gave him a wide grin. "Hey! You here to take me up on my job offer?"

Ralph just nodded.

"What about your grandpa? Doesn't he need you out there at the motel?" Chops asked.

Red and Ralph exchanged knowing glances.

"He died right after you left," Ralph answered.

But Chops didn't even hear him. He'd already set his sights on a blonde who'd just walked in wearing a miniskirt and white boots. She had big hair, was overly tanned, and Ralph thought her bright lipstick made her look like a clown.

Red came out from around the bar and slapped Ralph on the back. He was glad the boy had shown up. It would save him having to go back to the motel.

He had no doubt Tom had been at that motel. Red was good at a lot of things. But he excelled at tracking people and that's where

Tom's trail ran cold. He still didn't know if the kid had the bag, but he would figure it out. He just needed to keep the boy close.

"So did you ever find your friend?" Ralph asked.

Red didn't expect the question. He decided to go with the cover story he'd been told to use. "Yes and no."

Ralph just looked at him.

"Found out he was on a dinner cruise down in Miami. Something arranged by his company to thank their insurance agents. It's one of those ferry-type boats that takes people out to the ocean for a nice meal and some entertainment. Lots of booze and broads." He winked at the boy. "He was last seen talking to someone at the back of the boat. He'd been drinking heavily and told the man he was talking to that he needed to take a piss. Nobody saw him after that."

"Where did he go?" the boy asked, curiosity evident in his question.

"It's assumed he tried to pee over the side. Lost his balance. Nobody saw it, but there were witnesses who said he definitely got on the boat, but he never got off. They sent the Coast Guard to look for him. Couldn't find him. They're calling it an accidental drowning."

Ralph wasn't sure what to think. Was it possible this was a different man? Or was Red lying?

"Sorry. I know you said he was your friend."

Red got serious. "Thanks, kid. He was my friend. Left behind a wife and two daughters. The real sad part was that he was an insurance salesman and left his family penniless. Didn't have life insurance."

This wasn't true. Tom wasn't an insurance salesman, but because of his betrayal, his family wouldn't be cared for. It sucked.

Just then, a loud crash interrupted their conversation.

"Holy fuck, John, what are you doing?" Red asked as he turned to look at the man working on the renovation.

"Sorry, man. The kid dropped a bucket of nails," John answered.

"Have him pick them up. They're fucking everywhere." Red nodded toward John and the little boy, who was scurrying to pick up the nails he'd just dumped.

Red turned back to Ralph. "That's John Lawrence. Master

carpenter by trade. We're expanding. The kid in the overalls is his neighbor's kid. John has a soft spot for him. His parents leave him alone a lot, so John brings him along whenever he can. Picking up those nails will keep his little ass busy for a while."

Ralph glanced at the pair. John was a short and stocky fellow wearing blue jeans and a white T-shirt. He had on a carpenter's belt that looked full and heavy, but he worked in a sure and easy manner in spite of the bulk. The little boy must've only been four or five. About Ruthie's age, Ralph thought. He was wearing overalls with no shirt underneath. He had a buzz haircut and had spatters of blue paint all over his hands and arms, and even a smudge on one cheek.

Red noticed Ralph was looking at the boy. "He tried to help paint the bar stools. Got more blue paint on himself than he did on the stools. His name is Keith."

They were interrupted by a female voice from behind the bar.

"John, I told you already, your soup is getting cold." The woman motioned to a bowl sitting on the bar. Next to it was what looked like a peanut butter and jelly sandwich. That must've been for Keith. She muttered to herself as she walked away, "Don't know how one person can live on clam chowder. You'd think he'd be sick of it by now. Every day, chowder for lunch and chowder for dinner. Chowder, chowder, chowder—"

"You hungry, Ralph?" Red asked him.

"It's not Ralph. My name's Jason."

"You said it was Ralph at the motel."

"It *was* Ralph at the motel. It's Jason now."

Whoa, Red thought. This kid has an attitude. He might be more trouble than he's worth. He thought for a minute and smiled. Then again, he might fit in perfectly.

"Okay. You hungry, Jason?"

"Yeah. I'm hungry," Jason answered. "I can buy my own lunch."

Red nodded. "Good, because I don't give handouts. I'll give you work and you'll get paid, but you have to know right now, I'm not a nice guy. I don't do things for anybody without a reason. I'll pay you good, but you'll fucking earn it. You going to have a problem with that?"

"I know how to work."

"I bet you do," Red said as he motioned to the bar. "Patsy will take your order."

Jason sat at the bar and slowly ate the BLT he'd ordered, quietly observing everyone all the while. John and Keith had finished their lunches and were back on the other side of the bar working. Red was behind the bar, but talking to Chops and the lady with the miniskirt who'd come in earlier. Another man and woman had joined them. The waitress was serving beer and taking lunch orders from a few of the new customers who'd come in.

Chops was telling a story now, and his voice was rising the more excited he got. Jason wasn't paying any attention to the story and took a long swig of his soda. When he sat it down, he realized the bar had gotten quiet. He looked up and realized Red and his group were staring at him.

He stared back.

"Ain't that right?" Chops laughed, slapping his thigh. "Tell 'em, Red. Tell 'em how the kid sounded when he attacked Dusty."

"Sounded like a big old grizzly bear," Red told the captive crowd, a hint of a smile at his lips.

"Told ya. Told you he sounded like that. I swear we heard snarling and everything. After he clobbered Dusty, he pounced on him, too. Swear he pulverized him just like a grizzly. Big and mean. That kid is fucking dangerous, I'm telling you."

Miss Bright Lipstick took a drag on her cigarette while giving Jason an admiring once-over. They went back to their conversation.

Jason shifted uncomfortably in his seat and had to adjust his pants. She may have looked ridiculous with her big hair and bright lipstick, but the look she gave him made his dick jump.

Red took the towel that had been over his shoulder and threw it on the bar. He walked around to Jason and clasped a hand on his shoulder. "You finished your lunch. C'mon, take a ride with me."

Jason was taking his money out to pay for his lunch when he heard Red say, "Leave that there, Patsy. That's Stacy Ann's."

Patsy shook her head. "Red, you've had this bag of candy here forever. I was just going to offer some to the little guy. One piece of candy from the bag isn't going to hurt anything. He deserves a little treat. He's working his little heart out for John."

"I told you, I keep it there for Stacy Ann. It's her favorite. If she ever comes back around, I want it to be here for her."

"Yeah, yeah, yeah. Stacy Ann and her candy." Patsy picked up her tray and walked around the bar to clear a table.

Jason had laid his money on the bar and followed Red out the back door to a car. It was a nice car. "Who's Stacy Ann?" Jason asked as they pulled out of the parking lot.

Red gave him a sidelong glance. "My friend's daughter. The insurance salesman who died. Stacy Ann is his oldest girl. She was trouble before he died. She's really trouble now. I've been trying to keep an eye on her, but it's almost impossible. She's a wild one, she is."

"You keep the candy at the bar for her?" It seemed like an odd gesture.

"I mostly keep it there for me. When she was little, she loved candy. I can still see her face lighting up whenever I'd go over there for dinner. We made a game out of her and her sister checking my shirt pockets for where the candy was hidden. Guess it reminds me of happier times."

The conversation ended when they pulled into a gas station. It was big and had several garages attached.

"The guy you met back at the bar, John, this is his family's business. He's a carpenter, but this garage belongs to his family. You know anything about cars?"

Jason shook his head.

"You're going to learn."

They parked and walked up some steps that led to rooms above the garages. When they reached the top, Red knocked on the door once and flung it open. A boy, who looked to be just a little younger than Jason, was sitting on the floor. He had newspapers spread everywhere and each one held a variety of car parts. He was covered in black grease up to his elbows and was holding some kind of part.

Just then, another boy came out of what must have been a bathroom. He was wearing long pants and no shirt. He had darkly tanned skin and long black hair pulled back into a ponytail. Jason had never seen a guy with a ponytail before.

"Greg, Anthony, this is Jason. You're going to teach Jason everything you know. He's going to live here with you two now."

Greg didn't say anything, just nodded at Jason and went back to studying his car part. Anthony gave Jason the once-over and took a seat on the floor next to Greg.

"Anthony, remember to put your hair up under a cap before you go out. You stick out like a sore thumb already."

Red turned his back on both boys and Jason caught Anthony giving Red the finger. He tried not to smile.

"C'mon, I'll bring you back later," Red told Jason as they turned around and walked downstairs. On the drive back, Red explained that while both boys were young, they knew everything there was to know about cars. They would start Jason off small by teaching him what parts they needed and how to acquire them.

"You know how to drive?" he asked Jason.

"Yeah, but I don't have a license. Not nearly old enough."

"You look old enough. Well, you don't look old, you're just big. Might be able to get you a fake one."

They were heading back to the bar when Red took a sharp right into a parking lot. He threw the car in park and jumped out quickly, walking toward another parked car. A woman was bent over the driver's door, her back to Red. The person she was talking to must have said something because she turned around and registered instant fear as Red approached her. Jason could hear her from his spot in the passenger seat.

"I'm sorry. I'm sorry. I'm sorry, Red. I was going to call you. I swear." She started to lean back up against the car but lost her footing when it sped away.

Red grabbed her roughly by the arm. "You're sorry? You owe me, Meg. Where's my money? I know you worked that fucking convention. I know you're holding out on me."

"You're hurting me!" she cried.

Red must've squeezed her arm tighter because she let out another cry.

"This isn't hurting, Meg. You don't bring my money by the bar tonight, then you'll know what hurting is." He roughly shoved her away.

He climbed into the car and, without looking at Jason, shifted into drive and hit the gas.

Jason didn't say anything for a while. He was confused. He'd heard the man on the phone that night refer to Red as "agent." Weren't agents the good guys? He thought they were. But after spending just a few hours with Red, he'd already figured out he did something illegal with cars, and he knew what Meg did for a living. He was young and was raised in the sticks, but he wasn't stupid. Who was this guy who was on a special secret mission to retrieve a bag of money one day and kept underage kids on his payroll and scared hookers shitless the next?

Red glanced over at him, one hand casually holding the steering wheel. "So, you gonna stick around? Still want to work for me?"

He'd purposely put on a show for the boy when he saw Meg. He didn't want the kid to think he was a nice guy. He'd already told him he wasn't. Just because he kept a bag of candy behind the bar for his goddaughter didn't mean he was a softie. He'd been working both sides of the coin for years. He was in it for one person and one person only. Himself. He would let his *other* employers know about the kid, convince them it was in their best interest to keep the boy close. More than likely, if the kid had found that bag, he didn't know what he had his hands on. Red couldn't say one hundred percent that the boy had the bag, but if he had to bet his life on it, he would go with his gut. And his gut said that the kid did have it.

Yes, he would keep Jason close and use him. And he would let them know the kid could be molded and used—now and in the future.

He had no way of knowing then that the boy had a mind of his own and would never answer to anyone.

Red knew Jason was confused. The boy had been on the phone

listening that night and heard headquarters call him "agent." He knew Red ran an auto theft ring and he had working girls on his payroll. Jason looked at him now with penetrating green eyes brimming with uncertainty.

"So, Red?"

"Yeah?"

"Are we the good guys or the bad guys?"

Red looked over at him and smiled. "We're whoever the fuck we want to be, kid."

# Chapter Forty-Nine
2000

GINNY GAPED AT Tommy. She was at a loss for words. Finally, she quietly asked, "You're telling me that Candy, the lady I heard that night, was your mother and that Grizz killed her?"

"Yes, Ginny. That's what I'm telling you. And that's when I first suspected something, but I didn't know exactly what. I knew Blue had never had a girlfriend named Candy. I'd been at the motel since I was ten. He was juggling one woman named Sissy and another named Pauline, not to mention all the others in between." Tommy's face darkened. "After that, or maybe even sometime during all that, Jan came along. But I can tell you for sure there was never a Candy."

Tommy swallowed, continued. "I became curious as to who she could've been if she wasn't Blue's ex. Who was she that Grizz had to kill her? I didn't ask him because I couldn't be sure he'd tell the truth. Something told me it was important, though. That's when I started digging."

"And Karen? If she was your sister, then was Grizz her—?"

"I found out a lot of the story was true. It was just the players who were different. Karen was my aunt, not my sister, like I'd originally been told. She was my mother's sister. Candy's real name was Stacy Ann. She dumped me on my Aunt Karen and grandmother. Their mother, my grandmother, really was a waitress who ran off with a trucker. My mother and her sister really did lose their father to an accidental drowning. This all happened in Fort Lauderdale, not Miami like I told you. Parts of the story, all the stuff I told you years ago, were true. I was able to verify some of it."

Ginny couldn't believe what she was hearing. Tommy had already told her about the night Grizz came for him, but he'd lied then and told her it was Blue. Now, knowing it had been Grizz, churned her up inside. She didn't know what she was feeling.

"Did Grizz always know about you? What made him decide to go get you when he did?"

"No, he didn't always know about me, and he didn't actually come for me. He was giving Karen money to take care of me. When he found out that wasn't happening, he snapped and killed them. He could've left me there or taken me with him. He obviously took me."

"Did he tell you why he killed your mother?"

"Some of it. He just thought she knew too much about his criminal activities, and when she cleaned up her act and wanted to see me, she probably threatened to make trouble. I don't know. Maybe he was trying to protect me. He wouldn't have wanted his enemies to know he had a son. That's why I always had a hard time believing he married you when he did. I was always afraid for your safety. Grizz was a smart guy, but seriously, marrying you was the stupidest thing I ever saw him do."

It was evident by her body language that she didn't appreciate his last comment. He needed to change the subject. There was something else Tommy had to tell her. He didn't know if he was doing the right thing by telling her this. Hopefully, she would remember that he was a teenager then. He was counting on the fact that if he told her the truth, she would believe he was sincere.

He took a breath. "You know he told Leslie about me being his son out of anger after he found out about the billy club?"

She stiffened. "Of course, how could I forget that?" Sarcasm laced her words.

"Gin, I need to tell you something else about that." Tommy leaned forward in his chair and planted both elbows on his knees. He bent his head to rest his face in his hands. How would she react? He was willing to take the risk, but it was a big one.

"Ginny." He paused, gathered his courage. "I tricked him that night. He didn't ask me to take your virginity. Actually, it was my idea."

He had her attention now. She just stared at him. He couldn't read her expression. He took another deep breath and continued.

# Chapter Fifty
## 1975

GRUNT WAS SITTING in his motel room with Kit. He had just told her the story about his life before the motel and the night that Blue came for him—and killed Karen and Nate. Of course, he left out that it was actually Grizz who'd come for him. Grizz had told him never to breathe a word about that.

"Wow, I can honestly say that Delia and Vince did a great job of ignoring me, but they never laid a hand on me." Kit's eyes were filled with sympathy.

"I'll tell you one thing. Nobody will ever lay a hand on me again. That's for damn sure," Grunt's tone had a touch of bitterness. "Blue and Grizz made sure I knew how to defend myself."

"Yeah, I guess. It's hard for me to understand this lifestyle, though. Grizz hasn't hurt or touched me, but now that you told me how he dealt with Johnny Tillman, I don't know what to think." She shivered. "And Blue? He may have been defending you, but he murdered two people in cold blood. You just seem so, so—" She paused as she tried to come up with the right word. "You seem so normal compared to all that."

Grunt laughed at this. God, he loved her. She was sipping on the drink he'd offered her, skimming through his dictionary. She yawned. She looked like she was having a hard time concentrating on the pages.

He thought back to earlier that day when Grizz had called him into number four. Kit had been jogging around the paved area in front of the motel. It was an almost perfect oval track that surrounded the playground area and swimming pool. The pavement was old and pitted, but she still ran around it daily. It was really the only exercise she got and she seemed to like it.

"Did you figure anything out about me not hurting her?" Grizz had asked.

Grunt knew immediately what he was talking about. After Kit

had been at the motel for a short time, Grizz had come to Grunt, wondering if there was anything Grunt knew medically about not hurting a woman when taking her virginity. At the time, he'd been relieved to know Grizz hadn't been forcing himself on her. Somehow, he hadn't thought Grizz would; he had women throwing themselves at him all the time. Still, it was good to have confirmation. And he knew why Grizz was coming to him, just a kid, now. Grunt was the one who'd nursed Moe back to health after Grizz cut out her tongue. He had been stitching up the gang members since he was ten. If anyone would know something about this, it would probably be Grunt. Even if Grunt had zero personal experience with this sort of thing.

"I've been thinking about it since you first asked me, when you told me you thought you might've even hurt some experienced women because of your, uh, size." Grunt shrugged. "The only thing I can suggest is that you use something smaller than yourself her first time."

"Like what? My fingers?"

Grunt had to be cautious here. He didn't want Kit to lose her virginity to Grizz. He'd made an instant decision that he, Grunt, was going to be her first, but he had to handle this carefully. He was grateful Grizz had sought his advice; it would allow him to maneuver the whole thing to his advantage.

"I guess you could use your fingers, but it doesn't matter what you use. She'll hate you no matter what."

The statement caused Grizz's head to snap around. "What the fuck do you mean, she'll hate me no matter what?"

"Look at what you've done. You had Monster take her away from her home. You even told her you killed a guy."

"That fuck was going to rape her! And she wasn't in a happy home. Her parents were drunks who didn't give a shit about her. You know that."

"But it was still the only home she ever knew, and you took her away from it. I just don't see how you're not going to hurt her physically or emotionally. Not only that," Grunt added. "If you're as big as you say you are, I just don't see her getting over it easily."

Grizz didn't say anything for a minute. He just stared at Grunt with those intense green eyes. It was time for Grunt to make his move. Would Grizz bite?

"I could do it." Then he quickly added, "Without her getting hurt."

"Are you fucking kidding me? You're not sticking your dick in Kit. No man will ever be inside of her except for me." Grizz started walking toward him. Grunt forced himself not to back away. If he did, he knew he would look guilty.

"You don't understand. I don't mean *me*. I can do it with a small object. Fuck, man. Let her hate me instead of you. I can handle it. I don't want her to hate me, but she doesn't even have to know. I can give her something to make her drowsy. Make her sleep through it and she'll never know. Then the first time you're with her, it won't hurt like it would if she was still a virgin."

Grizz paused, turning the idea over in his head.

"I don't want to hurt her," he told Grunt.

"Like I said, I can take care of it while she sleeps."

Grizz didn't say anything. Grunt was afraid he'd lost him. "I guess you forgot I delivered Chili's baby when I was thirteen," he added.

Grizz looked at him closely, nodding. "Yeah, I did forget that."

"I did it all. Got the baby to breathe, cut the cord, took care of the afterbirth. I even stitched Chili up. Not bragging or anything, but I could go to medical school. I'm actually even thinking of changing my major." He continued to look straight at Grizz, careful not to look away.

"How exactly would you do it?" Grizz cocked his head.

"I have this small billy club. It's an old police baton. Even my dick is bigger than it is, so I know it's gotta be way smaller than you." Before Grizz could reply, he quickly added, "It's probably not much bigger than a speculum."

"A what?"

"A speculum. You know, that thing they use when they give a woman an internal exam. It's supposed to open them up to make it a little easier for the doctor to examine them."

"Yeah, whatever." Grizz shook his head. Too much information. He didn't say anything for a minute and Grunt realized he'd have to change tactics.

"I could give the baton to you to do it. You know, if that's how you want to remember your first time with her. Or you could do it yourself, but if your dick's so big, she'll probably wake up sore and know you raped her."

"What? What the fuck do you mean she'll know I *raped* her? I'd never rape her. I'd never force myself on her! When she's ready, she'll come to me, and I want to make sure I don't hurt her." Grizz was yelling now, the vein in his forehead starting to throb.

"Look, you asked me if there was any way I knew about medically taking a woman's virginity without hurting her." Grunt held up his hands. "No. None that I know of. So all I'm suggesting is that you let me do it, or you do it yourself, while she sleeps. She wouldn't have a single memory of it. And your first time with her won't be so bad after that. She'll never have to know."

Grizz just clenched his teeth and stared at Grunt.

Grunt continued, "I mean, you've been with women, lots of 'em, so you'll know how far you can go in without hurting her or damaging her, right?" He wouldn't break Grizz's gaze.

Of course, Grunt knew the proper medical terms. He'd been curious after he delivered that baby, but he sure as heck didn't know what he was talking about now. He just hoped Grizz didn't either. Grizz still wasn't saying anything. Grunt had to think fast.

"I see three options. One, you wait until she's ready and comes to you. Even if she's ready, you'll hurt her. No way around it. It's a given. You will definitely inflict pain on her, and I don't know if that kind of memory is something that sticks with a woman. Probably. She's only fifteen and very innocent. Even if it's consensual, I doubt she'll forget it. But that's option one."

Grunt held up a second finger. "Two, you do it yourself when she's asleep, whether it's your dick or the baton. But *you* have to live with that. Of course, you do a lot of things you have to live with, and they don't bother you. Why would hurting Kit be any different?" He knew he was hitting below the belt, but he continued. "But, if you do it with your supersize dick, she'll wake up knowing something happened."

Grunt shrugged, held up a third finger. "And three. You let me drug her and do it with the small club, and *she'll never know*. She'll wake up tired and not know a fucking thing. That I can promise. It'll be no different than a woman who goes for a gynecological exam. You would let a doctor examine her, right? As a matter of fact, a real exam would hurt more because she'd be awake. And you know, if you are going to be sexually active with her, you really need to start taking her for regular doctor visits."

Grunt threw that last comment in for good measure. If he sounded professional, maybe Grizz wouldn't see it as personal.

Neither said anything for a few seconds. Grunt acted casual. Disinterested, as if he was offering a matter-of-fact solution to a problem. He hoped his stomach didn't give him away. It was twisting and he could feel small spasms as his nerves started getting the better of him.

Grunt realized Grizz was actually, really considering it. Grizz was no dummy. As a matter of fact, he was the opposite, and if Grunt was going to be honest, he'd never given Grizz any reason to doubt him or mistrust him before now. Add to that the fact that Grizz had cared about Kit's well-being since she was a child. Grunt was counting on the fact that Grizz wouldn't be thinking straight when it came to her. He was counting on the fact that Grizz wasn't considering the future. How it would make him feel later to know that another man took Kit's virginity. Grizz was only concerned with the here and now, and Grunt took advantage of that one vulnerability: Without a doubt, Grizz would never, ever do anything to hurt Kit.

Grunt shrugged his shoulders and started to walk away. But to his great surprise and relief, he heard Grizz mutter, "Tonight, Grunt. Do it tonight. But make damn sure she's asleep and doesn't remember a thing."

That night, Kit rose from the bed and stood to leave. It was now time for the performance of his life, and he would have two things to his advantage. One, he was certain that when he pulled out that billy club he would make Grizz look like a rat bastard in Kit's eyes. Second, he knew she would never submit to the club. No, she would ask him to do it. He didn't know how he knew that, but he did. And he was right.

He was on top of her now and he gently spread her legs with his knee. They made eye contact then, and she asked, "Can you call me by my name, just once? Can you call me Ginny?"

"I'll try not to hurt you," and then after a pause he softly whispered, "Ginny."

"Please. Please tell me your name. I'll never tell. I swear!"

"I can't do that. You know that. You shouldn't have even told me your name." But, of course, he'd already known her name. He knew her first as Gwinny, and watched with Grizz, as she grew into Ginny.

She was starting to pass out now. Slowly, he slid himself inside of her just as her eyes were closing. They popped open when he entered her fully. He couldn't tell if he'd hurt her. She was starting to go under again and quickly opened her eyes in an attempt to stay awake. But to no avail. As they were closing for the last time and he was sure she was losing consciousness he whispered, "Tommy. My name is Tommy."

Had she heard him? Had she seen the tears in his eyes? If she had seen his tears, she probably would've thought it was because he was doing something against his will. She had no way of knowing his tears were from something else entirely. They were tears of joy and mourning. Joy at being her first, even in these circumstances. Mourning because he knew deep down that he would have to take a backseat after tonight and watch the woman he loved give herself to another man. It wouldn't be forever, but it would seem like it.

After she passed out, he stayed inside her while he buried his face in her neck. He wouldn't allow himself to have an orgasm. Not without her. He would just stay there and take in her smell while he waited. It seemed like an eternity before he could safely remove himself without exploding inside her. He got a warm washcloth from the bathroom and gently cleaned her.

He did it before he could stop himself. He did it before he even registered it as a thought or a decision to be made. He had to know. He hadn't realized it, but he was slowly lowering his face to the place he'd just wiped. He wouldn't allow his mouth to touch her, but he inhaled the scent of her and instantly got hard again. Fuck. Now what? He wasn't a pervert. He would never take a woman without her consent.

He hung his head in shame as he realized that this was exactly what he'd just done. But surely this was different, wasn't it? This was Ginny, and he loved Ginny.

He wanted to go further. He wanted to taste her. He was certain this was something she had never experienced before, and he also knew that it was something Grizz would introduce to her.

But with the greatest willpower he'd ever know, he stopped himself from doing anything. And very, very carefully he put her underwear back on her, pulling the sheet up.

I'll always be her first, he thought to himself. That was his only comfort and it would have to be enough.

# Chapter Fifty-One
2000

"I CAN'T BELIEVE what I'm hearing, Tommy." Ginny walked to him then. She stood there, looking down at him with her arms crossed in front of her chest. He didn't know if she was going to cry or yell. He didn't know which one he dreaded most.

"Gin, I'm sorry." He looked down at his lap. "I wanted to be with you for as long as I could remember. I actually don't remember a time when I was *not* wanting you. From the moment I saw you walking down the block and then setting up your lemonade stand, until today. And I know it was wrong to trick him, but—."

She was getting flustered. "You're telling me you actually, you know, you actually—"

She couldn't finish her sentence. She gestured with her arm to the space between her legs. "You put your mouth *there* while I was asleep?"

He tried not to smile. "As passionate as you are, Ginny, and you can't even ask me if I went down on you? No, I didn't put my mouth there. But I wanted to. Can't lie about that."

She punched him as hard as she could right in his face. He recoiled as much from shock as from pain. But it was a good pain. He wanted to hurt, after all she'd been through. Needed to hurt.

"How dare you sit there and tell me I'm passionate without thinking that something like this wouldn't anger me! That your so-called confession would make things right!" She clenched her fists, her body thrumming with fury. "I guess this is you trying to get something off your chest that made you feel guilty? But you know what, Tommy? It makes me feel used and cheap. How dare you and Grizz play with my life like that! I'm sitting here listening to a story about a decision you and Grizz made as to how I was going to lose my virginity! You could've been deciding on whether to order steak or chicken at a restaurant."

"Ginny, it wasn't a small decision. Don't make it sound like that."

"And it shouldn't have been *your* decision! Grizz's either." She punched him again, this time drawing blood from his nose. "That's the punch I should have given Grizz all those years ago, but I was only fifteen and naïve and hadn't realized the magnitude or seriousness of what had been done to me."

He recovered from the shock and looked at her.

"I deserved that. I deserve more than that." He swiped the blood that was slowly coming out of his nose.

He remembered how he'd gotten more than that. After she'd left his room that night and gone to number four, Grizz barged back in his door without knocking. Grunt had been sitting on his bed, his head in his hands. He was overcome with guilt. When Grizz walked in, Grunt stood up and started to say something, but he never got the chance. Grizz punched him in the mouth so hard that he fell back on his bed. He was lucky that his jaw hadn't been broken and he still had all his teeth.

"That's for not making sure she was asleep, motherfucker," Grizz said as he spun around and headed back to number four.

Grunt was surprised when Blue came down a little bit later and told him Grizz had given him permission to take her off the motel grounds. That shocked him, but he guessed Grizz was just feeling bad about her knowing what happened. Grizz had to leave on business and couldn't take her with him, and he sure didn't want her sitting in the motel all day thinking about what had been done to her.

Now, her body still tight with rage, Ginny turned her back on him. She walked to the railing and looked out over the massive yard. Once hers, now Carter's.

"I thought I saw tears in your eyes that night. Did I imagine it?" she asked him without turning around. She was still angry and her breathing was heavy.

"No, Gin. You didn't imagine it. I couldn't stand that I would have to wait for you after that night." He paused and then added, "Can I ask you something?"

She turned to look at him. "What?" Her voice was cold, distant.

"Why did you tell Leslie about the night you lost your virginity? Why bring that up?"

She shook her head. "It was stupid. She kept wanting to talk about how horrible Grizz was. She didn't believe me when I insisted he'd never forced himself on me. That I was the one who'd initiated the first time with him. She couldn't believe it. I thought I was making him look good by telling her he didn't want to hurt me, so he wanted you to handle it. When she was appalled that you, the man I was now married to, were supposed to rape me with an old police baton, I jumped to your defense. I told her I'd asked you to do it personally. Looking back now, I should've just left it alone. Let her think what she wanted about Grizz. It wouldn't have mattered now, anyway. I still can't believe he died knowing."

She cocked her head. "What would you have done if I didn't ask you to do it?"

"I wouldn't have done it. I wouldn't have touched you. I swear it. I would've rather told Grizz I changed my mind and didn't feel right about it. I would've rather done that than come anywhere near you with that stick."

She looked down at the deck they were standing on, slowly nodding her head as she took it all in. She didn't seem as upset as Tommy thought she would be. The punches were a surprise. He didn't think she had it in her. He'd never even seen her step on a bug. But still, he was a bit relieved.

She asked some more questions about the part Blue played in the deception. Tommy told her how Blue and Grizz worked on his memory from the beginning. How they did everything they could to convince him he was Blue's brother. He actually believed it for a while. It wasn't until he got older that he suspected maybe Grizz was his brother. But, as he'd told her before, he never suspected that Grizz was his father. And that was the absolute truth.

"Did you ask him anything else about her? About your mother? How they met? Did he love her?" She asked Tommy that last question without meeting his eyes. She could never admit that the thought of Grizz loving another woman, even so long ago, somehow didn't sit right with her.

"I wanted to know some things, but truthfully, Ginny, I really wanted to just put it behind me. I still do. He was in prison facing death in a few days and she was long dead. And at his hands. I was married to you, which is all I'd ever wanted. To be with you." He shrugged. "Why? Why dredge up an ugly past? I could live without knowing the answers. You were always my goal and I had finally reached it. It was then and still is about being with you, Ginny. That's all it's ever been about."

She bit her lip. "When did you find out about his real childhood? He told me a different story when I got pregnant that first time. Actually, it was the night I heard him talking with Candy."

"Could you blame him for not telling you the truth? Believe it or not, he told me right after you were raped by that son-of-a-bitch, Darryl. We had been taking turns sitting with you while you were sedated. He had been drinking. I can honestly say I had never seen Grizz drunk before that night. Ever."

"Neither had I. I thought he might've been a little tipsy the night I caught him with Willow, but that was it. I know he had an occasional beer and he never did drugs that I knew of."

"Your attack really messed with him. He just started telling me some things. The same stuff I told you about Sunday. I thought my childhood was bad. I honestly think Grizz's was worse. Not that he'd endured worse beatings or anything. But his helplessness at not being able to defend his sister. That seems to me like it would've made it harder."

"It was a horrible story." She shivered. "I can't imagine the Grizz I knew being a child and having that stuff happen to him. Did he ever tell you where he was raised? Did all of this happen here? In South Florida? I think he mentioned West Palm Beach once. And did he ever tell you his sister's name?"

She had a sneaking suspicion that she already knew her name, but she wanted to know if Tommy could confirm it.

"No, he never told me where he was born or raised, and he never told me her name. That's the truth." It was the truth. Grizz had told him the story, but never told him where it had happened or personal details about his childhood. The only name he'd ever heard was Ida.

Tommy wanted to go to her then, take her in his arms, but he was afraid of how she'd react. He wished that for a second he could read her mind. It had to be on information overload. After a few minutes of silence, he blurted out, "Ginny, I didn't know who I was in this world. Someone's brother, someone's son, a criminal, a student, someone evil, or someone kind. But when you came into my life, I knew who I wanted to be."

She started to get tears in her eyes and gulped back a response. She wouldn't allow her emotions to rule this conversation. She didn't want to remember that she liked waking up in his arms this morning. She looked away, and he could tell that she was thinking.

"Another thing, Tommy. Something else has never really added up or made sense to me. You used to spend a lot of time with me. Alone time. Wasn't Cindy ever jealous or anything? I mean, I'm still surprised Grizz even allowed it. That Grizz insisted I marry you. It seemed to go against everything Grizz ever did concerning me. Do you know why?" She frowned then and looked at him. She tilted her head to one side. "Tommy?"

He took a big breath. "Yeah, about that."

# Chapter Fifty-Two
1978

GRUNT HAD A very difficult time coming to terms with Kit's rape. He had a lot of guilt about moving out to live with Cindy. Would he have been able to prevent her attack if he hadn't moved out? It ate him up inside.

He'd actually moved in with Cindy as part of a bigger plan to be near Kit. He knew the only way Grizz would let him be near Kit was if he didn't think Grunt was a threat. The plan came to him quite by accident. He was still in college and studying architecture. A very prestigious firm had approached him to work part time. They had heard about him from one of his teachers. He hadn't graduated yet, but he was eager to work with them, knowing he could get some good experience designing homes. He wouldn't be able to put a certified seal on them, but one of the senior architects could review the work and make it official.

"Cindy, this is the nice young man I wanted you to meet," the woman had been saying as she walked into Grunt's office without knocking. It wasn't his office exactly, but a small one he had use of when he was working at the architecture firm, Monaco, Lay & Associates. The woman, Mrs. Jenkins, was a wealthy socialite who was having her house on the beach leveled and had hired the firm to do the work. She wanted to start from scratch with her own ideas, or so she said.

Mrs. Jenkins had noticed Grunt on a Saturday morning when she was there to meet with one of the other architects. She zeroed in on him immediately, insisting that he design her house. They tried to explain that he was still a student and pretty much interning with them, but she was adamant. Now, looking at the young woman being dragged along by her mother, he knew why.

"Michael, I want you to meet my daughter, Cindy." Grunt looked up from his desk and saw a cute, baby-faced girl walk in behind her mother. It was obvious that she was embarrassed. Her face was beet red. He took his glasses off and laid them on the desk. He stood up and extended a hand.

"Nice to meet you Cindy. I'm Michael. Michael Freeman." Grunt had continued to use the alias he had established after moving to the motel so many years ago, and the name rolled off his tongue easily.

"Michael, I want Cindy to be included as much as possible in the decisions for the house. It's going to be hers, anyway, so she might as well get what she wants."

"Mom, I love my penthouse. I don't want a beach house," Cindy huffed, barely concealing an eye-roll.

"Doesn't matter. One day, you'll thank me."

That was how it started. Mrs. Jenkins made use of every opportunity to throw Grunt and Cindy together. She was playing matchmaker, and why she set her sights on a wannabe architect and not one of her socialite friend's sons was a mystery to Grunt. But set her sights she had.

It was about three weeks after their introduction. Mrs. Jenkins insisted that Grunt go to Cindy's penthouse to have a meeting with her.

Cindy answered the door shaking her head. "I'm sorry, Michael. I know she's been pushing these meetings these last few weeks. I'm so embarrassed."

Grunt smiled. Cindy was a nice girl. Sweet, cute, and extremely likeable. He didn't mind spending time with her. He wasn't attracted to her, though. There was only one woman he was drawn to, and it was killing him that he had barely any time to spend with Kit. Between school and work, he rarely had free time, and if there was any, it wasn't alone time.

"It's okay, Cindy. I know what she's up to. I just don't understand why she picked me," he said as he followed Cindy into the oversized condo, looking around at the tasteful and expensive furnishings. It smelled like a combination of vanilla and lemons. He could hear the tinkling of wind chimes and "Sweet Talkin' Woman" by Electric Light Orchestra playing over an obviously state-of-the art sound system.

Cindy turned to look at him and laughed. "Don't take this as an insult. But basically, she's exhausted every other resource. I have turned down every guy that she has thrown in my face. She just won't stop. I guess she's not getting the hint. The beach house is supposed to be the dangling carrot."

He had followed her onto an expansive balcony. "She's not getting what hint?" he asked as he looked at the breathtaking view of Fort Lauderdale beach.

"That you aren't my type, either," she answered with a big sigh.

"And what is your type exactly, Cindy?" He was curious.

"For starters, you'd have to have bigger boobs."

Cindy invited Grunt to sit, then proceeded to pour her heart out to him. He guessed she'd had it bottled up for so long that it just came tumbling out. She didn't know how to tell her parents. It was the seventies. People weren't as open to homosexuality. She figured that if she excelled at school and showed up at the right social events, her parents would leave her alone. But her mother was relentless. Grunt listened as Cindy told him her story. She even confessed that she'd had the same girlfriend, Carla, since high school.

"My parents think we're best friends. Which we are," she quickly added.

Grunt glanced around the condo. "So does she live here with you? Is she your roommate?"

"No. My parents never approved of Carla, even as just a best friend. Said she came from the wrong side of the tracks. They are pretentious snobs. There's nothing wrong with Carla or her family."

They had been sitting at a table on the balcony drinking the lemonade that Cindy had offered. She looked at her glass. "I have another place. It's in Miami. My parents don't know about it. I spend as much time there as I can, but between school and this stupid house my mom wants me involved with—" She trailed off. She looked up at Grunt with worried eyes. "I'm afraid I'm going to lose her. I just don't have any time for her."

Grunt leaned back in his chair and looked at Cindy. He thought for a second and made his decision. Yes, he would do this.

"Cindy," he began, "maybe we can help each other out."

That's how the charade began. He started by designing the beach house on his own, telling Mrs. Jenkins the entire time that they were all Cindy's ideas. The persistent mother was thrilled. She was even more excited when they decided less than six weeks later that they would make it official. Grunt would be moving into the condo. Cindy was ecstatic. All that was required of her was for her to show up with Grunt on her arm at an occasional event. Her parents left her alone. She continued with her education and lived with Carla full-time, only stopping by the condo to get her mail and to make sure she said hello to the doormen and an occasional neighbor.

Of course, Grunt never told Cindy any details about his real life. As far as she was concerned, he was Michael Freeman. He wanted to be an architect, and he needed someone to think he had a girlfriend. She was only too happy to comply and never pried. As time went by and she was introduced to Kit and Grizz, it all became obvious to her. He told her a little bit more after she met some people that referred to him as Grunt. He explained more about the gang life and said he was sorry for involving her, even if it was peripherally.

She didn't care and told him not to worry about it. Her parents were so happy that she had a live-in boyfriend that they never bothered to do a background check on him or anything. When they asked about his family, he told them what he believed was the truth then. His father had drowned and his mother abandoned him. His sister and her husband, who had been taking care of him, had died tragically. He was raised in foster care and was smart enough to go to college. They never asked who paid for it or if he was receiving scholarships. They never seemed concerned that he was from the wrong side of the tracks. He guessed they were so self-absorbed and relieved to have found someone their daughter liked that they left them alone and went back to their lives. After Cindy was settled with her new beau, Michael Freeman, her parents started traveling extensively and rarely visited Fort Lauderdale. Mrs. Jenkins never even laid eyes on the beach home she'd had Grunt design.

**********

"You really think this will get mom off my back?" Cindy asked her father. It was several months before she'd even met Grunt—or as she knew him, Michael—and they were having a quiet cup of coffee in his study.

Mr. Jenkins smiled at his only daughter. "Don't you?"

"I don't know, Dad," she replied honestly.

"Look, I'll plant an idea in your mother's head. I'll suggest that maybe building you the beach house might be a good way to convince you to settle down. I have no doubt that when I send her to the firm where he works that she'll bite. She's been trying to tie you to a man forever. He's years younger than any of the men he works for, and he's a nice looking guy. I know your mother will notice him."

"And I don't have to do anything but become friends with him? Work with him on the stupid beach house?" she asked her father.

"Just become his friend," her father answered.

"Gosh, Dad. I don't know what your motive is and you don't have to tell me. But, if you'll help me keep mom off my back and keep my Miami condo a secret from her, I'll give it a shot."

"Your mom doesn't have to know about the condo or Carla," her father answered.

"What's in it for you, Dad? Without giving me any details, because I know you won't, what's so important about this architect?"

"I'm just trying to show some new friends that I can be trusted. That I can do my part. That's all."

"Sounds like you're trying to pledge a fraternity."

"In a way, I am."

Cindy never did figure out why her father wanted her to get close to Michael Freeman, but she didn't mind playing the part for years. She ended up caring very much about him, and it broke her heart to see him pining over Kit. She even remembered helping him along by trying to make Kit jealous. She didn't know if the little things she did helped or hurt his cause.

The only thing she did know was that Kit's husband, Grizz, was the scariest, meanest-looking motherfucker she'd ever met, and she never felt comfortable in his presence. He never did or said anything inappropriate, but he was obviously someone not to be messed with. At times, she actually feared for Michael.

She didn't want to let herself think what could happen to him if Grizz knew he was in love with Kit.

**********

The deception worked for a while. Tommy now remembered back to how he was almost caught by Grizz. He had graduated and was working full time at Monaco, Lay & Associates. Grizz called him one day.

"Come to the motel. Now." Grizz said into the phone. He hung up without waiting for Grunt to reply.

*What the fuck?* Grunt fumed. He had two meetings that afternoon and didn't have time to drive all the way out to the motel. But he sat back in his chair and thought about it. Grizz never called him. What if something was wrong with Kit? What if something happened?

*Calm down. You just saw her a couple of days ago.* He had taken her to dinner and then a movie. Grizz never cared. He believed Grunt had a serious girlfriend. Kit was Grunt's friend, and if Grizz wasn't able to take her out that much, Grunt didn't mind doing it. Of course, he always made it sound like he and Cindy would be the ones taking her out. He told Kit early on, "Cindy really does have a lot of studying and she doesn't mind if I go out with friends, Kit. But I just don't think you should tell Grizz that we go out alone. I know we're not doing anything wrong and you know it, but you know how he is."

"I know, Grunt. I just hate to lie. I don't lie, especially not to Grizz."

"Does he ever ask for details?"

She looked thoughtful. "No, I guess he doesn't. He never asks how you and Cindy are doing. He usually just asks if I had a good time. And stuff like, 'Did Grunt make sure you were safely in your car before he left?' You know how he is about my safety."

Grunt smiled at her. "Then you don't have to lie and we can still have some friend time together." He was relieved.

*What if Grizz somehow found out Cindy didn't make it to all of their little excursions? That he was alone with Kit more often than not?*

Grunt pressed a button on his phone. "Eileen, I have some personal business to take care of," he said. "Please reschedule my meetings."

Forty-five minutes later, he was sitting on the couch in number four. Kit wasn't there, and he didn't ask about her, telling himself she was out shopping or something. Everything seemed to be fine. No one was hurt. Grizz was in his recliner. Axel sat on the couch next to Grunt.

Grizz stared at Grunt for a minute before finally asking, "So, how are things with you and Cindy?"

The question caught Grunt off guard. Grizz never asked about him and Cindy. Not once. There was only one explanation. Grunt's earlier assumptions had to be correct. Grizz knew that Cindy wasn't going on the little "friend dates" with him and Kit. How did he find out? Kit must've accidentally let it slip. He was going to have to think of how to cover himself. He was mad at himself for not thinking about this before today. He should have had a ready answer. Maybe he was overreacting. Maybe he was thinking too much. He would play along and see where Grizz was going with this.

"Cindy's fine. We're fine," Grunt answered in a steady voice.

Grizz didn't say anything. He just looked at Axel, then back at Grunt. "Something you want to tell me?"

*This is it. He does know. Damn.* He would still play along.

"About what?" Grunt asked with as much sincerity as possible.

"It's okay to tell me," Grizz said in an even voice.

*Really?* Grunt thought. This was strange. Grizz never beat around the bush with anybody about anything. What was this really about?

"Tell you what?" Grunt asked, looking at Grizz and then Axel. "What is it that you think I need to tell you?"

"You wanna tell me why you live with a dyke?"

Grunt tried not to let his jaw drop. He never expected Grizz would know Cindy was a lesbian. How did he know? Grunt looked over at Axel. Bingo. In addition to running Grizz's car theft operation, Axel had a connection that did extensive background checks on people.

Grunt sighed. "Why did you check on Cindy? Why did you have to look into her background?"

"One of her father's companies came up in a meeting," Grizz said. "When I saw his name, I made the connection. I remembered Cindy Jenkins had a wealthy father. Wanted to see if it was the same guy. It was. I had to be sure she wasn't with you for any other reason. Like she wasn't with you because of business. My business."

"And?"

"They're clean. I'm pretty sure her father doesn't know exactly what his accountant is having him invest in."

This wasn't completely true, but Grizz wouldn't tell Grunt that. Grizz had his suspicions, but he couldn't be certain. Besides, if Cindy was there for the reason he thought, she wouldn't be getting anything from Grunt. He'd kept Grunt out of his other business for exactly this reason.

"But that's not the point. Why are you setting up house with a dyke? And I know she's not living at the condo." Grizz nodded at Axel then, adding, "I know about the parade of fags that show up there and stay overnight in that penthouse."

Grunt looked away from him then. He stared at something on the wall. It worked for a little while, his plan to have a girlfriend so Grizz wouldn't think he was a threat. So Grizz would let him spend time with Kit. What was he going to say? I'm in love with your wife and this was the only way I could think of to spend time with her?

But it turned out he didn't have to say anything at all.

"It's okay to tell me if you're a fag, kid."

*********

It was actually quite brilliant, or so he'd thought at the time. Letting Grizz think he was gay. Grunt hemmed and hawed after Grizz's last comment. He was shocked, but also relieved he had an out. So what if he had to let Grizz think he was gay?

Then he panicked. Kit.

"Don't tell her!" he blurted. He looked at Grizz, then Axel.

"Please! Please don't tell Kit. I'm not sure how she would react." He looked at the floor. "I wouldn't want her to think less of me. You know I care about her. She's like a sister to me."

Grizz didn't say anything at first. He didn't think Kit would care one whit about it. She'd seemed to accept Axel without judgment, though of course he couldn't be certain. Kit was religious, and even though he didn't know a damn thing about Kit's religion, or any religion for that matter, he thought maybe homosexuality was taboo. It certainly was in the biker world. That's why he covered for Axel and now he'd have to cover for his son.

Would she see Grunt differently? Would she act differently around him thus causing someone else to wonder about Grunt's sexuality? Grizz had a good thing going with Grunt. He couldn't take Kit out as much as she would have liked, and Grunt picked up that slack for him. Besides, he wasn't really a dinner and movie kind of guy, anyway. Okay, so his kid was gay. Big deal. Truth be told, he really didn't have an opinion on it one way or the other.

"She doesn't need to know." Grizz finally replied. Then, without another word, he got up and headed for the front door. He left, closing it behind him.

Grunt had been dismissed. He looked over at Axel, who had kept quiet the whole time.

"You're not a homo," Axel said to him matter of factly.

Grunt didn't know what to say. He remembered when he'd first discovered Axel's secret. He was maybe twelve or thirteen then. They had been sitting around the pit when, one by one, everyone got up and left. Grunt and Axel were the only two remaining when Grunt said to him, "You shouldn't watch them, you know. You make it obvious the way your eyes follow them."

Axel looked over at the boy. "What the fuck you talking about, kid?"

Grunt looked at him and with a kind expression said, "Don't worry, Axel. I won't tell. But you need to be careful. I know you try and put on a show. You take Moe in the room every once in a while to keep up appearances. I guess it's because she kind of looks like a guy with her short hair and combat boots?"

Axel didn't know what to say. His homosexuality could get him killed. How did the kid know? He was a smart little shit.

"You have to be careful," Grunt reiterated. "You don't realize it, but you look at some of the guys when you don't think anyone is noticing. I watch people a lot, and I notice it. Eventually, someone else will, too."

Grunt got up and left the biker sitting in the pit by himself. Axel stayed, absorbing what Grunt had said. If Axel valued his existence, he would have to watch it. Maybe it was a good thing the kid noticed. It might have actually saved his life. He'd been friends with Grizz since they were young and you would think that would offer him some form of protection, but there were no guarantees. Especially in the biker world.

Now, Grunt shot Axel a worried look. "How do you know I'm not a homo? And what did you tell Grizz to make him think I was?" Before Axel could answer him, he added, "Other than the fact that Cindy is a lesbian?"

"I just told him that I never saw you with a woman. Told him about the architect from Orlando. He's a regular who likes to stay overnight. Grizz thinks he's your boyfriend."

Allen? It all made sense now. Yes, Allen Ribisi was thirty-five, handsome, rich, and gay. He was a good friend of Cindy's and would stay at her penthouse when he had business in Fort Lauderdale, which was a couple of times a month. Sometimes as much as one or two days a week. He and Allen had become good friends and would often go to dinner. Allen knew Michael Freeman wasn't gay, and he never pried. He actually ended up being a good mentor. Grunt even went to Orlando twice to visit him. Of course Grizz would've thought he was gay.

Grunt was human, though. He'd had a few flings over the years. Cindy had straight girlfriends, too, and more than a few had come to stay at the penthouse and offered themselves to what they thought was their straight friend's boyfriend. Some girlfriends they were.

Axel interrupted his thoughts. "Why are you letting him think you're gay?"

Grunt looked at Axel and sighed. Could he tell the biker the truth? Axel cut into his thoughts. "Before you tell me anything, you need to know up front that I will never turn on Grizz or betray him. I like you, kid. I didn't want to tell him what I found, but if he ever found out that I didn't tell him, well, I don't need to tell you what I think would happen."

Grunt decided to go for it. When he gave it some more thought, the fact was that he could still make things difficult for Axel if certain members of the group knew he was gay. Maybe they could keep each other's secrets. "Kit," he blurted. "I just want to spend time with Kit."

"Seems like a major deception just to spend time with a woman."

"If you were talking about a normal woman, you'd be right. But, this is Grizz's woman we're talking about."

"What you do with your personal life is your business. If it involved the gang, I'd have a problem. But your secret is safe with me."

Axel was completely loyal to Grizz when it came to gang business. But as someone who'd experienced firsthand what it was like to deny your true self, he felt for the kid. Besides, he honestly believed that Grunt's crush, or whatever it was, would eventually play itself out. Grunt would pine after her like a lovesick puppy for a while longer and eventually move on to a woman who was actually available. He'd keep the kid's secret and maybe even have a little fun with it.

Axel stood then and stretched. "You want to make it convincing, you might need to learn a little more about being gay."

"I'm not going to have sex with a man, Axel. No way. You know I'm not gay."

"I'm not telling you to have sex with a man. But, you still need to play it safe. Grizz still might have someone besides me check on you. I'm telling you, you'd better play the part."

"Fine. What do you suggest?"

"I'll be parked at the beach across from your condo tonight at eleven. You can follow me from there."

"Where are we going?" Tommy asked.

"Time to introduce you to the underground gay haunts in Fort Lauderdale."

# Chapter Fifty-Three
2000

GINNY JUST STARED at him. "You are telling me you let Grizz think you were gay so you could be with me? That your girlfriend, Cindy, really was gay that whole time?" She threw her hands up in the air. "Tommy, this is crazy. I don't believe you."

"It's true, Ginny." He looked hurt. "I didn't do it on purpose, but I let it happen and used it to my advantage."

"No. No way. Grizz was too smart. He would've—"

"He would've what? Figure it out? He did. He caught me."

"Caught you? How did he catch you?"

"Somebody must've seen me out with a woman and said something to Grizz about me cheating on my rich girlfriend. Either that or he had me watched. He actually never told me how he found out. It didn't matter, anyway. He knew I lied and he knew why."

"What woman?" Ginny felt a stab of jealousy. A feeling she recognized from when Tommy used to occasionally bring Cindy on their "friend dates." Cindy was a big Rod Stewart fan, and Ginny remembered her always playing the song "Tonight's The Night" on the cassette player in Tommy's car. Cindy would even sing it to herself. Now that Ginny thought about it, she had been a tiny bit jealous, and as much as she loved Rod Stewart, she'd hated that song. Now she realized why. And to think there had been no reason to be jealous of Cindy. She wondered if Cindy played the part a little bit more than necessary just to needle her. The realization stunned her.

"Gin, there were women." His voice was soft. "I'm only human. And you were married. There were a few I tried to get close to discreetly. I tried. But I could never let myself get to the point of caring. It just wasn't going to happen. I wasn't getting over you just because I was with other women."

She tucked her feelings aside, pressing on. "Just forget it. So, after all that, you're saying Grizz caught you? What did he do?"

"You don't want to know."

"I'm so tired of hearing that." Her words were clipped. "*You're* the one who's been telling me I kept my head in the sand. That I've never faced the reality of what Grizz was capable of. Well, then tell me! Tell me what he did when he found out you had pulled one over on him. It couldn't have been too bad. You may have not known he was your father then, but he knew." She cocked a hip and leveled a smug glance at him. "What did he do to his own son?"

"He beat the shit out of me with his bare hands and put me in the hospital for two weeks. There. Is that what you wanted to hear?"

\*\*\*\*\*\*\*\*\*\*

That brutal night, Grunt was supposed to have dinner with Allen when Grizz called, saying it was imperative that he come to the motel. He looked at his watch. *I'll never make it.* He called Allen and told him he'd be late. Not to worry, Allen told him. He was friends with the restaurant's owner. They would have a table no matter what time they showed up. He'd just wait at the bar.

Grunt pulled into the motel and parked in front of Grizz and Kit's unit. He didn't see her car behind the office when he pulled in. *I wonder if he found the guy that raped her? Maybe that's why he wants to talk to me.*

He parked and got out of his car when he heard a couple of hellos from the pit. He waved back absentmindedly, then knocked once and let himself in number four. Grizz was sitting in his recliner.

"Don't sit," Grizz said as Grunt started to sit down. He rose to face Grunt, suddenly looking very tall in the motel room.

"Don't sit? Why not? What's up?"

"I want you to face me like a man when I beat the shit out of you."

Grunt blinked. "Beat the shit out of me? For what?"

"I need to know something." Grizz's voice was low, menacing. "Tell me now, because you won't be able to answer me when I'm done with you."

Grunt swallowed.

"You let me think you were a fag. I admit, I jumped to that conclusion based on what Axel reported to me. But you let me think it for a reason. And the only one I can come up with is because you're in love with Kit. You want to spend time with her. My *wife*."

The punch to his face caught Grunt off guard. He didn't lose his balance yet instantly knew he wasn't going to win this one. But he wasn't going down without a fight.

**********

"Grizz beat you up and put you in the hospital? His own son? Because of me?" Ginny's voice was almost a squeak.

"He beat the living hell out of me. I got my licks in too. I know I broke a couple of his ribs and gave him a black eye. We wrecked your place. How did you not know there was a fight there?"

"I think I remember that night. I came home once and number four looked like a bomb had gone off in it. Grizz told me two of the guys had come in and started fighting, and he'd gotten in the middle of it trying to break them up, which is how he got a black eye and a broken nose. *You* did that to him?"

"Yeah, I did that to him. He was bigger and stronger, but you have to remember, he's the one who taught me how to fight." A small smile played at Tommy's lips. "I broke his nose? Really?"

"You don't have to sound so proud of yourself." She rolled her eyes. "What happened after that?"

"Axel got me in my car and took me to the restaurant, where we found Allen. Allen got me to the hospital, then flew me to Orlando on a private jet so I could recover near him. He called my work and made up some story about me being banged up. Maybe he told them I was mugged. I don't remember. I do remember you asking me how my two weeks in Vancouver was."

"Grizz told me you went on a business trip." Her voice was small. Then something occurred to her. "Did he ever find out Axel deceived him by letting him believe you were gay?"

"No, I covered Axel's ass. I told him Axel reported the truth to him. I did hang with a gay man. Allen stayed overnight with me at the penthouse a couple of times a month. Why wouldn't Axel believe it?"

"But I saw you after that! I'm confused—we still spent time together. How did that happen? If he was so mad and he knew you were in love with me, why would he allow it? Something's not right."

"The first time I saw him after he beat the shit out of me, he told me he'd changed his mind, that it would be harder explaining to you why he wouldn't allow our friendship to continue—and that he'd kicked the piss out of me. Or maybe he just wanted to keep me close, keep tabs on me. Besides, he knew damn well that I would never, *never* try anything with you after that beating. And I never did. That beating was just a warning."

She let out a breath, stunned. So many secrets, so many lies. If she'd had her head in the sand, it certainly wasn't her fault. "But Tommy, you still brought Cindy around after that. You still stayed in her penthouse. Why?"

"A few reasons." He shrugged. "For her mostly; she still needed the ruse. And it was a comfortable situation. I lived in a million dollar condo close to work. And Cindy was a nice girl. We were friends. What else was I going to do at that point?"

Ginny shook her head, dizzy now with all the new information. "I'm still not sure I can understand why we were allowed to spend all that time together and Grizz never objected."

What Tommy wouldn't tell his wife, couldn't tell her was that he knew why. When he went to see Grizz a few days before the execution, they spent almost an hour together walking in the prison yard. He was the same old Grizz when it came to Ginny. He was still pissed about the billy club incident that Leslie had revealed weeks earlier. He told Tommy he was lucky it hadn't occurred to him to question it when he found out Tommy was pretending to be gay. He had no doubt if he'd thought of it back then, he wouldn't have put Tommy in the hospital for two weeks. Son or no son, he would've put Tommy in the ground. Grizz had also been angry when he found out through Blue that Tommy had fathered one of Blue's boys.

But then, Grizz went on to explain everything to Tommy, in great detail. Not leaving anything out. And after hearing about Grizz's involvement in something that went way past the dealings of his criminal activities, Tommy could only stare at him with his mouth open. It all made sense now: Going to prison without a fight. Letting Tommy stay close to Ginny. Asking Tommy to marry her when he got arrested.

Now Tommy knew why and didn't blame him one bit. He also knew why Grizz never told a soul. This was big.

"He was a criminal, Ginny. He knew he might need me one day. Need me to take care of you. I may have fooled him with the gay act for a little while, but it showed him something. It showed him that I loved you and I would protect you. Think about that. I didn't come to him and offer to marry you when he was arrested. He came to me."

She shook her head as she tried to take it all in. She needed a break.

"Do you want a refill?" she asked as she picked up his empty glass.

He nodded and watched her go into the house, closing the sliding glass door behind her.

Alone with his thoughts he silently berated himself for still holding back. But then he remembered. He had to. For her own safety.

His thoughts were interrupted when she came back outside, her cowboy boots thumping on the deck. She handed him the glass of water and took a seat.

"Going back to you being his son. Why was that so important to hide?"

"He had enemies, Gin. Enemies that could hurt me to get to him. He told me even Blue didn't know—Blue who knows *everything*, never even knew Grizz was my father. It wasn't until Blue went back to prison after finding Jan and his boys that Grizz told him about me."

"Do you really believe Blue never knew you were Grizz's son?"

"Yeah, I think I do. Grizz and Blue met when they were young, but Blue didn't really know Candy."

"When I heard them arguing, I remember she told Grizz something like how she'd introduced him to the people who put him where he was."

"It wasn't her. It was her dad's friend; she was just trying to take the credit, inflate her importance. Candy flitted in and out of Grizz's bed. He was young. He never remembered her crossing paths with Blue."

"Let me get this straight. I'm having a hard time organizing the sequence of events here." She took a breath and started ticking off the events on her fingers. "Leslie told Grizz during their face-to-face interview that you didn't use the billy club to take my virginity. He somehow managed to beat her up in the prison, but was so angry with you, with us, that shortly after that, he gave her a phone interview and told her you were his son."

"Pretty much." Tommy nodded. "By the time I'd told him the truth behind it, he'd already cooled off and ordered a hit on her so it wouldn't get printed."

"I think it was a bit drastic for him to order a hit, Tommy, don't you think? Grizz is intimidating. I think he could've made another type of threat. It's just a magazine article."

"Really, Gin? Think about how you reacted. Grizz didn't want to die thinking you might find out and do exactly what you've done, which is walk out on me. He always wanted you looked after."

At that, she slammed her hands down on the chair and stood up. "Looked after? I'm so tired of hearing this, Tommy." Her eyes blazed. "It's always been about protecting me. 'Ginny is too sweet. Ginny is too innocent. We can't tell Ginny. Ginny would be hurt,'" she mimicked. "Just because I went to church, tried to see the good in people, and looked at the world with a positive perspective never meant I was supposed to be treated like a child that had to be protected. I'm a grown, adult woman! I have an education and could support myself. I can think for *myself*, Tommy."

"I know, Gin. I know. I'm sorry. We both underestimated you for too long. I'm sorry for that."

"Go on." She sat back down, crossing her arms.

"I told Grizz everything I told you tonight. I told him why I tricked him into letting me take your virginity. He didn't like it, but believe it or not, he understood. Grizz had already realized by then that revealing he was my father would be so much more than just a little secret. It would've had a ripple effect that would've hurt Mimi.

Finding out her father, me, was really her half-brother? I don't need to tell you the shit storm that could've followed." He closed his eyes and rubbed at the spot between his brows. "Anyway, I talked him out of the hit and asked him to have it dealt with so nobody got hurt. I meant it when I told you Sunday morning that the time for killing was over. He could figure out a way to stop Leslie from printing the article without having to kill her. He agreed and told me he'd already come to his senses and called it off."

Ginny nodded at him and he continued. "Blue visited Leslie and told her that Grizz had a change of heart and not to print it. After that, and before Grizz's execution, Blue finally heard from the P.I. he'd hired to find Jan and his boys. They're grown now and don't live with their mother, but the P.I. sent pictures to Blue. After seeing the pictures and actually speaking to Jan, Blue visited Grizz in prison a week or so before the execution."

"Blue found Jan and the boys?" Ginny asked.

"Yes, and something came to light in Blue's last meeting with Grizz that angered Grizz again. That's when Grizz sent for me. That's why I actually went to see him before he was executed."

"Why did you have to go see him? Why couldn't you handle it on the phone?"

"I needed to have a sit-down with him. I needed to explain something and it had to be done in person."

"Why?"

"Because he found something out that made me look deceitful. Even though it happened a long time ago, years before the gay thing, it was fresh in his mind, and I was not looking good."

"What are you talking about? What did Grizz find out?"

"I need to tell you about Kevin."

# Chapter Fifty-Four
2000

KEVIN. BLUE AND Jan's youngest son. Ginny swallowed hard. She used to babysit him and his older brother, Timmy, whenever Blue and Jan were in a pinch.

Ginny bit her lip and pressed on. "Is it true? Were there any tests done to prove paternity or anything like that? And I guess what's more important: Do *you* believe Kevin is yours?"

"Yes. I do now. Jan tried to tell me he was mine, but I never believed it. Never wanted to, I guess. But Grizz showed me the pictures when I went to see him. He's mine, Ginny. I don't need a paternity test to prove it."

They were both quiet a long moment.

"Leslie alluded to the secret, you being Grizz's son, being put in the article Sunday morning when she called us on the phone. Grizz died two days before that. Whatever he was going to do to stop it, didn't work."

"Grizz died thinking it was handled. And it has been." He put up his hand to stop her next question. "I know Leslie needed more convincing, Gin. I know it's been taken care of, and I know nobody was hurt. He just never counted on her saying something to you before it was stopped."

She nodded her head in understanding. She could see the relief on her husband's face. They were making some headway with the secrets. The betrayals. The things that now seemed so easily explained away by Tommy.

Too easily?

Ginny knew there was still a lot more to tell. She could read her husband's expression, knew what he was thinking. He thought she would be going back home with him tonight. But she knew she wouldn't be. She still wasn't ready. She still hadn't decided what she believed and what she didn't.

And whether she could live with any of it.

She gave him a level look. "Tommy, this hasn't changed anything. All these secrets coming out. I still need time. You know that, right?"

He didn't know what to say. He thought by sharing so much and being truthful, she'd come home. She'd realize it wasn't all as horrible as she'd thought. But none of it was working.

He'd wanted to have this discussion in their home, needed to have this discussion in their home. Grizz had given explicit instructions about that. He hadn't even gotten to the part where Jan blamed Grizz's arrest on him. It was just too much information at once. He'd have to put that on the back burner until he could convince her to come home.

"No, Ginny, I *don't* know that." Tommy took her hands gently, but she pulled away. "I know you're taking in a lot of information, honey. But I don't understand why you can't come home to hear it. Why do you need to stay away from me? From our children?"

"Tommy, do not play the children card with me. Don't even try it. This has nothing to do with our children, so don't even attempt to go there. This is about our marriage. Maybe I can explain how I'm feeling in a way that you'll understand. A way *you* can relate to." She rushed on. The analogy had come to her this morning, and she liked it, "Let's say you've been living in the same house for years. It's not a perfect house, but it's the only one you've known, and—and you love it and accept it because it's yours. But many years later, you get a knock on the door. It's some city official, and they've just realized your house was built on ground that is not stable. Something is wrong with the land it's built on. You go and you pull out your original blueprint and you don't see anything wrong. You have a legitimate design with an architectural seal of approval. You look back over it and see some things you could've changed to make it better, but it's still a good house and you don't want to believe it could've been sitting on some massive sinkhole this whole entire time that could swallow it up whole!"

"Gin, this doesn't—"

"Let me finish! I know it's not the same thing, but bear with me. A city official has just told you that the foundation you built your house on isn't safe. You could be swallowed up in a second. So you start walking around your house and looking closer at all of the things you loved about it. And now that you're looking at it, really looking at it up close, you see the walls were built using substandard products. They could crumble at any moment. Your roof and windows wouldn't survive ten minutes in a bad storm. Maybe the paint on your walls contains harmful lead."

Tears began to fill her eyes, and he did what she asked. He listened. "Your contractor betrayed you, Tommy. He cut corners at every cost, cheated you out of knowing what you were really living in. Every step of the way. Aren't you *angry*? Aren't you just furious? He tried to explain it away by telling you it was okay that you didn't know. It was for your 'own good.'" She laughed derisively, one tear spilling onto her cheek, and then another. "You could never have afforded to have the house of your dreams, the house he'd built, if he'd used superior building products. And he wouldn't think of telling you he'd used low-quality materials to construct it. He reminds you that you would've never been happy in a house if you were worried it could collapse on you without warning. He did the right thing by not telling you what you were living in. He should be thanked and applauded for saving you from such distress. But you know what, Tommy? He never once considered how you would feel when that sinkhole, or should I say stinkhole, started to swallow you up."

Silence filled the air. He didn't know what to say. She was right. Both he and Grizz were guilty of letting her live a life based on secrets. How much better would it have been if they had told her certain things as they'd happened instead of letting them all swallow her up now? He wasn't being fair and he knew it. He tried to speak, but the words wouldn't come.

"I'm only asking you for time, Tommy, and I think it stinks you aren't even willing to give it to me. After *all this*." Her tears were gone now, replaced by the cold anger. "You are being selfish, and I'll be honest, Tommy. At this moment, I find that, that selfishness, a million times more repulsive than the fact that you slept with Jan."

He didn't get a chance to respond. Just then, she broke into a huge lopsided grin, staring at the sliding glass door that led into the house. "I didn't hear a car pull up!"

Tommy turned to see what she was looking at.

"Surprise! Hi, Mom! Hi, Dad!" Jason walked out on to the deck, and Ginny enveloped him in a big hug. "Aunt Carter and Aunt Casey said I could help take care of the animals tonight. Why is your nose red, Dad? It looks like it was bleeding. Why was your nose bleeding?"

"Bumped it on the barn door, Jason. Nothing to worry about," Tommy quickly said, forcing an over-bright smile of his own.

Carter and Casey had followed Jason onto the back deck. Quietly closing the sliding door behind them, Casey mouthed, "Sorry—he missed his parents."

Ginny and Tommy knew she was right. Poor kid had spent a couple of days at the Reynolds' while they were at the prison, and no sooner had Ginny picked him up to come home than she left for Carter's. Then Tommy had left after one night, replaced by Carter and Casey. He would start suspecting something soon. And God only knew what was going on inside Mimi's head. Ginny wrung her hands; she couldn't help but worry about her oldest child.

As if reading her mind, Carter chimed in, "Mimi's at someone named Courtney's house. Hope that's okay. Casey talked to her parents and they said it was fine."

"No, that's good. She's okay with them."

Carter answered the unspoken question. "She hasn't even asked."

Ginny nodded. She supposed she should be grateful.

Carter took Jason by the hand. "C'mon, I need help with the horses." Ginny could see Jason was only too happy to help. Carter called back over her shoulder as they walked down the deck steps and headed for the stalls, "If I had one ounce of his energy I could finish my chores in ten minutes."

Tommy hadn't said anything since the girls brought Jason home. He looked at Casey. "I know you just got here with him, but I really need another hour with Gin to talk. Do you think he'll notice if we sneak out to have dinner somewhere?"

Ginny started to object, but Casey wouldn't hear it. "He'll be fine. He'll be out there with Carter for at least an hour. We'll keep him busy. Go."

Tommy looked at his wife. "You up for dinner out somewhere?"

"I don't know. I haven't showered, but I am getting hungry."

"You're fine, honey. Just thrown on some jeans." He didn't want to have to deal with other men staring at his wife's long legs. They looked sexy in shorts with her cowboy boots. He never wanted to admit it, but he had inherited Grizz's tendency to be jealous.

After Tommy cleaned up, he talked quietly with Casey while Ginny changed into her jeans.

"Bumped it on the barn door?" Casey smirked. Tommy didn't answer her.

Ginny came out of the bedroom then. "All ready."

He followed her to the front door.

"So, where are you going?" Casey asked casually.

Ginny knew in her heart it was wrong, but she couldn't help herself.

"Tommy is taking me to meet his boyfriend, Allen."

# Chapter Fifty-Five
## 1980

"ARE YOU SURE you can go? Why don't you let someone else go?" Grizz asked Kit as they stood in the small living room of number four.

"I'm fine. The nausea isn't as bad as it was," she said as she looked up into his green eyes. They looked worried.

"What if you feel sick while you're driving? You know what? Give me your keys. I'll drive you."

"Grizz, you are overreacting. I think I can handle a drive to the grocery store. Just the fact that I'm feeling like I can cook again must mean the worst has passed." She cringed when she thought about how the smell of any kind of meat cooking made her want to empty her stomach. But she hadn't thrown up in three days. That was something. Maybe the morning sickness—or in this case, the all-day sickness—was finally gone.

She wrapped her arms around his waist and stood on her tiptoes to kiss him on the mouth. "I love how much you love me, and I love you even more, but it's just the grocery store." She laughed at herself. "Hey, I made a rhyme!"

He pulled her closer and deepened the kiss. "There is no way you could love me more than I love you, Kitten. And, if you really are feeling better, maybe you can stay here for a little while longer," he said in a teasing tone.

"Let me go to the grocery store and maybe I'll make it worth your while when I get back," she teased back.

He became very serious then. He gently took her face in his hands, rubbing her cheek with his right thumb. "I'm only teasing, you know." He nodded toward the bedroom. Without waiting for her to answer, he added, "As much as I love making love with you, Kitten, it's not about that with you. It never has been."

His brow creased as he tried to come up with the words that could describe how much he loved her.

As much as she wanted to hear the words, she knew how difficult this was for him. She smiled and grabbed his wrist, slowly turned it so her lips met the inside of his palm. "I know, Grizz. I know."

He was so overprotective. It was just the grocery store. Her heart swelled with love for him as she grabbed her purse and keys. Soon they would be moving into their new home. They were going to have a baby, and to top it off, Grizz was going to be finished with the gang. She couldn't have been happier.

He reluctantly let her go and watched as she walked out the door. He stepped to the window, and his eyes followed her as she strolled down the motel sidewalk, disappearing around the side of the office.

It was then that he noticed a car. Chowder was talking to the person behind the wheel. He squinted to see if he could make out the driver. He watched Chowder step back from the driver's side of the car and point to the highway. He must have been giving a lost motorist directions. It wouldn't have been the first time an unsuspecting traveler had accidentally turned into the motel.

As the car made its way around the pit and started to pass in front of number four, Grizz stepped back from the window so he couldn't be seen. But not before he recognized the driver.

What was Matthew Rockman doing at the motel?

Immediately, Grizz went to the telephone and dialed a number. "I have someone I need you to check out."

Less than a week later, Grizz pulled into the overgrown parking lot of an abandoned building in an older section of Hollywood. It looked like it had been some type of factory in better days. His contact had run a check on Matthew Rockman, then set up this meeting for him.

Two minutes later, an expensive luxury car pulled up next to him. The man got out and slid into the passenger side of Grizz's car.

"What do you need, Grizz?" The man, Carey Lewis, was dressed in a pricey, well-tailored suit. He reeked of confidence, expensive cologne, and maybe a little arrogance. Grizz was the only person he would ever meet in this type of circumstance. He wasn't a cloak and dagger kind of guy, but Grizz was different. He required special attention and he paid well for it. Carey had three ex-wives, five kids, and a twenty-two-year-old girlfriend. He was only too happy to comply.

Grizz handed him an envelope. "There's a kid coming out of law school soon."

"You need me to give him a job?"

"No," Grizz said slowly. "Not a job. I need you to get close to him, though. It's still too early to tell for sure, but I might need you."

"What's his name and what do you need me to do?" Carey asked.

"His name is Matthew Rockman."

"Okay, sure, Matthew Rockman. Do you know any more details? What kind of law he's studying, anything like that?"

"It's all in there," Grizz nodded toward the envelope now resting on Carey's lap.

"Okay, what else? What do you need me to do?"

Grizz looked at Carey hard. "You need to earn his trust." He paused. "And when you're certain that he trusts you implicitly—"

Carey waited. "Yeah, what?"

"You need to make certain he thinks you hate me as much as he does."

**********

After the meeting with Carey, Grizz drove to The Red Crab. He went inside and headed for his office. Chicky spotted him out of the corner of her eye and signaled him that she needed to talk to him. He switched directions and started walking toward her. He liked Chicky. She was one of the few women he'd slept with who he might actually consider a real friend.

He remembered how Chicky, who used to go by Rhonda, had tried years earlier to rope him into some kind of relationship. He never minded that she offered her body. It was when she tried to make it into something more that she used to piss him off. He was relieved when she set her sights on someone else. He even smiled when he remembered how Chicky had eventually passed the torch to Willow and how hard Willow vied for his love. How did that whore think he could possibly even like her, let alone love her?

Then his smile faded as he recalled something else. The night

Monster had brought Kit to the motel. How Willow had lunged for her. And later, Willow's involvement in Kit's rape. He should've broken her fucking neck that very first night.

Chicky interrupted his thoughts. "Hey, Grizz. Listen, just wanted you to know Guido's been looking for you. He stopped in here earlier and said he's been paging you and calling everywhere he can think of."

Grizz grabbed the pager off his belt and looked at it. "Didn't get a page from Guido."

Just as he said it, the pager went off, displaying a digital number with "911" next to it. Urgent. He headed for his office and dialed the phone.

"It's me."

"It's about time, boss. I've been trying to get a hold of you for hours!"

"Page just came through. What's so fucking important?"

"There's something you need to know. Her mother, your wife's mother—"

"What about Kit's mother?"

"I think she's looking for her." Guido took a breath. "Actually, I think she's looking for you."

# Chapter Fifty-Six
2000

GINNY SHOT SIDELONG looks at her husband as he drove them to dinner.

"So how come I've never heard about or met this supposed 'good friend' of yours?" she finally asked, more than a little haughtily. She refused to let herself feel bad about the comment she made to Casey about Allen.

Without looking at her, Tommy mumbled, "He had HIV and it weakened his immune system. He died from pneumonia."

She felt instant shame. She looked at her lap. "I—I'm sorry, Tommy. I didn't know and you never mentioned him." She looked at him now. "But why, Tommy? Why would you have never told me you had a dear friend who ended up dying? You had to be grieving. How could you have never once mentioned it?"

"I don't know, Gin. I guess I didn't want our time, our new life, to be about sadness and death and loss. I had enough of that for the first part of my life." He shrugged. "I got through it."

Her mind was still reeling from all his stories, which she realized went as far back as 1969. He seemed remarkably steady for someone who'd known so much for so long. She had her own reasons for being upset, but he'd had to be the one who lived it, day in and day out. He had known about Grizz's real childhood. Known what Grizz had really done to Darryl and Willow. Even witnessed some of it. He'd eventually found out Grizz murdered his own mother, Candy. And—she couldn't forget—he'd even played the part of a gay man just to be with her, then endured a beating that put him in the hospital for weeks because of that charade. And now he was telling her he'd lost a close and dear friend and she'd never known about it.

He was either the most caring and generous man in the world, she decided, or he was stone cold crazy.

She shivered and looked out the window. He was right when he said she'd stuck her head in the sand for years. It was her coping mechanism. She had played the part of naïve wife to two men. She wasn't stupid, and she was starting to get angry at herself for letting herself believe she was. She never saw it as avoiding truths. She really was a "glass half full" type of person, had tried for as long as she could remember to remain positive and upbeat regardless of what life tossed at her.

But with this new knowledge came a new realization that this was all she ever did: caught and dealt with whatever life threw at her.

She'd even allowed herself to be the victim of an abduction by making herself believe she was protecting Vince and Delia by not escaping. Sure, she could proudly pat herself on the back for making the best of whatever life tossed at her, but she secretly berated herself for not once thinking about tossing something back.

They didn't speak as they made their way through traffic. She wondered what Tommy was thinking. Was he remembering his friend, Allen? Was he thinking about what he was going to have for dinner? Was he wondering if his marriage was over? That's what she was wondering.

How much of Tommy's personality was actually the same as Grizz's? She blinked—her husband was her first husband's *son*. It sounded weird any way you looked at it. But was there anything about him that even remotely hinted at it?

She let herself drift back to a time when she was married to Grizz but spending some hangout time with Grunt. They were driving somewhere, she couldn't remember where, but she remembered what came next like it was yesterday.

"Grizz said he would meet us at Razor's," Grunt told her in the car.

"Razor's?" She wrinkled her nose. "Can't we meet him somewhere else? I hate to go to his bars. The women are all topless and it makes me uncomfortable. Not to mention the customers. They're all criminals."

"He has business there, Kit, and it's just easier for him to meet up with us there. I don't have time to drive you all the way home. Besides, it's still early, so I don't think there will be a lot of people there. Plus, I think Vanderline is working."

Kit smiled. She liked Vanderline. She was one of the few women who worked for Grizz that Kit actually admired. She was about Kit's age and only worked at the topless bar to pay her way through college. She was very up front with the customers that she wasn't a working girl and she wouldn't be serving up anything that wasn't on the menu. She had a tough, no-nonsense attitude, and the customers loved her.

They pulled up to Razor's, and Kit was glad to see there were only a few bikes in the parking lot. Grunt was right. It wasn't busy. She didn't see Grizz's car or one of his bikes. Maybe he was parked around back. She wasn't sure what he would be driving, but she hoped that he would get there soon. Hopefully, he had his car. She didn't have her helmet with her.

After their eyes adjusted inside, they found a seat close to the jukebox. There were a few guys playing pool on the other side of the bar. Vanderline, full-bosomed and bare from the waist up, made her way over to them.

Kit and Grunt both stood as she approached.

"Hey, you two, long time, no see," Vanderline said as she hugged them both. She smiled when she noticed Kit was blushing.

"Hey, Vee. We're just waiting on Grizz," Grunt told her. "He said he has business here and it was just easier for us to meet up so he can get Kit."

"Yeah, he called a few minutes before you walked in. Said he would be late, but he had something back in the office he wanted you to take a look at. Are you two hungry? I know it's a little early, but I'm pretty sure we can fix you up some lunch if you want."

"I'm not hungry, but I'll take an iced tea." Grunt said, then turned to Kit and gestured toward the office. "I'll be back in a few. Let me go see what it is he wants me to look at."

Kit told Vanderline, "I'll have an iced tea, too, and—"

"Lots of ice and lemon. I remember." Vanderline smiled warmly at Kit before she turned around and headed for the bar.

Kit watched the waitress walk toward the bar and remembered when she'd first seen Vanderline. Grizz had brought Kit to Razor's to pick something up. She sat in the corner and observed the waitresses in action. Vanderline caught her eye because she was the only black girl. She later asked Grizz about her. He told her Vanderline, who the regulars called Miss Vee, was about Kit's age. She had exotic good looks and a body that the men couldn't seem to take their eyes off of. With very large, full breasts and a rear end to match, she sported tattoos on both wrists and a small one just above her left breast. Vanderline was of mixed descent. When asked, she proudly declared that she had a black father and a Spanish mother. She had lost both parents when she was very young. Her mother died from cancer. And her father, who had never done drugs in his entire life, turned to them in his grief. He died of an overdose less than six months later. Vanderline had been passed from relative to relative until she finally struck out on her own at sixteen.

Kit had insisted on an introduction after Grizz told her Vanderline was working to put herself through college and refused to earn her money as a prostitute. They had hit it off, and Vanderline had impressed Kit so much that Kit began harassing Grizz about giving the girl a raise.

"She brings a lot of the regulars in. If I give her a raise, then she finishes school and is out of there," Grizz told Kit after she mentioned it that first time.

Kit just stared at him. "You just asked me what I wanted for Christmas. I want Vanderline to make more money. A lot more money."

"Kitten, you're killing me."

But Kit knew Vanderline had gotten her raise, and it wouldn't be long before she would be able to retire from Razor's.

Kit smiled at the memory as she dug around in her purse for some change. What had Grunt recently told her? That Vanderline would be graduating in a couple of months? Kit approached the jukebox and was studying the music selections when the door opened. She glanced behind her to see if it was Grizz. No, just two men. She went back to perusing the jukebox selections. *Hmmm, no Boston or ELO.* She would mention it to Grizz.

She heard the new customers settle themselves at a table near her.

She put some change in and made her first selection. Nothing. Was it broken? She heard Vanderline set two drinks on the table behind her, then approach the men.

"What can I get you guys?" she asked.

"What have you got on tap?"

"Screw that," the other guy said. "I'll have me some brown sugar, sweetheart. I heard this bar is good for some snatch. Didn't know they had a chocolate version."

Kit could hear them, but wouldn't turn around. She winced, but relaxed when she heard Vanderline's reply.

"The only brown something you're going to get is my fist down your throat if you don't take your hand off my ass right now."

"Whoa, whoa, didn't mean anything by it! Sorry!"

"What can I bring you?" Vanderline had to handle jerks like this before. She wasn't fazed by it at all.

"Whatever you have on tap is fine."

Kit heard Vanderline walk away, and out of the corner of her eye saw her approach the bar.

"Well, well, well, what have we got here?" One of the guys asked. "Hey, sweet thing. Why you wearing a shirt? Too good to show us your tits?"

Kit stiffened. Were they referring to her? She turned around and met the one's gaze. They looked like bikers. The larger one smiled at her. She realized he was missing his two front teeth. He was used to fighting. The smaller one had a cigarette dangling from his mouth. His hair was pulled back in a greasy ponytail, and his baseball cap was so dirty she couldn't even make out the logo.

She ignored them and turned her attention back to the stubborn jukebox. She pressed K13. "Hush" by Deep Purple. Nothing.

"Whatsa matter, Princess?" the bigger one said to Kit. "You too good for us or something?"

Vanderline had just returned with their beers. "If you know what's good for you, you'll leave her alone. She doesn't work here," Vanderline informed them as she placed their drinks in front of them. "Can I get you anything else?"

"How 'bout something to gnaw on? Got any pretzels or

something?" the bigger guy asked. Before Vanderline could answer, he added, "Hey, Princess, my friend was talking to you."

"You two must not be from around here." Vanderline raised her voice. "I'll say it again. If you know what's good for you, you'll shut up. I told you she doesn't work here. Both of you back the fuck off!"

"Whatsa matter, slut, jealous we're moving on? You missed your chance, sweetheart. C'mon, girly, let us see some tit."

Almost as if on cue, they both stood at the same time, their chairs scraping the rough floor. They began walking toward Kit. She turned and saw them approaching. *This isn't happening!* What was she going to do?

She backed up against the jukebox and stared at Vanderline. But Vanderline's eyes were glued to something over Kit's shoulder, a surprised look on her face. Before Kit could blink, Grunt was on both of them.

She knew her jaw dropped when she saw how effortlessly he handled the two men. Somewhere between the office and the jukebox, Grunt had managed to grab a pool cue. He cracked it over the bigger one's head before anyone saw it coming. Then he turned his attention to the smaller one.

"Go get in the car, Kit," he yelled over his shoulder as the bigger one started coming at him. The pool cue had stunned him, but it didn't knock him out like Grunt had hoped.

Vanderline grabbed Kit by the arm and started steering her toward the front door. "Do what he says, honey. I'll call the police. Go."

Later, Vanderline filled Kit in on the details. Somehow, she'd pushed aside the particulars, tucked them into a neat little place with all the other bad memories she didn't want to remember.

But she remembered them now—and remembered the look on Vanderline's face when she'd told it all.

Grunt had taken a couple of hits that day, but he gave as good as he got. A few minutes later, both men were on the floor. Grunt had headed for the bar and picked up the phone as Vanderline looked on.

"Eileen, it's Michael. I need you to reschedule my meetings. Push them out about two hours." He paused. "Yeah, I'll see you then. Thank you."

He hung up the phone and addressed Vanderline. "Tell Grizz I decided to drive Kit home. Call the police and see if they'll clean this up before he gets here."

"Will do," Vanderline said as Grunt headed for the front door.

She walked to the larger guy and kicked him in his face. "That's for the slut comment." Then she walked to the smaller of the two, who was looking up at her and moaning. She stomped on his genitals hard. "And that is for saying nasty things to my girl, Kit."

"What nasty things?" came a voice from the rear.

Vanderline turned to see Grizz standing there. He'd come in the back door right after Grunt went out the front. What was she going to tell him? Grunt had wanted her to call the police.

But she didn't have to say anything. The smaller of the two men was curled up in a fetal position. He had puked on the floor and was still moaning from the kick to his groin. The bigger of the two had recovered from Vanderline's kick to the face and was now trying to sit up. He gave Grizz the once-over, assuming he had an ally.

"Hey dude, maybe you can help a couple of fellow bikers out. That stupid fuck that just left and his frigid ice queen think they're better than us. Wanna help us finish what we started? Could use some help from a big motherfucker like you."

Vanderline actually snorted. Finish what they started? It was the two of them against Grunt. They couldn't fight their way out of a paper bag. Grunt had literally wiped the floor with their asses. And they were asking Grizz to help them finish the job? They should've shut up when she told them to.

She inhaled deeply and let out a long sigh. She knew she was going to witness something she wouldn't be able to erase from her memory. The stupid assholes didn't realize they'd just signed their own death warrants.

Vanderline walked out quickly to the car then, her tray covering her still-bare chest. A car honked as it drove by. Vanderline gave them the finger.

"The police are on their way," Vanderline fibbed to Kit, peering into the car window and giving them both a reassuring smile. She was doing it for Kit's benefit, and Grunt knew that, even if Kit hadn't known it then.

Now, Ginny shook her head at the memory. She had seen how Tommy had handled those two men years ago. He'd handled himself like a badass. Like Grizz.

What she wouldn't allow herself to remember was the look she'd seen in Tommy's eyes in the thick of that fight.

They were cold, ice cold. And utterly, completely emotionless.

# Chapter Fifty-Seven
1980

"COME TO THE Red Crab. Now," Grizz told Guido and hung up without waiting for a reply.

Twenty minutes later, Guido found Grizz in his office. He was sitting at Mavis's old desk and drinking a beer. Guido walked in and shut the door behind him.

"Tell me everything," Grizz said.

"Not a whole lot to tell," Guido began, perched in one of the little chairs set before the desk. "I started noticing little things a few months back."

"What little things?"

"I used to get pissed because the morons never properly bagged their garbage, and when they'd put it out on the curb, all the beer cans and liquor bottles would spill over onto my driveway."

"So you deduced that Kit's parents were looking for me because of an ongoing garbage dispute you've had with them?" Grizz snorted.

"No, no. There aren't any more cans or bottles. What I'm trying to tell you is that they've sobered up. I see them leaving every Sunday morning all dressed up. I think they're going to church. Last Wednesday night, there were some cars parked at the house. Some kind of meeting. Noticed when they left that they looked like a bunch of Bible thumpers."

Grizz didn't say anything. He was thinking.

"But the reason I needed to talk to you is because her mother, Delia, saw me sitting on the porch this morning. She fucking came right over to talk to me, like it was the most natural thing in the world. She asked me if I remembered her daughter."

"What'd you tell her?" Grizz sat straight up in the chair now, his body rigid.

"I acted casual. Told her, yeah, she ran away a few years ago, right? I told her I didn't remember a whole lot about the kid. Then her mom asked me something else. Asked me if I ever remembered seeing a big, scary-looking guy with a lot of tattoos around their house when they weren't there." Guido paused and frowned. "I think she was asking me about you."

Grizz was anxious during his drive back to the motel. It was an emotion he wasn't used to, and he wasn't sure he liked it. He didn't know why, but he felt a desperate need to hold Kit in his arms. To smell her, inhale her scent. Breathe her in. Kit. His wife and one true love. His only love. He'd never thought in a million years that he could actually fall in love. But Kit did something to him. He couldn't explain it. It was like she melted him from the inside out. She was the only woman he made love to. The only woman who ever fell asleep in his arms. And the only one that ever would.

He smiled when he remembered how happy Kit had been when he'd told her he would be giving up his criminal activities. He honestly didn't know if he would truly be able to stay away from this life, but he would try. For her. Especially with the baby coming. He didn't do drugs or drink much, but he didn't have to. In a sense, Kit was his addiction. He couldn't get enough of her.

A horn honked, pulling him back from his thoughts. The light had turned green. He thought about getting out of his car and punching the person in the face who was beeping behind him. When he looked in his rearview mirror, he saw it was just a kid. He could be taught a lesson. But Grizz was too restless to get home to Kit. He waited until the light turned yellow. Several cars had started beeping by now. A split second before it was going to turn red, he gassed his Corvette and sped through the light, leaving the long row of cars behind him stopped.

That kid didn't know how damn lucky he was.

A minute later, he saw flashing lights in his rearview mirror. He took a quick right into a gas station. The police car pulled up behind him. Grizz took his wallet out and had rolled the window down before the policeman walked up to it.

"May I see your license and registration, sir?" the young cop asked.

Grizz handed both to him. "You must be new."

He allowed his mind to wander while the policeman walked back to his squad car to check him out. So many ties from the past recently. Matthew Rockman showed up at the motel a week ago. Delia and Vince had sobered up and were looking for Kit. Both coincidence?

Grizz had been watching from number four last week, so he knew Kit had followed Matthew onto State Road 84 after Matthew had asked Chowder for directions. Grizz ran outside as soon as they'd both pulled onto the highway. He ordered two guys in the pit to follow each of them and report back to him immediately.

Less than an hour later, both guys returned and reported that Kit had gone to the grocery store and the other guy had headed north on University Drive. There hadn't been any interaction between either vehicle. Kit apparently had stayed behind the other guy until she turned off on Flamingo Road. She never passed him or even pulled up next to him. There was no contact at all.

He would have to think about this, give it careful consideration. If her mother was indeed nosing around and asking questions, it could interfere with the life he'd made for himself with Kit. That nosy nun didn't get anywhere when he'd first had Kit taken, and she finally gave up. But with Delia's renewed sense of sobriety, who knew what kind of trouble she could stir up? He would have someone keep an eye on Delia to make sure she didn't contact the police. And if she did, he knew who to talk to on the inside to make sure it didn't go anywhere.

In the meantime, he would have to think about this and come up with a plan. And for now, he would be happy to go home to his beautiful and sweet wife. She had recently told him the morning sickness was gone. She was feeling better. He would go home and make love to her until she screamed in pleasure.

Yeah, he was in love with a screamer. He grinned at the thought.

The cop pulled him back from his thoughts. "Sorry to have bothered you, sir," he almost squeaked as he handed Grizz his license and registration. The cop's hand was shaking so hard he almost dropped them.

Grizz swiped them out of his hand and gave a snort of disgust. He shifted into gear and sped off. He didn't have to look in the rearview mirror to know he'd covered the rookie in a hailstorm of stones and loose gravel.

# Chapter Fifty-Eight
2000

GINNY AND TOMMY had finished their quick dinner and were getting ready to head back to Carter's house. They had settled on a little diner tucked away in a shopping center. It was the same plaza where Grizz stole her wheel cap all those years ago. They were heading to their car when Ginny said, "Tommy, can you wait for me in the car? I used the last of Carter's aspirin and I want to replace it."

Before Tommy could answer, they heard someone say, "Those are very nice cowboy boots you're wearing, young lady. My wife had a pair of cowboy boots like those. Met her in Texas. She was the real deal. A real cowgirl."

They both turned to see who was talking to them. It was an old man. He was sitting on a bench between the entrance to the little mall they had just exited and the grocery store. He had a cane leaned up against the bench and an oxygen tank sitting next to him. He was ancient. They smiled at him.

"Keep him company," Tommy said to Ginny. "I'll run in for the aspirin."

Ginny smiled at her husband as he headed into the store. She made herself comfortable on the bench and listened as her new friend took a stroll down memory lane. They were enjoying their chat when a fancy sports car pulled up. It parked in the handicapped spot right in front of them. An energetic guy in his thirties got out and headed for the doors of the mall. Ginny recognized him as the owner of the hair salon a few businesses down from the little diner where they'd just eaten dinner. Ginny had actually gone to his salon once years ago. They were too snooty for her. And the owner was rumored to be a drug-using womanizer. His name was Jonathan Joyner.

"Young man," her elderly companion politely said to him, "you really should save those spots for people who really need them."

Jonathan Joyner stopped dead in his tracks and looked at the two of them.

"Yeah, and you should go fuck yourself," he said. Then he smiled at the old man—not a warm or kind smile, but a smile that said, "There, what do you think of that?"

Ginny couldn't help herself. She was on her feet in two seconds flat. "You don't have to be so mean or rude, buddy. He wasn't being nasty to you. He was just pointing out the obvious. You don't need a handicapped spot. Maybe you should save it for someone who does need it and be grateful that you don't."

Tommy had just come out of the grocery store. He'd seen Ginny stand up and was near enough to hear what she said.

"Who are you?" Jonathan sneered. "His little whore? Well, fuck you, too, and your sugar daddy and—"

He never got the rest out. Tommy had him on the ground before he could finish what he was saying. A woman who'd followed Tommy out of the store looked the other way, heading quickly for her car. The old man, however, just watched and grinned.

"Owww, you're breaking my arm!" Jonathan screamed.

"Apologize to the lady."

"I'm sorry. I'm sorry! Oh my God, you're going to snap my arm!"

Ginny spoke up. "He doesn't need to apologize to me. He needs to apologize to this nice gentleman here. He was awfully nasty to him," she said, nodding toward the old man.

"Don't break my arm, man. Please don't. I need to use my hands to make a living. I can't do it with a broken arm. I'll tell the old guy I'm sorry. Just let me go. Please."

Tommy let go of Jonathan Joyner's arm and stood up. Jonathan was now on all fours. He looked up at the old man and said with a sneer, "Sorry."

"I don't think you mean it," Tommy said. Before Jonathan could reply, Tommy came down as hard as he could with the heel of his boot crushing Jonathan's hand. Jonathan screamed in pain and pulled his hand to his chest as he fell onto his side. He curled up, sobbing, his knees to his chest.

Tommy bent down to pick up the small grocery bag he'd carelessly tossed aside. He took Ginny's arm and started to walk her toward their car.

She looked back at the old man as they went. He was still smiling.

"Don't worry, young lady. I didn't see a thing. Nope, didn't see a thing."

# Chapter Fifty-Nine
1980

GRIZZ DIDN'T HAVE to think long about a plan to handle Kit's mother, Delia, and her newfound sobriety and search for her daughter. It was obvious she was feeling guilty about a lot of things from the past and wanted to make things right with the child she had neglected her entire life.

Less than a week later, he answered a page from Guido.

"Gee, boss. You sure work fast," Guido said to him when he called.

"What are you talking about?"

"Her parents. I don't know how you pulled it off, but it was brilliant. No one would ever suspect."

"Pulled what off? What are you talking about?"

"That wasn't you? Now that I think about it, it would have to be a perfect plan, and I can't think of how you could actually get someone to do it."

"What the fuck are you talking about, Guido?" Grizz roared.

"Her parents. Your wife's parents. They're dead. Killed in a head-on over the weekend. I wouldn't have even known about it, but some neighbors knocked on the door and said they heard and wanted to know if I knew of any next of kin to contact."

Grizz was momentarily speechless. The person who'd been watching Delia hadn't reported this. He hadn't seen her in a couple of days and had told Grizz he thought they might've gone out of town or something.

Grizz was still hashing out a plan to get rid of them, but hadn't pulled the trigger on it yet. He was still working on the details with his contact. Now, it looked like he wouldn't have to do anything. The forces of nature had intervened and handled a problem for him. *Hot damn.*

Then he thought of something.

"Guido, I need you to do something, and I need you to do it

immediately."

Guido listened as Grizz told him what to do.

The next day, Guido was waiting for Grizz in the office of The Red Crab. Grizz went in and shut the door behind him.

Grizz looked around the office. "Where's the stuff? In your car?" he asked as he took his seat behind the desk.

"No, it's right here." Guido held up a leather bound book in his right hand.

Grizz hadn't been certain how he was going to get rid of Delia and Vince. He knew he wouldn't have had them killed. He could never do that to Kit. Even if she never found out, he didn't think he could look her in the eye. But he'd been planning to find a way to persuade them not to look for her. The car accident changed everything. And he realized he didn't want anything that belonged to Kit to come to the notice of any authorities who would be in that house. He didn't want a reminder that Delia had had a runaway daughter five years earlier. Bottom line, he didn't want anyone to start searching for her again. He wasn't certain that would happen, but he had to make sure it didn't.

"How long were you in there?"

"Almost three hours," Guido said seriously. "I checked everything and everywhere. The attic, the walls, the mattresses." He paused. "I also made sure nobody would notice the search. You know I know how to handle this kind of thing without causing attention, right?"

"Yeah," was all Grizz said.

"This is all that was there." He handed the book over the desk to Grizz.

It was a Bible. Grizz opened it and saw the inscription on the first page. The name Guinevere Love Lemon was neatly printed in what was obviously a child's handwriting. Kit's handwriting.

"You went through the entire fucking house and this is *all* you found of hers?"

"That's it. There wasn't a framed picture, a stuffed animal, an old report card, or a drawing. Nothing. My ex-wife used to keep all her kid's drawings on the refrigerator. They were all over our house. It's like Kit never existed. Her old bedroom was set up like an office or something. Didn't even have a bed in it. Guess when she left, they really cleared her stuff out. You remember when I got her guitar at that garage sale, a lot of her stuff was out there with it. That was, what? Five years ago? Guess Delia just got rid of everything." Guido shrugged. "Well, except for a few things. There are a couple of mementos in the back of the book."

He nodded at the Bible that was now sitting on Grizz's desk.

Grizz leafed through the pages and pulled out what was stuck between them. He stared at the picture and stiffened. It was a picture of Kit when she was young. He looked on the back. It wasn't dated, but he knew it was during that time when she wasn't being fed properly. He could tell by the hollowness in her cheeks. Her big brown eyes stared back at him. She had dark circles beneath them.

This was the only picture Delia had kept of her daughter?

Grizz then looked at the other item tucked in with the picture. It was several pieces of paper, some notebook paper, some copy paper, folded in half and held together with a thin paper clip. He unfolded them and read the handwritten note first. It was three pages long and written in neat script on notebook paper. He skimmed the first couple of paragraphs, then set the papers aside. Next he turned his attention to the four pieces of paper attached to it with a paper clip. Something on one of the pages caught his attention. He squinted in concentration, his brows furrowed.

"The note explains it," Guido said. "You have to read the whole thing, though." Guido grimaced. *Shit.* Maybe it wasn't such a good idea to tell Grizz he'd read it.

Grizz reread the handwritten note. Finally, he murmured, "This is beautiful. This is fucking beautiful."

The letter and documents sure explained some things. It also tied in with what Steven Marcus had told him all those years ago. Marcus, the scumbag who'd been abusing his kid. The boy Kit used to babysit. Marcus had come clean about what he had on Delia, but he didn't mention this. Maybe he'd never looked into it because it wasn't as big as Delia's real secret. Or he'd never found it because the note explained Delia had just received some of this recently.

Grizz folded the pieces of paper back up and tucked them, along with the picture, back into the Bible. Handing it back to Guido, he said, "Hold on to this for me. Keep it in a safe place."

Then he leaned back in his chair and laughed. "Delia," he said out loud. "You clever, fucking piece of shit." Then he laughed harder.

# Chapter Sixty
2000

GINNY SILENTLY WATCHED Tommy as he drove them back to Carter's.

"Don't say it, Ginny. That asshole had it coming."

She didn't say anything. Didn't know what to say. She'd seen Tommy mad before. She knew he'd nailed a grown man to a fence when he was sixteen. She'd seen him beat the daylights out of those two men at Razor's. But she could honestly say she'd never seen him show any violence to anybody, not once since she'd married him. Why had he behaved so harshly to Joyner? Why the last minute decision to crush the man's hand? Was it anger that had been pent up for years and the stress of the last few days that all just made him explode?

She didn't know what to think, but she did know one thing for certain. If it wasn't obvious before, it was obvious now that he was his father's son.

They had talked over dinner. She was still curious about his conversation with Grizz before the execution. She knew she was asking him to repeat himself, but it was important to her to know Grizz died peacefully. Not with any pent-up anger in his heart.

They'd arrived back at Carter's to find Jason was still out back helping her with the animals.

"He doesn't even know you left," Casey said. She gave Ginny a questioning glance. She was curious about Ginny's last statement before they left for dinner.

"I'll tell you about it later," Ginny said, slinging her purse on the counter. "It's a long story."

"I'm gonna see if they're hungry." Casey slipped out, leaving them alone.

"So you won't be coming home with me and Jason tonight." Tommy said quietly.

It was a statement, not a question. She didn't answer him.

"Ginny, please, honey." He turned to her. "I know you can't come home tonight. Maybe you won't come home this week. But I need to know our marriage is good. That this is just time you need to yourself to absorb all of this. Please, Gin—you're not concerned about our marriage, right? We have a solid marriage, right?"

She just stared without saying anything.

"When you come home, I'll tell you the rest," he promised. "And I think we should consider moving. We can even leave Florida. Start fresh somewhere new. How about the Carolinas?"

"The rest?" Ginny shot him a look. "And now you have us *moving*? Tommy, we can't just pick the kids up and leave. What about school? What about your job?"

"We have enough saved to live comfortably until I get a new job. The kids will be fine. They'll make new friends in new schools. Ginny, let's sell this house, too. Let's get rid of it all and start over. Please."

They were interrupted by Jason and the women coming in the back door. Jason walked out to the living room where they were standing.

"Aunt Casey's going to make me a grilled cheese," Jason said, running to his mother and hugging her tightly around her waist. "You're coming home tonight, right Mom?" He looked up at her, then over at his father. "You're both going to come home, right?"

Tommy looked at Ginny with a pleading expression.

Ginny ruffled her son's hair. "I don't think so, sweetie. Casey has to head back to her job, and Bill is still going to be gone. Carter sure could use my help."

Jason was starting to protest when Casey yelled out, "Jason! Come help me with your grilled cheese!"

With a shrug, he closed his mouth and headed for the kitchen.

But Tommy wouldn't stop wheedling her about coming home. Finally she'd had enough.

"No!" she bellowed, so loud Tommy shot a quick glance toward the kitchen. No one came; they must have gone back outside to eat. "Stop asking me, Tommy. Do you realize I have not made a decision for myself in twenty-five years other than which bookkeeping clients to take on or what to make for dinner or where we'll go on vacation? Stop badgering me. I'll come home when I'm good and ready."

He was so shocked at her outburst, which was rare, that he actually took a step back and just stared at her.

But she wasn't done. "I have never made a significant or important choice for myself. Not ever. I didn't choose to be with Grizz. He chose me." She spat the words. "And I don't even know what to say about the night I lost my virginity."

She said the last sentence in a hushed whisper as she looked toward the patio, then back at Tommy. "Yes, I got to go to college, but I always felt like it was on Grizz's terms, not mine. It took a lot of convincing. I couldn't go dancing unless Axel took me. I couldn't do anything by myself. And then, even after he got arrested, he *told* me to marry you. He guilted me into it. He told me that if I really loved him, I would do it. Don't get me wrong, it was the right thing. At least I used to think that. Now I'm not so sure. But again, it wasn't my choice."

She knew her words cut. She didn't care.

He knew she was right. There was always somebody, either Grizz or himself, influencing her. Even that day he convinced her to go back to Grizz after finding her at the church involved scheming on his part. He felt a quick stab of guilt.

"If you really want to save our marriage, I'm telling you now you need to give me space." Her tone was softer now, and she was gazing at him with those big brown doe eyes. "You have just presented me with a list of too-crazy-to-believe stories. Not to mention the knowledge that I've been duped over and over again for practically my entire life. And do I believe you about any of them? Honestly, I want to, but I just don't know, Tommy. Do you understand me?"

He could only nod.

She started filling him in on some household things. Informed him of what she knew was on the schedule for Mimi and Jason. She was glad he'd taken the week off. It would help her to gather her thoughts guilt-free while staying at Carter's.

She thought of something then, but wasn't sure if she should bring it up. Curiosity got the best of her.

"Moe's journal. Have you been reading it?"

"A little."

"Anything I need to know?" she asked. "Should I read it?"

"Honestly, Gin, I don't know if you should read it. I don't know what good it'll do. So far, it's nothing really bad, I guess. Not exactly nice, but hey. That's life." He gave a small smile. "She keeps talking to someone named Elizabeth."

"What?"

"Elizabeth. Beats me. All the entries, they all start out the same. 'Dear Elizabeth.'"

"Did we ever know her mother or sister's names?"

Before Tommy could reply, Jason's voice came from behind them. "Just like the horse!"

Ginny and Tommy turned around.

"What?" Ginny asked him. "What horse?"

"Elizabeth!" Jason said, nodding now. "That's the name of the brown horse in the picture that's in your bedroom. The horse has a little ribbon on it, like it won an award or something. The ribbon says Elizabeth. If you look real close, you can see it."

# Chapter Sixty-One
2000

ALONE IN THE house, Tommy sat in the bed he shared with Ginny. It had been a little over a week since she'd gone to Carter's. She hadn't come home yet. Maybe she would never come home.

He couldn't say he blamed her, especially after all the things he'd told her. They had done quite a bit more talking on the phone, but he still hadn't told her everything. Ginny still didn't know Jan had accused him of setting up Grizz all those years ago. But he wanted to tell her that in person. He needed to gauge her reaction. It wasn't true and he needed to make certain she believed him.

Tommy blew out a long breath and reached for the journal that had been sitting on his nightstand. Holding it, he studied the picture proudly displayed over Mavis's chess set in the alcove in their bedroom. It was the picture Moe had given Ginny that first Thanksgiving, when she'd begged out of going to Blue's. Ginny had kept it all these years, had it custom-framed and everything.

At Carter's, they'd both been shocked to hear Jason blurt out that Elizabeth was the horse in Moe's drawing. It made sense; Jason loved that picture. He used to stare at it when he was younger. Of course *he* would notice the small ribbon they had overlooked for years.

Tommy snorted to himself. The irony was them trying to live their lives as if there had never been a gang, and here they had a damn shrine set up in their bedroom. He shook his head and took a sip of the beer he had carried in with him. He sat back against the headboard and opened the journal.

*********

*Moe's Diary, 1978*

*Dear Elizabeth,*

*It wasn't supposed to happen like that. She wasn't supposed to be hurt. I promise she wasn't supposed to be hurt. Wendy swore to me when I gave the signal that the coast was clear, somebody was going to come and kidnap her back and take her to the police station. They'd find out where she came from, and Grizz would probably go to jail for kidnapping. I wanted to get him back for what he did to me. That's all. I didn't want that man to do what he did to her. She didn't deserve that!*

*I think Wendy must have planned all along for the guy to torture her. When I went in her room the next morning to get the dog food, I didn't have any idea she'd be there. She was supposed to be gone. But it was awful, Elizabeth. I thought she was dead! Then, when Damien found Gwinny, I wanted to die myself.*

*I can't believe that guy did that to Kit and then killed Gwinny, too. I didn't mean for any of it to happen, Elizabeth. I swear it wasn't supposed to happen like that. Wendy told me Grizz would get what he had coming to him. He was supposed to go to jail and she was supposed to go home. Wendy said it would be tit for tat.*

\*\*\*\*\*\*\*\*\*

Tommy almost spit out his beer when he read the passage. "No way. No fucking way. I don't believe it."

How had he not seen it then? Was he so absorbed in Ginny for so many years that he'd missed the obvious? He swiped his hand through his hair. Chicky must've figured it out, too. That's why she didn't want Grizz to know about the journal. Chicky was worried for someone. Who?

Realization slowly dawned.

He knew Wendy, the person responsible for setting up Ginny's attack all those years ago. He knew exactly who she was. He heaved his beer at the wall, the shatter and fizz a welcome release. Elizabeth and her unnoticed ribbon crashed to the small table that was sitting below it, scattering Mavis's chess pieces everywhere.

# Chapter Sixty-Two
2000

THE WOMAN LOOKED at her watch as she threw some last minute things into her briefcase. She had an important meeting this morning and she couldn't be late. The day was perfectly planned. Like a well-oiled machine, she meticulously organized each day down to the minute. Her planner was open on the kitchen counter. She took a minute to look at it as she sipped the last of her coffee. Work appointments were written in black. Family appointments were written in red. Soccer game, ballet recital, pick up her husband's suits at the dry cleaners. No, she would take that off her list. His secretary could pick up his dry cleaning.

After updating her list, she closed her day planner and tossed it in her briefcase. She put her coffee cup in the dishwasher, added some soap to the dispenser, and pressed start. She went to the refrigerator and took the crock pot out, carefully placing it into the warmer on the counter, and plugged it in. *There. Dinner will be ready at six and I can make Cheryl's ballet recital with time to spare.* She carefully surveyed her kitchen. All cleaned up. The babysitter would be here when the kids got off the bus from summer camp. Her oldest was spending a week in Arizona with a high school friend that had moved there over the summer. The younger two knew the chores they needed to do when they got home. All she had left was to go back into the bedroom and get her shoes on.

She smiled as she made her way there. She was happy and content. Her kids were healthy, smart, and talented. Stan was a great husband and father. He was a highly respected and sought-after surgeon who'd received job offers from around the world. Of course, she would never allow him to accept a job away from South Florida. She'd worked too hard to make her hometown exactly as she wanted it. Clean of the evil and corruption she'd known since she was a child.

She felt enormous pride in the job offers Stan was getting, but this was home and always would be. She was a registered nurse by profession and had been a damn good one. She was certain that was how she'd caught Stan's eye. After she'd become burned out by the emotional and physical aspects of caring for patients, Stan suggested she go into administration. She had been there ever since. With Stan's salary and success, she didn't need to work, but she wanted to.

She glanced around her beautiful and organized house and had to agree it had been the right career choice. She ran her home and her office with almost perfect precision.

Shoes on and grabbing her briefcase out of the kitchen, she was getting ready to go through the door that led into the garage when the doorbell rang.

*Who could this be?* It was eight-thirty in the morning. Probably Mrs. Kravitz, she decided. Yes, there was actually a real, live Mrs. Kravitz who lived in her neighborhood. Just like the nosy neighbor on that old television sitcom from the sixties. They had a new mail carrier who'd been occasionally transposing their addresses. Mrs. Kravitz wasn't really nosy; she was just lonely and always used the excuse to return the mail in person instead of just sticking it in the mailbox. She opened the front door.

"Hi," was all he said.

"Hi," she answered, a little stunned. He never just showed up without calling. Was something wrong? Was his family okay? Was *her* family okay?

"I need to talk to you."

"Not now, Tommy. It'll have to wait. I have a meeting first thing."

"It can't wait."

"What? What's wrong?" He was acting very serious and it was starting to unnerve her.

"A lot is wrong."

Before she could ask him what he meant by that, Tommy continued.

"You have some things to tell me about." He paused before adding, "*Wendy.*"

# Chapter Sixty-Three
2000, Northern Florida
A Week Before Grizz's Execution

GRIZZ STEELED HIMSELF as he prepared to speak the words. "Grunt is not my little brother." A long pause, then, "He's my son."

Blue stared at Grizz and leaned back in his chair, slowly nodding. "I should've seen it," he told Grizz.

"No, you shouldn't have seen it. I did everything I could to convince you and him from the beginning that it was anything but that. I should've told you early on, but I didn't think it mattered."

"Does it matter? I mean now that Jan told me on the phone that he set you up, does it matter that he's your kid?"

"No. Doesn't matter," Grizz answered Blue. "Besides, we both know she's lying."

"Is she? I have to tell you, Grizz, there is no doubt that Kevin is his kid. I know you've made peace with him since Leslie told you about the billy club, but he's not looking good. At least in my eyes. I saw it in your face just now, too. You thought about it again and it bothered you. You're wondering if he was truthful about what he told you. Seems like every time we think we know something, another Grunt bomb is dropped."

"You leave Grunt to me. Why your crazy ex decided to implicate him is something you can find out when you go to see her. Maybe she'll tell you. Maybe not. Either way, you be sure to tell her you believe her and you want revenge on him, too. If she thinks you believe her, it'll only help us more."

Blue nodded in understanding. "How come you never told me to find her?"

"I didn't have to. I knew you'd never stop looking for your boys. When you found Froggy a few months back, I knew it wouldn't be too long before you found Jan, too. Too bad the fuck isn't still alive to get what he had coming, but I still need her to finish this. You got a problem with that?"

"Fuck, no. She has it coming." Blue got quiet then and looked at Grizz. "You're scheduled to die next week. What if I'd found her after that?"

"I'd have gotten something to you telling you how what you've been setting up was supposed to end. It's all been written down and would've been delivered to you after I'm dead. I would've trusted you to make it happen as I'd planned it. I knew you'd never stop looking for your kids, and once you found them, you'd handle it for me. I consider it a bonus that you found her before I'm gone. At least I'll die knowing she has what's coming to her. Too bad fucking Froggy isn't still alive to be at the party."

"You're right. I would've handled it. I *will* handle it." Blue started to smile as he stared at the blotter on Grizz's desk.

Then something else occurred to him. He became very serious, glancing back up at Grizz. "Some recent shit has come to light about Grunt. Does the fact that he fucked my wife give you any new doubts about him?"

Grizz had to think hard on this one. He'd had a very long conversation with Grunt after Leslie told him about the billy club. They'd planned on meeting again before Grizz's execution. Grunt would be here in a few days, Grizz reflected. He had a lot to tell Grunt and would use the opportunity to ask about Blue's kid, Kevin. He didn't think he was wrong about Grunt, but he figured he should still have a back-up plan. As much as he wanted Kit to be taken care of, he wouldn't leave her with Grunt if Grunt wasn't the person he said he was. He would think on this a little bit longer.

In the meantime, he knew for certain he wouldn't be able to meet with Blue again before the execution. Blue would be leaving to go see his ex-wife in person. Grizz wasn't sure if they'd be able to have a secure phone conversation, either. They needed to finalize the plan now.

"You still have a plant who'll be in the execution viewing room?" Grizz asked.

"Yeah, she'll be there," Blue answered. They'd decided early on to have someone there to watch for any eleventh-hour signs from Grizz.

"I'll give a signal."

They discussed the plan Grizz had in place to handle Jan, expanding it now to include Grunt. How it would involve Grunt would be determined after Grizz met with him one final time. If he was clean, he would be able to continue his life as it was now. If Grizz detected even a hint of anything that was off, he'd have Blue take care of it. Son or not, nobody fucked with Grizz. Nobody except for *them*.

He would signal Blue's informant accordingly, and Blue would know how to wrap things up.

Grizz changed topics. "You said Leslie needs more convincing. What do you have planned?"

"It can't go down until a few days after your execution. But it'll definitely happen before she submits her article. She tried to be cute when I caught up with her at the grocery store. Believe me, she'll know we're serious. She won't print it. Kit will never know."

"Good. Very good. I don't mind about the fucking article. But I don't want Kit to be hurt by finding out Grunt is my son. I shouldn't have told Leslie, but we can stop it. Kit never needs to know."

"She won't know. I'll handle it."

The conversation was over and Blue knew he was going to be dismissed. He thought this might be the last time he would ever be able to ask Grizz something. Something that had nagged at him. It really wasn't important. He didn't have to know everything about Grizz, and he obviously didn't. He was floored by the admission that Grizz was Grunt's father. He'd known Grizz since they were kids and had no idea. Though truth be told, Candy hadn't come around much, and nobody at the The Red Crab had even known she was pregnant.

But there was something else that had aroused his curiosity.

"You told me if you'd died before I found Jan, you would've had me pull the trigger on the plan by getting a message to me."

Grizz nodded.

"Who? Who is the person all these years you've been communicating through? You get messages to and from certain people. Even me. Who are you using?"

Grizz stared hard at Blue. "Does it matter?"

"No, I guess it doesn't. I'm just curious."

"You'll have to stay curious. It's not for your protection. It's for theirs. After I'm gone, the gang, or what's left of it, is yours. Handle the Jan thing, and keep Kit away from anything and everything gang-related. You shouldn't have a problem with that. She was never cut out for that lifestyle and has stayed away since I've been here. In spite of that, keep an eye on things if you can."

"No, she wasn't cut out for that lifestyle, was she?"

Blue looked sheepishly at Grizz. Like he had something to say and wasn't sure how to say it. Grizz detected it.

"What is it?"

No answer.

"Tell me. What's up?"

Blue sighed. "I don't know about taking over when you're gone."

Grizz gave him a half smile and cocked his head to one side. He wasn't surprised.

"Blue, I'll be dead. I don't give a fuck what you do. You can shut it down, sell it to the highest bidder, just walk away from it. Do whatever you want." He paused and became serious as he added, "I should've done that a long time ago. Probably wouldn't be sitting here."

He honestly couldn't say if his last statement was true. But, believe it or not, he felt for Blue. He knew Blue had recently become involved with a woman. A woman who had turned his world upside down and inside out. Her name was Dicky, and Blue had told Grizz he finally understood Grizz's attraction to Kit. Kit's goodness and complete disdain for anything criminal was endearing.

Dicky was a cop. But Blue couldn't help himself. He fell quick and hard for the redhead who'd actually just been promoted to detective. He'd been brought in for questioning about a recent drug arrest. He wasn't worried about it; he hadn't been involved so he had nothing to hide. But during questioning, he couldn't take his eyes off the detective. She was in her late twenties or early thirties and very attractive in an eclectic sort of way. Curves in all the right places. A beautiful face with intelligent, bright green eyes that rivaled Grizz's. Short, red hair that stuck out everywhere. He couldn't tell if she'd styled it that way on purpose or if she'd rolled out of bed and left it that way. He felt a stirring below the belt when he thought about her rolling out of a bed. He liked what he saw.

He'd been sitting in the interrogation room when she charged in, apologizing to her partner for being late. She went to set her coffee on the table. But she'd been holding it by the lid and the lid came off, spilling coffee everywhere. Returning with paper towels, she proceeded to wipe up the coffee mess but accidentally elbowed her partner in the nose. She had just thrown away the soggy paper towels and was heading for the table when her cell phone rang. It was attached to her belt. She reached for it a little too quickly, and as she whipped it off her belt clip, it flew out of her hand. Narrowly missing Blue's head, it hit the wall behind him and shattered to the floor.

She was a bumbling klutz. Blue was fascinated.

"That's the third one this month, Dicky," her partner said dryly. "They'll start docking your pay."

Without missing a beat, she countered, "No problem, Charlie, I have stock in the cell phone company."

"Good, cause you'll need it. Just like you'll need stock in fender parts and the dry cleaners down the street."

Ignoring her partner's reference, Dicky sat down and looked Blue in the eyes. Her gaze was unwavering. She wasn't embarrassed by her recent mishaps. She wasn't put out by her partner's comments. She stared hard at Blue, and he thought he detected a bit of dislike in her gaze. No. He was wrong. She didn't dislike him. She downright hated him. Did his dick just twitch?

"I'm Detective Fynder, and I'm sure Detective Connor has already told you why you're here, Mr. Dillon."

Blue burst out laughing. "Finder? Your name is Dicky Finder?" He'd never thought he'd hear a name more ridiculous than Kit's real name, Guinevere Love Lemon.

"Yes, Fynder with a "Y" and we are not here to discuss my name."

Blue couldn't explain it. He'd never been attracted to someone like her before. And he wasn't certain if that was what he was feeling now. He'd tried settling down and having a family. As much settling down as he knew how to do. He would never try that again. So he'd stuck to easy women who were only interested in the same thing he was. An occasional fuck session, no strings attached. Woman had tried to snag him into something more. Eventually, even Pauline gave up and set her sights elsewhere.

He'd tried, too. He really thought that by marrying Jan he could find some semblance of a normal life, but he just didn't have it in him. He was a whore chaser and would always be a whore chaser. He didn't give a shit what women wanted, what they thought, or how they felt. He hadn't felt anything in a long time and didn't plan to.

Until now. Something tugged at him.

There was no logical reasoning behind his instant attraction to her. But it was there and he couldn't deny it. He felt a spark of something new and exciting. He felt a personal challenge. He wanted to get to know this woman. He wanted to know why she hated him so much. As crazy as it sounded, he found her contempt for him attractive. *How fucked up is that?* He grinned.

"Ahhh, Dicky," Grizz said now, leaning back in his chair. "So, it's getting serious?"

Blue looked away. "Yeah, I think so. Shit, I don't know. She needs me. She's so smart and everything, but she's a fucking mess."

"After all these years and all the women who chased after you because of the bike and the ink, and you're just now figuring out you're attracted to women who aren't attracted to that? That's pretty fucking funny, Blue."

Blue just shrugged. "Dicky's different, Grizz. Can't explain it."

Grizz nodded knowingly. Blue hadn't done his homework. Dicky was no mess. And Dicky didn't need Blue, but she wanted him to think she did. She knew exactly what she was doing. Should he warn Blue? Should he tell Blue what he'd found out about her?

No. He'd let Blue find out for himself. It's not like his life was in danger or anything. Grizz did have a small regret at not being around to witness it for himself, but he also knew his loyal friend was capable of handling himself. So Blue was in love with Detective Dicky Fynder. *Good luck, buddy. You'll need it.*

"I'll say it one more time, Blue, and I mean it. It's your life. Do what you want. I'm just asking that you take care of the last few things we discussed after I'm gone. You don't have to watch Kit or Grunt. Just keep your ears to the ground to make sure they are as far away from anything gang-related as possible. I don't think it'll be an issue, but it would help me as I face that table knowing that you're out there."

He stood. Blue was being dismissed.

Blue stood, too, and grabbed the file with his family's pictures. Grizz snagged it out of his hand.

"I'll hold on to this until I have my last face-to-face with Grunt," Grizz said.

They stood there as the seconds ticked by. No last words between friends. No hugs or pats on the back. Blue wouldn't be coming back.

Finally, he nodded slightly at Grizz and headed for the door, but not before Grizz saw a light sheen of tears covering Blue's dark eyes. He would've cried, too, but he'd made a vow a long time ago that he'd never shed another tear. And he hadn't.

# Chapter Sixty-Four
2000, Nashville, Tennessee,
Three Days Before Grizz's Execution

BLUE STUDIED THE woman sitting in front of him. He hadn't seen her in fifteen years. On some level he knew she was still attractive, but somehow she disgusted him. She still wore the same perfume. It used to make him hard. At least it had early in their relationship. Now it only nauseated him.

"Just so you know, I left an envelope to be opened if I don't return." She held his gaze. "I wrote that I was meeting you."

She swallowed then and looked away from him. She was afraid of Blue. If she never returned from this meeting, she wanted someone to know he was responsible.

"Jan, if I wanted you dead, you'd be dead."

"I'm in the Witness Protection Program. After you called, all I had to do was dial a number and I'd have been immediately relocated. You would have had to start looking all over again. But I didn't. I believed you, and I want you to get to know Kevin and Timmy again."

"I know you dialed the number. I know you thought you'd be relocated immediately. Witness Protection isn't completely without its flaws. It just took longer than I wanted to find its weaknesses."

She wriggled uncomfortably in her seat in the hotel room, a low tremor starting. Of course. Blue had someone on the inside. The quick jolt of fear caused her heart to begin racing. A lot of people had seen her walk into the hotel lobby. There would be plenty of surveillance footage. She knew he knew that, too. She was safe. But she also wasn't stupid. That's why she'd left the note.

"I told you I wouldn't stop you from seeing the boys." Jan folded her hands. "Why did you need to see me?"

"We'll get to the boys later. You've done well for yourself. Divorced your rich husband. No kids from that marriage to have to take care of. Ours are grown."

She didn't say anything, just stared at him.

He looked down and pinched the bridge of his nose with his fingers. He'd driven thirteen hours straight to have this conversation in person. He was tired, but still focused. A flash of wild red hair and passionate green eyes invaded his thoughts.

He had a half smile on his face when he finally said, "Tell me more about Grunt."

*Blue drove all this way to ask about Grunt?* Jan cleared her throat, "What more do you want to know?"

"For starters, how long was he fucking you?"

Blue hadn't wanted to ask this question, but he'd blurted it out before he could stop himself. It wasn't his main objective for having this meeting, and truth be told, he really didn't care who his ex-wife had screwed. He was more curious than anything.

Jan stiffened. She couldn't tell Blue the truth. What was she going to say? I was pissed that you were screwing women at the motel so I drugged your little brother and handcuffed him to our bed?

She remembered when she'd first found out Blue was sleeping around. She'd had her suspicions, because their lovemaking was becoming less frequent. It was after she'd had their first child, Timmy. She purposely stayed close to Willow after Blue insisted a couple of the girls stay with her when she was pregnant and not taking her medication. Blue had been careful about not letting her have any connection to the gang, so it came as a surprise that he allowed Willow, Chicky, and Moe to spend time with her. She knew she would need a friend at the motel. Someone to keep her clued in as to what was going on there.

After Timmy was born she stayed in regular contact with Willow. If she hadn't known better, she would've thought Willow actually took some pleasure in telling her Blue was sleeping around.

None of that really mattered now, anyway. Yes, she'd been angry with Blue, and her way to get back at him was to sleep with his little brother. She never actually did it for Blue to find out. She was afraid he would've killed them both. She did it because she could, to get back at him. It was her only way of feeling like she was getting some kind of retribution for his infidelity.

She recalled how she'd tricked Grunt into coming to the house while Blue was at work. She made up some excuse about needing Grunt to help her set up a household budget. She'd said Blue was giving her a hard time about her spending and she wanted to surprise him with a financial plan. Of course, it was a lie. If there was one thing that Jan did like to do, it was spend the money that poured in as a result of Blue's active participation in the gang.

Grunt was only too happy to offer his services. He had Moe drop him at his brother's house, and Jan said she'd make sure Blue drove him back to the motel later after dinner. Grunt was so unsuspecting then. He had been hardened somewhat by living at the motel, but there was still an innocence about him.

Grunt sipped on the drink she offered him while they chatted and she told him what she thought she needed help with. Then she told him she kept all their receipts in shoeboxes in the master bedroom closet. Would he mind helping her get them down?

When he woke up, he was groggy, naked, and handcuffed to the headboard. She flushed now when she recollected it hadn't exactly gone like she thought it would. She thought she would have this teenager eating out of the palm of her hand. She needed that. Needed some kind of validation. She would be any man's dream.

But that's not what she got from Grunt. He was angry.

"Unlock the cuffs, Jan," he'd growled after he regained conscious.

She had been fondling him while he was knocked out. It didn't take long for him to be fully aroused after he woke up. She couldn't understand why he was mad.

"Why don't you let yourself just enjoy this?" she'd asked him seductively.

"Get your fucking hands off me!"

She looked him in the eyes. "I don't think you want me to take my hands off of you."

She caressed his erection.

Grunt struggled. "This isn't right, Jan. It's not fair to Blue. Uncuff me and we'll forget it happened."

She couldn't believe what she was hearing. This little shit was turning *her* down? No way. Quickly she straddled him. He wouldn't look at her as she gently lowered herself on to him and started gliding up and down. She knew the minute she'd won. She felt his seed filling her and slowly came to a stop.

"I was your first, wasn't I?" she cooed. He still wouldn't make eye contact.

"Uncuff me," was all he said.

She bent down and started to nuzzle his neck. His next words made her stiffen.

"Get these fucking handcuffs off of me now, you sick, psycho bitch!"

That's when it started. The more repulsed he was by her, the more obsessed she became with him. She couldn't understand it. She was an attractive and sensual woman. She was offering herself freely. Any male would've taken the opportunity in a heartbeat to be with her.

She was certain that after they had sex, he would be finding all kinds of excuses to spend time with her when he knew Blue wouldn't be around. She'd even fantasized about how she'd let him down easy.

She never expected the look of revulsion she'd seen in his eyes. Yes, that was when her obsession with him started. She didn't remember how long it was before she realized she didn't give a shit anymore what Blue was doing at the motel. She started asking Willow about Grunt. Of course, she disguised it as sisterly concern for his well-being, but she wanted to know everything that concerned him. His rebuffs only made the fascination worsen.

And then she heard about that girl. Kit.

Willow didn't realize she was fueling Jan's fixation about Grunt. "I don't know why Grizz just can't let Grunt or someone else have her!" Willow had angrily confessed to Jan one afternoon. "I mean, Grunt is always looking at her. A lot of the guys look at her, but she's perfect for Grunt. They're the same age. I really don't know what Grizz sees in her."

Jan knew the story. Something about the girl being presented as a "thank you gift" to Grizz. She didn't remember seeing anything on the news or in the papers about a missing girl. She was probably a runaway. Nobody knew for certain.

"Why don't you just call in a tip to the police? Maybe if they come out to the motel they'll check in to who she is or something."

"It would never work," Willow huffed. "For starters, it would get back to Grizz. I showed my ass the first night he got her. I was going to strangle her. He would know in a second it was me."

This was interesting. Jan would file that information away for later. In case she ever had a bone to pick with Willow. Jan could call in a tip of her own, but she wouldn't. If Kit was returned to her family and Grizz went to jail for her kidnapping, it would just make it easier for Grunt to actually be with the girl.

Jan had no way of knowing then that a call to the police announcing Kit's presence at the motel wouldn't have gotten past the person who answered the phone. Grizz owned so many people back then. Besides, she didn't need to call the police. She had just given birth to Grunt's child. He would be hers one day. Somehow, some way.

The day Kit spent with her was agony. Especially when she saw how Kit filled out the bathing suit Jan had given her. Jan remembered herself at that age. She was an awkward, gangly teen and flat as an ironing board. Kit had curves. And she was genuinely sweet. Smart. She helped with the boys and doted on them. They loved her too, which only made it worse. No wonder Grizz had wanted her. Their time together was pure torture.

It was all too much for Jan to handle. She was ready to explode by day's end. And she did. In her anger, she was careful not to mention it was Willow who'd told her she saw Grunt watching her. She told Kit that Blue had said it. But it didn't really matter anyway. She could care less if she got Blue in trouble. He was screwing everything with tits and all she wanted was Grunt. And she couldn't have him.

Grunt avoided going to their home as much as possible. He never accepted a drink from her again. She wondered if anybody ever noticed that besides her. Probably not. Grunt was never around enough for it to be obvious. He flat-out ignored her when she told him Kevin was his son. He had been quite the creative tormenter.

If she let herself be honest, Grunt didn't actually do anything to torment her. She tormented herself. She had never been able to accept his rejection.

Now, sitting across from Blue, she decided yes—she was glad Blue had found her and discovered Kevin was Grunt's son. Maybe it would help destroy Grunt's little happily-ever-after with Kit. Jan may have been in Witness Protection, but that didn't stop her from doing some snooping of her own. She knew they had married before Grizz even went to trial. She also knew Grizz was about to die and Blue was angry. Maybe she could exact even more revenge for Grunt's denial of Kevin.

"He raped me," she blurted. "He had Moe drop him at the house when you weren't there. He made up some excuse about wanting to see Timmy. Of course, I never suspected what he really had in mind. You must remember it. It was that time you came home and he was there. We told you we were trying to set up a budget. You didn't really seem to care."

Blue looked at her sideways. "He raped you and you got pregnant with Kevin? Just that one time?"

Blue didn't question a teenager's ability to rape a grown woman. Grunt was big for his age, and he'd learned how to handle himself. He wouldn't have had a problem overpowering Jan. But he just couldn't see Grunt doing that. Blue knew she was lying.

"Once is all it takes, Blue," she answered, looking at her lap. "I couldn't tell you because I didn't want you to kill him. After all, he is your brother and I knew you cared about him. I couldn't ruin that."

Before Blue could respond, she quickly added, "I don't know if you ever noticed, but he stayed away after that. I guess he got what he wanted and that was the end of it. Maybe he felt guilty every time he was around me so he just stayed away as much as he could. I really hated him after that, Blue. I tried not to. I tried to forgive him because he was your brother, but I was always afraid that he might show up again when you weren't there. Especially after he got his license and started driving."

She looked up at him then. Was she convincing him?

"How was he involved with taking down Grizz?" He'd already disregarded the rape story. It didn't matter anyway. He thought he already knew the answer to this question, too, but he had to let her talk.

"I take responsibility for the whole affair thing. Yes. I did cheat on you, but let's be honest, Blue, there was no love lost between us. It was over long before it was over."

If she threw a little confession of her own guilt in there, Blue might be more easily convinced.

He nodded and urged her to continue.

"He came to me during the custody battle." Jan sighed. "Told me he'd been waiting to be with Kit and he was tired of waiting. Said maybe we could help each other. That's all. He just started the ball rolling, but left me and Froggy to carry the weight of it. He got what he wanted, her, and he was done."

This, too, was a lie, but Jan would never tell Blue who had really been instigating everything from behind the scenes. The man who'd come to her during her custody battle had said that he could offer a solution. The perfect solution. By then, she'd moved on from her obsession with Grunt. He had moved on from Kit, too. Or so she'd thought. He always brought that rich bitch, Cindy, to the few gatherings she attended. She didn't care. She was dating attorneys and even a judge behind Blue's back. Let both of them screw whomever they wanted. She wanted to get as far away from the gang as possible by then. She wasn't "old lady" material. She was too good for that low-life group of degenerates.

Blue just looked at her lazily as he asked some more questions. She answered them as best she could. There was a lull in the conversation. The air conditioning unit kicked on, breaking the silence in the hotel room.

"I don't know what can actually be done about any of it now." Jan shrugged. "I mean, it's water under the bridge, Blue. It's been years. Grizz is supposed to die in, what, two, three days? Why does it matter?"

Blue shot her a scornful look. "If you hated Grunt so much for raping you, why didn't you turn him in when you turned in the rest of us? Why wasn't Fess on the list?"

He was just playing with her now. He wanted to watch her

squirm.

This caught her off-guard. She didn't remember who was or wasn't on the list. The person she'd been working with said he'd take care of it all. She remembered that neither Grunt nor Fess had been questioned or interrogated early on, but she thought it was because they weren't really hardened criminals like the others. And after Grizz cut that deal, they were left alone, anyway. She wasn't supposed to know all of this. She had been whisked away long before the trial, but her contact had kept her updated. He, too, must have had an insider. He'd stopped contacting her after Grizz was sentenced to death. She hadn't heard from him since.

She stuttered then. "Isn't it obvious that he wasn't on the list because he was working with someone on the inside? Of course, he would've kept himself off the list."

"And immediately raised our suspicions? I'm telling you, Jan. I know it wasn't Grunt, and I know it wasn't Fess who helped you or got you to help them." He cracked his knuckles and leaned way back in the seat. He was just as big, just as strong as she'd remembered. "Who was it?"

She was really starting to shake now. She was scared, knew she'd backed herself into a corner. "Why don't you find Froggy?" she blurted. "Why don't you ask him?"

"I did find Froggy, but I was too late. Drank himself to death about two years ago." Blue switched tactics. "Look, Jan, you're telling me my kid brother raped you. I believe you. I knew he always had a crush on you. But I know he didn't set up Grizz. I know there is a bastard out there who is responsible for taking my boys away from me. If you tell me who it is, maybe we can help each other."

The words hung between them. She stared at him, eyes wide. She wondered if he knew she'd already spent the large divorce settlement from her second husband. She needed money, and she knew that the man behind Grizz's arrest was very successful. At least he'd been back then. She knew Blue would kill him, but maybe they could work together to extort some money first.

"Okay, I'll tell you." She said quietly as she chanced a glance at his face. "But you have to help me, too. I could use some—"

"Yeah, yeah, I know you're broke. What's his name?" Blue already knew, but it had to be played this way.

"I'm not ready to tell you. I'm not sure I completely trust you, Blue."

"You can trust me, but I understand why you're afraid. You want to hold on to that until I can show you I mean business. It's okay. So we work together. We both get revenge on Grunt and the man responsible for breaking up my family."

"You're not going to kill your own brother, are you?"

"I don't have to kill him, but he'll pay. He'll pay in a big way. We'll work it so that he goes to prison and gets a taste of his own medicine. He may be my brother, but he raped you when you were my wife. That won't go unpunished."

She smiled thinly now. "So what do you need me to do?"

"I need you to come back to Florida with me. Maybe for just a week. Maybe a little longer. We should be able to get enough money out of the guy, assuming he's still alive and still lives there." Blue already knew the guy was alive and living a very comfortable life in Florida. "If not, we can still come up with a plan for Grunt."

"What if we find him and he's not successful? I'm just assuming he is."

"Who do you think has been taking care of Grizz's money while he's been in prison?

She frowned. "If you have Grizz's money, why do we need to extort the guy?"

"It's not about the money for me. He'll pay for taking my kids away. If we can get you some money before I deal with him, then it's just icing on the cake."

She smiled and actually licked her lips slightly, like a cat stalking a bird.

He looked at her seriously then. "If I find out you're lying about any of this, I *will* kill you."

"I have just as much reason to hate them as you do, Blue. Witness Protection wasn't exactly good to me. I had to scrape by as a receptionist at an advertising agency. They wouldn't let me work in a law office because it was too close to what I used to do. If I hadn't met Richard or he hadn't been able to take care of me, I don't know what would've happened to me or the boys. I was a week away from applying for welfare. No, Witness Protection is not a good place to be. Whatever it is, I'll help you."

It was true. She couldn't care less about the guy who'd convinced her to help him go after Grizz. She wanted some money, and she'd be happy to let Blue do whatever he wanted to the man. But Grunt was a different story. Grunt had rejected her. He would pay for that. She listened to Blue's plan.

Then she opened her cell phone and made a call.

"I keep the key hidden in the fake rock. Just water them every couple of days. Maybe you could turn a light on at night. I'm in such a hurry I didn't have time to plan." Jan waited while the person on the other end of the phone said something. "Oh, you are a gem, Connie. Thank you. I'll see you in a week or so."

Jan closed her phone and looked at Blue. "All taken care of. My neighbor will water my plants and make sure the house looks lived in."

Blue nodded and reached into his pocket, pulling out a wad of cash. He'd convinced her to leave with him without going home to pack. The promise of a new wardrobe was too enticing for Jan to pass up. He knew she was on the brink of losing her house. Instead of getting a job when she divorced, she lived the life of a socialite and believed she would be able to snare another wealthy husband before her money ran out. She was wrong. That's why she was jumping at this chance, and Blue knew it.

He also knew she hadn't had any contact with the boys in over a year. She wouldn't be missed.

"We'll take my car and leave yours here. I'll fly you back next week. This hotel is pretty fancy. Why don't you take yourself downstairs to that boutique I saw in the lobby and buy yourself something nice to celebrate our new partnership."

She actually squealed when she grabbed the money from his hand. "You want to come with me and help me pick out some expensive lingerie? I know they have it." She batted her eyelashes.

It was all he could do not to roll his eyes. "I'll be down in a sec. I have to take a piss."

She picked up her purse and headed for the lobby. He knew she couldn't resist the green stuff.

Alone, he looked around the room. Nobody would ever trace her back to this room or this hotel. The credit card he'd used to hold the room was stolen. The room would be cleaned and used over the next week, anyway. He pulled his own cell phone out of his pocket and dialed a number.

"It's a go. You'll need to get in the house. Key is under a fake rock. The lady next door will be keeping an eye out, so be careful. You need to find some kind of envelope or note she left saying she's meeting with me. She's not the sharpest tool in the shed, so it's probably on the fucking counter."

He paused then. "No, the keys won't be in it. I'm sure they're in her purse. Just get her car away from this hotel. Strip it, dump it, I don't care what you do with it. As long as it can't be traced back to her."

The person on the other end of the line said something else. Blue replied, "I already swiped her phone. She didn't even notice. I'll get rid of it."

He snapped his own phone shut then and went downstairs to find his ex-wife.

# Chapter Sixty-Five
1985, Washington, D.C.,
Federal Bureau of Investigation Headquarters

LESTER FOREMAN TOSSED the file on his desk and looked at the agent sitting in front of him. "Who is this hotshot attorney that's screwing with him?"

"Matthew Rockman is a punk." The agent smirked. "He's young, slick, and thinks he's invincible. The only connection we can make is that he went to the same high school as the wife. That's it. He's a defense attorney, but is secretly working inside the D.A.'s office to target the gang. Specifically, Talbot. He's been buddies with Talbot's attorney. Seems like Lewis took him under his wing a few years ago."

Foreman nodded. "Carey Lewis. Yeah, he's another slick piece of shit. Does he know Rockman is working with the state to bring down his best-paying client?"

The agent shook his head. "We don't think so."

Foreman wasn't sure what to do with this new information. He'd taken over as special director a couple of years back after Spiro retired. He knew the case in detail, though truthfully there wasn't a whole lot to know. Still, he was the best choice to take over. He also knew nothing they'd tried in the past had worked. Talbot had been getting away with shit for years. Nobody seemed to be able to stop his criminal activities. Worse yet, they seemed to let him get away with it because of the occasional help he provided them. Supposedly, he was one of theirs. Foreman knew something was rotten about this particular operation, but he'd never been able to figure out what.

They'd tried. Tried their damndest over the years. Sometimes, it didn't seem like much was happening. Years would go by, and even though they watched and still had their man on the inside, there was no movement toward a resolution. Then, someone would be promoted, an election would be won, and it was stirred up all over again.

One thing he knew for certain. Talbot had something. Something that somebody with immense power wanted. They'd even thought about using the wife as a pawn, but Talbot was too smart. If they so much as went near her, they knew he'd blow the lid off something that would bring powerful families to their knees. If they killed him, they knew he had something set in place upon his death to do the same thing.

The simple fact was, they were fucked. They'd tried to make deals over the years. He'd never budged. It was a waiting game. They even had to let their inside man go rogue to prove he could be trusted. They didn't even know if their inside man was still their guy or not.

Foreman did know the FBI had the same experience with Talbot's predecessor, Donald "Red" Enman. Like one big cat and mouse game. A pissing contest over who had the upper hand. Red and Talbot were both considered agents, yet had to maintain their own criminal activities to be believable. But in Foreman's opinion, Talbot went too far. Even for an undercover FBI operative with a very long leash.

Foreman stared at his agent hard. "We've let him get away with shit for years without interfering. I say we don't interfere with this, either. Let's see what Rockman can get done. He must have some powerful friends to take on Talbot without exposing himself. Let them do it. Let them shake up his world and his life. Knowing him, he'll get out of it, but let's wait and see." He made a face. "Shit, who knows, maybe he'll come to us and we can use it to our advantage."

Foreman steepled his fingers. *Maybe we can even use it to get back whatever it was he supposedly stole all those years ago.*

# Chapter Sixty-Six
2000

"I CAN'T BREATHE! You're choking me!" She started to cough and sputter. After she was good and scared, really scared, Tommy relaxed his grip on her throat.

"I did it for all of us, Tommy." Sarah Jo clutched at her throat and backed away toward the stairway.

Moments ago, he'd practically shoved her inside her front door, kicking it closed behind them and pushing her up against the wall. He controlled his rage now. For the moment.

"Call your office and tell them you can't come in today," he said. His voice was calm. Dead calm.

Sarah Jo shivered. "Look, Tommy, I can't call in sick. You have no idea what I have going on today. We can talk about this tomorrow, the next day, whenever you want." She tried not to show her fear as she straightened her blouse and retucked her clothing.

But her attitude sent Tommy over the edge.

"Call them now, dammit!" He screamed at her, and she literally jumped back, fear pulsing through her once again. She'd never seen Tommy lose his temper. Never. She didn't even know if she could trust him right now.

She didn't think she'd ever been so scared.

Jo fished in her purse for her cell phone, eyes still on Tommy. Then, with her back to him, she dialed a number.

"Hi, it's me," she said, affecting a weak voice. "Uh, listen, sorry, but I'm going to need you to cancel all of my appointments today. I was ready to walk out the door and had to run back to the bathroom. I don't know what hit me, but I am so sick." There was a pause in the conversation. "No, I think it's a bug. I threw up my breakfast and now I have a blazing headache. I just have to lay down." Another pause. "No, I'll be okay. I just got off the phone with my friend, Tommy. He's stopping by on his way to work to drop off something for my headache. I don't have anything in the house."

She looked back over her shoulder at Tommy then, and he rolled his eyes. She snapped the phone shut, then motioned for him to take a seat on the couch.

He did, crossing his arms in front of his chest. "Nice move, Jo. Dropping that little hint that your friend Tommy was stopping by. I guess that's in case I decide to kill you, so the police will know who to go after. You should write crime novels for a living."

"Oh, just shut up, Tommy. Just shut up."

"I am shutting up. And you're going to spill it."

She stood on the other side of the coffee table, facing him. And told him everything.

Ten minutes later, Tommy couldn't take it anymore. He was ready to explode with anger.

"You are going to stand there and tell me you had Willow send Darryl to rape, beat, and almost kill Ginny *for you and me and her*? To be fucking *helpful*? That you somehow convinced poor Moe to assist you? You are delusional, Jo. You are fucking insane if you think I am going to believe that."

"Yes, Tommy, that's exactly why I did it. But he wasn't supposed to hurt Ginny." Jo's eyes were red. "He was supposed to just deliver her back to the police. You aren't listening to me. I didn't hate Ginny. I loved Ginny! I loved you, too, Tommy. But Grizz? I *hated* Grizz." Venom laced her words.

"And it never occurred to you that Willow's hatred of Ginny might have resulted in what actually happened to her? You knew that by getting Willow to help you, you were risking Ginny's life, Jo. You knew that damn well."

"No! I didn't know that! I thought Willow would've been just as happy to see her returned and away from Grizz. I didn't know she hated Ginny enough to have someone almost kill her."

"That is bullshit, Jo! You knew Willow despised Ginny. I don't care if it'd been years. Ginny was the reason Grizz tossed her out on her ass. How could you not even suspect it could've turned out as bad as it did?"

She didn't answer him. Her shoulders were shaking now, and she gripped her thighs to control herself.

"Moe said in her journal that someone named Wendy told her that Grizz had taken something from her. So. What did Grizz take from you, Jo?"

"Journal?" She looked genuinely bewildered. "And what did Grizz take from me? Are you serious, Tommy? He took my father. He took my mild mannered, sweet loving father who could never even bring himself to spank his own kids. He paid my father to keep his ledgers or whatever it was Dad did for him. Do you know how many times over the years our home was raided by the police looking for those stupid ledgers?"

Tommy didn't expect this. He knew there was a certain price to pay for being associated with Grizz, but he hadn't realized that it had affected Sarah Jo so much.

But he forced himself not to cave. A raid was nothing compared to what had happened to Ginny. And all because of Jo.

"An occasional raid?" Tommy snorted. "I know that's tough if you're not used to it, but it couldn't have been that bad. Especially if they never found anything. They must've eventually backed off."

"Okay, so how about the fact that my father went to the motel to fuck a two-bit, good for nothing, mute whore?" she screamed at him. "And after *she* died, another one started coming around! Trying to act like she was better than a used-up piece of biker shit. Trying to act like she was the lady of *our* house. Chicky had the audacity to come to my home and cook for my father like she could ever replace my mother."

Jo stood up then and strode to the window. "That's what Grizz took from me, Tommy," she said, her voice soft now, so soft he had to strain to hear her. "He took the father that wouldn't have given Moe or Chicky the time of day because he knew what it was like to be with a real lady. My mother was a class act and because of Grizz my father stooped to eating out of garbage cans."

She was breathing heavy now, her face turning a dull, deep red. Tommy could only stare in disbelief. He never knew Sarah Jo had so much hostility for Grizz or the group. Especially for Chicky and Moe. He understood her pain. But he couldn't understand her hatred.

Chicky and Moe might not have been ladies, but they weren't bad people.

Tommy raised an eyebrow. "If it weren't for Grizz, you and your family would've been living out of your car. You do know that your father was on the brink of bankruptcy, right? He was going to lose his house. Your mother's illness devastated him financially."

Her face turned even redder now, if that was possible. "How dare you!" she yelled. "How dare you accuse my mother of being the reason my father had to earn extra money to feed us and keep a roof over our heads by rubbing elbows with the lowest form of scum in this city. My mother was perfect! She was perfect in every way!"

Jo was yelling so hard she was losing her voice. A slow thin line of blood trickled from her nose. She used her arm to swipe across her face. Tommy jumped up and ran to the kitchen, quickly returning with a dishtowel. He blotted at her nose, then roughly guided her back to the couch.

It was obvious to Tommy Sarah Jo had some serious issues. Issues she'd kept bottled up for years. Apparently he'd just witnessed what happens when you try to pretend that a volcano will remain dormant.

He swallowed as he waited for her to regain control of her emotions. He never knew. Never even suspected she resented Fess's involvement with the gang.

Turning to face her now, he asked, "Why did you have Darryl attack Ginny? Why, Jo?"

Her shoulders slumped. "I already told you, he wasn't supposed to *hurt* her, Tommy. I love Ginny. I swear on my mother's grave I had no intention of anyone getting hurt. In a million years I never thought Willow would incite Darryl to do what he did. I really thought she'd be happy to have Ginny dropped off at the police station. And then Grizz would get in trouble, real trouble. Maybe do some time. My intentions were not hate-filled, Tommy."

She whispered the last part, her eyes filled with tears now, any remaining anger forgotten for the moment.

"Yes, they were, Jo," he said gently but firmly. "You may not have realized it, but you did hate. You hated Moe because your father cared for her. You hated Grizz. And you may have thought you were getting Grizz back by taking Ginny away, but your hatred went far deeper than you cared to admit."

They were quiet a moment, then something else dawned on him. "Fuck, Jo. Now that I think about it, you gave Ginny a really hard time about naming Mimi after Moe. You raised a fit over her name, saying it was old fashioned, that the baby would grow up to hate it. It was *you* who hated it. I should have sensed something way back then. I just trusted you too much."

Sarah Jo ignored the last comment. "She wasn't supposed to get hurt. It was supposed to be simple: Grizz goes to jail. Ginny goes home. You could have been with her then. Everybody would have been happy. Don't you see how I was looking at it?"

"I want to see it, but I can't. You do realize you are responsible for your best friend's torture, rape, and near death? And you are as guilty of Moe, Willow, and Darryl's deaths as if you'd killed them yourself."

She didn't answer him, but just stared at the wall. He was right. She'd lived with that guilt all these years, masking it as best she could. But it would never go away.

"And the Chicky you accused of caring for your father actually saved you."

This caught Sarah Jo's attention. She cast a wary glance.

Tommy looked at her steadily. "You never asked how I found out it was you, Jo. After Moe died, Chicky found her journal and she read it. And she recognized something in it that Grizz might've recognized, too. When Moe wrote about being contacted by Wendy, she wrote that Wendy said it would be 'tit for tat.' *That's* how I knew it was you. I've heard you use that phrase a million times. I guess Chicky heard you say it, too, from those times at your house when she tried to start a relationship with your dad. Moe didn't recognize the phrase or your voice because you never let yourself anywhere near Moe. She wasn't good enough for you or your father, so you snubbed her." Tommy rubbed at his eyes. "I'm ashamed I never noticed it. She was a good person, Jo. She'd been through a lot. God only knows if you'd ever said it around Grizz, but if you had and he read that journal and recognized it, nothing on earth could've protected you from him. I don't care if you are Fess's daughter or Ginny's supposed best friend. Grizz would've hung you out to dry and Fess wouldn't have been able to stop him."

Sarah Jo swallowed audibly. "I was really rude to Chicky when she used to come to our house," she said in a small voice. "Nobody would've blamed her if she'd showed Grizz the journal or told him what she'd figured out. When did she give it to you?"

"She didn't," he answered. "Her daughter brought it to our house after Grizz's execution. Said that she'd been holding onto it since Chicky's death a few years ago; said her mother specifically told her to wait until after Grizz died to give it to me and Ginny."

Sarah Jo sat up a little straighter on the couch. "I guess she's no angel then, is she? She could've gotten rid of it, but no. She hung on to it all this time just so she could hurt me."

"No, Jo." His voice sounded tired. All those years, throughout their long friendship, he had no idea this was who Sarah Jo was at heart. "Not so she could hurt you. So that Ginny and I would know the truth about what happened back then. To know the real reason behind Moe's suicide. Moe killed herself because of guilt. She felt that by helping Wendy, you, she had caused Ginny's near death."

"Ginny didn't die," Jo protested. "I don't know why Moe felt she had to kill herself."

"Sarah Jo, who *are* you? Are you even hearing yourself? Maybe it wasn't the only reason Moe killed herself. Maybe she was lonely and sad, and you sure as shit didn't help with that."

"And you did? You were so busy slobbering after Ginny and then moving in with Cindy that you forgot about Moe, too. Admit it. She was nothing to you. Not really. Don't pretend like she actually meant something. Moe was invisible. At least I'm honest about what I thought about her. You're hiding behind some kind of self-righteous, superior attitude like you cared. Yeah, you cared so much you left her at the motel with that beast when you moved out. I knew he'd gone too far the day I saw him make that poor drifter eat his own puke in my garage. Believe me, I was doing the right thing when I tried to get Ginny away from him. And I don't care if you tell Ginny. I'll tell her myself. She'll forgive me. She loves me and she'll understand." Jo sniffed. "Besides, she lived with Grizz. She had to forgive him every day of her life."

When he spoke, his voice was hard. "No, I don't think she'll understand this, Jo. Ever. Do you know the mental anguish she has suffered feeling responsible for Moe's death? For Willow and Darryl's deaths? She felt indirectly responsible for all of it, and you're going to sit there and smugly tell me my wife will forgive you? No. That's not going to happen. For starters, we've been through hell since Grizz's execution, and I'm not piling one more thing on her."

"Well, then good." Jo straightened her shoulders again, like she was trying to tuck everything—all the chaos, all the drama, all the anguish—back into one neat little box. "It's agreed then that she doesn't have to know. And we can pretend this conversation never happened."

She glanced at her watch and started to rise from the couch. "I have just enough time. I can change and still be at the office for my ten o'clock."

"No." Tommy stood, too. "You're not going anywhere, Jo. You are going to spend the morning on the phone with your husband. You are going to convince Stan to take one of those job offers he keeps getting from different countries. I want him to start interviewing before the end of this month."

A harsh laugh escaped her lips. "You are crazy if you think I'm moving, Tommy. Our life is here. So is my career."

"Jo, I don't know what happened to you. I don't know where you snapped. Maybe it was the actual moment your mother passed away. Maybe it was the day you first discovered your dad was sleeping with Moe. Maybe it was the day you saw some guy eat puke. I don't know, and I don't care. I just know I will not let you stay in the same city, state, or country and pretend to be a real friend to my wife."

"I *am* her real friend, Tommy." She crossed her arms. "I'm yours, too."

"No. I can't stand to even look at you anymore."

This took Sarah Jo by surprise. "Fine." She exhaled slowly. "I'll break off my friendship with her, but that's only going to hurt her more."

"Which is why I want you out of the country. Your friendship will die off slowly. Knowing Gin, she'll try to keep in contact with phone calls and emails, but you'll be too busy to get back to her. Just one of those things. People drift apart all the time."

"You aren't hearing me, Tommy. I *genuinely* love Ginny." Jo's brow creased. "I genuinely love you and your family. I'm sorry, Tommy. I don't know how to say it enough. I didn't do it to hurt her."

"But you did hurt her, Jo. You did, and you will remove yourself from our lives," he told her matter-of-factly. "Forever and permanently."

"She trusts me, Tommy. She called me to cry on my shoulder after she found out Grizz was your father. She wasn't going to tell me because she was afraid I knew, too, and she didn't want to think we'd deceived her together. Did you know any of that, Tommy?" She blinked, watching his face. "Doesn't sound like you've been very truthful about things, either."

Tommy smiled at Sarah Jo. A long, slow smile. But it wasn't a kind smile. Not at all. As a matter of fact, it was a smile Jo had never seen before.

"Why don't you say what this is really about, Tommy? Huh? Why don't you admit why you really want me out of the country? You finally got what you wanted. He's dead and you have your happily-ever-after with Ginny. I'm a reminder of that old life and you want as far away from that life as possible. Am I right? Why can't you face...,"

Before she finished her sentence he was gripping her arms tightly, so forcefully it hurt. His face was so close she could feel his warm breath.

"Jo, you should know better than to fuck with me." His voice was cold as ice. "Especially now that you know whose blood is running through my veins. Get your ass out of town, or you'll be sorry. This is your one and only warning."

He walked out the front door without looking back.

Sarah Jo followed him and stood in her doorway as she watched Tommy slip into his car and away from their friendship.

She stared through narrowed eyes, and in barely a whisper, she said, "Yeah, I know whose blood runs through your veins and he's gone for good. I never realized what an arrogant, scary son-of-a-bitch you could be, Tommy. If I'd known that, then I wouldn't have tried to help you be with her. It's *me* who shouldn't be fucked with. And I guess you'll have to learn that the hard way."

She watched him drive away and closed the door. She had to clean up so she could get to work.

# Chapter Sixty-Seven
2000

GINNY SAT IN her Sunday school classroom and stared at the blank dry erase board on the wall. Whenever her heart became heavy, she always seemed to find herself at church. They'd started locking the church years ago, but the Sunday school teachers were each given their own keys. Many times, after just sitting in the church by herself, she would wander up the stairs to her second grade classroom. She didn't know exactly what pulled her there; maybe she found something comforting in the innocence of the young children. Even empty, the room seemed filled with their presence and sweet joy. She looked at the walls and started to smile as she saw their hand-printed names on the angel pictures they'd drawn the Sunday before Grizz died. Laney. Jonathan. Noah. Eduardo.

She looked away then and down at her left hand. She moved the wide wedding band so she could see his name. Grizz.

She knew right before the execution that Grizz had wanted to see she still had his name there. She knew it was his way of confirming she still loved him before he died. She'd wanted him to have that last consolation— and the fact that Tommy approved of her doing it told her something else. That in spite of it all, he wasn't a lying, deceitful person. At least not anymore. He'd stood in the shadows and waited to be with her for years. It was his idea to name their son after Grizz because he knew it would mean something to her. Just like she'd asked, Tommy had taken her to see Eddie after the execution. She didn't have the tattoo removed. What she did do was have Eddie put the finishing touches on it. A date. The date Grizz had died. It was her way of actually saying goodbye to him. She was so proud of herself for not passing out while Eddie worked on it. She remembered it burned, kind of like a bee sting. It itched for a little while after that. She absently rubbed at it now.

She took a deep breath and allowed herself to think about everything that had transpired since Grizz's death. Not just the trauma of his execution, but all of the secrets that came with it. Then just this morning, Tommy had called to tell her Sarah Jo's husband, Stan, was interviewing for some of the job offers he'd received from other countries. She felt like she was losing a little piece of herself with Sarah Jo moving.

But she was also starting to believe in new beginnings. She glanced out the window at the bright sunshine, the vivid Technicolor blue sky. Carter's husband, Bill, would be back in town tomorrow, and she really didn't have any excuse to stay there anymore. She missed her children. She missed her home.

She missed her husband.

She thought about the hours and hours of conversation she'd had with Tommy. The explanations. The real stories. She'd probably asked him the same questions twenty different ways, trying to trip him up, trying to catch him in a lie. Liars forget their lies so they eventually mess up. But every story matched. Every question was answered the same way.

Did she believe her husband? Yes, when she thought about it, she did. At least she *wanted* to believe him. He seemed to be forthcoming about everything.

But could she move on from here? Could she put the past behind her and start fresh with Tommy? Could she accept that he was Grizz's son? Mimi's half-brother? Could she live with it? Those were the real questions.

She wasn't sure if she knew the answers. But one thing she did know—she wouldn't be able to make a decision until she went home. Until she went back to her marriage and her house to see if she could live a life that had not been of her choosing, but one she had grown to cherish.

Did she love Tommy? Yes, she believed she did. But she was starting to doubt herself, and the only way to figure out the truth was to be with him. To see what she felt.

She had an instant thought and felt immediate shame. If she'd learned these secrets when Grizz was still alive would she have stayed with Tommy? Or would she have settled for a life that had her visiting Grizz in jail regularly up until his execution?

Anger rippled when she realized the answer. No. She wouldn't have done that because Grizz wouldn't have let her. She'd tried to tell him when he was in the county jail that she would've gladly lived that life, but he wouldn't allow it.

Again, a decision that had been taken away from her.

Her anger provided some resolve. She would go home to see if she could work it out with Tommy. She would give him a chance. She did love him, and not just because Grizz had pushed them together, but because he really was an amazing man, husband, and father. She didn't like the lies, but that had been a teenage Tommy. A teenager who had fallen in love with her. She would go home. She would try.

The fact that she found herself wanting to try felt like a weight had been lifted.

Her cell phone rang, interrupting her new revelation. "Hello?"

"Ginny." It was Tommy.

She smiled when she heard his voice. It must've been a sign. "Tommy, I'm so glad you called. I'm at the church. I—I'm going back to Carter's now. I'm going to get my things and come home." She paused, but he was quiet. "I'm not saying everything is fine. I'm just saying I'd like to try."

He didn't say anything at first. What was wrong? This is what he wanted, wasn't it? He'd been begging her to come home. Why wasn't he excited that she'd made up her mind?

"I need you to come home right now." That's when she heard it—the undercurrent of concern in his voice. Something was wrong. "Some detectives are here. They want to talk to us."

"Talk to us? About what?"

"Apparently, they just found a body down by the beach. It's a woman and she's been murdered. They say it's Jan. They're questioning me, Ginny. They're making it sound like they think I could've had something to do with it. I think I'm being set up."

"What? Jan, Blue's wife? What's going on? Oh my God, Tommy!"

"I can't go in to it now, honey. I just need you home. Okay?"

"Do I need to call our attorney? Or maybe I should call Vanderline. Should I ask her what we should do?"

Vanderline had made quite a good life for herself. After saving her money and putting herself through law school, she had become a respected attorney. She was now a judge in New York.

But the line had already gone dead. Shakily, she laid her phone on the little table next to where she was sitting. Jan's murder? Tommy told her Blue had recently found Jan. What had Blue done?

She felt a crushing weight on her chest now. Would they never escape the darkness associated with the gang? Without even needing to ask for details, she knew her husband was right. He was being set up. It was probably something Grizz had ordered in retaliation for what he saw as Tommy's deception. Between the billy club revelation and Tommy being Kevin's father, Tommy clearly had not been forgiven. By Grizz or by Blue.

That nod to Tommy at the execution hadn't meant anything. And it didn't even matter that Grizz was gone. He was a formidable and powerful enemy, even from the grave.

Quickly, she gathered her phone and purse. Tommy needed her. She would get answers as soon as she got home. She still wasn't sure where she was emotionally. But she'd felt an urgency to defend him at all costs after hearing this latest news. Did that tell her anything?

She headed down the stairs and out to her car. Moments later, she was headed for home.

# Chapter Sixty-Eight
2000

TWO WEEKS LATER, Ginny and Tommy talked quietly in their bed, legs tangled loosely. Tommy had been questioned by the police, but to their surprise, soon they zeroed in on a bigger suspect: Matthew Rockman, who was now behind bars.

"I still can't believe Matthew Rockman's in jail!" Ginny told Tommy as they laid there, wrapped in each other's arms.

Earlier that day, Tommy had told her what he'd learned from the police: that Matthew had apparently had a vendetta from the start and had never gotten over Grizz threatening him and then abducting Ginny. He'd harbored a grudge for a very long time and had used Jan and Froggy to take the focus off of who was secretly going after Grizz. Himself. He manipulated it to look like it was all Blue's wife's idea because of the custody battle. It was pretty clever. Or so Matthew thought at the time.

Matthew must have panicked when Jan showed up back in town demanding money.

"I guess Matthew just freaked out and killed her," Ginny said while resting in the crook of Tommy's arm.

"I guess he knew he didn't have enough money to keep Jan quiet forever. She would suck him dry and hold it over his head that all she had to do was tell Blue that Matthew was behind the arrests. He knew he would be killed for his part in taking on the gang, putting Grizz on death row, and sending Blue's family into Witness Protection."

She sighed. "All these years and I blamed myself for Grizz's arrest. I really believed Jan was behind it because she found my wallet. Of course, it looked that way, but Matthew always knew my real name." She bit her lip. "He really did use Jan well."

They lay still awhile, listening to the tick of the ceiling fan, the hum of the air conditioner.

He pulled her closer now, whispering, "Ginny, it's over. Can we really try to put all this behind us now? Can we really start over, sweetheart?" He pulled back so he could look directly into her eyes.

She fiddled with her ring. "But what about Kevin, Tommy? If he's your son, shouldn't we acknowledge it or something? I mean, we could do a DNA test to be sure, but I've seen his picture. You're right. There's no doubt he's your son. You were super young when you got her pregnant."

He'd already told her the story about how Jan had forced him. It still made her sick to think about it. That woman had been crazy. And now she was gone.

"Grizz must've been super young when he got Candy pregnant with me, too, come to think of it." Tommy raised an eyebrow and chuckled a little. "Guess it's in our genes."

She squeezed his hand. "Sometimes I thought I had a déjà vu about something Jason did or said. I would tell myself that it was probably something you did at his age, but then I would remember that I didn't know you when you were a little kid. But I knew Kevin. That's what it was. I remembered Kevin as a boy. Knowing that Kevin is Jason's older brother, it makes sense now."

"I've talked to Blue about this, Ginny. I want Kevin to be in our lives, and he can be, but I don't know if it's necessary to tell him I'm his biological father just yet. Unless there was a medical crisis or something, I don't see how that would be good for anybody. Blue loves those boys and never stopped looking for them all those years. He was pissed at first until I told him what really happened. He knew his wife. He knew I wasn't lying about that. He wants to try to start a relationship with them again. He's not interfering with their lives, but he does want to try to get to know them. We will tell Kevin one day. I just don't think the time is right. I think we could both benefit from some counseling first. You know, to make sure we're handling it right. So much has happened in such a short time and I don't want to jump right in. I know we're both anxious to get the truth out there and move on from everything that has happened, but we need to consider how it could affect Kevin. We need to know *how* to approach him.

"You're right. It's complicated enough with all of the ramifications of you being Grizz's son. Hopefully, Kevin will remember us. Maybe we can work our way back into his life when the time is right. I agree. We need to talk to a therapist or someone that can help us." She paused then. "Will we ever tell Mimi about her father?"

"I'm her father, Ginny."

"I know that, Tommy, I mean—"

He cut her off. "I know what you mean. But I don't want our lives turned into some stupid afternoon talk show where people throw chairs at each other on stage. I know you resent living all of these years with the secrets and the lies."

"Exactly, Tommy," she said, sitting up and turning to look at him. "And I don't want that for Mimi."

"Neither do I." He sighed. "We'll tell her. She needs to know. Has the right to know. This is something else we can talk to a therapist about. She's my daughter. I'm not going to risk losing her, Gin. But I want to make sure we handle it right. We'll tell her, but only after seeking counseling. Agreed?"

"Agreed." She nodded and lay back against his shoulder.

"In the meantime, how about a getaway?" he asked.

"Just the two of us?"

"As much as I would love to do nothing but make love with my wife for a week on a tropical island, I know the kids have felt neglected this past month. Staying overnight with friends, both of us coming and going as we tried to sort through all of this. I want my family back. How about a cruise with that big mouse? The one with the high-pitched voice," he teased.

She grinned. "That sounds good, Tommy. Maybe I can get us booked before school starts again so they won't have to miss any days so early in the new school year."

"Sounds like a plan." He reached over to turn off the lamp on his nightstand.

She turned to him in the darkness. Slowly, she began kissing his neck, then made her way over until she found his lips. Her hand made its way down his stomach. It was the first time they'd made love since before Grizz's execution.

"I've missed you, Tommy," she said as her hand found his

erection.

It was obvious he missed her, too.

Tommy deepened the kiss, then quickly flipped Ginny onto her back, kissing his way down her neck, her breasts, her smooth, flat belly.

He swallowed back nausea as he blocked out what he knew. He'd have to act like everything was okay. It was a good thing his dick was cooperating. He was getting ready to go down on his wife, and the thought of it made him want to vomit.

# Chapter Sixty-Nine

2000

IT FELT GOOD to be in Tommy's arms again. Ginny hated to admit it, but early in their marriage there had been times she'd been making love to Tommy when she would think about Grizz. She'd felt like she was committing adultery against Grizz.

But now, even though she mourned Grizz and would always love him, she felt she was able to give herself over to Tommy without feeling like she was betraying Grizz. His death, although extremely painful, had provided some closure.

Ginny burrowed deeper into the crook of Tommy's arm.

"I need to spend some time again at Carter's, Tommy." Before he could object, she added, "Not now. Maybe when we get back from our cruise. I need to clean out the garage."

She felt him relax. "Let's do it before the cruise, honey. I'll go and help you."

"No, I think I should do this myself." She snuggled closer. "Besides, when we get back from our trip, you'll go back to work and the kids will be in school. I've been thinking about it a little. I'll start by putting the cars and motorcycles up for sale. Then I can tackle the guest room above the garage. It shouldn't be too hard. Grizz really didn't have a lot of personal stuff."

"Ginny, I don't know if you should do this alone. Going through all those things—it could be really tough. Tougher than you realize."

"I won't be all alone. Carter will be around taking care of her animals. I'll let her know if I need her." She turned to gaze up at him in the darkness. "Tommy, I think this is something I have to do without you. You have to understand that. I know you do."

"Yes, honey," he said and kissed her forehead. "I understand."

She fell asleep almost immediately. Tommy lay in the dark for a long time listening to the sound of her breathing. He told himself he had a clear conscience now. At least as clear as it could be for someone who had lived the life he'd lived. All the lies and deceptions over the years had given him a false sense of self-righteousness. When you told yourself, convinced yourself, you were doing something for the good of someone you loved, it didn't seem so bad.

He'd told Ginny in great detail about his last meeting with Grizz in prison before the execution, leaving out only the things they'd both agreed she shouldn't know. Things too dangerous for her to know. He'd made the hard decision not to tell her about Sarah Jo's part in her rape, which had led to Moe's suicide. He didn't know whether that was the right thing to do or not, but it felt right. As much as he wanted Sarah Jo to pay for her brutal dishonesty, he felt telling Ginny about Jo's real reason for moving out of the country would have only caused more pain. He was afraid one more revelation would break her.

He had to admit to himself: his wife was strong. Stronger than he'd ever realized. She could've handled knowing about Jo, and maybe one day he would tell her. Just not today. Chicky had been right to keep that journal from Grizz. It had probably saved Sarah Jo's life.

He thought more about his last meeting with Grizz, right before the execution. Tommy thought he'd have to convince Grizz he wasn't the one who'd gone to Jan about taking down Grizz, Blue and the gang along with them. But to his surprise, he didn't need to do any convincing at all.

**********

"I know it wasn't you. But Grunt, I was pissed." Tommy and Grizz stood in the alcove to the prison yard, the hot sun blazing beyond the covered overhang. It was three days before the execution.

Grizz huffed out a breath, then kicked at the cement slab. "You have to remember what that fucking reporter had told me about the billy club. I talked to you, we worked it out, I didn't like it, but what was I going to do? Have you killed and leave Kit alone? But then Blue waltzes in with pictures of his kids, says one is yours. Tells me Jan said it was you behind my arrest. It all came back how you manipulated me that night. Other nights, too. Admit it, Grunt. It looked bad for you. Real bad."

Tommy nodded. It did look bad.

"But I know why you did what you did. You did it for her."

Surprised, Tommy stared at Grizz. "Always, Grizz. It's always been about her. Look." He exhaled sharply. "You're going to the table soon. I have no reason to hide anything from you. I know you think I set you up. I know you think I fucked Jan."

Grizz put his hand up. "Stop right there. I don't give a shit about Jan, and I know Blue doesn't either. When she told us it was you who set it all up, *that's* what pissed me off. But just for a second. Nobody double crosses me—"

"I didn't double cross—"

"Shut the fuck up for a minute and let me finish. I know it wasn't you. Okay? How many times do I have to say it? You were a kid when you pulled all that bullshit. I can't blame you for being in love with Kit. I'm still in love with her myself. I've done a lot of things that would make another man cringe. The only thing I ever did that twisted my gut into pieces was telling her to marry you. To stop coming to see me. To make sure my daughter never knew me. I get it, kid. I get it all, and I understand it. I don't like it, but I accept it. Because I love her."

"You can stop calling me kid," Tommy said with a smirk. "I'm as big as you."

Grizz ignored that last comment. No one was as big as him. "I've had a lot of time to think in here, Grunt, and the more I thought, the more I wondered how Blue's slutty wife could've pulled it off. I could've kicked myself in the ass for not thinking about it sooner. I was pretty certain I'd been right in my thinking the first time."

"Who? Who was it?"

"That little prick, Matthew fucking Rockman. Rockman is responsible for bringing that shit storm into my life, and thanks to him, I'm going to the table in a couple of days. Can't do anything about it now but trust Blue to handle it."

Tommy blinked. Matthew Rockman? He had a quick flash of the guy. The young attorney who suggested to Ginny that she use Carey Lewis's firm for Grizz's defense. *That* punk was the one who'd caused all the dominoes to fall?

"So, we good now?" Grizz was saying to Tommy.

"I'm good if you're good," Tommy answered, relief evident in his tone.

"Wanna take a walk around the yard with me? I want to hear everything about my daughter and grandson. I want to know everything about them before I die."

Tommy hesitated. The yard? Was Grizz setting him up? Were there guys waiting in the yard to jump him?

"Are you allowed to take visitors in the yard?"

"I'll be dead in a few days. They let me do what I want. C'mon."

Reluctantly he'd followed Grizz out to the yard. It was empty and had an oval track, much like the track Ginny used to jog on back at the motel.

It was there that Grizz told him everything. Everything from the very beginning. Grizz started by explaining why he wanted to talk outside. Apparently, even with his clout, the prison still might have ears, and he had to be certain nobody would hear what he had to tell Tommy.

Grizz told him not to be surprised when he was questioned about Jan's upcoming murder. Tommy should've been surprised, but he wasn't. This was Grizz.

"When Blue was here last, I told him I would signal someone in the viewing room as to whether or not to take you down. I believe what you've told me today, so I'll signal accordingly. It'll all play out like I planned, but you need to know I have things in place that look like it might lead to you, but they won't. They'll only look like Rockman's sloppy attempt to frame you. I'm only doing it so you can offer up some more information that will further implicate Rockman. Got it?"

He then told him the real reason he'd been sitting on death row all this time. What he had been involved in since he was a kid. What they wanted from him. *They* had nothing to do with Grizz's arrest. That was all Matthew Rockman, but *they* let it happen to see where it would go. To see if they could use it to their advantage. *They* didn't have a name. In fact, they did, but Grizz wouldn't offer it up to Tommy. He didn't need to know it, but for the sake of this explanation he would refer to them as the NNG. The No Name Group.

The FBI thought they were reporting to the White House when in fact, Grizz was certain based on names he'd learned many years ago, they were reporting to people even more powerful than the United States government. An organization more secret and connected than the CIA. Actually, the NNG was more powerful than *any* government. Privately elected within their own ranks, they came from all different walks of life—politicians, educators, CEOs, philanthropists. They were the ones calling the shots. They made sure the correct person was in the Oval Office. They controlled the world's economy. They did it all.

And yet a nobody biker from South Florida had something in his possession that scared them shitless.

"What did you find that freaked them into letting you think you could bring down the people that ran the world? You know this sounds farfetched, don't you, Grizz? I mean, come on—people who 'run the world'?" Tommy made air quotes.

"This is the part Kit can never know. This is the part that will offer you an explanation. It's the least I can do for you, and you need to be able to handle what I'm telling you."

Tommy frowned, then nodded at him to continue.

"I told you about my little sister. How I killed my parents and made my way to Fort Lauderdale. But that was just the beginning."

As they made their way around the prison yard track, Grizz proceeded to tell Tommy the rest of the story. The motel. Pop's accidental death. What he'd found after Red and his guys showed up. He told Tommy everything.

"A bag of counterfeit money with the plates to make more? Was that supposed to finance something?" Tommy's eyes were wide.

"Yes, but I didn't find out the rest until I was older. I burned almost a million dollars that night in the pit. I thought I'd stumbled across plates to make counterfeit money. I hadn't realized these had been real plates, real money. Real plates that were in the possession of the NNG. No wonder they were so fucking wealthy. They owned the fucking mint, Grunt."

Tommy exhaled sharply. This was far bigger than he ever expected. "How was Red involved?"

"Red was undercover FBI. He was good friends with Candy's father, Tom. That's who she named you after. Tom was Secret Service, although his family never knew that. They always thought he sold insurance. Maybe he was undercover Secret Service, if there was such a thing back then. I really don't know. Anyway, the Secret Service is responsible for sniffing out and dealing with counterfeiters. That's probably what Tom thought he'd stumbled on. The NNG used their power to have Red, Tom's friend, put on his trail to get that bag back. But it wasn't the money they were after. There was something in the bag I'm not even sure Tom knew about. But I sure did. I found it."

Tommy slowed to look up at Grizz, but Grizz tugged him along, mumbling under his breath, "Keep walking and don't act surprised. This is supposed to be a friendly goodbye chat between father and son. We need to look like we're clearing the air so I can die a happy death."

"Got it." The sun was bright as they walked. Bright and hot. "So what'd you find?"

"A big fat document, that's what I found. Neatly typed, a logo and everything, very official looking. Names, dates, events. There were small explanations, notes under each one. It was basically an outline of major world events."

"Events? Like what?"

"The Berlin Wall. The Cuban Missile Crisis. The Vietnam War. Names of men who would be president. Watergate. The gas crisis. AIDS—"

"What's the big deal about that, Grizz? Everybody knows those things. You didn't stumble on any big secrets. Pick up a fucking history book."

"You're not as smart as I've always given you credit for, Grunt. You're hearing me, but you're not really listening." In a very low voice laced with anger, Grizz continued. "I found this document in the fifties. The Berlin Wall wasn't built until 1961. The Cuban Missile Crisis was in 1962. This letter said who would be president, who would assassinate him and who would assassinate the fucking assassinator. Said there'd be a president who would fall in a scandal called Watergate. That was in 1972. It said there would be a gas shortage. That they were working on a virus that would eliminate what they called 'the undesirables.'"

Tommy's jaw dropped as what Grizz was telling him actually sunk in. "You're telling me that you saw a map of our future? Like, a Nostradamus document or something?"

"That's exactly what I'm saying. And even though I was just a kid, I knew it was important. I just didn't know how important. I don't think Red even knew what I'd found. He died thinking it was a counterfeit operation. He was obsessed with that bag of money and his hunch was right that I'd found it. He convinced the FBI that I could be an asset. They didn't even know the entire truth about what I'd found. They always thought they were reporting to some White House official, and maybe they were, but that official was reporting to a higher power."

"And you used this knowledge to keep them at bay? To let you get away with so much for so many years?"

"I fucked with them big time. I let them think they talked me into working for them where they could keep an eye on me. I tossed them an occasional bone to let them think I was theirs and I'd—"

Tommy cut him off. "Why didn't they just threaten you, torture you, kill you?"

"They tried. I almost didn't survive their first and only attempt at torture. It was then that I let them know I had something in place for their shit to go public. And it would only happen in the event of my death. It was the truth. I had it all set up to be released if I died. Fuck, they even protected me for a while. They must've been shitting themselves when I'd piss off a drug cartel bad enough for them to want to kill me. I played them like that for years knowing I could get away with whatever I wanted and they wouldn't let me die." He clenched his jaw. "That's when I overplayed my hand. Thinking that when I got arrested for Kit's kidnapping and all that other shit they'd get me out. Especially if I got the death penalty. They risked exposure with my death."

Tommy nodded. Now some of it made sense. "But they didn't," Tommy finished quietly. "They didn't come to your rescue."

"No, they played me back like I deserved. They told me to make sure Kit and the baby were out of my life. It would be too obvious if my woman was waiting for me. They were right. I know a lot of men who were taken out because their women refused to move on. They made it apparent they were waiting for their men." Grizz gave a bitter laugh. "Of course, I told them that if they even so much as laid a hand on her head I'd expose them, and I would have. But it backfired on me. I did what they said. I told her to marry you and I never told her why. I could never offer her an explanation without putting her in danger."

Tommy didn't know what to say.

"They let me rot in prison after I did what they told me, thinking they'd get me out. Shit, Grunt, I expected to be out in a few years under the guise of a false execution. I didn't think I'd be away long enough for Mimi to remember you as her father. I stupidly thought I was going to get out and give them back their shit and they'd relocate me and Kit and the baby and leave us alone." Grizz shook his head. "It all went to hell, though."

"And it never occurred to you that I really loved her? That if your plan had worked you'd have been ripping her and Mimi away from me?" He understood Grizz, even had sympathy for him. But shit, it hurt.

"Honestly, Grunt? I was using you. I knew you loved her, but truthfully, I didn't care."

The only sound was their feet on the prison yard track. After a few minutes, Grizz added, "I'm sure you never suspected it, but I'm certain Cindy was a plant."

"Cindy?"

"I'm pretty sure her father was a wannabe. Trying to get in with them by showing them he could help out. When I guessed it I wasn't worried about it because there was nothing Cindy would ever learn from you. You never knew anything."

"And now? Now that everything in those documents has come and gone, does it even matter anymore? Anybody could create a document to look like it was written in the fifties by some clandestine group with a secret name, and they could make it look like it was mapping out future world events. You said you even found pictures. These days, photos can be doctored. Anything can be done in hindsight."

"It didn't stop at the seventies, Grunt," Grizz said softly. "It didn't stop at the eighties or even the nineties. That document mapped out future events for the next seventy-five to a hundred years. This world is being controlled by forces that have been around forever and they plan on staying around. Fuck, man, they've named kids who haven't even been born yet."

It was dizzying. Tommy blinked. "How did they eventually figure out you had all this? You said they suspected it, but how did they confirm it?"

"I showed my ass. I was in my early twenties and had always kept an eye on the property where my sister was buried. It's where I hid the shit after I got a license and could drive there by myself. I would occasionally call and inquire about the property. When I found out it had been sold and was going to be developed, I had her remains secretly exhumed and gave her a proper burial. At that time, I decided to look over the documents again. I hadn't read them in years. I noticed a company name that had been in the news. I decided to buy some stock and made a ton of money. They noticed, and it only confirmed to them that I had what they'd suspected all along. They knew I wasn't lying or dicking around with them. It was stupid of me."

He told Tommy more details then. How more recently a new player, one with brass balls, had stepped in and decided he wasn't going to let Grizz fuck with them anymore. Grizz had run out of time. They weren't giving him any leverage. They wanted their shit back and they wanted it now. The NNG's newly elected official made sure Grizz knew he could release what he had to the public and the NNG might falter temporarily, but not before they would let Grizz watch

Ginny die a slow and painful death.

Tommy tried to show no emotion, but the thought of Grizz putting Ginny in danger made him angry.

"So it's over for you, then? No more standoff?" Tommy tried to sound casual, but his throat burned. He swallowed thickly.

"No more standoff."

"Too bad you just didn't give it back when you were a kid. You know, before you actually understood what you had your hands on. But how would you have known what would happen?"

"I wish I had, Grunt. Believe me. But let me warn you: If they think for a second that you or Kit know any of what I've told you, you're dead meat."

"Then why are you telling me?" Tommy asked in disbelief.

"Because I have to be sure they leave you both alone after I'm gone. They have to be certain you know nothing and you won't be touched. I need to make sure you or Kit don't say anything, not a single thing by accident that would even let them think you know any of this."

"But we didn't know any of this! And I'm definitely not going to tell her. Besides, how will they be able to verify that we don't know anything without interrogating us?"

Grizz put his arm on Tommy's shoulder. "They might even be watching us now. So you can in no way react to what I'm about to tell you. Understand? You just nod and laugh like I just said something funny."

Tommy did as he was told, and with a smile on his face, he asked, "How, Grizz? How can they know for certain Ginny and I don't know any of this?"

"Your house has been bugged for years."

# Chapter Seventy
2000

TOMMY COULDN'T EVEN begin to describe his anger after hearing Grizz's last statement, but it all made sense now. The NNG could never be sure Grizz hadn't shared his story all those years with his wife and son. He hadn't, and the NNG should've known it. But Grizz was convinced Tommy needed to play out his part after the execution.

Tommy was supposed to take Ginny home after Grizz's death and come clean about some horrible things. He was willing to do that.

"You have to give them something," Grizz had told him. "You understand? Coming home like life is perfect will only keep them listening. They keep listening because you're so fucking tightlipped. Nothing has ever come up about the gang, her life with me, nothing. It's almost overkill, like you're purposely hiding something."

"We're *not* hiding anything." Tommy's voice was low. "We live a normal, average life. I'm an architect. She's an accountant-slash-soccer-mom. Doesn't that count for anything?"

"You need to give them something. My execution will be the perfect time to let it all out. You tell her everything you can remember about growing up at the motel."

"No. I've spent years not telling her stuff. I don't want to hurt her."

"I spent years trying to protect her, too, Grunt. I was wrong. She was smart and strong enough to handle some truths. But she's never been allowed to know this truth."

Tommy had been prepared to tell Ginny some things after they'd wrapped up the phone interview with Leslie. He knew they'd be listening, and even though it would be hard for her to hear some things, he knew Grizz was right. He had to give them something.

What he hadn't counted on was that Leslie would allude to the secret about him being Grizz's son. He hadn't counted on Ginny actually leaving their home, going to Carter's. They couldn't be listening if she wasn't there to have any conversations. If not for this, he wouldn't have hassled her to come home. He would've given her the space she needed. But he was desperate to move on with their lives, and he needed to give them what they wanted by dropping some small tidbits.

He could only pray that it would be enough for them to leave his family alone.

Grizz never said anything about the chess set. Tommy didn't know if Grizz sent it or the prison did, and he still hadn't figured what the missing king meant, if anything.

Now, as she slept, he held Ginny closer and tamped down his growing anger. They'd listened to everything that went on in his home. Every whisper, every laugh, every intimate secret. Then, to have to make love to her knowing they were listening? And to make it worse, they'd not been together for almost a month. They were both ready to explode with need, and he hated it. Hated *them*.

He should've been reveling in their lovemaking instead of grinding his jaw and making the appropriate moves and sounds for Ginny's sake.

# Chapter Seventy-One
2000, Northern Florida,
Three Days Before Grizz's Execution

AFTER THE WALK in the prison yard, they casually made their way back to a room that may or not have been bugged. In the event that it was, Grizz had told him what they would be discussing. Just like he believed that Ginny and Tommy needed to give the NNG something to listen to, he believed he and Tommy had to do the same.

"Why did you even bother with me?" Tommy asked him as they entered the room. "Why did you take me from Karen's that night? Why did you let me think for years that Blue was my brother? I'd still think it if I didn't suspect Candy was my mother. I did some investigating after your trial. She was my mother, wasn't she?"

"Yeah, Candy was your mother, Grunt. She got pregnant with you and dumped you off on her mother and sister, Karen."

"I knew that much. But how did you find out about me?"

"Your Aunt Karen showed up at The Red Crab with a picture of you when you were about seven or eight. It was a school picture. You must have been in foster care when it was taken because you looked good. Looked cared for.

"Yeah, that's possible. I was in and out of foster care. Some good, some not so good, but I was fed."

"Anyway, she insisted that you were mine. Karen said her mom had run off and she didn't have the money to take care of you. Candy had been long gone. Karen said if I didn't give her money she would pack up and not be there when you got home from school one day."

"You gave her money based on a picture of me? If my mother was a prostitute, I could've been anybody's kid."

"True. But a couple of things made me believe it. First, I thought you looked like me at that age. Second, your birth date was telling. It lined up with a time when Candy was off the streets and staying with me and Anthony in the garage apartment. Red had been trying to get her off the drugs. He dumped her on me and Anthony. Made her a prisoner. We had to take turns not letting her out of our sight. When we weren't there, Red would stay with her. She definitely wasn't hooking. Axel was spending a couple of months in juvie so he wasn't around. He wouldn't have slept with her, anyway." Grizz gave Tommy a knowing grin. "But me and Anthony banged her every chance we got. She was willing. Used it to try to convince us to let her back on the streets. We were young and horny little shits. Red let her leave after he thought she was clean." Grizz shrugged. "I never saw her again. Not until that night she came to the motel looking for you."

Tommy just stared. He didn't say anything.

"You sure as hell ain't half Indian." Grizz blurted out. Then he shook his head and added, "Hell, maybe you're not my kid. Maybe I assumed wrong all these years."

Tommy frowned. "You didn't assume wrong," he said softly. "I thought early on *you* might've been my older brother, not Blue. But I didn't suspect you were my father until we heard the testimony about Candy at the trial. I started digging further then, getting nowhere. It took years to be certain. It wasn't until about a year ago, when they found Moe, that I thought to have some tests done." He waited a beat. "Mimi and I share the same DNA."

Grizz didn't say anything, just nodded. Tommy thought he saw a flicker of satisfaction pass over Grizz's face, but he couldn't be sure.

"So why did you have to kill her when she came to the motel that night?" Tommy pressed on. "All you had to do was tell her to lie and say somebody else was my father and that Blue was her brother or something. Why did you kill her?"

"Didn't want her stirring up shit. Didn't want anybody to know you were my kid."

Tommy laughed. "Come on. Who would've cared if I was your kid?"

Grizz stared at him seriously. "I had good reason to kill her. You don't know how many enemies I'd made over the years who wouldn't have thought twice about coming after you to get to me. I was saving *your* life when I killed her."

"Yeah, whatever, Grizz." He was playing along now, just like Grizz had told him to. Just in case they were listening. Grizz had explained during their walk that Candy's sobriety had actually caused her to start digging into her father's death. She'd started remembering some things Red had said. *They* had caught wind of it, telling Grizz that if she ever showed up, she needed to be eliminated. Immediately. She was a threat. Grizz was following an order. He was honest with Tommy, though, admitting he'd felt no remorse in killing her. It was just part of the job.

Now in the room, Grizz slammed a hand on the table. "Dammit, Grunt, listen to me. I know you waited a long time to be with Kit. Do you want that to dissolve? Do you want to stir up all the bad shit that I used to be involved in? Blue will stop Leslie from putting in her fucking article that you're my son." He ran his hand through his hair and mumbled to himself, "I still can't believe I let you talk me into it. Fuck! You told me Kit said she needed the closure and I wanted her to have that. I knew the stupid bitch didn't work for the big magazine she claimed to. I figured it would just fizzle out. I almost didn't do it until Kit called me."

This last statement caught Tommy's attention. He was going off script here. "Ginny called you?"

"Yeah, I had already spoken to you and I was still chewing on it when I heard from her. I almost fucking dropped the phone when I heard her voice. She told me she really needed to do this interview. She felt she hadn't completely healed from all of those years with the gang, from seeing and knowing the things they did. It was important to her, but the reporter needed more. Needed to talk to me, too, to see she was telling the truth in the interview. Kit was very matter-of-fact. Said I owed her."

"Grizz, Ginny never called you."

"Don't tell me she didn't call me," he growled. "I fucking talked to her."

"Before that, when was the last time you spoke to Ginny?"

"She called me to tell me you named your boy after me. When was he born? Ten years ago? We talked for less than a minute back then."

Tommy sat there shaking his head. "I cannot believe this. I cannot fucking believe this."

"What can't you believe?"

"It's not your fault. I've mistaken them on the phone, too."

"What the fuck are you talking about?"

"It was Mimi," Tommy said. "You were duped by Mimi."

Grizz leaned back and looked at Tommy hard. "Are you fucking kidding me? How do you know that? Why would she do that?"

"I'm not exactly sure, but I'll find out. She was working Ginny on our end, too. After Leslie came around, Mimi acted very interested. Told her mother maybe it would help her to forget the past. To give the interview as a way to have closure on the gang life. Mimi has withdrawn from us the past few years. Typical teenage stuff, I guess, but I know Ginny saw the article as a way to bond again."

Grizz got very serious. "I don't like it. I don't like it one bit. You figure out what the fuck that was all about and fix it. I trusted you with my child. I've stayed away for fifteen years believing that you were on top of it. You're telling me now that Leslie got the interview with me and Kit thanks to *Mimi*? My time is almost over. You get this fixed, Grunt. You hear me?"

"Yeah, I hear you. It could be nothing, but I'll make sure I get to the bottom of it."

The one thing Grizz didn't tell Tommy was that after Jason had been born, he'd stopped running his own surveillance on Mimi. He'd been able to see some pictures of her growing up, but he'd stopped when Kit moved on with her life and had another baby. The pain was too unbearable.

"Good. And you have to give me something else." Grizz was now going back to the script they'd discussed in the yard. "You asked me to believe it wasn't you who set me up. I do. You asked me to understand your deceptions when you were younger and you wanted to be with Kit. I do. I'm giving you that. But I'm telling you that I am going to my death, giving you the freedom to move on with the woman I love. The *only* woman I have ever loved. Now you have to give me something. Just take care of her and my daughter." He paused then, looking at Tommy hard. "And my grandson. Take care of all of them. Can you do that?"

"Yeah, Grizz. I can do that."

"And one more thing," he quickly added. "Tell Kit— Ginny—I'm sorry. Okay? Tell her I'm sorry for a lot of things, but I'm not sorry for loving her. I'll never be sorry for that. And she's not responsible for me being here. She probably thinks it's because of Jan finding her wallet, but it's not. I'm here because of the things I've done. Not because of her."

In their bed now, Ginny let out a big sigh. Tommy shook his head free of the memory and pulled her closer. Her scent was intoxicating. He held her in his arms as he breathed her in, remembering how he had loved her from the very first glance. Up until a few weeks ago, she'd thought it was when she was brought to the motel. Then when he'd told her about being with Grizz a few times to check on her, she'd thought it was when she dumped lemonade on Curtis Armstrong's head. He smiled at that memory.

Then he carefully removed her from his arms and silently made his way downstairs to his office. He flicked on the light and went to his desk. He pulled out a drawer and released a hidden compartment. Then, very quietly, he took out a small box.

The same box he'd had in his dresser the night Grizz came for him. The same box he had kept for the past thirty-two years.

**********

"Hey, new kid? Is it true you don't have any real parents? That you're on loan to some loser family who shaved you bald because you were full of bugs?"

There was a round of laughter. Tommy just stared at his library book and pretended not to hear them. It was 1967. He was eight years old.

"Maybe he has bugs in his ears, too, and can't hear us," another one piped up. More laughter.

Tommy continued to read his library book and refused to look up. It was morning recess and he was sitting on the ground with his back against a tree. He'd only been in this new school for a day. He didn't think his foster parents were losers. They were nice people, and he didn't blame them for shaving his head. He was actually relieved.

He stared at the pages of his book and continued to ignore them. Before he knew what had happened, they swiped it from his hands and pulled him to his feet by the front of his shirt. His first thought was, please don't rip my new shirt.

But before he could react, the bully had let go of him and was stumbling backwards. Tommy managed to gain his footing. All he could do was stare.

He hadn't seen her approaching. She was taller than him and had her back to him as she stood over the boy she had just shoved to the ground. With her hands on her hips she said to the boy, "Stop being such a bully, Arthur. Maybe *you* should try reading a book once in a while."

Before Arthur could get to his feet, there was a shout from several yards away. "Guinevere! Get over here this minute."

The girl looked at the three bullies and reluctantly marched toward her teacher.

One of the bullies looked at Tommy. "Better watch your back. Won't always be a scrawny girl around to fight your battles."

Before Tommy could reply, Arthur and the other boy had already started walking away. They called over their shoulder, "C'mon, Curtis, we'll get him later."

"Guinevere," Tommy said out loud. He picked up his book and headed for the line at the water fountain.

The rest of his morning wasn't too bad. He enjoyed his studies and some kids even gave him nice smiles. He wondered which class Guinevere was in. Maybe he would see her in the lunchroom. His class was quiet. They were working on their multiplication tables. He rushed through it very quickly and realized he hadn't used the restroom all day. He'd been too nervous to go when they went as a class. He stood and slowly approached his teacher.

She looked up with a kind smile. "Yes, Thomas?"

"May I use the restroom, ma'am?"

She nodded and asked if he knew where it was. He told her he did and quietly left the room.

He had left the boys' room and was heading back to class when he heard her name. Two teachers were talking in a classroom. He slowed down before he passed the door.

"I can see Guinevere is at it again," one said with amusement in her voice.

"Yes, she does seem to have her nose in everything lately."

"What's the latest crusade?"

"Potholders. She's making potholders to sell because she wants to buy Kenny Schultz new shoes. He's wearing his brother's hand-me-downs and they're too big. He keeps tripping over his own feet."

Tommy heard the sound of a desk drawer being pulled out.

"Where did she get the money to make potholders? Isn't she from a needy family herself?" the other teacher asked, bewilderment in her voice.

"I think one of the cafeteria ladies gave her a potholder kit. Said her neighbor's granddaughter got it as a gift and didn't want it, so the neighbor asked her if there were any kids at the school who might want it."

"It's very sweet that she's using it to help someone else. Why are you keeping them in your drawer?"

"I feel bad, but it's school rules. I told her she could only sell them before or after school, and to be quite honest with you, I don't know how much money she's going to make charging a nickel each."

Tommy heard the desk drawer close, and he ducked behind some lockers. He hoped they would come out of the classroom and go the other way.

"C'mon, we better catch up with our classes or we won't have time to eat lunch," the one said as they walked out the door and headed in the opposite direction.

Tommy breathed a sigh of relief that he hadn't been caught eavesdropping. He walked to the door and turned the handle. Unlocked. He quickly ran to the teacher's desk and opened the top drawer. Nothing. He opened the next drawer, and there he saw them. They were little potholders, all weaved together with different strands of colored fabric. He saw they were in a clear plastic bag, and at the bottom of the bag he could see three nickels. She had sold three. He reached into his pocket and took out the two coins his foster parents had given him for lunch. He carefully picked two potholders out of the bag and tucked them in his shirt. He dropped his thirty-five cents into the plastic bag, returned it to the drawer and gently closed it.

As he headed back to his classroom he felt something he'd never experienced. Happiness. He was happy to do this for Guinevere. He had always been the recipient of either hate from his sister or pity from strangers. He was never in a position to actually give and he liked how it felt. He wasn't worried about not having any money for lunch. He'd gone hungry before and he would go hungry again today. For her.

Now, in the cool darkness of his office, Tommy sat at his desk and looked at the potholders in his hands. He remembered being disappointed that he'd never gone back to Ginny's school after that day. Some government worker had decided his home life wasn't really that awful and couldn't justify the expense. So he was returned to Karen. He remembered being happy his foster parents had let him keep his new shirt. His smile faded as the bad memories started again, but he immediately stuffed them down with memories of when he'd found her again.

He knew he gasped that day he saw her walking down the street. The day she set up her lemonade stand.

His thoughts were interrupted by her voice.

"What do you have there?" she softly asked.

Tommy looked up, surprised. She was casually leaning in the doorway to his office. How long had she been standing there? He didn't hear her follow him down the hall. He stared into her big brown eyes and tears started to form in his own.

"I need to tell you about the real moment I fell in love with you, Ginny. I need to tell you about the very first glance." He looked at her with a love that transcended time. "I've waited a long time to give these back to you, honey."

# Chapter Seventy-Two

2000


"YOU WERE THE most beautiful bride in the world," Tommy told her as he passed her the sweet potatoes. "Tell your mom how beautiful she was, Jason."

"You were real pretty, mom. How come you don't look that pretty every day?"

Tommy almost dropped the bowl he was passing, but Ginny just laughed. "Because it was a special day and I took extra care to look beautiful for your father," she replied.

"I don't know why you had to wear white," Mimi chimed in. "You're too old to be wearing white, Mom. It's not like you and Dad haven't done it."

"Done what?" Jason asked innocently as he reached for a roll. "What did you do? I wanna do it, too!"

"Mimi, don't try and hide behind the sarcasm. I saw you watching your parents say their vows and you had tears in your eyes," Carter chimed in.

They were all sitting around the dinner table. Tommy and Ginny had just returned from a short but long-overdue honeymoon. They hadn't been able to get their weeklong cruise reservations for the family on such short notice, so they decided to put that cruise on hold until Christmas. It was Tommy who'd determined he wanted a real wedding for Ginny, not just the courthouse formality they'd had all those years ago. He remembered vowing back then to walk her down that church aisle. And it was as long overdue as the honeymoon.

They were able to put something together very quickly, only inviting a few close friends. He was the one who insisted she wear a white gown. And just like the Ginny he'd known and fallen in love with, it was beautiful in its simplicity. They had a small and modest reception and asked that, instead of gifts, donations be made to a local charity that helped children to adapt better in foster homes. Mimi and Jason had stayed at Carter and Bill's house.

Tommy and Ginny had just arrived home and were thrilled to

find Carter and the kids there. Carter had Mimi and Jason help her prepare a surprise dinner.

"Don't know if I can stand seafood for a fourth night in a row," Mimi said under her breath.

"You know Carter doesn't eat meat. You were at her house, so you lived by her rules," Tommy told his daughter. "And as far as this meal is concerned, I'm sure she bought and made it, so again, you don't have a say-so."

"Still, a roast would've been nice," Mimi said, rolling her eyes.

"Oh, Mimi," Ginny said, in a false singsong. "I cannot wait until you have a teenager of your very own. You know what they say—something about paybacks being heck?"

"Hell, Mom," Jason chimed in innocently. "I think it's hell, not heck. Corbin said it about his older brother once."

Just then the doorbell rang. Jason got up and ran to open it.

Ginny looked over at Carter then and quietly told her. "The kids are back in school next week. I'll be over to clean out the garage."

Carter nodded at her.

"Uncle Bill!" Jason shouted from the door. "Uncle Bill's here. He made it and he brought a present!"

Seconds later, Carter's husband, Bill, followed Jason into the dining room. "Sorry I'm late. More traffic than I expected."

He planted a kiss on Carter's head, then grinned at Tommy and Ginny. "How was the honeymoon?"

Before they could answer, Jason piped up, "What's in the box? Is it a wedding present? You know they didn't want presents, right? Why does the box have holes in it? You brought them a present with holes?"

Bill laughed and said, "No, not guilty. This was on your porch when I arrived."

He walked towards Ginny and handed it to her as she stood up.

"What could this be?" she asked.

"Open it, Mom! Open it now. Wait, can I open it?" Jason peered over her shoulder, almost bouncing with excitement.

It was a fancy white box with a big silver ribbon tied around it.

She handed it to Jason and moved some things out of the way.

"Here, honey. Set it on the table."

Jason planted the box on the table and quickly untied the ribbon. When he pulled off the lid he gave a squeal of excitement.

"Look! Look what someone gave us!"

He carefully lifted something out of the box and held it to his chest. It was a tiny black kitten.

"Aww, you're a cute little thing! And look, Dad, look what's on its collar. I better get it off. It's heavy."

"What is it?" Mimi asked as she tried to peek around Carter.

"It's the dark king. Just like the one that was missing from Dad's new chess set."

Tommy and Ginny's eyes met. He knew she didn't know what to think.

"I wonder if it's a boy or a girl," Jason said, ruffling its fur. Even Mimi was standing up now, fussing over the kitten.

Carter joined them and was untying the ribbon that fastened the chess piece to the kitten's collar.

"We can keep it, right, Mom?" Jason asked as he looked at his mother. Without waiting for an answer, he looked at his father. "Right, Dad? We're keeping it, aren't we?"

"Yes, son," Tommy answered him, smiling broadly. "We can keep it."

This was the signal that Grizz had promised from the grave. Their home was theirs again. The NNG was gone, and whoever had been able to confirm this for Grizz must've sent the kitten, too.

Tommy would later explain to Ginny that he thought it was Grizz's way of telling her it was okay for her to be happy. The nod hadn't been enough. He needed to reassure her it was okay to move on and have a life. She agreed.

"What should we call it?" Jason asked.

# Chapter Seventy-Three
2000


GINNY OPENED HER car windows and enjoyed the warm breeze as she drove to Carter's. The kids were back in school, and she planned to clean out the garage before she took on a new bookkeeping client, hopefully next week.

She sang along with her favorite seventies station as she thought about the potholders Tommy had returned to her the first night they'd made love after their short separation, right before they renewed their wedding vows. She knew the moment he told her how long he'd held onto them that she'd made the right decision to believe him—and to trust him with their future. She had no more doubts about his genuine love for her.

She felt bad that she hadn't remembered the exact incident he'd described in the schoolyard, but she remembered the potholders. He teased her that he was going to have them framed and hung in his office, but she'd finally agreed with him that he was right earlier that night: It was time to put the past away. All of the past. It was time to pack up the potholders along with Grizz and Mavis's chess sets, Moe's drawing, and even Grizz's jacket.

He was glad she had agreed.

**********

They'd sat on his office floor, cross-legged, after they'd talked about the potholders.

"Ginny, I'm curious about something. You said in the last interview with Leslie that she missed the real love story. A story about a man that had loved you from the beginning, from the first glance. I know you were talking about me. Did you mean it when you told her I was always your soul mate? Did you ever consider Grizz your soul mate?"

She pulled her knees to her chest and wrapped her arms around them, hugging them tightly. She didn't answer right away, just tilted her head to one side, considering what she was about to say.

Before she could say a word, he added, "I can tell by your body language that you're trying to decide whether or not to tell me the truth. You don't need to lie. You can tell me."

"I told Leslie the truth. This is the only love story now."

He nodded his head at her last comment. He couldn't help himself. He knew what her answer was going to be, but his question was out before he could stop it.

"It's the only love story *now*, but it's not the only love story, is it?"

"I know what you want to hear. You want to hear that you are my one and only true love and soul mate. I don't want to hurt you. God knows I don't want to hurt you, but I will never deny that he was my first love and a true love. I meant what I said about you being my soul mate, Tommy. But I also think a person can have more than one. I still consider Grizz a soul mate, too. I say consider because I believe his soul still lives on."

She toyed with Tommy's hand. "I was very much in love with Grizz. I still love him in my own way, even though he's gone." Absently she played with her wedding band.

Looking quickly back up at her husband, she added, "Don't let what I've said take away from what we have now. I can't deny my past and my love for him. But that doesn't mean I love you less than I loved him. He's not here anymore. You are here, and I am in love with you. That is the truth. I am not pining away for Grizz. Am I mourning him? Yes, because he's gone for good. But it's getting a little easier each day. Sorry, there was more to that answer than what you asked."

He kissed her hair. "I understand."

She frowned then. "You know, I always resented Sam's insinuation that I suffered from Stockholm Syndrome. I can see why he thought it, but it was never true. Nobody ever glimpsed into our marriage."

"Who could? Grizz kept you in a protective bubble. Kind of like one of those snow globe things."

"Tommy, Grizz and I had a good marriage and, yes, I despised the gang, his activities, some of his so-called friends. But I really loved the man. It didn't happen right away, but slowly, I started to draw things out of him. Did you know Grizz loved the stars? I bought him a telescope for our anniversary one year. I think it must still be in the guest house over our old garage." She had a faraway look in her eyes.

"How would I know something like that? Grizz rarely discussed anything personal."

"He used to take me on midnight picnics. We would go places he knew would be vacant or empty. The zoo, an amusement park. We even laid on the deck of someone's yacht and watched the stars one night." She paused before adding, "He liked building, construction. Did you know that?"

"No, I don't think I knew that either."

"He practically lived at our house in Shady Ranches when it was being built. He couldn't get enough of it. And I guess you already know about his soft spot for animals. Especially after hearing about what happened to his dog. I think it's why he was so agreeable to Carter living at the house and keeping her animals there."

She looked at a spot over his shoulder and he knew she wasn't finished. He would let her talk. It's what *they* would want, anyway.

"I would get up and go to church every Sunday by myself, then come home to find Grizz in his favorite chair with the newspaper scattered everywhere. He would get embarrassed when I caught him reading the comics. For someone with such a mean streak, he had a certain quality of vulnerability that I fell in love with, Tommy. I really was in love with him."

Tommy just nodded.

"You probably didn't know that he was afraid of the dentist. That his favorite color was blue, and believe it or not, he was a better cook than me." She smiled, still that distant look on her face. "He took me fishing once. There were some kids nearby and they were using their slingshots carelessly and aiming for little animals. Squirrels and birds. Grizz stopped them and told them that they should never hurt an animal, any animal, just for sport. I think they were too scared to disagree with him, but he won them over after giving them slingshot lessons. He was an excellent shot. It was the cutest thing I ever saw."

Tommy didn't say anything, just continued to listen.

"I lost my job because of him. Did I ever tell you that? When I was working for that accounting firm in Miramar?"

"No. I thought you quit."

"I let Grizz think I quit. The owner's daughter drove me home one day. My car wouldn't start and I couldn't get ahold of him to come get me. She practically jumped at the chance to take me. For some reason, I was a curiosity to the people in the office."

"What happened?" he softly asked.

"The reason Grizz never answered the phone was because he was in the garage working on one of his bikes. When he heard the car pull up he walked out to see who it was. He was wearing a dirty tank top and he was carrying a wrench. My friend thought he was robbing my house. She was embarrassed when I told her it was my husband." She looked away from Tommy then. "They started hinting the next day that they were probably going to start cutting back and that I should maybe consider looking for another job. I knew that was their way of telling me they would be getting rid of me. I quit before I put them in the awkward position of having to fire me."

"And you never told him?"

"No. I didn't tell him because as surprising as you may find this, Grizz had feelings, too."

"I never doubted he had feelings, Ginny. I just never saw him show them."

"Well, he showed them to me. Losing the job wasn't a big deal, anyway. They went under less than six months later. They were caught helping one of their clients in some tax evasion scheme. I was shocked. They seemed like an above-board firm to me."

The room was quiet for a minute. Tommy looked at her, and she knew what he was thinking.

"What?" she asked. "Say it. You know what? Don't say it. I know what's coming. You're going to tell me Grizz had something to do with them getting in trouble. Don't say it and don't think it, Tommy. Just don't!"

He didn't have to say anything. Tommy knew Grizz would've

noticed the surprise on the face of the lady who drove Ginny home. He was too smart not to have seen the coincidence in Ginny resigning immediately afterwards. He tanked that company because they had dared to hurt Ginny's feelings. He was relentless in his protection of her. Almost overboard. No. Definitely overboard. He was trying to make up for what he never was able to give his sister.

Come to think of it, Tommy realized he himself was a lot like Grizz. Relentless in the pursuit of what he wanted. And he'd gotten it. He'd gotten her. The only thing he'd ever really wanted. It hadn't gone like he'd originally planned, and it took a lot longer than he'd expected, but he'd won.

Tommy interrupted the silence with another question. "So when did you fall in love with me, Ginny? You told Leslie that if it weren't for Grizz, you wouldn't be married to the man you were completely in love with today. You resisted me for years after I married you. When did you know you were in love with me?"

**********

"But both programs concentrated on architecture and classical arts from Ancient Greek and Roman culture. This was the only school of architecture in the western world until Jonathan Seely graduated from the University of Illinois as its first student of architecture in 1874."

Ginny stopped short when she heard Tommy's voice coming from the den. She peeked around the corner and tears came to her eyes. It was 1988. Tommy was sitting on the couch and had Mimi situated in the crook of his arm. He was holding up one of his architectural magazines with his other hand and reading it out loud to her. He was using voice inflections that had her captivated. His story made absolutely no sense to the almost three-year-old, but she was mesmerized by him. She was looking up at him, hanging on every word.

Ginny's heart melted at the sight.

"Okay, sweetheart, I'm finished with my story," he told Mimi. "How about I tell you another one?"

She heard Mimi clap her hands. "Nudder tory, Daddy! A fun tory!"

She smiled, then leaned against the wall next to the door. She listened as Tommy started to tell Mimi another story.

"Once upon a time, in a faraway land, there lived a beautiful princess—"

Ginny closed her eyes as she listened to Tommy tell Mimi about a princess who was so beautiful she was likened to a pot of rubies and emeralds as brilliant as the sun. The princess's name was Ginny. She actually lifted her hand to her heart and had to stifle a sigh. How sweet was this?

"If you marry my daughter, you will have to take all of the rubies and emeralds in my kingdom," the king told the brave knight.

"I would be honored to marry your daughter and take the precious gems that represent her brilliant beauty, and I will guard them all with my life," the brave knight answered the king while bowing before him.

"But wait!" the king added. "If you take my daughter and all of my precious gems, you must also take something else."

The king told the brave knight to stand, and when he did, the king handed him a beautiful baby girl. This is my granddaughter, the Princess Miriam. She is the rarest gem of all. Rarer and more beautiful than her mother. You cannot take one without the other, and you must take this pot of flawless diamonds for they represent the purity and innocence of the tiny princess."

The brave knight looked into the eyes of the Princess Miriam, and he knew that his heart had been forever changed. He would love Miriam as his own. He would protect her with his life. He would put her on the highest pedestal of his heart and never let her fall from it.

"It is my honor, Your Highness, to protect and love that which you value most dear. I would lay down my life for both of your princesses."

Ginny'd had to stifle a sob as she'd quietly made her way down the hallway and into the small bathroom off the kitchen.

**\*\*\*\*\*\*\*\*\***

"That was the day, Tommy. The day I eavesdropped on you telling Mimi that story. I was so broken up over how you were making it sound like someone was giving you a pot of rubies and emeralds, but in order to take the pot of rubies and emeralds you had to take a pot of diamonds, too. It wasn't like you had taken on the burden of a child. Rather, it was like you saw it as a gift. You welcomed her and loved her in spite of knowing that she was Grizz's daughter and that I had been in love with him; I think I may even still have been in love with him then. But you loved her without question. You didn't have to love her, but you did because you loved me." Ginny blinked, surprised to find her eyes wet with tears. But they were happy tears. "I had been holding back, denying the feelings I'd had for you when I was younger. I still remember struggling with feelings I was having for you back then. I was only fifteen. I was confused. After I heard you tell that story, I let myself feel again."

He smiled at her. "Ginny, of course I loved her. She came from you. How could I not love her? She *is* my daughter. Never let yourself think otherwise."

She sniffled and smiled back at him. "Can I go back to your original question?"

He nodded.

"Yes, I consider you my soul mate, but I consider Grizz one, too. I hope you understand that. I hope you can accept that." She looked at him questioningly.

"I do understand it and I do accept it." He smiled warmly at her. But he couldn't deny that his heart suffered a small blow.

As if reading his mind, she quickly added, "And yes, Leslie did miss the real love story. The real love story is the one I'm living now."

She grabbed both of his hands in hers, there on the floor of the office. "Did I have a real love story with Grizz, too? Yes, I did, in spite of the stupid Stockholm Syndrome accusations. But I guess my story with him ended when he told me to marry you, Tommy. You are the only love story there is now, but it doesn't mean I didn't have one before you. Does that make sense?"

He breathed a sigh of relief. That was what he'd really wanted to know, anyway. That she loved him now. He had subconsciously wanted to hear that her love for Grizz wasn't real to her. As much as it hurt to hear about her feelings for Grizz, at least he could appreciate her honesty. He knew she was telling him the truth about her love for him in the present.

It was more honesty than he'd given her for most of their marriage.

"I've been meaning to ask you something," she said then. "Moe's journal. I haven't read it yet. Do I even need to?"

It was time. He knew they'd be listening, and he'd been waiting for this moment. He was glad she'd brought it up so he didn't have to figure out a way to work it into the conversation.

"I don't think you need to read it if you trust me to tell you the highlights."

She frowned, but he added, "I know you're worried about trusting me, but you really don't need to read it. I can tell you everything."

"Okay, then. Tell me what you think I need to know."

"For starters, you had nothing to feel guilty about. Moe didn't kill herself. It was an accidental overdose. She'd been writing about how she'd been having difficulty sleeping and kept taking more and more pills to help with it. She was so little, Gin, I guess her body couldn't handle it."

He wasn't being completely truthful. Yet. He couldn't tell her that Moe committed suicide because she felt guilty for helping someone named Wendy set up Ginny's attack. He would've felt like he had to spill it all. The whole Sarah Jo being Wendy thing. He would definitely tell her all of it. But not yet. It was too soon and there were still too many emotional bruises. The counseling they'd agreed to get would help. He would have to wait.

"Really? Are you serious, Tommy?"

"Yes, Ginny. I'm serious. It had nothing to do with feeling guilty about having the dogs that night. Yes, she felt bad. She mentioned that a few times. But she didn't kill herself because of it."

"I'm so relieved to hear that! I've had enough guilt of my own over the years about different things. It's a miserable feeling. I almost envy that Grizz never seemed to feel guilty about some stuff. Lots of stuff, actually."

"Oh, and this you might find interesting. When Jan told you why Grizz cut Moe's tongue out because of a comment she made about me? Not true."

"What?" Ginny practically shouted.

"Nope, Moe saw Grizz with some gussied-up fancy dude in a suit and told him about it."

"And he cut her tongue out? That can't be right!" Ginny replied, the doubt in her voice obvious.

"Think about it, Ginny. It was the late sixties. He was starting to make his drug connections with the South American Cartel. She was a blabbermouth. He really probably thought he was doing her a favor. He concocted the blow job story for everybody else, including Blue."

"I'm sorry to have to admit this, but yes, I can see Grizz doing that." She shook her head then as if waking from a dream. "So what do we do with it? Do we save it, turn it in to the police? Find Moe's remaining family and give it to them?"

"Can I make a suggestion, Gin?"

"Of course, Tommy. What should we do with it?"

"Tomorrow is garbage day. I say we throw it away."

# Chapter Seventy-Four

2000

GINNY FELT ODDLY elated as she sat idling at a red light on her way to Carter's house. She'd watched Tommy the next morning as he'd ceremoniously tossed Moe's journal into the kitchen garbage and, after tying it up, walked it to the curb. She thought about the church ceremony and honeymoon that followed. She thought about the counseling sessions they'd been going to regularly. They were helping, and she was glad that Tommy had suggested it. She even thought about the tiny black kitten that had shown up when they'd arrived home from their honeymoon. The black kitten that had been creating havoc in her home ever since. She smiled.

She was still enjoying her seventies music and had reached blindly into her purse to dig for a pack of gum she knew she had in there somewhere. She felt something at the bottom of her purse and was trying to figure out what it was when it appeared in her hand. She stared for a minute and just smiled. She brought it to her lips and gently kissed it.

"Goodbye, my love," she whispered. "I guess I must've still had it in my hand the night Casey found me in the garage."

She didn't remember shoving it in her purse, but she probably had. She lifted her right hip and slid Grizz's blue bandana into the back pocket of her jeans. She would return it to the motorcycle in Carter's garage. Where it belonged.

The morning traffic was worse than she expected, and forty-five minutes later she pulled into her old driveway. Carter was off to the side doing something with the animals. She waved as she approached. Carter let herself out of the gate and told Ginny, "You got a delivery today."

"A delivery?" Ginny gave her a quick hug. "Here? Are you sure it's for me?"

"Yeah, it says Kit on it. I'm assuming it's for you."

Ginny stopped in her tracks. Carter knew her old gang name, but she hadn't gone by Kit in fifteen years.

"C'mon," Carter urged. "I can stay with you while you open it, if you want."

"Who delivered it?" Ginny asked as she followed Carter inside.

"Couldn't tell you. I found it this morning on the porch." Carter closed the door behind them. She snagged the package from the coffee table and gently placed it in Ginny's hands. It was wrapped in brown paper with "Kit" written in black marker on the top. Ginny didn't recognize the handwriting and couldn't imagine who'd delivered it.

Slowly she removed the brown paper, then fell onto Carter's couch with a plop, her mouth open.

"It's my Bible!" Ginny said incredulously. "It's my Bible from when I was just a little girl."

She smiled then and opened it, noticing her name where she had written it in bold block letters: Guinevere Love Lemon.

"I wonder who's had this. I wonder why whoever had it never gave it to me before."

Carter sat next to her. "Are you going to be okay?"

"Yeah, I'm fine. It's actually kind of a nice surprise. I'm shocked, but glad to see it. It's like—like running into an old friend." She'd thought about Grizz's chess set and jacket showing up. The kitten with the missing king. Even Moe's journal. What else might show up?

She shook the thought off. She didn't do dark and she wouldn't start now. Not when she was so close to starting over.

"Do you want something to drink?" Carter was asking. "I'm dying of thirst."

"No, I'm not thirsty, but I may be later. I want to make a serious dent cleaning out the garage by the end of the day."

Carter broke into a wide grin. "Good for you." She stood then. "I'm getting my drink and heading out back. Call me if you need me?"

"I will," Ginny told her friend.

She leaned back on the sofa and gently fanned through the pages when she realized something was stuck between them. She took out some papers. An old school picture was paper-clipped to them. She stared at it. The picture didn't invoke any good memories. She would throw it away.

Then she noticed the rest of the papers and spotted Delia's handwriting immediately. It wasn't hard to recognize. She'd learned how to emulate it perfectly when she handled the family's finances. It used to be slightly shaky, but this handwriting was neat and precise. It was definitely Delia's, though.

Ginny had a hard time calming her own shaking hands so she could read what was carefully written on the old notebook paper, now slightly yellow with age:

*My Dear Ginny,*

*Where do I begin? Where do I even begin to tell you what you have deserved to know from the very beginning?*

*I should probably start with your father. I wasn't living in a commune when I got pregnant with you. I know you always believed that. That was only one of many lies I fabricated. I was actually married to a man I was deeply in love with. You were conceived in love, Ginny, but it went horribly wrong and I blame myself.*

*Your father's name was David Dunn and my name was Alice Crespin. We married right out of high school and were working our way through college. It wasn't easy, but we were young and motivated and excited about our future. We wanted to wait until after we graduated to have a baby, but we were both elated when we found out I was pregnant.*

*I don't remember exactly how it started, but your father was invited to a student rally at the college. It was a time when nuclear weapons were being protested. I remember him telling me he didn't want to raise a child in a world that wasn't safe. He started getting more and more involved in politics and the rallies and protests. I adored your father and I went along with him to some of them, but I was so wrapped up in work and studying and my pregnancy that I didn't realize how truly involved he'd become. I didn't see it in time to save him. To save us.*

*It was a total surprise when you and your sister were born almost two months early. We didn't know we were having two babies. We were afraid we were going to lose both of you, but in spite of your size, you were a fighter. You had to stay in the hospital for almost two months before we were finally able to bring you home. Your sister was much smaller and had to stay longer.*

*You were only home for a few days when your father came home from work one night and told me he was going back out. He picked you up out of your bassinet and told you he was going to do something important. He was going to do something that would make the world a better place to raise his beautiful daughters, Josie and Jodi.*

*You were named after my parents. My father was Joseph and my mother was Diana. That's your real name, Josephine Diana. We called you Josie.*

*I'm smiling as I write this. Your sister's name was a little more challenging. Your father's father was Jedediah. We spent days trying to shorten the name Jedediah. We couldn't so we named her Jodi Marie. Marie was your father's mother's name.*

*As God is my witness, I didn't know what your father was really going to do that night. When I asked him if it was another protest, he just handed you to me and smiled. I never saw him or your sister again.*

*I was woken up that night around midnight by banging on our door. I was shocked to find two men I knew from the protests. They told me something had gone horribly wrong. The group had been planning to make a big statement. They had planted a bomb in the college library. They didn't want anyone to get hurt, so they made sure to do it at night when nobody would be around. They hadn't known some students were given permission to use the library after hours to hold a study session. Your father realized it too late and ran back in to warn them. Your father, along with seven students, were killed in the blast.*

*The two men that came to the house told me I needed to leave. I needed to pack up and move before they identified your father. They said they were going home to get their things and get out of town, and if I didn't want to go to prison and have my babies taken away, I should, too. I was too stunned to even answer them. What could your father have been thinking? Didn't he realize that even if nobody had been killed, bombing a school was serious and the authorities knew about the protests? It would've only been a matter of time before they made the connection. I was angry at him, not fully taking in the fact that he was* dead.

But then I started to get scared. I did pack you up. I took a small file that contained our personal information. Our marriage and birth certificates, social security and school identifications. I took what little cash we had and walked to the closest bus stop. I carried you, a diaper bag and a small suitcase. I left everything else behind, including your sister. I would've gone straight to the hospital to get her, but she was still too little. It would've been the same as signing her death warrant. She was too small to live outside the incubator.

I had a horrible choice to make that night. To risk losing both of my children or just one. I chose the latter.

I don't remember how many days I spent switching buses. I ended up in Miami and slowly started to rebuild our lives. Your father and I didn't have any family to turn to. I was afraid and I was alone, except for you. It didn't take me too long to establish a new identity as Delia Lemon. I found a low paying job and an elderly lady to care for you while I worked.

I thought I was doing okay for a while, Ginny. Then something changed. I was miserable, exhausted and lonely. I remember holding you one day and you messed in your last clean diaper. I was sitting in a hot, cramped, one-room dump without a clean diaper in sight, and something in me snapped. I looked into your eyes and I remembered what your father said the last night he was alive. He said that he was doing it for his daughters. He was doing it for you and Jodi, and she was gone from my life.

So I blamed you. I convinced myself I had been forced into the life I now had, a life on the run, because of what your father supposedly did for you. Looking back, I was naïve. I'm certain I could've gone to the authorities and told them I hadn't been involved. The men who came to the door that night were probably there to scare me away so I wouldn't implicate them. Still, I convinced myself I was guilty by association and didn't want to go to prison.

Something happened that day. Something I have regretted every single day since my sobriety, but not something I knew I should've been regretting then. I left you alone in your dirty diaper, walked to the closest liquor store, and bought something to drink. Something to numb *the pain. The pain of losing your father, your sister, and the life we knew. And even worse, I allowed myself to blame it on an innocent baby girl. You.*

*That was the beginning of the end, and I don't need to tell you how the rest of your life played out. You were living in a nightmare and probably didn't even know it. You were always a happy, positive child, and it only made me hate and resent you more. What kind of woman can hate her own child? I treated you as badly as I could and you persevered. You never stooped to my level.*

*You're probably wondering why I never abandoned you. Just got rid of you. I've had time to reflect on that and I'm ashamed to say that looking back, it was because I saw you as my excuse to wallow in my addictions. You were the reminder that told me it was okay to continue drinking and doing drugs. You were the cause of my pain and I deserved to get stoned and drunk.*

*I remember thinking that if the authorities were looking for me, they would've been looking for a woman with a daughter your age named Josephine. It was then that I started calling you Guinevere. I can't even remember how I came up with that name. I'm certain it was during a time I was experimenting with the heavier drugs. I was using LSD by the time I'd met Vince. He was the only reason I stopped. And even then I hadn't stopped completely. I was still doing some heavier drugs even after we were married.*

*When I finally made the move to Fort Lauderdale, two years had passed that you should've been in school. I had a fake birth certificate made for you with the name Guinevere and a false birth date. You were always small and had grown only a little by the time I enrolled you in kindergarten. Even though you were seven, you easily passed as a five-year-old, and nobody questioned it.*

*You pretty much raised yourself from that point on. I was relieved when food showed up on our doorstep. A normal parent would've been grateful. Maybe even a little embarrassed. Not me.*

*Even though I was horrible, and I can admit it, I still never sent Johnny Tillman to rape you. He was supposed to scare you. He was supposed to tell you to back off the Steve Marcus thing. After you figured out what Marcus was doing to his kid, he came to me and threatened me. He knew I was growing and selling pot, but worse, he had someone break into our house. I had gotten rid of our real birth certificates and other identification years earlier, but I kept my marriage license, and they stole it and did some digging. Marcus told me he would expose me. I would go to prison as an accessory to murder or worse because it was a bombing, I would be tried in a federal court and the sentence would be that much more severe.*

*And just so you know, Vince was never part of that. He didn't know I sent Johnny Tillman to our house that night. Ginny, I'm sorry for not even being nice to you after it happened. A real mother would've comforted her daughter. A real mother wouldn't have asked her how she could've done something so dumb. A real mother wouldn't have sent a monster to scare you.*

*Looking back, a real mother wouldn't have bullied her daughter into going on the birth control pill. By then you had found such comfort in your church, and I even tried to take that away from you. I knew birth control was against the Catholic faith, but I made you take it, anyway. I think I was jealous of your happiness and faith, and I tried to ruin that, too, by forcing something on you I knew you would feel guilty about. I couldn't stand to see you happy. I can see now that Johnny Tillman wasn't the monster. I was.*

*More than a year later some big tattooed man showed up at my work. He told me he was taking you and he threatened me and Vince. Then he showed me what was left of Johnny Tillman. Worse yet, he told me that he knew about my past. He was responsible for scaring Steve Marcus away and he knew about the bombing. Marcus must have told him. I was afraid for myself and Vince. I wasn't afraid for you, Ginny. I am so sorry. So very sorry.*

*I've been trying to find you. Vince and I have finally sobered up and I told him about my past. I told him everything. He's sorry about you too. We've gone to the police, but they just take notes and tell us they'll get back to us. I asked Guido just yesterday if he remembered a man like that coming around our house. It never occurred to me the man must have seen you somewhere. Maybe he even lived in our neighborhood back then and I'd never noticed him. Of course, I was too wasted to notice* much back then.

I'm writing this letter as part of my therapy. I don't know if you'll ever get to read it because I don't know if I'll ever find you. But if I do find you, I will look you in the eyes and tell you I'm truly, truly sorry. I will let you read this and I will ask for your forgiveness. God has taught me about forgiveness. And if you don't forgive me, I will have to accept that. I'm not even sure I forgive myself at this point, but I'm trying and God knows that.

I tried looking for your sister, too. I'd had high hopes that she would've been adopted by a nice family. Instead, I found a death certificate. She died a week after I left her there. I have nothing to remember her by. Not a picture, a piece of clothing she would've worn. Nothing. All I have is a memory of a lovely nurse who cared for her as if she was her own. I don't even remember the nurse's name, just that she had a pretty accent. She used to call your sister Cricket because when Jodi would take a deep breath, her exhale came out sounding like little chirps.

I don't have much to remember you by either, Ginny. After that man took you, I started cleaning out the house. Told myself that by removing any memory of you, I could remove the guilt that had slowly sunk into my soul. Maybe it was there all along and seeing your things called attention to it. Your Bible was something I could hide in the bottom of a never-used drawer, and that's where it's been for all of these years. I hate the picture of you I found tucked inside. It was taken during a time I know you were being horribly neglected. But it's now all I have along with yours and Jodi's original birth certificates, which I recently was able to track down.

Vince is taking me on a trip back to the city where I went to college. I'm going to face my past and admit my part in the bombing. Although my part was never anything more than going to a few protests, I was married to the man who helped plan and plant that bomb.

When I get back, I will continue my search for you. And I will continue writing this letter. Maybe you'll want to know more about your father. I can do that. I can tell you more about him.

She hadn't signed it. Through blurry vision, Ginny stared at the three-page note as tears streamed down her cheeks. Delia never signed it because she'd never made it home to finish it. Ginny looked at the date on the letter; Delia and Vince had died in a car accident less than a week later.

Attached to the back of the note were four pieces of paper: The fake birth certificate that Delia had made for Guinevere Love Lemon all those years ago and the two real ones showing hers and Jodi's real birthdays. They were born in 1958. Jodi's death certificate was also attached.

Just then, Carter walked in and said, "I just came back for my—oh, Gin, what's wrong?" She ran to her friend. "Why are you crying, honey? What's wrong? Bad memories? Do you want me to call Tommy?"

Ginny tried to smile. "No, I finally got some answers. That's all. I finally got some answers."

It was bittersweet to find out she wasn't an only child. At least not for the first few months of her life. What would her life have been like if her father hadn't helped plant that bomb? What would it have been like to have been raised by a sober Alice Crespin and a father? Her heart felt heavy. Was it possible to mourn a life you didn't have? If she'd had that life, she most certainly wouldn't have been raised in Florida. She would never have known Grizz. She would never have known Tommy. She wouldn't have her children.

It had been difficult to read Delia's note, and yet there was something freeing in it as well. She got a little angry when she realized someone had held on to this Bible for years. Delia had died in 1980. Why was it only being given to her now? And in an envelope addressed only to her gang name. Was there any significance?

No. There wasn't. She was certain of that. Maybe it had just been forgotten about. It didn't matter now, anyway. None of it did actually. None of it.

She took a deep breath and remembered her reason for being at Carter's. She would handle cleaning out the garage now. She passed the note to Carter and told her to read it for herself. She wiped her tears with the back of her hands and smiled. "I'm going to go tackle the garage. I am so ready to start over, Carter."

Carter looked up from the note and smiled at her. "I can come help you."

"No. I'll do it myself."

She walked with long sure strides to the side of the garage and tried to ignore the pain in her chest. The pain of a life she hadn't known, wouldn't know, but yet somehow still grieved. *You've made progress, Ginny. Don't fall apart now. You should be happy to know the truth. To know Delia had regrets about you.* She couldn't deny, though, that even with Delia's confession, it stung to not read somewhere in the note that Delia had loved her.

She opened the door with the key that had been put back under the ceramic frog. She went in and flipped on the light, then pressed the button to open all three automatic garage doors. She was looking down as she walked toward the motorcycles. She smiled as she caught a whiff of fresh air from the newly raised doors. She reached into her back pocket for the blue bandana and stopped dead in her tracks.

Grizz's favorite bike was gone.

She held the bandana in her hand and stared at the spot where she'd laid on the ground and cried over a month ago. Then she looked up and walked out of the garage, gazing across the expanse of the property. She looked at the bandana in her hand. And she remembered all those years ago when Grizz was first incarcerated in the county jail.

"If you ever need anything," he'd said then, "I mean fucking anything, and Grunt can't be there for you, you put your hair up in one of those high ponytails you like to wear and you wrap my bandana around it. You hear me? You wear my bandana, and it might take a day or two, but you'll get whatever help you need. You understand me?"

Now she knew. She knew what he meant. But how? Who? Who would've gotten a message to Grizz in jail or prison that she needed him? Who was watching out for her if it wasn't Tommy?

Movement in her peripheral vision caught her attention and she quickly glanced at the front porch. Carter was sitting there in a rocking chair. She had her right leg perched on the edge of the chair and had one arm resting on it casually as she rocked. The note from Delia was dangling from her hand. Their eyes met. Carter gave her a small smile.

Carter? Her dear, sweet friend Carter had been keeping an eye on her for Grizz? Grizz, the man she'd accused of not caring about other people. All those years ago, when she'd told Grizz about her new friend that she met at college, Carter, and the stalker causing her so much fear. The stalker that left her alone after she went to the police and took out a restraining order. Ginny realized now there had been no police report or restraining order. Grizz had taken care of it and gained an ally for life.

Tears filled her eyes again. Did she want to know? Did she dare to ask? Could it be? She looked at the blue bandana in her hand and at the empty spot where Grizz's bike used to be. Then she looked back at her friend. They locked eyes, and she knew Carter would tell her the truth. Carter nodded slightly.

Hope was replaced with an immediate and intense anger. An anger she hadn't expected. How dare he! How dare he do this to her! If she was reading Carter's nod correctly, then it meant he was alive. Grizz was out there, and he was alive.

Did Tommy know?

She thought about her husband's behavior since Grizz's execution. No. Tommy didn't know. She was certain of that. She could tell by his actions. If he even suspected Grizz was still alive, he would be acting even more protective of her. Tommy wasn't behaving like a man whose life was still on hold while he waited for the other shoe to drop. No. He was behaving like a man who had just started to live. He really believed the kitten was a signal from the grave that all had been forgiven. She had naively believed it, too.

She dropped to the paved driveway and sat cross-legged as she digested what she was learning. Still clutching the bandana, she started to cry again. But it wasn't a melancholy, soft cry. It was an angry, loud one. She felt Carter's arms try to hug her from behind and she shook her off.

"Don't! Don't, Carter. Leave me alone," she wailed as she rejected her friend's attempt at solace.

Carter stood and walked around to face her. Looking up, Ginny cried, "Carter, leave me alone. Just go away and leave me alone."

Carter squatted and grabbed Ginny's face with both hands. Using her thumbs to wipe away Ginny's tears, she quietly asked, "What did you expect him to do, Gin? Did you expect him to show up on your doorstop and announce it? Did you expect that he should've given you a choice? Put you in the position of having to decide whether to leave your family and disappear with him? To live under new identities? Or leave Tommy and take your kids with you to be with him and start over somewhere? Can you imagine the two of you trying to raise children who would question why they'd been taken from the only father they'd ever known? Think about the choices you would've had to make if he'd shown up."

"Stop making excuses for him." Ginny swiped at her tears. "I never asked anything of him but the truth, Carter. That's all I ever asked of him from the very beginning. He wouldn't even tell me his real name. And don't think for a second I don't know I probably named my son after an alias. He never trusted me enough to really let me in. I got pieces here and there, but he never told me a thing."

Her voice got very low then and came out in almost a growl. "I'm not stupid. I know he had Blue set Jan and Matthew up. I'm sure Tommy thinks it, too, but we would never talk about it. That's what we've done in our home for years. Deny our past and try to pretend we weren't part of something so horrible. And if Grizz thought for a second that Tommy was the one that helped Jan, he'd be paying for it."

"Ginny, don't—"

"I hate him! I hate him, Carter!"

The sobs began anew, became loud and uncontrollable. Carter reached for her again, and this time, Ginny let herself be held and comforted.

"How could he do this to me? How could he make me love him so much only to leave me? Then to make me mourn him, and now, to know that he's alive and purposely chose not to be with me all those years ago? I hate him for that, Carter."

Carter spoke softly. "I don't believe you hate him, Ginny." She looked at her friend. "I don't know any of the details and I don't want to know. But I do know one thing. I know the choice to be with you must have been taken away from him. Because I have never seen a man, any man, maybe not even Tommy, love a woman like Grizz loves you. I've never seen a man go out of his way to protect someone he couldn't be with. You may be having a lot of doubts about him now, and I don't blame you. But one thing you should never doubt is his love for you."

Carter pulled back from Ginny and could see by her expression that Ginny had heard her. She was starting to take in big gulps of air, and the tears were subsiding.

They sat like that for a few minutes. Ginny used the bandana to wipe at her tears as she tried to calm her breathing.

"I'm fine now," she said in a small raw voice. "He made the choice for me, so I'm done talking about it."

Carter gave her a questioning look. This was so like Ginny. Brave, resolved, determined.

"Seriously, Carter. I'm fine. It's been a rough day. My Bible and now this, but I'm okay. Well, I'm not okay, but I will be."

Carter nodded at her. She knew Ginny needed a little space, some time to process all this. "I'll be out back with the horses if you need me. I love you, Gin."

Ginny watched her friend head for the horse stalls while she took another deep breath. She tried to collect her thoughts. Twenty-five years of memories washed over her in a single moment. She knew without a doubt there was truth in what Carter had said. She never once doubted Grizz's real and genuine love for her. And if she was remembering the Grizz she'd married and fallen in love with all of those years ago, then this situation wasn't of his choosing. He wasn't with her because he couldn't be, not because he didn't want to be. She didn't know why, and she didn't know if it was something she should try to find out. And if she did find out, then what would she do?

No, Carter's explanation made sense. How could she have

chosen?

Her head was spinning and she realized Grizz had done her a favor. He had loved her enough to spare her from having to make that choice. Still, he needed her to know he was there. He would always be her protector. But did she really need to know that? Was this his way of ruining her life with Tommy? She knew subconsciously she'd let Grizz cast a shadow over her marriage. It wasn't until his death last month and her return home to Tommy that she really let herself put her past where it belonged. In the past. That didn't last long.

She couldn't exactly say what she was feeling. Anger, relief, remorse, grief. She was so conflicted. It was just too much. Delia's letter, and now this.

*Don't lose it, Gin. Don't lose it now. You've come too far.*

She looked at the bandana clutched so tightly in her fist that her knuckles were turning white. She wouldn't make a decision today. She would do what she came here to do: Clean out the garage and her past with it. She wiped the last of her tears with the already-soaked bandana and, lifting her right hip off the pavement, she tucked it away in her back pocket. Maybe Grizz was right.

After all, she had no way of knowing if she might need the bandana one day. She had no way of knowing if she might need *him* one day. Him. Jason William Talbot.

# Chapter Seventy-Five
2001, Six Months Later
Somewhere in Louisiana

HE DIDN'T KNOW how long he'd been riding. He barely remembered the roads, the little towns he passed through, the crummy diners, the dilapidated old motels. He shook his head. The motels.

Memories pierced and taunted his heart. Big brown eyes, an innocent stare, tears, laughter, passion, love. The passion. There had been a lot of passion. The love. There had been even more love.

He shook his head as he tried to reason with himself. He tried to remember why he'd done the things he had. Nothing, not even fifteen years in prison or the near-death experience he'd had on the lethal injection table, had prepared him for the emptiness, the hollowness of a soul that didn't love. Or worse yet, a soul that didn't think it could love again, found it with Kit, only to lose it.

Lose it by his own stupidity.

Twenty-five years ago, he'd seen a spark of light. He lived in the radiance of that light for ten years. He hadn't realized how bright that light truly was until he had to live without it while he was stuck in that prison. And then he'd actually died on that table and saw what darkness was like. Real darkness.

Kit had tried to share her faith with him for so many years. To introduce him to a God he was certain didn't exist. He had been wrong. He now knew Kit's God existed, because he was pulled from what he was certain was the pit of hell. If hell was real, and he now knew it was, then heaven had to be real, too.

But he was certain it wasn't there for the likes of him.

He remembered at his execution motioning to Kit to show him her ring tattoo. He couldn't see his name, but he knew it was still there, and that was all he needed to see. He knew they, he, had permanently removed her from his life, but they couldn't remove him from her heart. She could've had that tattoo removed years ago, especially when he'd told her she had to move on with her life and leave him behind. She had finally fallen in love with Grunt, had a child with him.

But she didn't have Grizz's name removed. As small a consolation as that was, it was all he had gotten and more than he deserved.

He'd fucked up big time in more ways than he cared to admit. Regret, an emotion he rarely admitted to, pierced his conscience, and as hard as he tried to bury it, it was there all the same. He'd had no way of knowing all those years ago he would fall in love with her. He didn't care about people back then and he certainly didn't love. Especially after Ruthie.

But all of that changed after he'd had her brought to the motel.

And what the hell was he even doing in Louisiana? He knew he was looking for some connection to the woman who'd been torn from her home as an infant and forced to live under an assumed name by her foolish mother. He hadn't seen Delia's note from Kit's Bible since the day Guido had showed it to him all those years ago. But he thought he remembered the city on Kit's real birth certificate. The certificate Delia had tracked down. So, he mused, Kit had been seventeen when he took her, not fifteen. He should have felt some relief at knowing she was slightly older back then, but honestly, he didn't care. Her age was never a factor in his decision to take her.

He couldn't remember the name of the hospital but found one he thought could've been where she was born. He sat on his bike and stared at it. Idiot. He didn't even know if he was remembering the city right, so the chance he was sitting in front of the hospital where she was born was slim to none. What had he been hoping to find here, anyway? Nothing, really. He knew there was nothing to find. It was just his last feeble attempt at grabbing onto something that was part of her.

Two days later, he was still wandering the back roads, slowly taking him away from what he thought might be his last connection to her. Clinging to the speck of hope that she might one day need him. For someone who'd thought he was so smart, he was actually a stupid motherfucker.

He slowed down and squinted to see if the little diner he was approaching was open. Nope. Another locally owned business that had sunk under the weight of trying to make a living in a small town. A small town in this country. He scoffed to himself as he thought about what was really going on with this country. With this world, actually. Restaurants were tough. It wasn't like they could sell off their inventory. When the customers didn't come, the food eventually rotted. As did dark souls who thought they could be rehabilitated.

He'd felt tricked by fate.

His mind drifted back to a good memory. He didn't like to remember good things because it made it all the more painful when the memory was over and he was brought back to the bleak reality that had become his life. Riding worn and pitted roads, staying off of *their* radar, just in case. Staying off the world's radar and mourning the life he'd carelessly let be taken from him.

He smiled at this memory. He might even let himself laugh at how adorable she'd been. He'd been patiently waiting to introduce her to oral sex. He'd been driven mad by the smell of her, and not going down on her had been pure torture. His smile widened when he remembered her scooting down the bed. How she'd thought she was being subtle while dodging his attempts. He had known all along she'd been avoiding it and had let her have her space.

His hands gripped the bike tighter when he remembered she'd told him she needed to save something of herself for her future husband. He'd been stunned when he realized she hadn't seen him in her future. That she was going to save something of herself for the man she would marry "one day." Fuck that, he'd thought then. There was never a question in his mind. Never an instant where he had to think about marrying her. She'd fallen asleep in his arms that night and he reflected on what had been so special about her. What had drawn him to her like a moth to a flame.

It had started out as nothing more than repaying a kindness to an obviously neglected child. When she'd walked out of that convenience store and handed him a box of bandages, he'd been overcome with an unfamiliar feeling. What was it then? Was he grateful that he'd seen a spark of kindness, even if it was from a child? Maybe that was it, but he couldn't remember for sure, and he really didn't see himself as anything more than a silent partner in her care and protection. It was all Mavis. Yes, he was responsible for putting Mavis there, but he really didn't do anything other than shell out some money for necessities.

He had to admit that when he'd found out about her quest to bring down a prominent businessman and local political figure, that Marcus fucker, he'd started to admire her. And that was rare. As a rule, Grizz admired no one but himself. He'd prided himself on being a self-made and successful businessman. He shook his head. No, he wasn't a businessman. He was a thug who'd used the excuse of his childhood to inflict terror and wreak havoc wherever he went.

It hadn't started out that way. He really believed early on he'd been ridding the world of filth. He didn't remember when he'd invisibly crossed over that threshold himself. When he'd started becoming the filth. Eventually, he allowed himself to think he was entitled to whatever he wanted. He'd told himself he'd not only outsmarted the government, but he had the real power players by the balls. He'd gotten cocky and slack, and it'd cost him Kit.

Maybe he'd fooled himself. Maybe she was never really his to begin with.

The first wrong move he'd made was abducting her because he saw Matthew Rockman kiss her. He wasn't in love with her then. How could he be? He didn't know her. Besides, he didn't love back then. But witnessing that kiss had unnerved him in a way he hadn't expected and couldn't explain. He hadn't entertained thoughts of kissing her himself, but he couldn't ignore the twist in his gut when he saw Rockman do it. Rockman. That fuck.

He remembered the first glimmer of light in his soul the night she was brought to the motel. The night she'd first seen him and looked up at him from the lawn chair with those wide, innocent brown eyes. Even though he'd seen her from afar over the years, he wasn't prepared for the jolt he received when their eyes met. The fear she'd tried to replace with false bravado. The smell of her. Oh, fuck, the smell of her when she passed by him as Moe led her to number four. He'd never been close enough to inhale her essence before. It permeated his very being that night and never left. It was there now, in his mind, torturing him.

Another smile as he remembered her defiance when he told her she would never use her real name again. That ridiculously, beautiful name that had been branded on his soul. Guinevere Love Lemon. Of course, he hadn't even known then that that wasn't her real name. Delia had been clever at covering her tracks. It didn't matter, anyway. She would always be his Kitten.

He thought more than once what it would've come to when she was recognized so many years ago in the vet's office. What if she admitted to her high school acquaintance that, yes, she was Ginny Lemon? He'd told her then that he would've grabbed her and run, and he would have.

Would it have turned out any different if that had happened?

His second mistake was marrying her. Not because he didn't want to marry her. He wanted to marry her with a desperation that riled him to his core. To make sure that there would be no other man in her future.

But he'd fucked that up, too. The mistake was in letting *them* see he cared. He'd made himself vulnerable.

He'd only ever loved two people. The first was Ruthie. The second was Kit. He loved Kit, and his actions showed it, and they knew it and used it against him. And that's where he went wrong. He should've given it up then. Given them what they wanted in exchange for a new life with her away from South Florida.

A few things stopped him from doing that. One, his ego. He was Grizz. He could have it all. He had been wrong. Two, he'd become complacent; let himself forget they were still out there. He told himself that the "powers that be" had died off or gone away. Even after they had told him to get rid of Candy he hadn't heard from them again for years.

And, third, there were no guarantees that instead of relocating them with new identities, they wouldn't just have had them eliminated. There was still no guarantee, but he'd stayed around long enough to be pretty sure they'd kept their word. He knew they'd listened closely in those last few weeks to everything happening in Grunt and Kit's home. They were certain the couple who had been so tightlipped for years about Grizz would finally slip up and talk about what they knew. There was nothing to know.

He'd been with them that day, listening to snippets of the last conversations between Grunt and Kit. Grunt was smart to throw the journal in the garbage. He knew they'd be listening and would need to make certain nothing important was in it. Grunt knew they would retrieve it from the trash, and of course they had.

He was also glad Grunt never revealed the truth behind Moe's suicide. According to the two agents, Moe had felt guilty for inadvertently helping someone named Wendy set up Kit's rape and attempted murder. This was old news to Grizz. He never did find Wendy. It was probably Willow tricking Moe from a phone. Isn't that what Willow had told him? That Wendy had called and had a Southern accent? It had to be Willow all along. He remembered the agent's smug attitude as they sat there listening to the tapes.

"So, looks like your son is still lying to her. Never told her someone named Wendy was behind her attack," the younger of the two agents said. He had a baby face and a head full of wavy, black hair. "What a fucked up mess you left, Talbot, or whatever the fuck your real name is."

It took all the strength that Grizz possessed not to beat the shit out of the man right then and there. He'd been sitting in an isolated office behind a small pool supply store somewhere in Tallahassee. It was the agreed meeting spot. He gave them the documents, pictures, and money plates, and they were to give him his life and Grunt and Kit their freedom from the NNG's inexcusable invasion of their privacy.

There were no guarantees that the electronic versions of what Grizz was turning over wouldn't go viral, but they didn't care about that anymore. Hadn't cared about it for a while. Anybody can pretty much do anything they want on the World Wide Web. Isn't that what they called it? It was the hard documents they wanted. Grizz surmised that with the advances in forensic technology, even though so many years had passed, there was a way to pull DNA and fingerprints from those documents, pictures, and metal plates. Of course, Grizz's would be on them as well, but it wasn't Grizz's that concerned them. Somebody powerful wanted all of it back.

He was certain the two agents took sadistic pleasure in letting him listen to some of the tapes. He tried not to wince when he listened to them making love. He tried not to breathe a sigh of relief when Kit confessed that Grizz had been a true love and a soul mate to her. He needed to hear that. To have that validation. He even felt a stab of pity for Grunt when he heard her tell him her love for Grizz had been real and she wouldn't deny it.

His hands gripped the bike's handlebars tighter as he remembered hearing of Jan's confirmation, that his suspicions were correct about Matthew Rockman. Rockman hadn't been working for or with the NNG. He had taken Grizz on all by himself without knowing he was helping *them* out. They could've helped Grizz find Jan a lot sooner than Blue did. But they didn't.

Grizz could admit he'd been an egotistical ass, priding himself on being two steps ahead of everyone and everything. He didn't find it exhausting. He found it invigorating. And yet he'd fucked up royally. Then they'd fucked with him over the years while he was in prison. He knew only *they* could pull off a fake execution with lethal injection. Yet they made sure the bills in place to legalize lethal injection in the Florida prison system continued to get vetoed, furthering his stay on death row.

He lied to Grunt that day in the prison yard. There was no new person in charge who didn't care if he exposed them. In fact, it was the opposite.

Someone new had been moved up the ranks within the NNG, and almost immediately lethal injection had been legalized. Someone was finally ready to play ball. And after thinking about what he'd seen in those documents and realizing what would be happening later this year, he could understand why. It was something that would bring this country to its knees.

The men who sat before him allowed him one last parting gift. They hadn't interfered in Blue's set-up to get rid of Jan and frame Rockman. He felt a pang of conscience. After having a near-death experience, he was almost sorry he'd had Jan murdered and Rockman framed for it.

"You should probably know that the last thing Blue handled for you has been thwarted. You're not going to find your money in that offshore account. You're stone-cold broke."

The younger of the two men practically spat this last comment at Grizz. The second guy was older with a ruddy complexion, thin lips, and a comb-over that consisted of maybe ten strands of gray hair. The older agent sat silently with a tightlipped smile as the younger agent informed Talbot of this latest information.

*Good*, Grizz thought to himself. They had followed the trail he and Blue set and thought they'd found his money and were going to prevent him from getting it. Let the fuckers think it. At least this told him something. He would be walking out of here. He already had proof they'd pulled surveillance from Kit and Grunt's home. He'd had his own reliable contact who was able to confirm they were telling the truth about that. The same contact who'd had the kitten delivered. They thought he was walking out of here a beaten and broken man. They thought they'd consigned him to a fate worse than death.

Unbeknownst to them, he still had a lot of money so he wasn't broke, but he was still broken. He no longer had her.

Their business was concluded. Grizz got up and started to leave, but as he turned, he asked one last question. "This journal. This journal that they keep talking about. It was Moe's, right?"

"Miriam Parker? The girl you maimed? Yeah, it was hers. Rhonda Bailey had it. Why?"

"What are you going to do with it?" he asked them.

"Toss it. There's nothing in it, Talbot. You want it? Kind of like a keepsake or something?" Mr. Comb-Over asked.

"Yeah. I want it."

That was almost six months ago. He'd finally given it back. He'd given it all back and walked out of that meeting not certain if he would be getting a bullet in his back. But, they gave him the journal and let him go. They were certain he'd find himself in trouble again soon and would meet his own demise. They had what they wanted and he would no longer have their protection. His death would no longer expose them.

He still hadn't read Moe's journal. He wasn't ready. Besides, he was certain it was full of nonsensical ramblings from someone who'd hated his guts. Could he blame her?

Grunt thought he was dead. Blue thought he was dead. They all thought he was dead. Everybody except for Carter and Bill. He should've let Kit think it, too, but he couldn't. He just couldn't walk away without letting her know he would always be there for her. He waited until after she renewed her vows with Grunt to make himself known by taking his bike. And by leaving and not facing her, he took away any turmoil he might've caused by forcing her to choose.

What would he have expected? That she would leave her family for him, or leave her husband and take her children to start a life over with him somewhere? Neither option would've been a good one for her, and he loved her enough to know that.

He scowled to himself when he realized something else he had done. He hadn't meant to. He had told Grunt the truth behind the NNG, and yet Grunt couldn't share it with Kit. Then, he had let Kit know he was still alive—and knew she wouldn't tell Grunt. She wouldn't want to hurt him or let him think Grizz would show up one day and try to reclaim her.

Without even realizing it, he'd forced the couple into keeping more secrets from each other. He shook his head as he drove. He realized he hadn't consciously done it, but it had turned out that way. Maybe he really didn't know how to be anything other than a first-class rotten son-of-a-bitch.

Her Bible. He had completely forgotten about it until Guido got a message to him before his execution asking what should be done with it. He'd given instructions for Guido to have it delivered to Carter's after his death.

He was startled from his thoughts when a cat ran in front of the road and he had to swerve. Pulling off the road then, he gazed around. *Where the fuck am I?*

He noticed a restaurant up ahead. His stomach growled as if answering an unspoken question. Gotta eat. Hope it's open.

He pulled in and noticed one car in front. It was a small restaurant with a tidy exterior. Though an older building, it had what looked like a fresh coat of white paint. There were three steps leading up to a front porch that spanned the width of the front. The building's window trim and porch railings were painted an avocado green. That's when he noticed the sign. The Green Bean. Okay, not avocado green, he smirked. Green bean green. What the fuck did he know?

He chuckled to himself as he parked and got off his bike. He was stretching when a sign on the front porch railing caught his eye: "Bikers not welcome."

This surprised him. He scratched his jaw. *We'll see about that.*

His heavy boots resounded off the wooden deck steps as if the loud bike pipes wouldn't have already announced his visit. He noticed the restaurant entrance was a screen door. No doubt they'd heard the bike. Maybe they would be waiting inside with a shotgun. He hoped so. They'd be doing him a favor, he thought to himself as he swung the screen door open and went inside, letting it slam shut behind him.

He immediately caught the scent of a savory aroma and had an instant déjà vu of coming home to one of Kit's home-cooked meals.

Before he could adjust to his surroundings, his ear caught a familiar tune. He immediately zeroed in on an old-fashioned jukebox in the far corner. It looked like one he'd had in his bars back in the seventies. "Don't Look Back" by Boston was playing. It wasn't loud. It was actually kind of quiet, but it taunted him. He was never a fan of Kit's music, but he'd heard enough of it over the years to recognize it. Where was the person with the shotgun? He'd like one healthy blast to the chest, please.

Just then he heard her.

"Another fucking biker with shit for brains. Can't you fucking read, Granddad? The sign says 'Bikers not welcome.' I heard you pull up, you dirty-arse piece of shit biker with bollocks for brains!"

He didn't know what shocked him more: Being referred to as Granddad or the voice that said it. Yeah, he was old enough to be a grandfather, but so what? He took a quick glance to his right and checked himself out in the mirror behind the cash register. His hair was dirty blonde and the few streaks of gray were barely noticeable. He subconsciously swiped his hand through his hair and wondered if it was time for a shave. Kit liked him when he was clean-shaven.

Would he ever be able to not think about her?

But it was the voice that assaulted his senses even more than the Boston song and the smell of food. It was a voice he knew. A voice that had been implanted in his brain. A voice he would never, could never forget. One he'd heard twenty-five years ago when Kit talked in a British accent to the girl that recognized her at the vet's office.

He smiled to himself when he remembered her awkward and totally adorable attempt at dirty talk in that same accent.

He swung around to see where the voice had come from and he almost stumbled backwards. He couldn't think. He couldn't move. He sure as heck couldn't speak. He was certain that he looked like an oversized ape with his arms dangling at his sides and his mouth open.

"Don't you hear? Are your ears filled up with piss or something? You and your kind aren't welcome. Get your big, tattooed, hairy face out of my restaurant. You get back on your bloody bike and keep going."

She stood there with her hands on her hips and looked up at him with a defiant tilt to her chin. A defiant chin that he knew. He was looking at a blonde, blue-eyed version of Kit. He could tell her blue eyes were too bright, almost exaggerated, and he realized she was probably wearing those colored-contact things they made nowadays. He had to forcibly stop himself from reaching out to caress her cheek, run his hand down her jaw. He could picture himself tilting that jaw up toward his face to kiss her lips. He'd done it a thousand times before. He shook the thought from his head.

*This isn't Kit. But other than the hair and eyes, it looks exactly like her.*

He slowly scanned her, from what had to be bleached blonde hair down to her painted pink toenails. He knew every inch of this body. He'd sucked on those toes. No tattoos and no piercings. He blurted out the first thing that popped into his head.

"You afraid of needles? They make you faint?"

She hadn't expected this, and he could see in her expression he'd caught her off guard with his comment. She quickly regained her composure.

"Oh, so you're the amazing fucking Zoron? What the fuck would you know about what makes me faint or not? You bloody, cocky shit. You're all alike. Dicks for brains."

He looked at her questioningly at the Zoron comment.

"He's a fuckwit that read minds for a living back in the seventies." She rolled her eyes. "Fucking American men. You've never ever heard of the Amazing Zoron? You know, Zoron, rhymes with *moron*! You've been living with your head up your arse?"

Without waiting for him to answer, she pointed to the door.

He started to walk toward her. She didn't back away and instead appeared to adapt a more forceful posture, folding her arms now. Like she was ready for the challenge. "Don't let the door hit you in the arse on your way out."

Just then, he heard another voice coming from behind the lunch counter. "Don't be so mean to the guy, Cricket. He doesn't look like he wants any trouble and he's by himself."

Grizz looked up and saw an older woman peering through the pass-through from the kitchen to the counter area.

"Yeah, he's by himself. Probably sucks his own dick all day long. You can wait on this balls for brains, Edna. I'll be in the back doing my paperwork."

Kit's lookalike huffed her way past him toward the back of the small diner. He watched her pass through two swinging doors. Actually, he watched her ass. It was an ass he knew intimately.

He had no doubt he was looking at Kit's twin. Kit's twin who was supposed to be dead. Not living in the back country of Louisiana with a British accent and a vocabulary that would make a sailor blush.

He'd read the note from Delia. He knew she'd tried to find her other daughter and found a death certificate instead. What was her name? He vaguely remembered the nickname Cricket from the note, but he couldn't remember her real name. What had Delia written? Joanie, Jenny, Jeanie? No. They weren't ringing any bells. He couldn't even remember Kit's real name. Just that they both started with a J.

He decided against a table and took a seat at the counter. Edna had come out from the kitchen and handed him a menu. Without looking at it, he asked her, "Got any specials?"

She nodded. "Meatloaf, mashed potatoes, and green beans."

"Yeah, that and a large water."

Before she could turn around, he nodded toward the swinging doors that led back to the kitchen. "What's her beef with bikers?"

"Oh, don't let Cricket bother you. We've had some trouble with them in the past, is all. She's really a good person."

"Cricket? What kind of name is Cricket?"

Edna smiled. "It's Jodi. She's gone by Cricket since she was a baby, though. I've always known her as Cricket."

"You've known her since she was a baby?" he asked, and before she could answer, added, "Her accent isn't from around here. Yours is."

Edna set his water down in front of him. "I was friends with her mother. We'd worked together at a hospital. She was a nurse and I worked in the cafeteria. She went back to England when Cricket was a baby. She was raised over there. Her mother and I stayed in touch over the years. When she died, I asked Cricket to come here and help me with my diner. I think she was missing her mother or maybe having some trouble of her own over there. She's been here a year and has taken on the role of self-appointed watchdog of me and my restaurant. It's hers now. She bought it from me. She's not a bad girl, really. Well, she's obviously not a girl, but you know what I mean."

Grizz didn't reply and Edna headed back through the swinging doors. He could see her in the kitchen fixing his plate. He would like to pick Edna's brain some more.

He sipped his water and thought about the blonde-haired, blue-eyed woman who had spoken to him like nobody, *nobody* ever had before. A foul mouthed, British version of Kit with a boulder-sized chip on her shoulder.

No, she was not his sweet little kitten. She was more like a tiger. A dirty-mouthed, obnoxious, nasty tiger, and if he hadn't been certain he was looking at Kit's twin, he'd have shut her up instantly. He'd actually had a moment when he almost grabbed her by the throat, but stopped himself because he kept seeing Kit's face in spite of the blue contacts and blonde hair.

He would have to think about what to do with this information. Should the twins meet? Should they know about each other? And if so, how the hell would he arrange it? He smiled when he thought about how much fun it would be to drag her ass back to Florida and drop her on Blue's doorstep. Blue had confessed he was attracted to Dicky because of her dislike for him. If that was true, then this one would certainly have his dick hopping all over the place.

His thoughts were interrupted when Edna set a plate in front of him.

"What's today's date?" he asked her.

After she told him, he motioned to the TV in the corner. "Does that thing work?" he asked before taking a bite of his food.

She grabbed a remote and pressed the "on" button.

"Want to watch anything in particular?"

"How about national news?"

She switched it to a national news station and laid the remote down next to his plate.

He ate his food and listened with half an ear as the newscaster talked about snow in the North, the search for a sailboat lost in the Caribbean with a famous actor's fiancé on board, and the latest stock statistics.

"We now return to a tragic story we brought you yesterday," the newscaster droned on. "A married father of two in South Florida is still in critical condition and barely clinging to life after police believe he tried to intervene in a convenience store robbery that left the store clerk dead and the perpetrator still at large. There are no witnesses, but police believe the forty-one-year-old architect from Fort Lauderdale—"

Grizz's head snapped around to face the TV and he grabbed the remote to turn up the volume. He saw a convenience store with crime tape and several police cars on the scene.

The newscaster continued in a voice laced with concern. "In an ironic coincidence, the surviving victim is slated to testify later this year in the trial of prominent South Florida defense attorney Matthew

Rockman. Rockman is expected to go on trial for last summer's murder of a woman he'd placed in the Witness Protection Program over fifteen years ago. It's not clear whether or not this shooting is related to the trial, or whether the victim was just in the wrong place at the wrong time. We'll bring you more as we follow the investigation."

He felt a sadness that he couldn't identify with. Grunt was near death and he was sorry for that. His shoulders sagged. He realized he was genuinely sorry, and the revelation surprised him. He hadn't allowed himself to love his son all those years, but he'd cared for him, and couldn't deny their connection. He'd always had a soft spot for the kid, even if he did want to put him in the ground a time or two.

He reached for the pager on his waist. He knew everybody carried a cell phone now, but that wasn't his way. He was still stuck on old technology. One person knew the pager number. Carter. He placed it on the counter and felt the last spark of hope leave his soul. Grunt had been shot yesterday and was in the hospital clinging to life and yet there had been no page. If he had to think of a time when Kit might need him, he would've thought it would be now.

But he guessed not. She had really moved on. She was surrounded by friends who loved her and would see her through this. She had accepted that he was gone and he couldn't blame her one bit. Still, the realization brought a crushing weight to his soul. He could feel the darkness creeping back in. Would he fight it or allow it to consume him?

He stared at the pager on the counter, and something caught his eye. He squinted and noticed the light wasn't on. That was strange. It was always on. He reached for it and looked closely. He must have flipped it off accidentally when clipping and unclipping it to his belt. How long had it been off?

His gigantic fingers fumbled with the tiny "on" button. When the light went on he set it back on the counter and stared at it. Nothing.

He started to take another bite of food and realized he'd lost his appetite. He was going to ask Edna for his check when a loud buzzing caught his attention, and the pager practically hopped across the counter.

He picked it back up and read the message. Three words were digitally displayed in red: She needs you.

He was going home. To her. It was about fucking time.

# Epilogue

CARTER SAT IN the hospital waiting room and surveyed the strange mix of people that were gathered.

There was a group of bikers in one corner. She recognized a few, especially the big, handsome Native American who'd been at her house so many years ago to collect Grizz's chess set. Anthony Bear. The pretty blonde talking to Ginny was his wife, Christy. They'd never been formally introduced before this tragedy. Anthony was Grizz's friend, not so much Tommy's. The Bears had moved to this coast just this past year, and even though Christy and Ginny were friends, Carter still hadn't crossed paths with them until yesterday.

Another corner harbored men and women in business attire. They had to be some of Tommy's work associates. Some were dressed more casually and it was obvious that others had made their way over from the office. She recognized Tommy's secretary, Eileen, who'd been with him for years. Her red nose and swollen eyes made it obvious she'd been crying.

A bigger, louder group was huddled together in the center of the room. It looked like some of Ginny's friends from her church and neighborhood, as well as some of the parents of Mimi and Jason's school friends.

Carter noticed when one of the bikers glanced at someone who had just walked in. She turned and recognized the reporter from the execution viewing room last summer. *What could she possibly want?* The biker, who she now recognized as Blue with much longer hair and a beard, headed straight for the reporter and, grabbing her by the elbow, roughly escorted her away from the waiting room. *Glad I'm not in her shoes.*

Her gaze then fell on Mimi. Her nose and eyes were red. She had been crying. She was sitting next to a very handsome young man. He had been introduced as the oldest son of Anthony and Christy. His name was Slade, and Carter had no doubt he and Mimi were trying to conceal something. They had known each other since they were children, and Mimi looked at Slade with a desire Carter recognized. Carter couldn't tell by Slade's demeanor if he felt the same way.

She could tell, however, that Slade's younger brother, Christian, didn't like it. He was sitting across from the two with his arms crossed as he glared at his brother the entire time. Even though she'd never met the family before today, Carter had heard enough about them over the years to know Christian was about Mimi's age. And it was obvious by his stare that he did not like seeing his older brother with her. Carter tried not to smile. *The complications of young love. I'm so glad I'm past that.* She felt a rush of love for Bill, her Bill, always so steady and true. She'd take that over passion and drama any day.

She looked at her watch and wondered when Bill would be back with Jason. He had taken the kid out to get him away from the hospital for a little while. Jason was having a really hard time with the trauma of Tommy's attack, and Carter was grateful Bill was in town and doing his best to provide a distraction.

A loud wail from behind her brought her out of her observations. Everybody in the room stopped their conversation and watched as Sarah Jo came into the room and dramatically launched herself into Ginny's arms.

"I'd have been here sooner, Gin. I got on a plane as soon as I heard."

Carter knew Sarah Jo had been out of the country with her husband. He had been interviewing all over the world since last summer and had yet to accept a job. They just couldn't agree on which country they wanted to settle in.

Ginny started crying all over again as Sarah Jo clung to her, trying to calm and soothe her. Everybody went back to their discussions and left the friends to console each other, but Carter just stared at Sarah Jo. Something was off. She didn't look as upset as she should. Wasn't Tommy a childhood friend? Shouldn't she be sporting red eyes and a red nose? As if reading Carter's mind, Sarah Jo started crying, too, as if on cue.

"Thank God you and Stan haven't moved yet, Jo," Ginny babbled, sniffling. "I can't imagine dealing with this without you. Just thinking about you moving to another country is too overwhelming."

Sarah Jo continued to hold Ginny tightly. "We could never move now. I would never move and leave you here to deal with this. This is just awful, Ginny. Don't give it another thought. I don't even need to talk to Stan about it. We're staying."

Ginny let out a loud sob. Christy walked over and handed her a clean tissue.

"Stan's in there now consulting with Tommy's doctors," Sarah Jo added. "He'll make sure Tommy's getting the best care possible."

Carter shifted uncomfortably in her seat and watched Sarah Jo with suspicious eyes. Something wasn't right. Sarah Jo was crying, but Carter didn't see any tears.

Ginny's ponytail swung slightly as she and Jo hugged. The ponytail was sporting the blue bandana, but was sagging under the weight of yesterday's trauma. Carter had never forgotten the favor Grizz had asked of her all those years ago; she had only been too happy to comply. He had told Ginny to use the blue bandana as a way to signal him if she ever needed him.

Carter had watched her friend for years. It wasn't hard. They spent a lot of time together. They belonged to the same church. Carter went to all of Mimi's piano recitals and whatever sporting event Jason happened to be involved in. There were family dinners, barbecues, shopping trips, vacations. Not to mention all of the animal rescue fundraisers they'd both attended. That blue bandana stayed on Grizz's bike for years.

Even after Grizz's fake execution last summer and Ginny's realization that he was still alive, that blue bandana had never been worn, and Carter purposely made sure to be around her friend even more than normal.

She hadn't noticed any difference in Ginny's behavior after finding out that he was still alive. She was the same Ginny, same attentive, loving, and giving wife and mother. That had never changed and never would. Ginny was just Ginny.

But she also detected a new hollowness behind Gin's eyes. Carter regretted confirming Ginny's suspicions that day in the driveway, but that's what Grizz had wanted. To make sure she knew. Carter now questioned the wisdom, or lack of, behind that decision. It was probably the worst thing Grizz could've done.

But she understood it. She honestly believed what she'd told Ginny that day. She had never seen a man love a woman as much as Grizz loved Ginny. She had wondered to herself if Ginny would ever talk to her about it. And besides, if she needed him, wouldn't she just come directly to Carter and ask her to get in touch with Grizz?

Carter smiled to herself and shook her head. No. Ginny was too smart to mention him. Carter was certain Ginny would understand the instructions were there for a reason. She wouldn't risk mentioning his name even to Carter. No. Her friend would wear the bandana if she ever needed Grizz. The short discussion they'd had in her driveway last summer had never been mentioned again, and Ginny had seemed to accept it and move on.

Carter had received a call from Ginny just two days ago. It was a reminder that Jason had an important basketball game the next day.

"He's in the playoffs. You're coming, right?" Ginny had asked her friend then.

"Bill and I wouldn't miss it. You know that, Gin."

Carter and Bill had been at Jason's playoff game. They sat in the bleachers and cheered his team on with Ginny, Tommy, and even Mimi.

Ginny had been wearing the blue bandana at that basketball game. Carter had excused herself to go to the restroom and sent a page within twenty minutes of seeing the bandana.

And that had been almost twenty-four hours *before* Tommy had been shot....

**The End**

# Acknowledgments

*This is the hardest part for me: expressing my feelings to the people who have made such a difference in my life—from the moment I typed the first word in my debut novel, to when I typed "the end" in this one. I've been the recipient of so much unconditional love that it continues to amaze and astound me on a daily basis.*

*First and foremost, I would like to thank my Heavenly Father for seeing me through this journey. He alone knows the personal struggles that went into writing this novel. He alone knows my heart and how it has swelled with love for the people who have shared their love for me and the whirlwind that has been Nine Minutes.*

*To Jim, Kelli, and Katie Flynn, my husband and daughters. You have selflessly given a part of yourselves to help me realize my dream. I always tell people "family first," but each of you has allowed yourself to become last so that I could do my best to continue to bring this story to life. Your patience, love, understanding, and willingness to support my newfound love of writing is a blessing, and I could not have done it without you.*

*To Joseph and Patricia Blasi. Thank you for being the best parents in the world and my biggest fans. Your love and support means more than you could ever know. I love you both so very much.     To Jennifer L. Hewitt. Thank you for taking me by the hand and patiently introducing me to the online book world and for helping me navigate it ever since. I will be forever grateful for your love of Nine Minutes and your determination to get it "out there." It worked!*

*To Adriana Leiker and Nisha E. George. Thank you for being the better two-thirds of our Three Musketeers Club. Your daily devotion to helping and supporting me cannot be measured. I value your friendships and could not, would not, have gotten through this book if it weren't for the two of you. I love you both to Jupiter and back. But you already know that.*

*To Jessica Brodie. Thank you for being the best editor an author could ask for. I am so very grateful for your hard work and dedication. I just came up with the story, but you are responsible for making it shine. Thank you, my friend.*

To Cheryl Desmidt. Thank you for your eleventh-hour saves. You swoop in when I need you the most and go above and beyond. Your love and dedication to my story causes my heart to swell with love and gratitude.

To Josie Melendez. Thank you for "stumbling upon" my story and sharing it with your friends. You were there from the beginning, and I am so glad you never left. You are the first person who told me you would not accept the fact that Grizz was dead. I was okay with that because I knew the truth all along.

My continued love and heartfelt appreciation also go to the following people who, in their own special way, are responsible for contributing to seeing this novel come to fruition. My apologies if I accidentally left someone out: Aleksandra Adamovic, Allison M. Simon, Anitra Townsend, Beverly Tubb, Catherine Gray, Charity Pierce, Chelsea Cronkrite, Cheryl Desmidt, Christine Pappas, Christy M. Baldwin, Connie Thompson, Corinne Regan Bridges, Denise Sprung, Eli Peters, Ellen Widom, Erin Thompson, Eva McFarden, Heidi Wiley, Jackson Tiller, #JamieOskavarek, Jessica Frider, Jodi Marie Maliszewski, Kate Sterritt, Kelli Blasi, Kim Holden, Lisa Mondragon, Liz Himsworth, Louise Husted, Lynsey Simpson, Marcia Miller-Rogers, Maria Angie Mendoza, Mary Dry, MJ Fryer, Melissa Rice, Nicole Sands, Nicky Boutte, Paola Cortes, Samantha Cobb, Samantha O'sarah Deonarine, Sara Lopez, SE Hall, Shasta Baumgarner, Sunshine Lykos, Suzanne Perry, Teresa Childress, Tesrin Afzal, Vanderline Thorpe and Wendy LeGrand.

Again, my deepest gratitude goes to you all.

Made in the USA
Middletown, DE
15 September 2015